In June, 1861, Raphael Semmes' Confederate cruiser Sumter makes a daring escape through the Federal Blockade of the Mississippi...

So began the commader's career as the Southern Seahawk. With a hand-picked crew of Southern officers and mercenary seamen, Semmes seized eight enemy ships in four days — a record never surpassed by any other captain of a warship. By the time the cruises of the Sumter and her successor the Alabama ended, Semmes had taken and burned more than eighty prizes. The most successful maritime predator in history, Semmes eluded a pack of pursuers for two and a half years, and almost single-handedly droves marine insurance rates so high in the North that many Yankee ships refused to sail until he was caught.

Back in Washington, Semmes' predations fueled feuds within the Lincoln cabinet and incited the spy games of historical figures like courtesans Rose Greenhow and Betty Duval, detective Allan Pinkerton and the commander's lovely mistress.

Southern Seahawk, the first novel in the Seahawk Trilogy, grows from the true story of Commander Raphael Semmes' rise to infamy, becoming the Union's "Public Enemy Number One." Using intriguing historical fact melded with his unique and insightful literary style, Randall Peffer has breathed life into a legend of the seas, the Southern Seahawk, Raphael Semmes.

Also by Randall Peffer

Waterman

Logs of the Dead Pirates Society

Killing Neptune's Daughter

Provincetown Follies, Bangkok Blues

Old School Bones

southern
SEAHAWK

RANDALL PEFFER

southern
SEAHAWK

A Novel of the Civil War at Sea

BLEAK
HOUSE
BOOKS

Published by
BLEAK HOUSE BOOKS
a division of Big Earth Publishing
923 Williamson St.
Madison, WI 53703
www.bleakhousebooks.com

This is a work of fiction.
Any similarities to people or places, living or dead, is purely coincidental.

Library of Congress Cataloging-In-Publication Data has been applied for.
ISBN 13: 978-1-60648-012-0 (Trade Cloth)
ISBN 13: 978-1-60648-013-7 (Trade Paper)
ISBN 13: 978-1-60648-014-4 (Evidence Collection)

Printed in the United States of America
12 11 10 09 08   1 2 3 4 5 6 7 8 9 10

For
Commander Chester R. Peffer,
an officer and a gentleman

... And
Marian L. Smith

His sun, his moon, the star he steered by.
The angel on his shoulder. Fair winds.

PROLOGUE

USS Brig *Somers*
DECEMBER 8, 1846, MEXICAN WAR

An instant before the norther strikes. The sultry air seems to freeze. The brig's young captain senses what's coming. And he sees how his life will be if he loses his ship today: Court-martial, humiliation, years of puny postings. Perhaps assignment to the reserve list. Or a mustering out of the service. The word "cursed" branding his name in the wardrooms of ships and the salons of Washington. Forever, really.

He has harbored such delicate dreams of glory. He thinks he's made to rise to flag rank. Can hardly believe that thirty-six years of living, decades in the navy, has led him to this moment. Blockade duty off Veracruz. A fight to the death with a faceless devil on a malignant sea. His first real command and already grappling with wind and water like few mariners ever face. He wants to howl at the face of his god, "Why?!" But he bites his tongue and seizes the main shrouds to larboard. Spreads his legs, tries to brace his body with bent knees. It's all that a man can do.

Bring it on!

The ship stalls in a swell. The sails fall limp from the yards. Foredeck boys and officers gape to weather. A flock of seabirds screech, wheel across the surface of the water, vanish off to leeward. Then the storm shows its claws. It comes charging toward the ship out of blue sky, tearing over the Gulf of Mexico, a roiling wall of wind and water from the north. Thundering down on the *Somers*.

"White squall!" screams the lookout from the main truck. He leaps for a backstay, with hopes of a fast slide down to the relative safety of the deck. But the norther catches him. Flings him off into the blue.

"Bear off!" shouts Raphael Semmes to his quartermaster on the helm. "Run for it!"

The screech of the wind carries his words away. A torrent of salt air lays the brig down on her side. The starboard rail awash. The tips of the lower yards already snagging in the waves. The mainsail dragging in the water. Filling like a pool. *Jesus.* Men tumbling into the sea, scrambling from below decks in their long johns. They hug the rigging, and anything else to anchor them, with both arms. A cannon breaks loose from its breaching ropes to windward, skates across the deck. Crashes through the lee rail. Is gone.

"Bear off!"

Semmes dives from his post at the shrouds to help at the helm. Tells himself that God is testing him for greatness. *Buck up, man.* If he could just help the quartermaster crank the wheel over, get the rudder to bite, the ship might yet turn her stern to the norther and right herself. Run off safely before the squall. But a sea sweeps over the *Somers* and slams the captain into the fife rail at the base of the mainmast. He feels something crack in his chest as the air goes out of his lungs.

The wind is howling, cutting his face with blasts, sharp little nails of spray, as he comes up into the air again.

"She's not answering the helm, sir!" The sailing master has joined the quartermaster at the great cherry wheel.

Shouts and cries for help rise from men trapped below decks.

"Beat to quarters. All hands on deck!"

"She's down flooding by the head. Sailing herself under!" A voice from midships.

The foretop mast splits right down the middle with a crack that muffles the shrieking of the wind. A second later a topsail carries away to leeward, a winged thing on the loose. Sails shred to rags in the blink of an eye.

"Cast off sheets and braces!" He grabs the ax from its sling by the companionway, scrambles back to the main sheet and hacks it in two. "She will rise. She must rise!"

But she does not. Even cut loose from the wind and sails that have pinned her down, the *Somers* wallows on her side, larboard beam to the wind and seas. Hills of foam raking her. The starboard side of the ship feet below the surface. The deck a wall for scaling. One of the ship's boats hangs high from her davits on the windward side. Unusable. A cruel joke. Another drifts off to leeward, ripped from its slings by boarding seas. Smashed and awash. Only the gig, dangling from the stern davits, might yet serve.

He claws his way forward along the windward rail, hoping for a miracle, willing the bows buried in the black water to rise and shake off the seas. Yells to his men to heave the leeward guns overboard. Move aft, move to windward. Redistribute the weight.

"To the axes, boys! Cut away her rig!"

They are the best of crews. And so they bend to the order. Swinging their axes in a fury. Parting the windward shrouds. The luff and his gang are hacking away great chips from the foremast when a sea comes crashing down on them. When it passes nothing remains but a sailor's blue kerchief dangling from a foot rope to leeward. The air stinks of fish.

The fat cook named Seymour is swimming over the spot where the cook shack has recently been.

"Here, man." He throws the cook a line and pulls him back to the windward deck. "Hang on, I've got ..."

An explosion like the roar of a cannon drowns his words. A geyser shoots into the air from midships, spewing broken hogs heads of salted beef, sacks of corn, sweet potatoes. Rats.

He knows instantly that the main hatch has blown. Driven down by wind and waves, the ship has finally yielded to the building air pressure in her hold and exploded. Now, her hold, the great source of her buoyancy, is flooding. He can already feel her sinking under his feet, knows that he has lost her.

He grabs midshipman Clark. Tells him to lower the gig. Fill her with his best oarsmen, row for the fleet anchored just a few miles away. Bring help. Then he gives the order to abandon ship.

"Over the side, men! Try to stick together ... until the rescue boats get here."

The order is unnecessary. The better part of the crew of seventy-five men is already in the water, trying to cling to anything in the wreckage that will keep them afloat.

The air fills with the shouting of swimmers, calling the names of their shipmates for comfort. Begging their god for mercy. Or cursing the navy and the captain as whoreson floggers. The ship a cold-hearted sea bitch. Goddamn the ship. Goddamn this blockade duty, this fool's errand that has sent them off chasing after a strange sail on the horizon. Goddamn this ridiculous war with the Mexicans. Goddamn the *Somers.*

He feels the sting of prophecy come true. Knows that there are those who have quit the navy rather than take orders to sail in this ship. But he has rejected such superstition. Until now. His ears wither from the screams and curses of his crew. His mind racing back to 1842 when the *Somers* was the site of an ugly hanging. A young officer on board, Philip Spencer, along with two other conspirators, charged with plotting a mutiny and executed from the yard. An extraordinary punishment in a service where crews' insubordination was commonplace. Especially rare since neither the ship nor the United States was at war at the time, the *Somers* merely on a sail-training cruise with cadets. Especially harsh since Philip Spencer was the son of the Secretary of War.

She is a doomed ship, said the scuttlebutt. A lightning rod for death, terror and injustice. It is just a matter of time until fate strikes her again.

And now it most surely has.

His stomach knots as he kicks off his shoes, flings away his coat, dives into the water. He's a strong swimmer. Soon he finds an upper half-port on which to float. The water washing over him feels like ice. He presses his face to the wood, listens to the fading cries of his men. Wonders how many will die from the cold and sharks before Clark comes back with help from the fleet. If he comes back.

1

District of Columbia
JANUARY 12, 1861

He leaps off the little sofa bed, shivering. Drags the sweat-stained sheet around his shoulders. He's wet, freezing. In the sheet, his compact body seems to glide across the floor. Thick, shaggy graying hair falls over his ears. Here is a face made to play Shakespeare's rakes—heavy brows, gray eyes almost always set on a distant horizon, sharp nose, broad mustache and a tuft of whiskers above a pointy chin. Commander Raphael Semmes, USN.

"Goddamn. Goddamn these wretched nightmares!"

To think that after more than thirty years in the Federals' navy, his career has come to this. Hallucinations of death, a sweaty toga, a dark, cold cell in Mudville on the Potomac and an obscure post as Secretary of the Lighthouse Bureau. He has not been to sea for eleven years, and now he thinks and dreams of little else. But when the salt spray washes through his sleep, it rarely sweeps him back to his pink-cheeked years as a middie aboard the *Lexington,* nor to his West Indies cruises as sailing master on the *Constellation* during her victories over French frigates. More often his night voyages land him on the *Somers.* He sees the sails ripped to rags, masts buried in the sea, men washed overboard or leaping into the foam. Gone. Many men. Good men. More than half his crew. Then, like tonight, he dreams of punishment and vengeance. Until he wakes awash in regrets and impossible hopes.

His whole body shakes as he moves toward the moonlit window to check the time on the church tower. He's glad that he sleeps in the study so that his wife cannot see him so reduced by terror. Anne, his nearly loyal spouse. She's still his stately, handsome girl. After fourteen years he can forgive—but not forget—her betrayal, the bastard child named Anna who she conceived while he was away in the Mexican war. Anna, who has long been cloaked from his sight, ensconced at Eden Hall boarding school in Philadelphia. Anna, the cool, dark space between his wife and him. Anna, whose very existence has given him permission to hold back his heart at home, tender it elsewhere. It has been years since he nuzzled his wife's breasts with the wings of a mustache that she used to call the "bird of paradise."

Two thirty by the church clock. The moon freezes Capitol Hill in harsh, silver light. It is a light such as seamen sometimes see during a winter's midwatch offshore. A night when the shadows of sails and masts vibrate and sway across the deck, looking like valkyries ready to come crashing down on your head with the next roll of the ship. So seems the distant shadow of the unfinished Washington Monument wrapped in scaffolding.

Suddenly, he drops to his knees before the window, crosses himself, clutches his hands to his forehead in prayer.

"*Mea culpa*. Gracious and merciful Father, I have become the miserable pawn of Pharaoh's rule. Forgive me my trespasses. Let Satan lead me not into temptation. Grant me the strength to deliver myself, my family and my country from evil, greed, torpor and cowardice."

He shivers, catches his breath with a sharp gasp, squeezes his hands together with tightening, interlaced fingers. The shape of prayer. Now, on his knees and draped in his sheet, he looks like one of those monks he saw during the Mexican War, the monks who slept in their coffins.

His mind turns to the poet Tennyson for words, and he mumbles aloud the lament of Ulysses, idle king, the landlocked gray man of the sea matched with an aged wife.

"Oh Lord my God, how dull it is ... to rust unburnished, not to shine in use." He spits into his hands. "Fifty-one is a pathetic age. I am become a name."

Below in the street a hansom carriage clatters up the cobblestones. Beneath its hood a woman shrieks in delight at secret fondling. A man laughs.

"Maude." The name rushes from his lips.

It's not Maude below in the hansom, but he hears her youth and her joy in the woman's voice. He pictures her round, lightly freckled face, sparkling candle light in her emerald eyes, her hive of copper hair. His nose sniffs at the air as if he might catch a scent from the lavender on her neck.

"Sweet child."

The hands that have been praying against his lips suddenly draw back together from the kneeling figure, then swiftly reverse their course. He slams his clasped fists against his forehead as if driving a knife into his skull.

"Curse me, but love be damned. It's now or never, sir. There may yet be time for some act of greatness. Rise up!"

The voice sounds guttural and raw. A thing from his nightmares.

Still dizzy from the blow, he staggers to his feet, lurches across the room, knocking over a globe stand before finding his desk. The officer who so many know these days as the gold-braided dandy of Washington cotillions seems a man of sticks and rags as he rummages through his desktop for a match.

When the candle's lit, he settles into his chair. His left hand begins unconsciously to twirl the tip of his broad mustache, while his other puts pen to paper.

January 12, 1861

The Honorable Senator Clement C. Clay
Esteemed Delegate from the State of Alabama

Sir:

I have had news this passing night that the legislature of our great state has voted to join South Carolina, Mississippi, Florida and Georgia in secession from the Federal union of states. In this regard I request the honor and privilege of visiting with you to speak on the matter at your earliest convenience.

You know me as a naval officer of considerable experience, and you will now find me a man with fire in his very soul ...

He pauses. Then nearly adds, *A man who would sell that soul for a fighting ship. Give me a ship!*

2

District of Columbia
FEBRUARY 13-14, 1861

"I love to look at your body."

Maude Galway lies in her bed beneath a crimson comforter, propping herself up on an elbow. Thick, copper hair covers all of her bare skin except milky-white forearms as she surveys her man's back from across the room. Stepping into his small clothes, he stares out the window at the railway tracks leading to the station near Capital Hill, says nothing.

"Aye, but I mean it, Raffy. Your back is so broad, and the cords in your hips ... You look like—"

"Stop, lass!"

"A gladiator." She says this word with the triumph of discovery. The image of her lover as a Roman warrior has just popped full-blown into her mind.

"Don't flatter me. I'm old enough to know a lie when I hear one." There's rebuke in his voice. A hint of amusement, tenderness too.

She bunches the top sheet into the warm wetness between her legs and sighs.

She did not mean to patronize. Truly, as these shadows of late afternoon in mid-February bathe the boarding house room in a fuzzy, violet light, the man who spends his days shuffling paper for the navy appears to have the raw-boned body of a Bantry Bay waterman.

She suddenly sits up in bed, holding the comforter over her breasts.

"What's wrong?"

"Nothing, lassie. Nothing's wrong."

He stops watching the smoke belching from a locomotive as it puffs its train south. Turns, stares at the green-eyed witch smiling up at him from her bed. His eyes soften with each second she holds his gaze. His mustache begins curling into a subtle grin.

I'm a selkie to him. He called me that once. His West Irish mermaid. She can still hear some of that delight in his voice every time he says "lassie."

"I have to go back to the office." A complaint. Not an excuse.

He snatches his white shirt from the back of a wicker chair, is midway through jamming his right arm into a sleeve, when she speaks.

"It's Saturday. Come to me again."

She reaches out her hand. He crosses the shadowy room to her as if on wires. When he stands almost directly above her, she takes his fingers, rises to him, kisses the light fur on his belly.

"Lord have mercy."

Then he is on her like a mink, fumbling the nightstand for his lambskin sheath.

"Now who do you love?"

His breath burns her neck.

It's after seven thirty in the evening on St. Valentine's Day when they finish their poached rockfish and oyster stew in a dark corner of the Ebbitt Grill on Fifteenth St. There is a long pause in their conversation. She can hear the piano player across the room shuffling through a slow and dissonant "Oh, Susanna."

Finally he speaks.

"I'm leaving Washington. Perhaps as soon as tomorrow, lassie." His voice sounds hollow.

Her ears prick beneath the coils of hair pinned to the sides of her head.

"Another lighthouse to see somewhere?"

He says nothing and stares at the glass of Bordeaux in his left hand.

She sees a cloud forming over his face. His uniform seems to be pinching his shoulders, neck. His breath comes fast, shallow. A cat's.

"Raffy?" She wipes her lips quickly with her napkin and stuffs it back in her lap to hide her fingers that have suddenly started to tear at each other.

"I'm on the first train I can get to Alabama." He inhales deeply, pulls a yellow telegram from his inside breast pocket, passes it across the table for her to read.

Montgomery
Sir—On behalf of the Committee on Naval Affairs, I beg leave to request that you repair to this place at your earliest convenience.
Your obedient servant,
C.M. Conrad, Chairman

"I hope to get a ship and fight for Jefferson Davis and my new country. Even though the South has no navy whatsoever now, I have thought long about her naval defense. It is right clear to me that the best defense is a bold offense. So if Davis gives me my chance, I will raid the enemy like an avenging angel, a demon from their worst nightmares."

He has a dreamy look, stares right over her shoulder and out the front window of the restaurant.

Her cheeks flush. She raises her hands to the corners of her jaw.

"Damn you. Damn you!" she says under her breath. But he must not hear her because he rambles on.

"Anne and the children will be leaving for her brother's house in Cumberland."

He takes a slow sip of wine.

Her gaze rises from the table to his face.

"My god, Raffy. Would you look at me? Just *look* at me?"

His gaze leaves whatever it is beyond the window of the restaurant, sees for the first time the lightning in her green eyes.

"Raffy, listen to yourself! Spewing on about your wife and children. Do you even know who you're talking to? Can't you see? You're killing me. Killing us. Snuffing us out like a ..."

Her voice chokes. She rubs her cheeks with the palms of her hands before continuing.

"And here I sit trying to hold back bloody tears. For what? For a man who wants to make himself a demon or an angel? Jesus, Mary and Joseph, Raffy!"

He raises his chin as if to look cavalier, but his thick brows sag as he pulls a fresh kerchief from inside his dress-blue jacket with one hand. His other takes her right hand across the narrow table. The hand on which she wears the silver band set with emeralds. The band that he gave her for her twenty-sixth birthday almost a year ago, when he first told her he would love her unto death.

Tears begin rolling down her cheeks. He laces his fingers through hers. Then he leans toward her across the table and begins wiping the tears off her face with the kerchief. She thinks he suddenly looks older than her father did when he was laid out at his wake. How very, very pale.

"Maude ... lassie. This is the hardest thing I have ever done. Forgive me. Leaving you ... "

Her body shudders then slumps in the cane chair, the purple organdy dress folding up around her ... before she gathers herself and pounces.

"I hope you die! Right here before God and the bloody Congress."

Barely have her words begun to explode over the other diners at Ebbitt's, when she hits him with a gale of wine from her glass. It turns his shirt a slick, dark red.

"Oh dear," says a matron at another table.

"I've heard enough of your boyish fantasies of glory ... you faithless coward!" She stands up, throws her napkin on the table. Storms off to the coat check for her fur.

"Bravo!" A woman cheers from across the room.

He's not drunk when he shows up at her door some time after midnight. But he's wobbling like a loose jib. The north wind has been swirling snow along Pennsylvania Avenue since sunset. Now, he has a white paste covering him from head to foot as if he has been walking into the blizzard for hours.

"Go away!" She stands in the doorway wearing the blue satin robe she keeps for his use.

"Lassie, I'm on my knees."

"Then crawl home to your wife."

"I love you."

A man of snow is crumpling at her feet in the hallway of her boarding house.

"You're too late, Raffy. Damn you for coming here!"

"I've been a fool. I did not see what I was doing to you. Forgive me. I've been so bound up in the Southern cause, so moved by the idea of going to sea again ... May the Holy Redeemer strike me down if I lie. You are the best thing ... "

She bites her lower lip, stares at him with the curiosity of a woman who has discovered St. Jude, the patron of lost causes, on her doorstep. How different he is now from the officer and gentleman she met twenty-two months ago. Aglow in the blue and gold of his full-dress uniform, he had sliced a sprig of apple blossoms from a tree outside the Smithsonian castle with his saber, presented it to her with a courtly bow. *Lady, may these blossoms bring you some small measure of the pleasure that gazing upon you has brought to me on this noontime in May.* Later he bought her ice cream, made with the first strawberries of the season, before she returned to her pupils at the little school on Capitol Hill.

"Knock it off with the noise!" The shout comes from somewhere down the hall.

She throws her hands up in the air as if begging God for a sign as to what to do next.

"Let him in or throw him out. People are trying to sleep!" A woman's voice echoes through the drafty boarding house on H St.

He catches her eye with his lost little boy face. She groans.

"Come on ... before you catch your death of cold."

She reaches out, brushes the slush off his brows, cheeks, the mustache drooping in surrender.

Later, after drying him before the coal stove, after filling him with onion broth, after the apologies and the love making—after it all—he holds her with a force that almost scares her.

"My heart breaks from what I must do. Believe me, lassie."

She feels her chest heave.

"But my mind is right firm in its resolve. And my soul knows that to do anything else but serve the South at this moment would be to render myself so clearly an abject cretin and coward that I would not be fit for your arms. Let me go."

He nuzzles the hollow between her neck and gleaming shoulder.

"Let me do what I must, and let me have your love and blessing. Pray for me that I can do what must be done to bring this secession conflict to a quick end. Then I swear with all the fire in my soul, I will make my peace with Anne and come to you as an obedient servant if you will still have me."

She feels his tears running down the plane of her chest, sliding over a breast. Remembers how home and hearth kept her soldier father from a campaign and the regiment he loved. How the bottle took him early because he used it to mute the calls of duty and his own strange passion for the warrior's life.

"Will you stand by me?" His voice is pleading.

3

The Hudson River
MID-MARCH, 1861

The waves look black even though it is morning.

"Lord how I hate rivers."

He stands high up on the promenade deck of the packet *Queen of the Mohawk* as the steamer beats her way north against the current. She's bound for West Point, then Albany, to the rhythm of laboring pistons, churning side wheels. A squadron of low clouds rush overhead trailing fits of sleet and showers, casting the rocks of the Hudson Palisades in an eerie, violet light.

"Confounded rivers!" He speaks as if there's a shipmate standing next to him to listen. "No sea room. Nowhere to run. No place to set a sail. Wind and current always on your nose or tearing at your ass."

A woman passenger who's standing at the rail nearby when Semmes lapses into his soliloquy casts a sidelong glance at the figure in the black overcoat, listens to his rant for a while, then shrugs him off as a drunk, a looney. She slips away.

He takes a sip from a mug of coffee a steward offered him a few minutes earlier. It tastes like snake blood, and he walks to the larboard rail to spit the poison overboard. Then he stands there hugging the shoulders of his coat and watching the broad river ahead vanish in a haze of blue. He purchased the coat, made of a puny worsted, before leaving Montgomery on this mission to the North. It was good enough to keep the March chill off him in the South and even in Washington. But ever since he came north from purchasing gun powder from the Du Pont people in Delaware, he has suffered.

He shivered in New York. Then just plain froze his tail off in Hartford and Springfield. His warm, blue sea coat molders in a closet because he quit his post as Pharaoh's pennyboy to be Jeff Davis' special envoy. Meanwhile in places like Charleston, Savannah, and Biloxi, other men—less seasoned mariners—are outfitting privateers, preparing to put to sea, waiting for the first shots of a civil war to be fired.

He's not what the politicians, neither Yanks nor Rebs, think of when they picture an officer of the line. To the politicos he's a good old boy, born and bred on the Potomac in Charles County, Maryland. A fellow with talents for impeccable dress and small talk over tea or sour mash. An officer who knows the diplomatic and supply sides of the military trade. A gentleman and lawyer, who came of age at his uncle's home in Washington's Georgetown amid the balls, cotillions, society outings to the race course. He's an agent who can carry a secret letter from Jeff Davis tucked in his small clothes, or talk to himself on a steamer, without raising much suspicion.

Present circumstances have conspired against his dreams of sea duty, and he's more than disappointed. But he gave Jefferson Davis his pledge to serve the South "however needed," right there in Jeff's room at the Exchange Hotel.

"I will not recant!" He scowls at the river.

The crack of small explosions like gunshots sounds at his back. Old habits from his soldiering days ashore in Mexico after the wreck of the *Somers* take over. The Rebel envoy drops into a crouch alongside the cabin house on the promenade deck of the *Queen*.

"Die, you fuckers! Piss off and die!" Someone's shouting from the stern.

More cracks.

He sees no one on deck. He reaches inside his coat and draws a new, husky .44 Colt revolver from its shoulder holster.

His knees ache as he moves toward the shooting in a low crouch.

"Eat shit and die."

A single crack, two more, then a man's laughter. The voice is coming from the deck below at the very stern of the ship.

He stays low as he approaches the balcony railing overlooking the main deck and the fantail stern.

Another shot. He's close enough now that it makes his ears ring.

"Ashes to ashes, hag!"

Almost overhead, one of the terns that some mariners call "hags," the birds that follow river and coastal ships, explodes into a cloud of feathers as it swoops above the stern.

Bang. Another bird off to the left literally bursts into flames, cartwheels down into the Hudson.

"Hot damn! Wings of fire."

He feels his stomach churn. Someone's killing birds. He cocks his gun, creeps to the balcony rail, looks down.

Below on the fantail stands a lumpy-looking fellow in the powder blue uniform of the steamship company. Semmes recognizes him as the purser who took his ticket after boarding. He has a glowing slow match wedged in a joint on the stern rail, and he's using it to light firecrackers that he throws up to the birds like pieces of toast.

Now as the purser fishes another firecracker out of his pocket and reaches toward the slow match for a light, Semmes takes aim with his pistol and fires. He surprises himself with his total lack of hesitation, his instant impulse to redress a wrong.

The slow match shatters in a hail of sparks. The purser's jaw drops open.

"My next bullet's for you, friend, if you ever try that jackass stunt on another bird."

"Who ... who in Hell are you?"

"Somebody who likes birds ... You don't want to cross swords with me."

"Tough guy."

"Don't make me show you. I got a cannon, and I'm in a right mean mood, son."

He cocks the .44, steadies it with both hands at arms' length and points it at the purser's head.

The man raises his arms in surrender, retreats indoors.

"Lard-ass lubber."

He pulls a cap and ball from the ammo pouch tucked in an inside coat pocket. Then he reloads, holsters his gun, strolls toward the steamer's bows where the wind, spitting sleet and rain, braces his face. When the hot blood in his forehead and ears cools, he turns his back on the weather and takes a letter from inside his coat. The letter is almost three months old, and the author his son Oliver, a third-year cadet at the United States Military Academy at West Point.

Father,

I am feeling most wretchedly torn asunder, sir. Even though there is not yet war between the states, we Southern boys, like Custis Lee (I think you may know his father Robert of Virginia who was once superintendent here) and yours truly, roam this academy like restless shadows, cut off from our own souls. Is war to come now that Lincoln has been elected as the next president? Or will the Union let the South go its own way? If the split is amicable, and the North and South should become American allies in the future, could I finish my schooling and accept my commission in the Federal army? Will you stay with the navy?

He had finally written back last month.

What do I know, Son? I have no crystal ball to help me read the future. After much soul searching, I have resigned my commission. But my circumstances of age, career, family, and loyalty to the South are so different from yours, I can hardly hold my choice to leave the Federal service as a model for you.

His letter was balderdash. Cowardly horse manure. A half-truth at best.

"You must give the boy an honest answer," Anne said. "Go to him, Raphael, when you are in the North. Please. The boy needs you."

So now he's coming to his son. To talk. For better or for worse. He promised Anne that he would make this visit, and he will not renege on a promise to her. So what if he and Anne ceased to kindle flames

on a promise to her. So what if he and Anne ceased to kindle flames in each other's loins years ago? They have a shared history. A man has to respect that. And family. His own baser needs be damned.

West Point smells like war. The acrid scents of fear, brass polish, and gun oil ooze from everything, even the leafless oaks around the parade ground. But the rain and the sleet have passed off to the east, leaving a sunny afternoon that warms with a southerly wind and the promise of spring.

On the muddy parade ground the regiment stands its afternoon muster. Hundreds of cadets box themselves into platoons and companies to the calls of unit leaders. The superintendent and his officers sit upon chestnut mares, prance around the perimeter. When the fife and drum boys march past playing a popular march from the Mexican War, "The Rose of Alabama," he almost raises his right arm in salute. Then he remembers he's not in uniform ... and this is the enemy army's camp, a Yankee nursery for young vipers soon be at the throat of the South. Yet, right now, the whole confounded gaggle look like toy soldiers with gray tunics, gold chest buttons, shiny black campaign hats painted over the bodies of boys, framing the faces of cherubs.

Once he believed in all that West Point stood for—the honor of national service, the duty of protecting home and hearth, the comradeship of warriors. And so he supported his son Oliver when he sought senatorial appointment to the academy. He even envied Oliver the chance to come of age at this grand institution of learning in company with the brave and the strong. There was no academy when he joined the navy back in 1826. No classes in engineering, tactics, leadership. Just a dank midshipman's berth on the Old Lex and officers looking to bust you out of their ranks and down into the fo'castle with the jacks.

"Father?" The word jolts him from his thoughts.

The superintendent had dismissed the regiment while he was brooding, and now Citizen Semmes looks into the rosy face of a stocky youth. The boy seems almost giddy with surprise.

"Mother wrote that you were in the North, but I did not expect ... "

He gives his son his right hand. The boy takes it, hesitates long enough to find his father's eyes, then embraces him for several seconds. A stiff hug. But a hug nonetheless.

"Ollie."

"It is so good to see you, sir."

"You have been much on my mind, Son."

"And you on mine. It is so odd to see you out of uniform. Have you gone back to practicing law in Mobile?"

"Let us walk somewhere less public."

Semmes fixes his gaze on a forest of bare trees in the distance.

"I have an hour before mess."

The young man with the long arms and thick chest of a wrestling champion leads his father to a wooded path. It traverses a bluff that overlooks the river hundreds of feet below and Cold Springs on the opposite shore. There's a cannon foundry over there, and the smell of coal smoke and smelting iron hangs above the river.

"They work day and night," says the boy when he sees his father eyeing the cannon manufactory. "There is a rumor that the engineers have begun employing a thing called rifling in their cannons. It is like screw threads inside the barrel. The threads spin the shell as it leaves, increasing the velocity, range and accuracy of the projectile."

His shoulders hunch up slightly. "The South cannot yet produce even smooth-bore weapons."

The boy sees the scowl on his father's face, changes the subject.

"You look good in civies, Father."

"I look naked."

The boy shrugs. He meant to reach out to his father, but he has offended. "Sorry, sir."

"No. It is I who should be sorry, Son." He grinds his back teeth, gives a tip of his mustache a sharp twist. "I owe you more than I have given, Ollie."

"These are difficult times."

"Aye." He hears Maude in his own voice, and he hopes that she will stand by him now. Lord, he hopes he's about to say the right thing.

"I am not reading law, Son. I serve the South. Mr. Davis has made me one of four commanders in his new navy."

Oliver pauses on the trail, bends his head, puts his left hand to his mouth and squeezes his upper lip to stifle strong emotions.

"When?"

Semmes takes a step ahead. Stops. Then wheels to look at his son the cadet. "It has been some two months."

"Why did you not write to me of this? Your decision would have made my own choice of service so much easier."

He shifts his weight from the left foot to the right then tugs on his mustache again.

"I thought it best not to unduly influence you right much."

Facing off with the father, the boy extends his arms, the wrestler testing his opposite.

"You're my father. How can you not influence me? By denying me the whole truth, you influence me. Don't you see that?"

He adjusts the maroon muffler at his neck and clears his throat. "It is not that simple, Ol."

"Why not? You join the Confederates, and you don't tell me?"

"Some things are better left private."

He starts to walk again. The boy pursues.

"From your family?"

"From the world, Son."

Semmes stops again, turns his back on his son, gazes off toward the gothic towers of the academy.

Oliver puts his hand to his upper lip once more, squeezes, stares into the purple haze gathering over the Hudson as the sun sets. At last his hand drops. He casts his father a sidelong glance.

"You're a Reb agent, aren't you? That's why you're here in the North."

He swallows a mouthful of saliva.

"It is a right dirty piece of business, Ol. It might even be an evil business. I hate every second of it except this chance to see you. I have come north to buy cases of powder, service revolvers, muskets from the Du Ponts, Sam Colt and their competitors. Then I ship my purchases off to Beauregard in Charleston with the word "Bibles" stamped on the packing cases. Lots of packing cases. Now they want me to buy a fleet of steamers."

Oliver's eyes widen. The sun has set. A fog of coal smoke and smelting cannon iron rises over the river from Cold Spring. The hour of the cadets' mess approaches.

"What next, Father?"

4

District of Columbia
MID-APRIL, 1861

Gideon Welles bolts the lock on Room 8 in the Willard Hotel, turns toward the dresser mirror, sighs at the sight of his own image as he peels the gray wig off his pale dome.

"I swear if I hear one more knock on this door tonight, I'm through with Washington."

Thirty years ago when he lost his hair and started wearing wigs, he thought that his toupees, with a spit curl cocked over the left eye and thick curls roiling over his ears and neck, made him look stentorian or knightly. He pictured Seneca and Lancelot, and felt like one of the Chosen. But now with the wig off and the bushy white beard hiding his neck and collar, he thinks he looks like Father Christmas.

"Good Lord, how could Lincoln have chosen a man who looks like this to serve him?" He loosens the red tie at his throat. "I'm a clown. I'll be the darling of the political cartoonists within weeks." *Why not just catch the next train back to Hartford, Mary Jane and the children, avoid the whole wretched catastrophe. Secretary of the Navy! What do I know about ships or Horatio Nelson types? I'm a newsman.*

He whips the loosened tie from beneath his collar, flings it across the room onto the bed. Then he shambles in the same direction, his bunions aching with each step. The prospect of peeling out of his suspenders and all the rest seems entirely too daunting. He might just sleep in his clothes. It has been a long day trying to find competent and trustworthy officers to replace the more than one hundred and fifty senior men who resigned to join the South. And a longer night warding off the legions of opportunists and office seekers stalking the corridors of the Willard, currying favor. Total madmen, liars, scalawags. Someone even tried to sell him ships made of iron. *Imagine. A navy of iron ships. They'd sink like stones.*

After his large and weighty frame crumples on top of the lilac bedspread, he reaches to douse the flame in the oil lamp on the bed stand. He catches sight of the small tintype of the president, the man he worked so hard to elect, propped against the lamp. Photographs amuse and scare him; they seem to have the power to stop time and steal souls.

But that's not what the newly frocked Secretary of the Navy is thinking just now. He closes his eyes and begins to laugh aloud. A long explosion of sad and giddy mirth rises out of his belly as an odd discovery strikes him. He pictures the key players in the Lincoln cabinet. Treasury Secretary Salmon Chase, a free-soiler from Ohio and one of Lincoln's rivals for the nomination, looks like a bull-necked prize fighter. Si Cameron at War, a Pennsylvanian with the hooked nose of a hunting hawk and his own chip on the shoulder about having lost the nomination to Lincoln. Ed Bates, yet another of Lincoln's rivals, has already started presiding over the Attorney General's office with the handsome looks you see in drawings of Caesar. Worst of all, Bill Seward. The man who had been chief among Lincoln's rivals for the Republican presidential nomination is now Secretary of State. The former governor of New York and senator has the sharp looks of a fox or Iago. He and Welles have clashed at smoky political caucuses for well over a decade.

What a snake pit! None of us are here because of our talents. Lincoln has appointed us to consolidate the party and pay off political debts. And I am the president's only friend. His older, uglier shadow. We must be jokes to these boys.

He's still laughing at the sheer madness of it all when two sharp raps sting his door.

"What the hell is going on in there, Welles? Are you thumping a tart?"

Seward. Jesus Christ!

"It's eleven o'clock. I'll see you in the morning."

More knocks. Harder now.

"Open up. I need to talk to you! This can't wait."

He rolls out of bed, wobbles to the dresser to fetch his wig.

"Come on, Gideon. Where in Jesus' name are you?"

"Present." He swings open the door, then presses the wig to his temples with both hands.

Seward, followed by his son Frederick, a slick-haired rat in a suit, backs him into his own room.

"What the hell is this?"

Seward waves a telegram. "You've countermanded the president's orders. Nothing's happening in Brooklyn. The navy yard will not let David Porter take the *Powhatan* because the yard's got an order from you for some Captain Mercer to take *Powhatan* as flagship on this ridiculous expedition to rescue Fort Sumter."

Frederick slams the door.

"What? Porter? Who's Porter?" A chasm opens beneath his heart.

"He's a lieutenant. On a secret mission. That's all you need to know."

He bites his lower lip.

"A mere lieutenant has been sent without my knowledge to take command from a seasoned captain of one of the few first-rate ships I have that is not off gallivanting around the globe somewhere? The one ship that can assure the success of our expedition to resupply the troops at Sumter? The navy's ship? My ship? How in God's name? What secret mission? Tell me. What right do you have to order my navy ... ?"

He begins gathering himself, rising erect like a waking giant to tower over Seward.

The Secretary of State takes an unconscious step backward, bumps into his son. It makes him jump.

"Stop. Stop acting like a fool, Gideon. It's not *your* navy. It's the president's navy."

"How can this happen? The president approved sending Mercer and the *Powhatan* to Sumter!"

Seward smiles a tight-lipped grin. "And then he signed a secret order to have Porter take the *Powhatan*. He overruled you!"

He feels a knife sink between his shoulders and a great rushing of blood in his veins. His bunions seem to swell to bursting within his shoes.

"Everything would have worked out just fine. But you had to go and send a second set of orders to the Brooklyn Navy Yard underscoring your earlier orders for the *Powhatan* to go to Sumter. Now Brooklyn's doing nothing because they have three sets of contradictory orders. Great show, Gideon."

"You shat on your president, Mr. Secretary," says Frederick.

The little weasel. His fists tighten. "We'll see about that!"

The president squeezes his chin with his hand, paces the length of the parlor in the East Wing and waits for the butler to finish stoking the fire and quit the room. He's still in his black suit trousers, but his white shirttail sticks out around his pants hangers. His shoes are off. The sound of his silk socks on the oak floor makes a strange squeak.

Welles, Seward, the rodent son and a naval officer named Stringham, who Welles has brought along as a witness, stand just inside the doorway to the parlor handing their coats and hats to a small platoon of uniformed guards.

"Sit, gentlemen," says the president when the guards close the door and leave them alone. Lincoln motions to the divan and cushioned parlor chairs arching around an oriental carpet in the center of the room. The president's own chair is the huge leather wing-back affair facing the fire.

The case clock chimes twelve thirty.

"Excuse my appearance. Mrs. Lincoln says that I have a peculiar tendency to revert to my wood-splitting roots behind closed doors. She may be righter than right. You can take the boy out of Kentuck, but you can't take Kentuck out of the boy … "

The president pauses in his pacing in front of the fire, seems to think about sitting in his chair, then changes his mind, grabs a poker, reshuffles the logs in the fire.

"Now that's better, isn't it?" He smiles to himself, perhaps amused that he has not lost the knack for fire building. "I confess to a certain fondness to those first eight years of life I spent in Kentuck. We didn't have two coppers to rub together ... but still those woods and hills and creeks were all a boy ... But I'm rambling, gentlemen. It has been something of a long day, and by the looks on your faces it is not quite over. Or ... are we about to greet the morn with some new and wondrous tale of hard times in our little frontier town on the backwaters of Chesapeake Bay?"

Settled on the divan, Seward and the rodent cross their arms over their chests and cast each other pained looks in judgment of the president's homey monologue.

Gideon Welles cranes forward on the edge of his seat.

"Mr. President, I fear the relief mission to Fort Sumter is in grave danger."

Lincoln pivots away from the fireplace, jerks his head to one side as if someone has just fired a shot over his shoulder.

"Come again, Gideon?"

"No such thing, Mr. President. The relief convoy has already departed Brooklyn for Charleston. All is as it should be. The Secretary has just gotten himself into a snit about one ship that will not be making the journey."

Welles' eyes pop. "Who started the snit, Seward? Who came beating on my door at eleven o'clock at night to complain that I have balled up the orders for a secret mission with the *Powhatan*? I need that ship. Sumter needs that ship. The whole operation ... "

The president crosses the room and puts his hand on Welles' shoulder.

"Take a deep breath, Gideon. What is this *Powhatan*? *Powhatan, Pocahantas, Pawnee*? I'm afraid I can't keep the names of these ships straight in my head."

"She's a side-wheel frigate, *Saranac* class," says the rodent.

Lincoln either doesn't hear or pretends not to.

"What is she, Gideon?"

Welles explains. *Powhatan* was one of his, er ... the navy's, fastest warships. A steam frigate carrying sixteen heavy guns. A floating fortress. Her presence covering the landing of men and supplies at Sumter would be intimidating enough to General Beauregard's Rebels in Ft. Moultrie to make them think twice, and then twice more, before trying to interfere with the resupply of Sumter by firing off any of their peashooters at the operation. With Sumter resupplied and the *Powhatan* on station at the mouth of Charleston Harbor, the Federals could keep the port closed indefinitely.

Powhatan is just the ship to make South Carolina and the other seceding states realize that picking a fight with the United States of America would be futile, suicidal. Without the *Powhatan*, the resupply of Sumter would look like a half-hearted joke, an armada of mostly tugs and troop barges. The president knows this. He approved sending the *Powhatan* to Sumter under Captain Mercer. Stringham witnessed the order.

"That's ridiculous. A waste of a ship." Seward's on his feet. "The whole Sumter rescue is a shot in the dark, Mr. President. You know that. We've got bigger things to worry about than one puny fort in South Carolina. No matter what we do, it's lost. The Rebs have it surrounded. We give up Sumter now, or we give up Sumter later. It doesn't matter. Sumter has no strategic value if a war breaks out. Secretary Welles is focused on a short-term operation of little moment. As we have discussed, sir, the *Powhatan* is the lynch pin in a long-term, top-secret strategic plan known only to you, me and the operatives. You have signed her orders yourself. Look."

"I did?" Lincoln's face suddenly falls into a mosaic of ruts as he takes the paper Seward hands him, reads. Then, staring at the ceiling as if begging for some god to descend, he motions for Seward to sit.

Welles feels something pound in his chest. *Good Lord, the man doesn't remember his own orders.*

A smug, thin-lipped smile begins to spread over Seward's lips again.

"Lieutenant Porter and I were here with you not more than a week ago. We planned how Porter would take the *Powhatan* to Pensacola to reinforce Fort Pickens and give us a long-term strategic base on the Gulf Coast. You must remember."

Lincoln's mouth moves, but no words come out for several seconds. "I thought ... I thought it was another ship that young man was taking. Surely not the *Powhatan*. You handed me the order, Bill, and ... and I just signed off on it. I didn't note the name of the ship and ... "

Now the president pulls at his ears unconsciously, then hands the secret order to Welles.

"My god, Gideon. Can you forgive me? It seems I have given away your battle ship. Didn't you say she's still waiting in Brooklyn to resolve the confusion in her orders? We can send another order, send her as you planned with Mercer to Fort Sumter."

"Don't do it!" Seward's on his feet, pointing his finger at Lincoln. "You'll destroy the secret mission. We've got troops already committed. You'll lose those men and the Gulf Coast for a stupid little fort in Charleston."

Suddenly a massive tick begins to shudder above the president's right cheek. His lip curls.

"*Sit down*, Mr. Seward. Sit down right now. If you ever point a finger at me again, I'll break it off. Do you understand me, sir? We are not talking about some stupid little fort in South Carolina. We are talking about a symbol. And you know it. We give up Sumter, we are showing the nation's weakness. We are as good as giving the Rebels an invitation to war. Do you want that, Mr. Seward? Do you want Virginia and Maryland to go over to the secesh states? Do you want secesh militia shooting it out with us here on Pennsylvania Avenue? You tricked me, Mr. Seward, into something for your own mercurial purposes. I've been a fool. But once burned, twice shy, sir. Never again, Mr. Secretary! Perhaps it's still not too late to send Gideon's ship to Sumter."

Welles casts a sidelong glance at his companion. Harry Burlow, the blond—almost girlishly handsome—naval lieutenant looks far too young to be the secretary's aide. But Burlow is a Connecticut boy from New London seafaring stock, someone with deep Yankee roots, who he feels he can trust amid a department smothering in men of dubious loyalty.

He has never seen such a mess as the navy's current officer corps. His most active officers are Southerners just waiting for Virginia to go out before tendering their resignations and joining the Rebels. The most senior men in the service are dozens of doddering captains and admirals, in their mid-sixties or older. They do not understand the basics of steamship technology or modern weapons. They find excuses to avoid distasteful duties, and they manipulate squadron orders to make extended pleasure cruises of places like Italy. Worst, the Navy has hundreds of middle-aged lieutenants frustrated by their lack of promotion and opportunities for command within a moribund scheme that fails to retire senior officers. More than a few of these men are bright, ambitious mavericks like David Dixon Porter from well-connected, powerful commercial and political families. Officers who have all the makings to be, what they called in the service, "loose cannons."

"Sir!" Burlow nudges him in the side with an elbow and gives him a broad smile.

A fresh young woman in black silk curtsies before the two of them. She has a tray full of fluted champagne glasses spitting tiny bubbles in the air. With a twinkle in her eyes, she cups the delicate silver tray just beneath her breasts as if offering more than sparkling wine. His gaze slides right down her bare chest into the soft dark space beneath the bodice seam.

"My god, where have you brought me, Lieutenant?"

"Isn't this a gay place, sir?"

Women in reds and yellows are moving about in this brick manse at Sixteenth and I Sts. like butterflies on a spring afternoon. Naval officers in full dress uniform, cavalry colonels, diplomats in morning coats, congressmen, some of the cabinet are here, too. He has already seen Senator Henry Wilson of Massachusetts, the chair of the Military Affairs Committee, and Bill Seward engaged in hushed laughter with women too young to be their daughters.

"Rose Greenhow throws the best parties in Washington," says Burlow, handing him a refill of champagne to replace the one he just bolted. "Isn't this the best? The merry widow receives callers every Monday, Friday and Sunday afternoon. But these Friday gatherings draw the biggest crowd. And, sir, the fishing is easy ... if you know what I mean."

He grumbles.

"I'm telling you, Mr. Secretary, this will be just what the doctor ordered. Nothing else to be done but move on. Put it behind you, sir. Sumter has fallen. The *Powhatan* has gone off to the Gulf with Porter. Let it go. Bring a bit of fun into your day. Life is not all war and politics."

He gulps half of his second champagne, looks around, listens to the laughter, inhales the scents of perfume, powdered skin. *Good Lord, here's Sodom and Gomorrah. Mary Jane would just plain kill me, or throw me out of our happy home, if she knew I was ...*

"Mr. Secretary, what an honor you do us with your presence!" A dark-haired siren of indeterminate age approaches. She's wearing a crimson wool jacket over a navy blue silk dress, and she snakes her arm under his. "I'm Rose. They call me Wild Rose, and I don't have the slightest idea why. Can you guess?"

She presses a breast against his forearm, ushers him through the crowd out into the bright light of a garden where couples and trios are lining up in front of a tintype photographer's tripod.

He sees flashes of red and purple as his pupils try to adjust to the blazing afternoon light.

Where has my willpower gone? He has emptied a third glass of champagne. Across the garden a fiddler begins a romp through "Dixie." People cheer.

He stiffens. Jesus, he has fallen into a harem of secessionists.

"Forgive me, madam, I must go. There is unfinished business at ... "

Greenhow braces her arm tighter in his, clamps her fingers around his wrist. She presses herself against his body with more soft force than Mary Jane ever mustered even in the first year of their marriage.

"Don't leave me without a memory."

"Madam, I insist … "

"Just one second more." Her eyes dart over her shoulder to something or someone.

He tries to wrench her hand from his wrist with his free hand.

"Smile!"

And he does. He can't help himself. He smiles like a pig in shit … as she kisses him long and hard on the lips. The camera clicks.

"Got you, honey," she calls as he flees.

5

Montgomery
LATE APRIL, 1861

He feels the tremors starting in the fingers of his left hand again. He cannot say when he first noticed them, but he knows that they have grown worse since he returned to the South.

"Unacceptable, sir!" He begins fishing for the pencil and a leaf of paper in the little manila folio he has recently taken to carrying to distract his hands from the palsy.

When he finds what he's looking for, he closes the folio, takes the only seat in the barren little waiting room. Then he places the folio on his knee. Using the folio as a tablet, he begins to sketch a picture of a tall-rigged steamship of war with a saucy bowsprit, raked masts, gun ports along her sheer, a funnel belching a plume of smoke. With each stroke of the pencil, the tremors seem to arrest a bit. He feels sharp little currents passing through his hand, but as he draws, his fingers themselves almost cease their shaking. He has just begun to add a huge swivel cannon aft of the foremast, when the door opens to the office of Secretary of the Navy, Confederate States of America.

"Well met, Commander." Stephen Mallory stretches out his hand to take Semmes'. The secretary is a short, middle-aged leprechaun with a nose grown pink from his love of vintage, a belly plump on creole *etoufée* and a ready smile. He loves tossing off the mariner's greeting to another man of the sea.

Semmes returns a smile of respect and brotherhood. While Mallory has never sailed professionally, he has spent his life among ships in Key West. And as a U.S. senator from Florida, he brought his maritime experience to play as chair of the Senate Committee on Naval Affairs. And like Semmes, Mallory loves the study and practice of maritime law. To Semmes' way of thinking, here is a man who will be as valuable to the Confederacy as any man he can think of, including Bobby Lee.

"Well met indeed, sir. What a great day for the South, Mr. Secretary!" Word came earlier by wire that Virginia lawmakers have voted to secede and join the Confederacy. He heard shouting in his soul as well as in the dusty streets of Montgomery.

The two men settle into a pair of easy chairs facing each other over a smoking table. Mallory opens a humidor, pulls out two Havanas. He passes one to Semmes, whom he appointed head of the South's Lighthouse Bureau on his return from buying arms in the North.

"What a day? What a *week*! First, war breaks out in Charleston, then the Yanks give up Sumter. Now Virginia comes over and—as we speak—patriots are making a move on the naval yard at Norfolk."

Mallory says scores of naval officers are crossing over. Norfolk will belong to the Confederation before the week is out. The South will have that amazing arsenal of guns, power and shells with which to defend itself. Best of all the South may have a warship at last. The incompetent Yanks have left her vulnerable and tied at the docks. The *Merrimack,* one of Abe Lincoln's best. A prime warship.

Semmes wills his left hand not to shake as he brings the cigar to his mouth. Mallory leans forward with a match to light it.

"A ship, sir. A ship is the very thing that brings me here, Mr. Secretary. Now that we have war, I want to serve the South at sea. I want to go afloat." He exhales deeply, does not say all that is in his heart. But he can hear the words that had been rolling through his chest all day. *This is my time. It will never come again. I have already passed the prime of life and am going gently down.*

"You want me to give you the *Merrimack*?" Mallory leans back in his chair and blows a fat smoke ring into the air over his head.

He shakes his head no. Even if the South is lucky enough to seize the battle wagon, he could not be so bold as to hope for such a plum. There are officers more senior already in the service of the South, and a flock of younger mariners full of current command experience will be crossing over. The *Merrimack* is too much to ask.

"You found us *another* ship? Good boy, Raphael. I knew that your fishing expedition last month in New York would bear fruit. Jeff Davis was miffed that you did not find us a single ship to buy. But I told him. 'Trust Semmes. He's a sly old boy. He's not going to buy some hulk just so he doesn't have to return empty-handed. He's going to bring us a winner, just give him a little more time.'"

He suddenly feels dizzy. *Holy Mary, Mallory's gone off my mark here.*

"No one can buy arms and equipment like you. I've a mind to send you over to England and France with Bill Yancy to get us ships. How would you like that, Commander?"

A burst of smoke tears from his lungs. He can't catch his breath. A fit of coughing seizes him.

Mallory passes him a paisley hanky.

"Commander? Are you alright?"

He rises to his feet, hacking into the kerchief, staggering toward the open window. He suddenly pulls himself up short, strikes his sternum mightily with his left fist.

"My god, bubba. What are you doing?"

He strikes himself again in the chest. This time something sounding like a deep bark escapes his mouth. Tears roll down his cheeks. He can breathe again.

"A ship. I want a ship of my own." He wipes his face with the hanky.

"Sir?"

He can see Mallory looking at him with the pity of a man watching a friend in the final throws of consumption.

"Give me a ship, Stephen. Please! Give me a ship. I have been long thinking on a plan to rip the Yankee fleet to shreds. I am not as old as I look. God Almighty, I can do you some good."

There. It's out. He has said it. Not the way he rehearsed it, but he has said it. With wet eyes, a voice as horse as an old bosun's ... and a handkerchief waving wildly in the air.

"Sit down, Raphael. The South owes you a great debt already, and I am of a mind to grant you your dearest wish. But what ship can I offer you? *If* we get the *Merrimack*, she must go to one of the Virginians who has rescued her. And our surveyors have condemned everything on both our coasts as unfit for anything but river and harbor patrol. I have no ships."

He collapses into his chair. His shaky fingers tear open the folio he previously dropped on the floor. He finds the sketch he has been working on in the waiting room, hands it to Mallory.

"What's this?"

"A secret weapon."

"Sir?" Mallory studies the sketch.

"She's a cruiser. A steamer, to be sure. But a vessel that can cross oceans under sail if need be. Her stack can be lowered on deck and her rig altered to give her the innocent look of a merchantman. But she will be armed to the teeth. Hidden behind those plain, black bulwarks will be cannons of the first order and a swivel gun, lethal at any angle."

Mallory jerks upright in his chair, his ears pricked.

"And what do we do with this wolf in lamb's clothing?"

"We take her out into the sea lanes. We fly false colors, and draw the Yankees merchant fleet to us as one merchantman always hails another for news and mail and weather." He gets a far-away look. "And when they come within range of our guns, we show them our true colors. We fire across their bows. We stop them. We check their papers. And if they're truly Yanks, we seize our enemy's ship and cargo under the rules of war."

"And if you are short of a prize crew or she carries little of value?"

"We take her crew aboard our cruiser and light up the ocean with her. We render unto her master and men a sight to haunt their hearts, a glorious image of what men will do to protect their God-given rights to freedom and self-determination. We will make the North tremble to go to sea."

Mallory claps his hands. He seems to picture Yankee pandemonium.

"With a small fleet of such cruisers, we could drive insurance rates sky high. Masters would tie up their vessels and sailors would refuse to sail for fear of coming afoul of a Southern seahawk."

For the first time since he has entered the secretary's office, he smiles. *He sees. Mallory sees.*

"We are warred upon by a commercial people whose ability to do us harm consists chiefly in ships and shipping. We stop their shipping, we stop them. And when they feel the pain of their aggression against a people who only wish to be free and go our own way in peace, then they will reconsider their self-righteous palaver and let us be."

"You may be a genius, Raphael. But will the North not accuse us of piracy in the world court? Will they not point to the laws now on the books against privateering? Call us free booters and criminals?"

He feels his teeth set on edge. "Damn them! We are no such thing! A pirate acts out of pure self-interest and preys on innocents. We act in defense of a sovereign nation that has been aggressed upon. The enemy seeks to hold his forts on our soil by force. Mr. Lincoln is calling for seventy-five thousand volunteers to fight us in Virginia."

"Yes. But the world knows nothing about—"

"The world must see we are the victims here. Under the rights of a belligerent nation we have the duty to defend ourselves."

"They will say their merchant ships are not part and parcel of their government. That they act under no orders of the president or congress. That they are simply innocent businessmen going about making a modest living."

He feels the color rising through his neck into his cheeks.

"Rubbish. The world must be made to see—"

"*Tranquilo*," says Mallory, imitating his Spanish wife Angela. He waves the flats of his hands as if trying to stuff a very large rabbit back into a very small hat. "Be calm, Raphael."

"It makes me hot, sir!"

Mallory shakes his head. "Too hot for a diplomat ... by a league. I see it would never do to send you off to Europe with Yancy and his clan of pleasers. I had thought you the man to persuade the shipyards in Liverpool like Lairds and the Frenchy builders in Le Harve to build us a navy."

He takes a deep breath, groans. He knows it is the worst kind of rudeness, but he just can't help himself.

"I beg your pardon," Mallory shoots him a hard look.

He stutters an apology, catches his breath, continues. "There was a time when I might have done admirable service for the cause in this realm of diplomacy and negotiation. But I have measured out my life in teacups and—forgive me, Mr. Secretary—cigars. And now ... and now ... "

"Relax, Commander. You're twitchy as a squirrel on a picket fence ... I like your idea."

He swallows a mouthful of saliva. Something hard around his lungs seems to ease its grip.

"I really like it. We could spend years trying to match the Federals ship to ship, but with an irregular navy of these cruisers we could be at their throats almost immediately. Hurt them before the Yanks can blockade our ports ... as sources claim they are planning to do ... We will have your irregular navy. We will do it. On my word, we will do it, and leave it to the diplomats to make our case with the world, right sir?"

"Yes, but my sh ... I ..."

Mallory lifts his body out of his chair, flaps his hands beside his ears as if to drive off the sound of Semmes' plea, begins to circle the thread-bare hooked rug.

"Listen to you! The land has poisoned you, my friend. It will kill you. The only antidote for you is the roll of the deck in a gale. The thunderclap of cannons. We must get you afloat. But as I told you, I have no ships. Not one. Look at this mess. All condemned as unsuitable for service by our surveyors."

Mallory snatches a file of papers from his desk, hands it to the commander.

Semmes gives the secretary a quizzical look.

"Go on, Raphael. Have a look. Here's a report that came in this morning from New Orleans. Read it, see what you think."

Mallory lights another cigar, pours two fingers of sherry for himself and the commander as Semmes flips through the report.

The secretary is right. New Orleans seems in possession of nothing but worn-out trading vessels.

Save one.

The ship's name is *Habana*. She's almost new, having been built by Vaughn & Lynn at Philadelphia in 1857. She has been earning her keep as the New Orleans-Havana packet. A lightly rigged steamer of about 500 tons, 184 feet on deck. Small for a warship. She has a decent power plant, a vertical, direct-acting, low-pressure Merrick engine turning a single screw that can drive her at nine or ten knots. But she only carries enough coal for five days' steaming. That will never do ... Unless bunker space is somehow added and the rig altered to make her a better sailer.

Whatever the case, this little ship is hardly anything like the grey-hound cruiser he sketched in the waiting room. Still ... the South needs a warship now, not in six months. And who knows whether Mallory or anybody else will give a second chance to an old sea dog. The secretary said it himself, hadn't he? *Land poisoned.*

"Sir ... ?"

Mallory cocks his eye at Semmes as he passes him the crystal of amber sherry.

"Commander?"

Lord Jesus, help me in this, my hour of need.

"Mr. Secretary, give me that ship." His voice is almost a hush. "I can make her answer the purpose."

6

District of Columbia
EARLY MAY, 1861

She feels the sobs bubbling into her throat as the cab lurches. There's a throng of Sunday after-church traffic jamming up Fifteenth St. in front of the treasury building. Fiona O'Hare wraps long arms around her. Draws her face against her soft warm breasts as the flood of tears begins.

"Just go ahead and cry, Maudie. You're safe now."

"It's too much."

"Shhh. Let it go. Let it all go."

Fiona cradles her, runs her long fingers through the copper curls, kisses the top of that lovely head. The cabby casts them an odd look over his shoulder.

It has been two months since her lover left her. Even with his weekly letters, she feels like she's dying. Just bloody drowning. At first, she tried to fill her life with students. She spent sunrise to sunset organizing and reorganizing her classroom until it was, to her mind, the perfect learning nest for the five- and six-year-old daughters of some of Washington's most powerful lawmakers. At night when she couldn't sleep, she wrote. Her heart wanted to write to Raffy every day. But she knew he had a challenging life with the infant Southern navy, and she did not want to plague him with her heartache.

There really was not much more to tell him except how dull and muddy Washington had begun to take on quite a few aspects of a circus. Since the weather had turned warm, tens of thousands of soldiers were arriving to raise a vast village of white tents right outside the Smithsonian and around the still unfinished monument to George Washington. A legion of low and adventuresome woman had followed for romance and profit. And now the city's saloons churned out the piano tunes, operetta anthems, a sultry buzz, the smell of beer twenty-four hours a day.

To keep the circus and the emptiness at bay, Maude tried writing longer letters to her mother back home in Ballyheigue. But the letters were a farce because the only thing she yearned to write of—Raffy—was off-limits. You can't really write about your married gentleman to a woman who makes confession three times a week, rain or shine.

So she's sinking from loneliness, and now she's doing what she has been avoiding for the past year. Throwing herself at Fiona's feet.

"That bleedin' sod left you, didn't he?" Fiona puts her hand beneath Maude's chin, raises her face until the two have eye contact.

She stares up into a face that always makes her heart quiver a little. Fiona has the strong jaw, piercing dark eyes, bold nose, high forehead and straight, shoulder-length black hair of a young knight-errant. You could almost imagine her riding off on a crusade in a chain mail tunic. But the easy crescents of the brows, smooth pale cheeks, deep pink lips promise something more feminine, secret, wildly amorous.

"I love him and ... " The sobs come again, a squall of tears.

"Oh, lass."

Just hold me. Make it all go away.

She presses herself against Fiona and remembers nuzzling her mother like this so many years ago in the little white cottage on Tralee Bay when she had come home from the convent school to hear that her father had passed on. She could not catch her breath then, and she cannot catch it now.

"Pardon. Ah, ladies. Where to now?" The cab has come to a halt at an intersection to wait for a wagon train of artillery pieces and caissons to move on down Pennsylvania Avenue.

She raises her eyes, looks around. A strange new country. Ahead, across the canal to the south, the mall is a fairground of white tents. The sounds of fife and drum marches swells, fades, swells again. A herd of soldiers is filing from the encampment, heading into town. One, a rat-faced boy in blue, catches sight of the women in the hansom, nudges his brother.

"Gaddamn, Luther. Lookee there. Now I see'd everthing. Two tarts sweatin' on each other."

Maude hears, shudders. Pulls herself away from Fiona.

"I got three dollars. How about we ride on down there by the river and make it a threesome?" The rat-face steps up to the cab, leers at the women, licks the corner of his mouth with a tongue that flicks in and out like a fat pink worm.

She feels her face flush.

"I've got to get out of here."

"Driver, turn around!" Fiona calls.

The rat-face has a grip on the door of the cab with both hands. The worm is still licking his thin lips. He seems on the verge of popping open the door and leaping aboard.

Something flashes in her mind. A stiff bolt of fire shoots down her spine, turns her back to iron. Some basic polarity in her body shifts and her tears change into a different sort of storm altogether.

She leans forward until she's eye to eye with the rat. So close she can smell his chaw of sour tobacco.

"Bugger off!" She pulls back her head, a viper sizing up her prey, and spits right into the soldier's face. She can see the web of her phlegm stretching over his nose as the cab lurches into a U-turn on Fifteenth St.

"Let's go!"

The driver puts the whip to his horse. It breaks into a trot.

"Heathen cunny lappers! You'll burn in hell." The soldier wipes the spit from his face.

She falls back into her seat, folding her hands together, bringing them to her lips. Casts her gaze up to the cornices of the surrounding buildings.

"What's come over me?"

"These Yankees are a curse. They could make a person insane."

"He's just an ignorant boy. I don't know why I let him get to me like that."

"Because you're a tiger, lass."

She shakes her head at the idea. *No I'm not*, she thinks. *I'm just a silly school teacher in love with a married man.*

But what she says is, "Where are you taking me?"

"I didn't know until just this second, love."

Her hand presses down on the leather cushion between them. Fiona covers it with her own.

Until a year ago, they had shared a room together on Capitol Hill. They had met on the bark to New York from the Shannon River three years ago, and for their first two years in America, the two of them lived together like favorite sisters. Maude the younger free spirit; Fiona the older, pensive one. Both of them trailing their girlhood with them when they sailed from the West Country in search of a better life across the sea. They found each other in a women's reading group on the ship, discovered that each of them had trained as a teacher. Aimed for careers in the States.

"Together forever," Fiona said when they decided to seek their fortunes together in the boomtown that was the American capital. Fiona found a teaching job at the St. Mary's Academy for Girls first, brought Maude aboard almost immediately when a colleague left to have a baby.   Life for the young teachers was a laughter-filled adventure in teaching, homemaking, shared novels, candlelit confessions over glasses of peach wine. The pair made forays to museums, theaters, concerts. Attended lectures on the new art of photography, which fascinated them both. An amateur historian, Fiona read the dailies ravenously. She took a keen interest in the slavery question and came to favor Southern secession from the Union. For her part, Maude was infatuated with theater, particularly the work of the magnificent Booth family. She could not have imagined that anything was missing in her life ... until Raphael Semmes.

The day after she had spent a night with her navy man in a Foggy Bottom hotel, the roommates fought.

"I think you are making a terrible mistake with this man, Maudie," Fiona said. "And words cannot tell you how betrayed I feel. But God must judge you, not I. My job is to be here when you need me, to be here when you come to your senses. To hold you in my heart."

Maude still cannot say why, but those words cut her. They made her feel shame, resentment, something even darker that she could only cast off by moving to a place of her own.

Now, as she rides west on I St. in the cab with Fiona, those words echo in her head.

"I was cruel to you on a spring day like this last year. And you have always been so good to me. Even after. Even now. Will you forgive me?"

Fiona squeezed her friend's hand.

"Always."

Maude puts her head on Fiona's shoulder, inhales the scent of her musky perfume. Listens to the clopping of the horse's hooves. The time seems all too short before Fiona hails the driver to turn left on Sixteenth St., stop in front of Number 398, a redbrick manse across the street from St. John's Church.

"Let's go meet some interesting people."

"I don't understand."

"Just wait, love. I promise this is going to put a new spring in your step."

7

New Orleans
MAY 27, 1861

The one-time Havana packet shudders with the changing of the tide near midnight. Back aft the figure of a man who has been pacing the quarterdeck in the thin fog comes to an abrupt halt. His legs spread apart, his shoulders square as if bracing himself for a rogue wave. The shuddering timbers increase their vibration. Suddenly, the ship yaws away from her dock, comes taught against her spring lines with the screech of manila, then veers back toward shore, ramming a piling along the levee with the heavy crack of splitting wood.

"Oh, Lord, now what must I repair?" He holds his frozen stance, but his eyes wander away from his ship down the Mississippi into the foggy pitch south of New Orleans. "Will we ever get on, girl?"

He heaves a deep sigh, settles on a crate of muskets near the steering wheel. Runs his hands through his damp hair, stares forward over the length of his ship. He has renamed her *Sumter*; might as well have called her *Victory* ... so high are his hopes for her. But the last two months have been a desperate fight to ready her for sea. A race against the Yankees. Now, lookouts have sent word up to New Orleans in the afternoon that the *USS Brooklyn* has arrived off the Delta. The newspapers say she's the first of what is sure to be a flotilla of Yankees acting on General Winfield Scott's Anaconda Plan, the blockading of Confederate ports. Meanwhile, every day his hopes of commissioning his vessel, shipping the crew and making a run for deep water seem further delayed by a mountain of new problems.

Unconsciously his hand reaches out, grabs a spoke of the steering wheel before him and gives it a hard spin.

This can't be how we end. We have come too far, mustered too much energy to end our days rotting at a wharf. Surely, God would not tempt me with this dream just to rip it from my fingers when it's almost within my grasp.

What he, his officers, the shipyard mechanics in Algiers have accomplished already is nothing short of a miracle. In less than sixty days they have transformed a ship, which he judged on first survey to be nothing more than a dismantled packet-ship — as unlike a ship of war as possible. Over-loaded with upper cabins and other top-hamper, furniture, crockery. Working from his drawings, the mechanics have stripped the *Sumter* of her passenger cabins, strengthened the main deck to hold cannons. They have raised her freeboard almost ten more feet above the waterline to make room for a berthing deck to house a hundred jacks and marines. Carpenters have given the ship a flush deck, crafted officers' cabins, added water tanks, more coal bunkers. Protected the engine with an armor of timber, iron bars.

He and his officers have supervised the fabrication of magazines, requisitioned four thirty-two-pound cannons from the stockpiles liberated from the Yankees at Norfolk, designed almost from scratch an eight-inch pivot gun, ordered sails and yards to make the ship a more capable and weatherly sailer with a barkentine rig. But nothing was easy. The shipwrights of Algier, where the *Sumter* lay across the river from New Orleans, were not warship builders. He had to teach them a career's worth of knowledge. He even had to show them how to cast the shot for his cannons.

"The Yankee licks his lips at our door, and we are still not ready!" He mutters aloud to his empty ship, the fog, himself. Then he suddenly pops off his seat on the wheel box, dropping with a thud to the deck with both feet. He looks toward the bows of his ship and scowls at all the empty space he sees. The cannons have not yet arrived from Norfolk; their gun carriages are not finished. The iron track for the swivel gun has still not been firmly anchored to the deck nor the gun mounted.

But it isn't really these empty spaces, the snarl of loose ends, the repairs to splintered timber, the work that worries him. It isn't even the facing off with the Yankees at sea. He has written Maude that if truth be told, he likes this work. He has not felt so alive since he left her arms. It's a different kind of alive, to be sure, but still his blood hums. He relishes the challenge of building a warship almost from scratch to his own design. He loves being out-of-doors, likes feeling sweat on his brow, trickling down between his shoulder blades.

And he enjoys meaningful command. Officers listen to him here. Children come by for autographs from the commander of the first Southern warship. Women bring him bowls of tangy gumbo. Business men have cases of champagne and Burgundy delivered to the ship. And through all the sweat and sawdust and well-wishers, he finds himself in his work. Finds the confidence and energy of the young man who commanded the *Somers* before the norther tore her and him to pieces, finds the dreamer who fell in love with Maude Galway.

He puts his hands on his waist, walks forward along the larboard rail of his ship. He surveys the loose yards and bundles of sails yet to be heaved aloft. He moves in slow steps just as he knows he will when it comes time to muster his crew here on the main deck, inspect them for readiness, stoke their spirits with rousing words about freedom, bait their appetites by conjuring the sweet taste of victory known only to the underdog. And, of course, there will be prize money for dividing.

But now he feels his stomach churn. What weighs on him, what nags at his mind, after the tedium and struggles of preparing ship and men, is this race with the Yanks, this fear that he might never escape the Yankee blockade of the Delta. *What if time has really passed me by ... and I no longer have the wits and skill to sail a warship? What if after all of these machinations, my handsome and saucy ship is simply too small, too fragile and too short on coal to shoulder the titanic task I have set for her? What if I fail my family, my officers, my men, my love? What then?*

He's standing near the main fife rail. Suddenly his right hand grabs an unused belaying pin, draws it back over his shoulder as if preparing to throw a field knife, lets fly. The pin strikes a brass ventilator over the fo'castle with a loud clang.

"Jesus Christ Almighty!" he says aloud. *Save me. If I be fortune's fool.*
"Is everything alright, sir?"
His body jerks, surfacing from a dream.
"Who goes there?"
"Freeman, sir." The voice seems to come from the dark deck itself.
"I thought I was alone."
"Been below, sir. Burning the midnight oil, so to speak. Just tinkering a bit, you know."

Lantern light suddenly glows from midships. The face of engineer M. J. Freeman rises in the glow above the engine room hatch, cheeks and forehead streaked with grease as dark as the Vandyke around the mouth. A long mane of black hair is tied back in a ponytail. As Semmes approaches the hatch, he can see Freeman standing on the engine room ladder, his bare torso slick with sweat, grease, kinky hair. One hand holds a lantern, the other a massive pipe wrench.

"I thought you might be a Yank or a spy come aboard to play us some tricks."

He smiles, seems to picture this bear of an engineer assailing a legion of Yankees with his pipe wrench. Samson slaying the thousand Philistines.

"The Yanks are indeed afoot," says the commander as if to explain his own nocturnal patrolling of an empty ship.

"The *Brooklyn*, sir. We've all heard the news. Some of the deck officers say she can make better than twelve knots. That's the scuttlebutt, anyway. So I thought I better look to our tea kettle a bit more, eh? She's as good as they come for a low pressure system, sir. But I ain't guaranteeing us twelve knots. Only so much speed you can get out of a little hull like this. But one thing I'll bet on, Captain: she'll outrun anything her own size and weight. You picked yourself some boat. Fast and strong as a bull seal."

He squats next to the hatch, looks his engineer in the eyes. Suddenly wants to hear more from the man who was engineer aboard this ship when she was still the Cuba-New Orleans packet. Freeman came to Semmes and the Confederate navy as "part of the package," as the rugged Welshman says. Where the ship goes, he goes. "The man knows things," said Lawrence Rousseau, the Confederate captain in charge of the port of New Orleans who confiscated the *Habana*. "I'm not saying he's a guardian angel or a secret weapon, but pay attention to him, Commander, y'all hear?"

"You've been on a sealer?" He doesn't know why he asks this.

"Aye, one trip. Was enough, sir. Second engineer. Hellish brutal, it was. Cold and ice, blood and stink. Even though I weren't a direct part o' it, that kind of killing ... it was inhumane. Just got under my skin, to speak frankly, sir. A slaughter. Innocent seals. Not like your fish or even whales; they had souls, sure. You could hear 'em cry, even laugh sometimes, they do. This Irish bloke on the boat claimed ... well, he said some was what they call selkies. Spirits of women. Did you ever hear of such a thing?"

Maude. He almost says the name, feels something sharp in his chest, has to change the conversation, cast off a sailor's superstition ... and the sound of her laughter.

"How's the engine coming, Mr. Freeman? Will it be ready?"

"It's a right big box of puzzle pieces just now, sir. But she'll purr when I get her ... Would you like to have a peek?"

He nods, still in the thrall of Freeman. "As long as both of us are strangers to sleep ... "

"Night's a cursed thing sometimes." The engineer leads his captain down the ladder into the dark. "Just a bloody ordeal."

You don't know. But then again, maybe you know all too well, and I've shipped another maniac.

When they reach the bottom of the ladder, Freeman holds his lantern at arm's length overhead. Slowly the shadows resolve themselves into shapes. The engineer was not lying when he chose the words "puzzle box." Cylinder heads, pistons, rods, wrist pins, steam pipes, a couple hundred bolts, washers, leather gaskets spread over the coal- and oil-stained catwalk around the engine block. Tubs of grease, crocks of pipe dope, wrenches of every possible size fill almost every vacant space of floor so that he sees no place for his feet ... if he tries to take even a step away from the ladder.

"Good God!"

"Sorry about the dirt, sir."

"What are you ... ?"

"Changing out the bearings, sir. Trying to take some of the slop out of the piston rods and things, as it were. Increase the compression. Give her a bit more speed for certain."

He gasps for breath. Even with the boilers cold, the heat and humidity feel suffocating.

"This isn't a job, it's a life's work! Mr. Freeman, the Yankees are breathing down our necks, we've got just a few days left. We've got to run, and you ... you tear down my engine ...!"

8

District of Columbia
LATE MAY, 1861

What's going on here, Lieutenant? Who's gotten into my office?"
Welles glares at the plume of pipe smoke roiling from the open
door to the one room in his life where he felt safe from liars, cheats,
madmen and whores. He hates tobacco smoke.

Burlow, who has been reading the *Star* at his desk, bolts to his
feet, salutes.

"Stop that. I'm not some bloody prince. Now, tell me who ... "

He does not pause in his charge across the ante room toward the
smoke and light blooming from his inner sanctum.

"Ah ... admirals, sir. And senior captains. They call themselves *The
Curmudgeons*. Burst in here a half hour ago. Half-past eight it was.
Demanding to see you. Marched right in with the morning light, guns
blazing, as they say. I couldn't stop them. Said they wouldn't leave
until you give them a hearing. Claimed you've been putting them off
for weeks."

*Damn these entitled sons of donkeys. For years they have been doing
little but writing each other orders to keep themselves afloat in Washington and Annapolis society rather than at sea. Shore captains! Tea
party admirals!*

He crosses the threshold into his large office, whips the white summer cape from his shoulders. Flings it on the coat tree by the door. His
wig is cocked sideways a bit from the flurry, and he quickly presses it
back in place with both hands.

"Gentlemen, what is the meaning of this?"

Nine, possibly ten officers sit in a ring of cane chairs that they must
have dragged in here from the ante room.

"Just a friendly visit from your seniors, Mr. Secretary." The speaker, in dress blues and gold epaulettes, looks almost as pink and fat as a prized pig. As old as McCauley who gave up the Norfolk Navy Yard to the Rebs last month.

"We have grievances, sir." The admiral sucks on a huge meerschaum until his face goes gray.

"This Anaconda Plan, this so-called blockade of General Scott's is ill-advised."

"It is going to dismantle a naval service it has taken us fifty years to build."

"Wipe us out in one fell swoop."

"To build this impossible blockade of the South you have called home our Pacific, Mediterranean, Far East and South American squadrons."

"Left us one ship to deter the slave trade in West Africa. Gads!"

He has to pass right through the middle of the circle of officers to get to the relative security of his desk. And when he pauses there in the center of the navy blue rug surrounded by all this brass, he wants to growl.

"Would you gentlemen please do me the kindness of not smoking. I have a crippling aversion ... "

He finds his desk, stands behind it, slams down a paperweight that looks like a miniature half-hull model of the frigate *Constitution*.

"Now!"

The officers jump. One of them finds a brass spittoon and begins passing it around. One by one the men bang out the contents of their pipes into the urn.

"We were hoping this would be a cordial meeting. That you would be willing to hear us out and stand with us against the army's plan. But I see we may be headed for ... " The fat one is speaking again.

"Confrontation." A captain with white hair and a dyed black beard frowns.

"Perhaps so, gentlemen ... " He surveys the face of the officers, thanks God that Stringham and David Farragut are not among them. Perhaps he still has some allies.

Don't start fights, Gideon. Please don't get your hackles up. Pick your battles. He hears his wife Mary Jane's voice pleading in his head.

A chair screeches on the floor. He opens a window, waves the last of the pipe smoke away.

"Gentlemen, let's make a new start here."

He thinks he hears a collective sigh. But maybe it is just his own chest gasping for air.

"Like you, I take my orders from the commander in chief. One of those orders is to initiate a blockade of ten thousand miles of coast with a navy that has fewer than fifty active ships. Squadrons simply must be recalled. Priorities shifted. Still, I promise you I will give you a fair hearing."

"Then why have you made it so difficult for us to have this exchange?"

He feels the tips of his ears burning, hears Mary Jane's pleas again. Lowers himself into his chair at the desk, takes a deep breath, counts to ten.

"My apologies. The current cascading of events. All the recent defections. This war ..."

He pauses. *It's a monumental mistake; it's tearing all of us ...*

He closes his eyes and searches for different words. "It is a challenge to us all."

"Yes, sir." The black beard sees his opening. "And an opportunity ... if we could persuade the current administration to back us, to let us go on the offensive."

He cocks his head. *The offensive?*

"Closing the Southern ports is a job for the Revenue Service, not the navy."

"It is a waste of our resources and expertise. While we are marking time on picket duty off Charleston or Mobile, who will be protecting our merchant ships trading with Europe, the West Indies and South America? Who will be looking after our whalers in the Pacific? The South has already launched privateers to prey on our merchantmen and whalers. Every day the newspapers print stories about Rebel commercial raiders being readied for sea. We're the shepherds, and we're abandoning our flocks to the wolves, sir!"

"I say General Scott is too old to command. He's lost his nerve for battle. That's why he wants this blockade. He thinks he can starve the South into submission without a head-on fight. But he doesn't know these Rebs. They're foaming at the mouth."

He thinks about how the Rebs stole the navy yards at Norfolk and Pensacola. How they've been shelling vessels right here on the Potomac from batteries at Aquia Creek and Alexandria.

"This blockade is for the birds, Mr. Secretary. We must go on the offensive. Drive a squadron right into Mobile, or reclaim the James River. Bold attacks. That is what will stop the rebels!"

The room echoes, a collective "Aye."

The black beard speaks again.

"And 'blockade' is absolutely, let me repeat, *absolutely* the wrong word to use here. In the parlance of international law a blockade is the thing one nation does to an enemy's ports. But our fight is not against a foreign enemy, but rather to quell a local insurrection. To bandy about the word 'blockade' as has been done in print and public by the president and others for the last month is to acknowledge the legitimacy of this puppet so-called Confederate government as an enemy nation. To use the term 'blockade' invites other countries to acknowledge the same, give the South the status of a belligerent nation, belligerent rights. That means Rebel ships will have safe harbor in foreign ports, Rebel agents will have the diplomatic immunity of ambassadors. Rebel smugglers will have rights of legitimate trading partners. Shall I go on?"

He suddenly discovers that at some point during this last speech he began biting his thumb.

"I think I see your point." He speaks softly. *My god, these old fuss budgets could be right.*

"Are you with us, Mr. Secretary? Will you save the navy and the nation from a terrible error?"

The Thursday cabinet meeting has already lasted most of the morning. For the past hour he has not had a single chance to respond to the onslaught of fire aimed his way from his fellow secretaries after presenting his senior officers' case against the blockade.

Just now, a red-faced Bill Seward is holding forth ... again.

"We're a joke, Mr. President. The South and the press are calling Secretary Welles' boys the Paper Navy. Ships are passing with impunity to and from the Confederate States through his pretense of a blockade. And these admirals and captains want to abandon the operation? Nonsense. I don't understand them. We need to *add ships,* many more ships to the blockade. Give Welles the money to buy more ships. Show the South our teeth and claws, sir. Put some balls into this blockade!"

Lincoln's cheeks flinch.

"Enough of that kind of talk, Mr. Seward. I won't have it here! You've made your point."

"He speaks for the army and us in the War Department too, Mr. President."

The Secretary of War Simon Cameron shoots a wink at Seward.

Lincoln pushes his chair back from the Cabinet table, puts his hands behind his neck, leans back to stretch his body. It looks seven feet long.

"My natural inclination is to favor this blockade, gentlemen. I am not a military man, and so maybe it is harder for me to understand the urge to attack the South. Bottling them in seems the safer thing to do, puts the lives of fewer men and boys at risk."

He feels someone kick his ankle hard under the table.

"Maybe I'm just a poor country lawyer, but darned if I don't think Mr. Welles' officers have a point here about how we've been using this word 'blockade.' The last thing we want to do is open the door for the English, French, Spanish, Dutch or the South Americans to acknowledge these Rebel states as a legitimate nation. What do you think, Mr. Bates?"

Attorney General Ed Bates opens his mouth to speak, but Seward cuts him off.

"Silliness, Mr. President. Utter tripe. Semantic games to cloud the issue that Welles' senior officers are a defiant bunch who crave the glory of attack and battle at the expense of innocent, young lives. At the expense of the nation, sir!"

"Mr. Seward, I asked Mr. Bates ... "

"You must hear this, sir! There must be no doubt about the need for a strong blockade. My diplomats are in constant contact with foreign heads of state and their ambassadors here. If some nation wanted to pick a linguistic bone with us about this term 'blockade,' if some country is thinking about recognizing the Rebels as a legitimate nation, I would have heard about it. But I've heard nothing. The term is not an issue."

Welles rises halfway to his feet. "Come on, Bill. England is furious with us!"

"Yes, some of our allies abroad are concerned about this blockade. As well they should be. It threatens their trade for cotton and rice. But I see this as an advantage for us. When we hear these foreign complaints, this is what we're telling foreign governments at State: respect the blockade, keep your ships home for a month or two. Help us to starve these Rebels into submission. By the time summer is over you can have all the cotton and rice you want. At reasonable prices. Not on the inflated terms currently offered in Charleston, Savannah and Mobile."

Lincoln sighs.

"Secretary Bates, pa-lease speak!"

Ed Bates clears his throat. He looks toward Seward, Cameron.

"In the abstract, Mr. President, Secretary Welles and his officers may have a point about the misuse of the term 'blockade.' 'Closing' the ports is the proper term in the case of a rebellion. But according to Secretary Seward, 'blockade' may well be the only term foreign nations will understand. And understanding is what we want here, not a lot of abstruse sea-lawyer niggling. The British, the French, the Dutch, the Spaniards must cooperate. They must help us. They must believe that it is in their own best interest to respect this blockade and cease trade with the South. That is why I fully support Mr. Cameron and Mr. Seward. What we need here is not the dismantling of the blockade for the dubious purpose of a naval attack against our own citizens and families. Not even the changing of our terminology. What we need here is one monstrously scary blockade to make foreign traders stay home!"

"Well said." Sal Chase, Secretary of the Treasury, claps his hands together twice. Loudly.

"I agree," says the Postmaster General.

"Mr. Welles. Where do you stand now?"

The President has his hands clasped together propping up a massive, whiskered jaw. He stares at the Secretary of the Navy.

He shifts in his seat, feels a numbness in his left leg. *The Curmudgeons will be hate me.*

"Anything to prevent bloodshed, Mr. President."

The president raises his chin from his hands and smiles.

"Good boy," says Seward.

Welles is not finished.

"If we go on with the Anaconda plan, then Secretaries Seward and Cameron are most distinctly correct. I need money to buy a lot of ships and man them, sir." He pauses. Then he says the words he has not yet been able to give voice to ... even in his own mind. "And I need money to retire a lot of senior officers to make room for new leadership in the service, leadership more to our way of thinking."

"Sal?" The President turns to his Secretary of the Treasury.

"We'll have to go to Congress for a war appropriations bill."

"Then so be it. I'll meet with the Speaker of the House and ranking senators tomorrow. Gideon, we will get you your ships and a retirement plan. And to prevent any misunderstanding in foreign capitals, I will issue a public order to the Navy saying that heretofore we intend to 'close' rebellious ports with squadrons of picket vessels. I encourage all of you to avoid this double-edged word 'blockade.'

"The horse is already out of the barn," says someone under his breath.

The big brick fireplace at the Middleton Tavern in Annapolis stinks of sap wood ashes on the humid night when William Seward meets the Curmudgeons around a table for crab cakes and baked oysters.

"Gentlemen, Secretary Welles has stabbed you in the back. Not only has he cast his lot with those who want to strengthen the blockade, but he aims to assure loyalty within his service by ramrodding a bill through Congress that will force you into retirement."

"The poxy bastard!"

"We should send him home to Hartford with an ass-load of marlin spikes!"

"Exactly. Stick with me, sirs." Seward raises a mug of ginger beer and rum in toast.

9

District of Columbia
EARLY JUNE, 1861

Rose Greenhow opens her arms to Maude, draws her up against a chartreuse bodice of rich brocade.

"Congratulations, dear, you've passed the test."

After more than a month of visits with Fiona to the salons at the manse on Sixteenth St., Maude is used to Rose's forwardness, her almost constant need to touch people. So now she accepts the embrace, which always ends with a little squeeze under the arm to that sensitive place alongside her breast. But today's different. There's no salon.

The dozen or so women standing in the library of the manse clap as Rose embraces Maude.

"Welcome to the best kept secret in the District."

Maude scans the room of powdered faces, jeweled necklines, ruby lips.

"This is the surprise I promised," says Fiona, who stands by Maude like an escort.

Maude brushes a long copper curl from her right eye with a gloved hand, tries to smile at the assemblage.

"The first Saturday of the month is our time for ourselves," says Bettie Duvall, a tall, dark-haired beauty in crinoline and lace. She stands behind a petite widow, Augusta Morris, hugging her casually around the waist as if she were a child.

"No whiskery, cigar-stinking, chest-puffing tall children ... commonly known as *men*," says a musical voice. "Let them imagine what they will of us. But they will never bear witness to our private lives."

"Not in their wildest dreams!" Greenhow rolls her eyes coquettishly.

The group laughs.

Maude looks at the silk and lace, the pink and yellow spring gowns of the women eyeing her from across the room, and feels distinctly shabby in her second-hand blue satin tea dress. These women look so beautiful so ... so regal. And yet she has heard the gossip. Fiona lets things slip from time to time when she gets in one of her snippy moods. Such-and-such a widow is running a senator; the refined Miss so-and-so can be bought for fifty dollars a night; Rose Greenhow keeps a secret room with hoods and whips; quite a few of the ladies have a fondness for long, candlelit baths with each other. She has also heard rumors of blackmail and worse.

"Since Fiona started bringing you to my teas, we've all taken quite a shine to you, Maudie," says Greenhow. She draws herself between the two West Irish school teachers, slips an arm behind the back of each, ushers them across the room to where Bettie Duvall has begun pouring a pale pink punch into crystal glasses.

"We think the two of you are gems."

"I've never felt so at ease as I do here, Rose," says Fiona. "All my life, in Ireland and in Washington, I've always felt like a stranger. But when I'm here, I feel as if I've finally come home."

"You have, dear. You most certainly have."

Greenhow stretches her neck and gives Fiona a kiss on the neck just beneath the ear. She kisses her back, catches Maude's gaze out of the corner of her eye. Gives a little shrug—as if this kiss could not be helped—then blushes.

She looks away toward the punch bowl. *Does she aim for me to be jealous? Am I?*

"Let the monthly meeting of Women Warriors begin," says Augusta Morris, raising her glass.

"Long live Dixie." The group in unison.

She suddenly thinks of the man she has been trying so hard to forget, pictures him in his ribbons and gold braid staring out to sea from the deck of a ship he calls the *Sumter*. Something burns deep in her chest, and she wonders how she will fill this space Raffy has left, whether the answer lies with these women.

In the afternoon, the women shift their festivities to a huge red-checkered picnic blanket in a sun-dappled glade along the eastern side of Rock Creek. There's a picnic basket of smoked fish and French cheeses, chilled bottles of sweet Rhine wine. Betty Duvall has a mandolin with pearl inlays. She strums romantic melodies the minstrels sing at the summer Shakespeare offerings. Songs Maude loves like "Greensleeves;" songs with "hey-nonny, nonny" choruses that they can all sing; rude country songs like "Roll Me Over in the Clover" that bring laughter. Through all the music, women stretch out on the blanket. Some with their shoes kicked off, some plaiting and unplaiting a friend's long hair, a few with their heads reclined in a companion's lap. And with them is Maude. Reclining on an arm, blowing dandelion spores into the sky, watching with feigned disinterest as to what might happen next.

"You seem so pensive, Maudie. Will you walk with me?" Rose Greenhow is on her feet. She holds an open white linen parasol in one hand, offers her free hand to help Maude up from the blanket.

For three or four seconds she just looks up into Greenhow's face as if she's trying to read the woman's soul, or maybe her own. She feels Fiona watching her. Then she gives a shy little smile and takes the offered hand.

The pair stroll silently, arm-in-arm beneath their parasols, following a path downhill along the edge of the creek.

"What ails you, pretty lady?"

Maude takes a deep breath.

"I hardly know where to begin, Miss Rose."

"Just 'Rose,' dear. Call me as I am."

"My heart aches, Rose. It pulses with a riot of emotions I can hardly trace or name. I start every day thinking this will be the day I will find some peace ... and every day I seem to slip deeper into a swamp of sadness and confusion."

"You've lost your man. A naval officer, gone for the South, Fiona tells me." Greenhow tries to catch her eye, but she looks away into the deep, green woods.

"It sounds silly, doesn't it? When I look around at all of you women and how you sustain each other without any dependence on men, I feel such the bloody, little fool."

"I lost a man, too. Doctor Greenhow. The greatest shock of my life. Just gone. Dead. How I wept. You cannot help but weep. My poetess Sappho knows. 'Delicate Adonis is dying Cytherea, what shall we do? Beat your breast maidens, and rend your tunics.' There's no grief like it. And it is always, *always* happening to us. There are so many things that rob us of men, but war is the worst. And unless someone stops the coming calamity, it will be the worst of the worst."

She stops, lets her parasol slip off at an oblique angle, brushes a curl away from her forehead, peers into Greenhow's face.

"We all fear what Lincoln is bringing upon this land, dear. Almost all of us have lost men. Husbands, fathers, sons. Perhaps that is why we take so much comfort in women now. They support us, they understand us, they love us as themselves and they never leave. When a woman holds you in her heart, only death or wild horses will tear her away. And only in body. So we go on. Sisters. Think how your mother still holds a place in your heart across time and oceans. But your father?"

She shakes her head sadly, feels tears coming. There's something true in what Greenhow says. Her mother was always there next to her heart. But when her father died, he slipped away from her like the sixteenth summer of her life, leaving in his place a hollow pain from memories plucked out of her chest by time in tiny bunches.

"I wish I were as strong and confident as you, Rose."

Greenhow drops her parasol, places both her hands on Maude's cheeks and presses her forehead to the younger woman's.

"I'm middle-aged and scared to death, dear. But keep that to yourself, will you? I've got a big job to do. I have to play Lysistrata. We have to end this war before it begins. Have to stop Lincoln and the Yankees before they start their blood bath. Will you help?"

She smells the wine on Greenhow's breath.

"How?"

"Fiona tells me you are a tigress; I need a tigress. These loyal ladies you see today have their talents, and they have strong motivations to serve. But they are not tigers. To speak plainly, Maudie, they are lonely widows, courtesans, prostitutes and bored society women. They use their positions and connections in Washington to gain intelligence about Yankee war plans for me. I send secret reports off to Jeff Davis. For some of these women the motive is an abiding love of Dixie and loyalty to their sisters. For others, the motive is support for lovers, husbands, fathers, brothers and sons who will surely see combat for the South."

She takes a step back from Greenhow, gives a wild-eyed look of confusion and panic.

"Why me? I'm just a simple school marm."

"You have uncommon courage and a Southern officer grafted to your soul, a man whose life will be much at risk if the Yankee war-mongering is not stopped soon. You may be in a position to do nothing less than save his life."

She turns away, wrings her hands.

Greenhow steps close to her back, rubs a hand along the blade of Maude's hip.

"Here is the sad truth. Most of our Women Warriors have come into my secret service in search of a little wickedness to put spice in their lives. But none of them, not even sweet Fiona with her fiery words against the Yanks, is a tigress. None has the self-assuredness and pride to spit in the face of a Yankee soldier."

She pivots, faces Greenhow, feels fire rising in her head.

"Fiona had no right—"

"Peace, peace, child." Greenhow takes both of her hands again. "Save your spite for the government who would visit death upon tens of thousands of Southern boys and men—men like your Commander Semmes!"

She pictures Raffy amid a cloud of cannon smoke, smells burning wood, hears the crash of falling spars slapping decks and ocean.

"What do you say, Maudie? Will you join us? Will you be my tigress?"

Greenhow holds her in a deep gaze, draws so close their petticoats crush together at the waists.

10

Mississippi Delta
JUNE 29-30, 1861

He sits at his desk in *Sumter*'s great cabin, glares at a dozen river pilots who stand before him under armed marine guard.

They do not look like the angels of deliverance he hoped for. They appear ordinary men, some bearded, some clean-shaven, some youthful, many middle-aged. All dressed in open shirts, loose pants, the peculiar hemp-soled slippers of the clannish Cajuns who man the pilots' station. They live at the river's edge in a collection of stilt shacks known as Pilottown with their families here at Head of the Passes in the Mississippi Delta, seventy-five miles below New Orleans.

"I am putting an end to your delinquency, sirs. Right here, right now!" he says. The *Sumter* has been anchored off the pilots' station for nearly two weeks waiting for guidance to put to sea. Meanwhile Federals have moved more ships in to help the *Brooklyn* blockade the river. Now the *Powhatan, Minnesota* and *Niagara* are patrolling out there, too. Laying in wait for the *Sumter*.

He grinds his back teeth as he squints at the pilots. They stink of this infernal river, infest his cabin with the scents of crab, muskrat, goose grease and putrid, salt-marsh mud.

"We must break out of this delta, before an entire Yankee squadron arrives. You know this right well. Yet it seems you would have me, my ship and men rot here. You make excuses every time I get steam up and send for a pilot. Hell's blazes!"

A barrel-chested fellow steps forward and spreads his arms as if to sing.

"But *Capitaine*, we must wait for a dark night and a fog to take you out. The moon has been too high and ... and surely, you know what the Yankees will—"

"Hush up, man! We are done with excuses about time, tide, moon, stars, weather, shoals. I've heard them all. This ship WILL put to sea, or we will die trying. Hear me. We go on my order, not yours. The *Sumter* is a ship of war, not some broke-back cotton smuggler. Hence forth, one of you shall remain aboard my vessel ready to guide her to sea at a moment's notice." His voice booms. His mustache flicks with each word. "Understood?"

The air in the cabin suddenly seems piped straight from the boilers. No one speaks. The pilots shuffle their feet. He drums the desk with his fingers. Finally, the pilots stutter their reluctant compliance. Then all but one shambles out of the great cabin, escorted by the marine musketeers. The pilot he orders to remain behind begins to protest that he is but an apprentice.

"You'll do ... Or you will die like the rest of us in the service of the South."

June 30. Blazing sun, thick haze, burning the captain's eyes to squinting. Nowhere to turn for relief. High tide at Head of the Passes. The ship, the water, the marsh grass all look aflame.

This is Purgatory. I'm paying for my betrayals.

The voice of the luff, First Officer John McIntosh Kell, sounds faint, something from a daydream, as it orders the bosun to pipe the crew to attention for their weekly full-dress inspection. Semmes turns his back on the ship's company, slaps his left cheek hard as if to wake himself. Starts a measured march forward from the quarterdeck to begin the inspection.

Shouts from a Cajun fisherman break the cadence of the captain's boots on the fir planks.

"*Allons, allons.* Let's go, on the *Sumter*. Let's go!"

Second Officer Lieutenant R. T. Chapman, a blue-eyed ladies' man, dashes to the port rail, no doubt with the intent of quelling this disruption to the solemn dress inspection.

A moment later, Chapman rushes back to the captain's side, beckons him to the rail.

"Ship's company, at ease, Mr. Kell."

At the rail a flurry of French. First from the fisherman who's now alongside the *Sumter* in his boat. Then from Chapman, Semmes.

"*C'est vrai?*"

"*Oui, certainment, mon capitaine.*"

Now, in spite of the white hot sun, his eyes grow large, dart downstream toward the Gulf.

He turns, strides back to the crew who remain at ease in their ranks on the main deck.

"'Ten shun!" Kell calls to the crew.

They snap to as their captain starts pacing before them.

"Men, the cat has left the cheese unguarded. We have word from a patriot that the *Brooklyn* has gone off to the south chasing a sail, leaving the Pass á L'Outre unguarded. Now's our chance. At last we go. Take your stations. Mr. Freeman, give me every ounce of steam she can hold. We get underway with all haste. God bless us, God bless the Confederate States of America!"

The crew cheers.

Ten minutes after the drum beats the crew to general quarters, Freeman and the stokers have steam up. The foredeck men heave in the anchor. With a fair tide driving the little black warship, the *Sumter* churns downstream trailing a plume of black smoke as she races toward the sand bars at the mouth of Pass á L'Outre, the open Gulf. The third officer and five midshipmen are already overseeing the distribution of bags of cannon powder from the magazine when they hear shouting erupt on the quarterdeck.

Semmes looks ready to spit in the pilot's face.

"What do y'all mean, sir, you don't know the channel over the bar?"

"I'm a Southwest Pass pilot, Captain. I know nothing of the other passes."

"Damn you, man. Are you refusing to take a sovereign vessel of the Confederates States to sea from her home port? I ought to shoot you for your treachery."

He puts his right hand on the revolver in his belt holster, barrels toward the pilot, backs him against the mizzen shrouds. Then, just as suddenly, he turns away, releases his grip on his weapon. Speaks in a low, slow drawl to his second lieutenant.

"Mr. Chapman, hoist the pilot jack, sir. If those pilots don't send us a man worth his bacon, by god, I will take her over the bar myself."

"Damn all, he don't know the way," one of the gunners says to his mate. "He was a fuckin' lighthouse inspector. We'll shipwreck sure."

The luff approaches him with a look of alarm. Kell's a tall, well-proportioned officer of middle age, brown wavy hair, a magnificent beard inclining to red. A picture of professional confidence. But now his wide and affable face sags.

Semmes cocks his head toward the leeward taffrail.

"Walk with me, sir."

When they reach the stern of the *Sumter*, Semmes stops, looks up into the bigger man's face. The screw churns with a loud grinding beneath their feet. A trail of white froth spews behind in the muddy water.

"Do you think I am crazy? Is this madness, Mr. Kell?"

"It is not my place to second guess the captain, sir."

"Come, Kell, you are always the model of protocol and gentility, don't spare my feelings. Am I hell bound to lose this ship and these boys? Speak, sir."

The luff swallows hard. Says he's been twenty years in the navy. Sorely court-martialed and drummed out of the service for a spell, as Semmes well knows, for breaking tacks with his captain. But Semmes was his legal counsel. He fought for Kell and the rights of other junior officers when no one else dared.

"You are a maverick through and through, sir. I say do what you do best, Captain. Raise hell. Raise all hell with the Yanks, the pilots and ... and Neptune himself. Let's have at it."

He breaks into a rare smile, slaps Kell on the shoulder.

"I picked one hell of a first mate," he says quietly, then shifts to his command voice. "Carry on, luff."

The captain's heading back to his perch by the helmsman when he hears Second Officer Chapman shouting.

"There at the waist. Look to the starboard gangway. Boat coming. Pilot, sir."

He feels wind, for the first time all day, coming brisk in his face from the ship's speed—nine knots from her own power and another four to five knots from the current of the ebbing tide. Four black fellows in a pilot's bateau are pulling toward the *Sumter* with a swing and flash of oar blades. In the stern of the bateau, the pilot, a tanned young man in a loose white blouse, is waving his arms and cheering on his oarsmen. But they're losing ground.

"All stop."

The bell on the engine telegraph clangs. The deck shudders. All is silent except for a sharp hiss of excess steam blowing off from the top of the funnel. Slowly, the ship begins to lose way. Yard by yard the bateau catches up to the *Sumter*. When the bateau finally fetches up alongside, a middie lowers the Jacob's ladder, bends down at the gangway, stretching for the pilot's hand. Pulls him aboard while another middie ties the bateau off the quarter with the oarsmen collapsing on their benches.

"I'm for you, Captain!" The pilot mounts the starboard horseblock that's his realm.

"Let's make history, sir."

An instant later engineer Freeman has his pistons pounding hard again. The *Sumter* rushes past a little collection of stilt cottages near the lighthouse at Head of the Passes. Women with flowing hair and bright dresses wave at the crew from balconies, docks and windows with handkerchiefs.

As he passes, he removes his hat, gives a slight bow to return the ladies' salute. Then all of the crew take their hats in hand.

"Good Lord Jesus, but I love the fairer sex." He cracks his second smile of the day.

"Aye," says the luff.

No sooner has the *Sumter* passed the women than an officer with a telescope curses, points to the horizon. The *Brooklyn* has reappeared. She's about five miles to the southard, belching black smoke, racing toward the *Sumter* with canvas set aloft.

"The engineer says his boilers are starting to foam." Kell says. "We have to slow the ship 'til they settle down."

"Damn the boilers. Full speed ahead."

"Look to the bar, sir." Chapman has a frog in his throat.

On the quarterdeck all the officers and men turn their gaze from the *Brooklyn* to the muddy waves breaking less than a mile in front the *Sumter*. Dead ahead lies a steamer. She's flying a German flag and she's hard aground on a sand bar, lying almost abeam to the *Sumter*.

The captain stands beside the luff, who has a long glass up to his right eye.

"Tell me her every move, Mr. Kell." His voice is flat, his face clear of all emotion.

"She's got a kedge out ahead of her, sir, with the cable tight to her capstan. She's trying to pull herself out of the mud."

The pilot takes a midshipman's telescope for a look, swears in French.

"What, sir?" Semmes' voice has dropped an octave, grown quiet. It's the voice from his nightmares, the voice that ordered the crew to abandon ship as the *Somers* sunk beneath his feet so many years ago.

"The steamer, she's got her cable set right across the channel, Captain. She's blocked our way."

He cocks his head as if listening to a memory of a song, turns slowly away from the pilot and the officers at his side, stares out to the east into the Gulf. He tries to see the green forested Chandeleur Islands in the haze, thinks of *Hamlet*.

"If it be now, 'tis not to come; if it be not to come, it will be now; if it be not now, yet it will come. The readiness is all."

The muscles in his jaw flex as he turns back to face his officers.

"I wouldn't stop this train if I could, gentlemen. We're going to sea. Mr. Chapman, load your pivot gun and your starboard battery. If we have to blast ourselves free of the steamer so be it."

"On the double. There isn't much time, Chapman." A taut chord has settled into Kell's voice.

Now the steamer's so close he no longer needs a telescope to see her kedging cable stretching across his path. The saw grass marshes of the Mississippi Delta begin to fall astern, but the river's current still boils behind the ship. She hurtles toward the shallow sand bar, the grounded German, the Gulf beyond.

The pistons cough and sputter, catch their rhythm, then sputter again.

"The engine, *Capitaine*?" The pilot stands pale on his perch.

Semmes feels an urge to twirl his mustache. Stifles it, clutches his hands together behind his back. Wills his face stone, takes a deep breath.

So this is how you will test me, Lord. Fair enough, but let me find my strength.

"Sir, she's losing steerage! Shall I let go the starboard anchor?"

Kell has lost his cap somewhere. Now he rakes spread fingers over his bare forehead, back through his hair.

He feels the stern of the ship skid to larboard ever so slightly as the current starts to overwhelm her. Shoots another look to the east, imagines Mobile Bay and the place he called home somewhere out there lost in the glare. Sees the face of Anne and each of his six children, one at a time. Hears Maude call him a gladiator.

"Crew aloft, Mr. Kell. Make sail."

He casts a side glance at the luff. There's an odd twinkle in his eyes.

"They didn't raise us with steam and screws on the Old Lex or the *Constellation*, did they, sir? Light air or heavy, current fair or foul, we learned to get by with a bit o' wit and a few scraps of canvas. Just keep me in deep water, pilot. We'll sail her out of here if need be. She is a creature of the wind after all ... as once we were, too. Aim your guns for the steamer, Mr. Chapman. Give me the danger whistle, Mr. Kell."

Five deep-throated short blasts sound. The German and its kedg-ing cable lay less than two hunded yards ahead. In the distance the *Brooklyn* looms larger.

Now, the third mate's in the bows with a megaphone shouting, "Slack your cable! Slack your cable!"

Canvas cracks aloft as the t'gallants and topsails on the fore and main masts catch the southwest breeze.

"Jib and foretop staysail up," orders the luff.

He feels the ship begin to heel to port, accelerating under a press of canvas. Breaks his third smile of the day.

"She sails, Mr. Kell. Sweet Jesus, she sails."

Seconds pass while the two men face into the growing wind, drink it in.

"Prepare to fire the pivot gun into her bows. Sound the danger whistle again. Take her to sea, pilot." His voice sounds calm, sure now. He paces the quarterdeck with long, easy strides, feels strangely as if he's growing taller with each step.

"Come two points to larboard." The pilot.

The ship sheers. The engine coughs then catches its rhythm again. The cable still lies taught across the channel ahead.

"Shall I fire, sir?" Chapman.

A midshipman backs against a mizzen shroud, bracing himself for the collision with the kedge cable and the steamer.

"Ready, aim … "

"Hold your fire! Hold fire. She's slacking off."

The kedging cable droops into the water.

"Jesus Christ!"

Kell rolls his eyes.

"Exactly."

Three seconds later the *Sumter* sweeps past the grounded German. Her crew lets out a cheer as they spot the Confederate Stars and Bars flying from the cruiser's peak.

"Three fathoms, three fathoms. Four fathoms," calls the seaman with the sounding lead from the bows.

"Now, *Capitaine*, you are clear!" The pilot grins from ear to ear as he wipes the sweat from his brow with both hands. "Give her hell and let her go."

Turning his long glass south, he finds the *Brooklyn*, a full-rigged screw sloop of 2,900 tons, six times the size of the *Sumter*, billowing clouds of coal smoke. She's crowding on stunsails to enhance her working canvas. Gun crews swarm over their cannons. To the east, lightning flashes and the blur of a squall blot out sun and sea.

"What think you of our prospects, gentlemen? Can we outrun her?" The captain has his lieutenants with him at the taffrail.

Kell shakes his head *no*. The *Brooklyn*'s a twelve-knot ship.

"Then we must play the fox. Helmsman, take her up as close to the wind as she can stand. Set every sail. Give us the courses and spanker. On the double. Aim her right for that squall."

The officers look dumbfounded.

"Mr. Kell, tell the crew we're bound for heavy weather. You have the deck. I'm going below to see how Mr. Freeman fairs with his confounded foaming boilers. If ever there was a time for him to lay on the coal ... "

The second and third officers shoot questioning looks at each other. They have never seen such a commander. He's breaking all the old rules. Driving into a squall by choice with all sails set. Leaving the deck to visit the engine room with disaster threatening from all quarters. Is this madness?

He descends into a dungeon where heat burns the inside of his nose. Visibility drops to just a few yards in the smoke and steam. Light comes only from the glow of the open fire boxes. Men are mere shadows. The hiss of steam and the racket of pounding rods and pistons make his ears throb.

When he finally finds engineer Freeman, he shouts his questions at the man in the red bandana. But instead of answering, Freeman shakes his head *no* like a man lost in his own hell. He points to gray gobs of wax in his ears and shoves a small slate and stick of chalk into the captain's hands.

Semmes writes on the slate. "How go the boilers? We must lay on coal. Yank like to chew on our tail!"

The engineer sucks the insides of his cheeks, scribbles.

"Foam gone from boilers. We're hell on wheels!"

"Aye, that we are. Full speed ahead!!!"

Just as he reaches the main deck, the squall hits with a burst of wind, laying *Sumter* on her beam ends. He pictures the *Somers* again, driven down on her side by the norther off Veracruz, down-flooding through her hatches, sinking beneath his feet as the helmsman tried without success to bring her up into the wind. More than thirty dead. *Not again.*

"Keep her on the wind!" he screams at the helmsman. "She'll rise."

The lee rail disappears beneath white foam. All over the deck, men claw their way up to the windward rail. Cling to anything they can lay a hand on. He braces himself against the side of the binnacle. The wind shrieks in the rigging. He turns his back to the rain cutting through his uniform, watches the *Brooklyn* disappear astern in the fury, waits for his ship to rise. The engine shakes the deck with each revolution. A greasy cloud of coal smoke swirls over the *Sumter* so that no one can see if the sails have torn away. He feels the screw take a hard bite into the sea. The ship gives a shudder, almost as if she has struck a bar, then veers up into the wind a point.

"She's answering. She's rising!" The helmsman. A shout. Almost a cheer.

The screw bites again, drives her up another notch to windward. Decks rise out of the sea, torrents of water spill from the gun ports.

"Steady as she goes now. We're going to ride this monkey."

In his mind he bows down before his god.

At last the *Sumter* breaks into the sunshine. But he barely has time to ring the water out of his cap before the *Brooklyn* emerges from the storm. Now she's less than three miles off, nearly within shooting range.

The wind has clocked north, howls. Water roils over the starboard decks as the ship struggles to stay on her feet.

"Strike t'gallants?" the luff asks. The prudent course of action to save the sails and rig.

Semmes has a wild look, seems like he wants to swing on somebody or something.

"Not on my life, Mr. Kell. Welcome the breeze, sir! We haven't come this far just to be supper for some damn Yankee. Trim her full and by. Keep her hard on it, man! We aim to eat the Yankee out of her wind."

Sumter buries her starboard bulwarks in the foam, plows to the eastward. Green seas break over the larboard bow in sheets. He does not take his eyes off the sails. He prays that all the fresh canvas he had the sailmakers sew up for the new rig will hold, says ten Hail Marys that the new, taller topmasts he has given his ship will not carry off to leeward any second ... or that the crucial headsails will not shred themselves to ribbons.

"Look to the *Brooklyn*," calls a lookout from aloft.

The heads of more than fifty men who have taken shelter under the windward bulwarks crane to look astern.

"She strikes! Lord God Almighty, she strikes, Captain."

The Yank's rig is a shambles of back-winded and flogging canvas, slowing her as she begins to strike her sails.

"Long live the *Sumter*!" A sailor cheers from the masthead ... Just before smoke bursts from the Yank's pivot gun.

He hears the buzz of the shell. "It has only just begun, boys."

11

USS Powhatan
JULY 1-2, 1861

The signal officer on the side-wheel steam frigate raises the long glass to his eye, squints out across the Gulf. There's a ship steaming toward him from the east in the hazy light of mid-afternoon. Smoke rises from her funnel like a black tornado.

"Signal flags going up from the *Brooklyn*, sir!"

David Dixon Porter, captain of *Powhatan*, cocks an eye, stiffens. His barrel chest heaves against the double-breasted tightness of his sea coat. The full dark beard he has grown since putting to sea in April is still not bushy enough to conceal an inveterate boxer's thick neck, just now reddening around the collar.

"Let me have it when it is complete."

A mile to the east, chains of flags rise up and down on the *Brooklyn*'s signal halyards.

Forty-seven years of living, thirty years of naval service, has taught Porter to rue the arrival of all sorts of messages—both official and otherwise. They almost always bring bad news, usually put a major kink in his plans. Like the chaos surrounding Seward's secret plan to rescue Fort Pickens and Pensacola. After all of Seward's backslapping, whispering, promoting, planning to install Porter as captain of the *Powhatan,* the Secretary of State had sent a telegram, just as Porter was ready to set sail from Brooklyn, canceling his command. Too bad for Seward, that at Porter's insistence, his original orders to take the ship had been penned by the president himself. It gave Porter pleasure to ignore Seward's last minute change of heart and claim his ship with a stroke of defiance. He tossed off a terse telegram to Seward and headed to sea:

"I received my orders from the president and shall proceed and execute them." –D.D. Porter

But the Pickens-Pensacola mission had turned sour. Dispatches caught up with Porter in the Gulf, and he yielded to the senior commanders on the warships already stationed off Pensacola. Instead of the bold attack that he had imagined, chasing the Rebels out of the town, Porter found his ship acting as support for the resupply of Fort Pickens. His commanders were content to sit on their battle wagons. There was to be no attack.

Since then he has suffered the tedium of blockade duty. First off Pensacola, now the Delta. Furthermore, he has had a tough go managing officers whom he suspects are still loyal to Captain Mercer, the man he relieved.

Buck up. Your life is not totally mud.

There was that one glorious dispatch that had caught up with him at Pensacola. Lincoln took total responsibility for the bizarre way Porter had come to command the *Powhatan*. And he had been promoted! *Commander* Porter, after twenty years as a lieutenant. Indeed, it helped to come from one of the most prominent families in naval history and Washington society. But Lincoln's absolution had a double edge. It put him firmly under the command of the Navy Department, and a resentful Gideon Welles.

And what now? Something of import has caused the Brooklyn to leave her station and steam down here, throwing smoke like a funeral barge.

"Message complete, sir." The signal officer, bracing himself at attention.

"Go on."

"*Brooklyn* says the Confederate raider *Sumter* has ... has ... "

"Come, sir. What?" The captain's voice booms.

The second officer, who has the watch, waves off the bosun with whom he has been in earnest discourse and crosses the deck quickly to be at Porter's side.

The young signal officer's face winces, not from the harsh afternoon sun of the Gulf of Mexico, but like a dog smacked down too many times and now expecting another drubbing.

"It seems, sir, the Reb has put to sea, breached the blockade."

Porter stamps the deck so hard with his leather heel that the seaman at the helm, twenty feet away, jumps.

"Semmes? That drawing-room dandy! That snake! At liberty? How?"

He feels his fingers tightening into a fist, his right arm cocking at his side.

"How? How can such a thing happen? On our watch?"

There's a faraway look in his eyes ... as if he's already picturing Raphael Semmes putting a match to a crack Yankee clipper.

Still at attention, the signal officer winces again.

Steady as she goes, Commander.

He wills his fingers to uncoil. Draws his arms behind him. Faces the wind.

"At ease, son. I need your best efforts. Signal the *Brooklyn* to heave to. Tell them we are launching a boat. Send a steward for the luff. I want him to get up a boat detail, go over there and fetch every scrap of information from Captain Poor about Semmes' little stratagem. Maybe we can stop that mustachioed Mephistopheles!"

He paces back and forth in the *Powhatan*'s great cabin. With each circuit, he returns to the table and the chart he has spread of the Caribbean Sea. As he paces he pounds his right fist unconsciously into his cupped left hand. Through the stern lights he can see the last purple hues of sunset over the Gulf. The luff came back aboard an hour ago with his report on what he called the "*Sumter*'s balls-for-brains escape."

"I'm daunted twelve ways to Christmas," he says aloud. "Just flat out fucking fouled ... unless I catch Semmes before he raises all hell."

No one has to tell him how this sort of thing goes. He's seen it time and again. Someone screws up on your watch and everybody involved feels the heat coming down from up top. Once while he was a middie in the *Constellation* on her goodwill cruise of the Med, a boat crew accidentally smashed up the gig while lowering it overside to take Captain Wadsworth ashore in Barcelona. Only one middie had been present at the ill-fated lowering. But since small-boat handling was the general responsibility of the middies on the watch, the skipper called every middie on watch during the accident before a captain's mast, ripped them a new set of holes in their small clothes, swore that he'd write them such dank fitness reports that their next billets would be on a mapping expedition of the Arctic. None of those boys stayed in the service long enough to find out.

Porter had been lucky then. He had been off watch, but he fears that his buggering had simply been delayed. Time and again fate has taken a whip to the Porters. His father, a full commodore and a hero of the 1812 conflict, was drummed out of the service for alleged "over-zealousness." The incident occurred when Commodore Porter sent troops from his squadron to seize a Spanish fort in Puerto Rico after the locals had mistreated an American officer who had gone ashore in pursuit of pirates. Rather than retire on the beach, Commodore Porter went to work setting up a navy for the new Mexican republic and took two of his sons with him, twelve-year-old David and ten-year-old Thomas. In Mexico City, David Porter watched his favorite and closest brother die in a fit of yellow fever.

Two years later in 1828, Porter saw his cousin Lieutenant David H. Porter ripped in two by a shot from a twenty-four pounder. The man lay on the deck of his ship in two pieces spurting blood. And yet his legs moved like they wanted to get up and fight on. The mouth kept shouting orders for what seemed an eternity. That was when both Porters had sailed on the Mexican twney-four-gun brig *Guerrero,* raiding Spanish merchant ships in the Gulf of Mexico. But they had run afoul of a sixty-four-gun Spanish frigate off Mariel, Cuba, and were blown to bits.

When he thinks back on the dark events of his youth, he bites the inside of his cheek. He considers his own failure to move beyond the rank of lieutenant in twenty years, thinks how he has let himself be cast as the hijacker of the *Powhatan*. That's what his officers, Mercer's men, call him behind his back when they think he isn't within earshot. The Hijacker. He feels as cursed as his kin.

So here's fate's big move, and Raphael Semmes is a horseman of the apocalypse. He sees himself condemned to oblivion with Captain Poor on the *Brooklyn*, and the skippers of the *Niagara* and the *Minnesota*. The four of them had the watch at the Delta when Semmes slipped through the blockade with the *Sumter*. They have failed to do their duty. Now it's only a matter of time before orders come down from Washington replacing him. Unless he can find and destroy Semmes and his three-penny raider, the *Powhatan* will be his one and only command of a first-rate warship.

"No! I will not go quietly into this good night!"

He kicks the desk chair across the cabin. It hits the corner of a settee, falls into pieces with a crash.

There are no words for what he feels ... because he suddenly feels *nothing*. Absolutely nothing. Hollow.

He arches his back, stretches his arms out wide from the shoulders as if growing wings.

I am as clean and simple and heartless as that engine that turns the wheels of my ship. I am slave to no man. I have an iron will, and I may yet do something glorious for the sake of myself and my family. I may catch Semmes.

He flings his sea coat on his berth, loosens his cravat, turns up the light on the oil lamp that swings slowly over the chart table, puts on his specs. Then he crosses the cabin, picks up the chair, jams its legs back into their dowel holes, takes a seat at the table and begins twirling a pencil in his fingers as his eyes roam the chart.

Little by little a smile begins to spread over his lips; because here before him is the image of the Caribbean and the Gulf—Semmes' old cruising ground when he was sailing master on the *Constellation*, and later in command of the *Poinsett, Somers, Electra* and *Flirt*. But it was Porter's home turf as well. As a middie in the Mexican service with his father and cousin, he was here as a commercial raider himself, had hunted Spanish prizes aboard the *Esmerelda* and the ill-fated *Guerrero*.

"You did not count on this, Commander Semmes!" A smug smile spreads over his face. "You did not know that among the dull and bloated fish of this Delta, there's a shark who knows your hunting ground as well as you yourself do."

By sunrise he has it figured out, knows that Semmes' easterly track when last seen was simply his escape route and a feint to mislead pursuers. He has known Semmes for nearly fourteen years, barely missed serving with him in the Connie. They crossed paths often in recent years when they served in Washington. Both traveled in the highest social circles, both men had served off Veracruz in the Mexican War.

The tale of how Semmes lost the *Somers* was once common wardroom grist in the fleet. It etched itself into Porter's memory as a lesson in seamanship, survival, command. And from those details Porter thinks he has learned something about Semmes. Instead of heaving to under heavy weather canvas to face off with the norther in the *Somers*, Semmes had turned tail, tried to outrun it. The tactic was a perfectly sound one. Perhaps even the favored one. Sailors argue constantly and endlessly about the virtues of heaving to versus those of running before a storm as competing survival tactics. And the evidence supporting the choice of one over the other remains inconclusive. Ships have been saved and lost following both tactics. So it always comes down to fate and the captain's choice. Semmes had chosen to run in the *Somers*.

"He's a rabbit. No, more like a fox. Even looks like a wild dog with that ridiculous mustache." He mumbles to himself. *Doesn't matter. Rabbit or fox, they both circle back to their homes in a chase.*

In his mind the *Sumter*'s course is clear. She may have given signs of heading east to the Atlantic or the Old Bahamas Channel. But she will circle back to the Gulf and the Caribbean, start her hunting along the busy shipping routes off the south coast of Cuba. If he leaves soon, makes a direct run at full steam for Cienfuegos, waits, Semmes will sail right into his waiting arms. Any raider has to hunt there. Cienfuegos is the best natural harbor and the busiest commercial port on the south side of Cuba. And it has coal. Semmes will need coal. Even if he's playing his sailing master games and roving under canvas, he'll need coal by the time he reaches Cienfuegos. So it is there that Porter will meet him, give him a taste of the *Powhatan*'s big guns.

There are just two or three things to do before he leaves the Delta. One, coerce his officers, Mercer's men, to support his abandoning the blockade to take up the chase. Two, convince the engineers to risk *Powhatan*'s weak and corroded boiler tubes and give him full speed. Three, send word to his fellow blockaders—the *Brooklyn*, the *Niagara*, the *Minnesota*—that he's off to find and sink the *Sumter*.

He will be in violation of the standing order, perhaps, but surely new orders will be forthcoming from Washington demanding that he give chase. The current situation dictates that a captain take initiative if the Union's to carry the day, isn't that right?

12

CSS Sumter
JULY 3, 1861

The first ship was an unavoidable temptation. *Sumter*'s lookout had spied two vessels at three in the afternoon and run down the nearer one, sailing between the south coast of Cuba and the Isle of Pines.

The chase had been thrilling. Freeman's gang had thrown coal into the fireboxes with blind abandon while the pistons thumped and the crew close-hauled the sails taut as a dolphin's skin. Under sail and steam the little black Rebel cruiser romped at almost ten knots into fresh east-by-southeast trades and white caps. Sheets of spray broke like hail over the foredeck. When the *Sumter* raised her false flag, the British Union Jack, the brig hoisted the Spanish colors in response. Semmes stopped her with a shot across the bow, and sent over a boarding party just to make sure she was not a Yank in disguise. But in the end all her papers proved to be in order; she hailed from Cadiz, bound for Mexico.

"We've harassed an innocent merchantman of a neutral nation. wasted our time and coal, Mr. Kell." He stands along the leeward rail watching the boat crew retrieve the longboat, removes his service cap, beats the wind-buffeted peak back into shape. "I must do better. Time's not our ally."

"Couldn't be helped, sir. We have to take our prey as we find it. The chase, stopping her, boarding—good practice for a green crew."

He sees genuine good humor, optimism in Kell's face, wonders at the rightness or wrongness of his own impatience.

"Loyal Kell," he says, "you temper the fire in me."

"I would not wish—"

He shakes his head, waves the luff's words away with his right hand as if to put the Spanish ship behind him. He takes up his long glass and eyes an unknown bark, the lookout's "second vessel," laboring against the trades five miles to the northeast. She flies no flag.

"Yankee! I'll bet right much on it. Has a Downeast look."

"Most certain." Kell has his own glass on the bark. "Riding high, must be she is in ballast."

"I care not, Mr. Kell. Loaded or empty she serves the devil!"

He glances up at the angle of the sun, notes three squalls brewing off to the southwest, realizes that it's almost 1800 hours and time for the second dog watch. He has perhaps two and a half hours of daylight left. *Not much time.*

"Have the watch clew up the sails, Mr. Kell. Men aloft and furl. Brace up. But keep the jib, staysail and spanker on her for a bit of lift. Tell the engineer I want a fresh gang of stokers. Full speed ahead. Set a course to intercept her. On the double now."

Jesus, Mary and Joseph be with us now in the hour of our need.

"She still shows no flag, sir."

He tries not to bristle. Why did the young watch officer feel that he needed to state the obvious? *Good Lord, doesn't anyone teach these boys anymore that silence is a considerable virtue at sea?*

"Load the swivel gun, Lieutenant." He twirls the left tip of his mustache, surveys the bark that now sails just a mile to leeward on starboard tack. "Prepare to fire across her bow. Let's make her heave to and show her colors."

He does not need the glass now to see her. She looks magnificent with her courses, tops, t'gallants, royals spread against the violet of the evening sky. Seven hundred tons for certain, and by the look of her shining black topsides, saucy red bulwarks and gleaming spars, she's nearly new. A great albatross of a sailing ship. He suddenly thinks of his days as sailing master on the Connie, remembers how driving to windward into the trades on such a day as this could almost take your breath away with the power of harnessed wind and the plunging of the ship into head seas. He wonders if the merchantman will try to put up a fight when he shows his true colors.

"Take a good look, men," he says to the officers, warrants and men on the quarterdeck. "There sails the glorious past. Mark my words. When we have finished with the Yankees, the human race will think it folly to put to sea in such a ship. For better or worse, this crew and our little black tea kettle have been called by God to be the judge and executioner on the age of sail."

"Gun's ready, sir."

"Stand by to raise the Stars and Bars. Have the boatmen ready to launch. Lieutenant Chapman and Lieutenant Howell will board her with a detail of marines. Every man armed and ready. Fire away."

The swivel gun erupts with a deep bark that shakes the deck and sends a gray cloud of smoke curling aft over the flush decks. For an instant or two the crew hears the buzz of the ball burning through the humid air. A second later a geyser rises from the waves a hundred yards off the merchantman's bows.

"Look there," says Lieutenant Chapman. "Stars and Stripes going to her peak."

"That hateful rag was once our fair mistress, Kell." He watches the russet tones of the setting sun play on Kell's beard. "She did much deceive us."

"I don't look back."

"Right." *You're a lucky bugger.*

This is easy, just too damn easy ... and utter hell.

The Yankee has rounded up in the wind with great grace and superb sail handling almost the very instant that the *Sumter*'s signalmen doused the Union Jack and raised the Stars and Bars to the peak of the spanker gaff. Now she sits pretty as a picture. Just two hundred yards off to the north. With the coming of sunset the punch has gone out of the breeze. The two ships roll easily on a sea that looks like it has been calmed by a film of purple oil. In the west the sun has left fast-fading bars of red, gold, green on the horizon. It's dark enough to see lightning flash from cloud to cloud in distant squalls. Almost the only sounds are the cackling of gulls and the creaking of oars in tholl pins as the *Sumter*'s boatmen row back to their ship, transporting the captured crew and all the ship's stores the cruiser can use from the Yankee bark. The *Golden Rocket*, hailing from the state of Maine. As Kell suspected, she's empty, sailing in ballast in hopes of stuffing herself with a load of Cuban sugar. The worse for her. If she carried valuable cargo, he might have put a prize crew aboard her. But now ...

"Captain, I must condemn your lovely vessel to death." He sits at his desk in the great cabin, holds the *Golden Rocket*'s American document of registration and her U.S. Customs clearance form in his right hand, surveys the Yankee captain who stands before him.

The amiable looking Yankee in the black pea jacket reminds him of his grandfather. He has soft gray eyes. They do not blink as the Rebel captain delivers his verdict. He planned to say no more. But now he feels judged himself, feels the need to explain himself, show himself as an officer and gentleman—a man of culture, heart, high principles. He suddenly picks up the loaded Colt revolver he had placed on his desktop for credence, tucks it back in his desk drawer. Feels ashamed of himself for relying on such a crude and obvious instrument of intimidation.

"My duty is a painful one. To destroy so noble a ship as yours. But I discharge it without vain regret. And as for yourself ... you will only have to submit, as so many thousands have done before you, to the fortunes of war—yourself and your crew will be well treated on board my ship."

"You must do your duty," says the Yankee, laying a large neatly folded bundle on the desk. "Here you have her gold, her chronometer and her flag. I am your prisoner, and I do not judge you, sir. Only our God shall know whether what we do here this night is a sin or a sacrament."

"Amen."

The two captains both have their hands clasped together as if praying. They stare away from each other, gaze out through the stern windows at the black, tropical night while the oil lamps flicker within.

It's after ten at night when the boarding officer and his crew row off into the gloom to fire the *Golden Rocket*. But even before the first flame, the spectacle seems a dream to him. A new and unnatural nightmare to add to his collection. A thing that he already knows he will write down in great detail afterwards. Without a sign from Heaven or a command from his heart, he understands that from this time forth he's unconditionally bound to revisit the burning decks of the *Golden Rocket* again and again, much as he returns to the storm-wrecked *Somers*, day and night, waking and dreaming, until his very death. As if in returning to these ghost ships, he hopes to find something he lost, some part of himself that once labored face-to-face with the gods of fire, wind, water, war.

As he stands on the quarterdeck and stares off into the night, something like stale bread pudding catches in his throat. He hears his mind already telling itself the story of monumental waste and destruction.

The wind by this time is very light, and the night is pitch-dark—the darkness being the kind described by old sailors, when they say you may cut it with a knife. Not a sound can be heard on board the Sumter, *although her deck is crowded with men. The doomed ship lies at a distance of just a few hundred yards but cannot be seen even by those officers searching the dark with binoculars.*

Suddenly, one of the crew exclaims, "There's a flame! She's on fire!"

The decks of the Maine-built ship are of pine, caulked with old-fashioned oakum and paid with pitch. The woodwork in the cabin is like so much tinder, having been seasoned by many voyages to the tropics. The fo'castle is filled with paints and oils. So now the flames set by the boarding officer in the cabin, the main hold and fo'castle are not long in kindling, but leap full grown into the air at three parts of the ship at once. The flames rush up from these three nests with a fury. The draft of air sucking into the ship is like the deep whir of an enormous winged creature beating against the sky or the roaring of a hundred furnaces in full blast. Meanwhile the Sumter *lies off with her grim, black sides like some great sea monster, gloating upon the spectacle and on the sleeping sea whereon the reflection of the burning ship sails again, a second ghost.*

The Golden Rocket *lies to the wind with her main topsail to the mast, all her light sails clued up like so many hanging drapes. The forked tongues of fire race up the newly tarred rigging into the tops, then to the topmast heads. Thence to the t'gallants and royal mastheads. In a moment more they are at the trucks. Other currents run out along the yards and ignite the sails. A t'gallant sail, all on fire, flies away from a yard, sails leisurely downwind on the light breeze, lands far off, a patch of flame on the dark sea, burning, burning as if it has lit the water itself afire. Yards, long strands of thick flame, drop from high overhead, piercing the water with wails and hissing, glowing red and green as they dive down, and further down, beneath the oily surface.*

All at once, the entire intricate network of the ship's rigging traces itself like golden thread against the night sky, blotting out even the brightest stars. The threads begin to part, twisting and whipping like serpents in the throws of their death wounds. The ship lets out a sharp cry and the mizzen mast crashes on the poop, shatters, cartwheels over the side. Now the foremast totters, sways and collapses with a loud snap. The mainmast falls with a crash, and the flames rising fifty or sixty feet above the inferno burn the cheeks of men watching from the Sumter's *hammock rail. A plume of sparks churns hundreds of feet into the heavens.*

The captain of the Golden Rocket *watches from a place alone near the taffrail. He has the calm eye of a philosopher, but one must wonder well what thoughts of inexpressible disappointment, regret, anger, vengeance and self-loathing must roil within. There are no words to describe the torture of the sailor watching the dying agonies of his beloved ship, whether she be broken up by fire, winds or water.*

"Lord God Almighty, forgive me," he says. "The enemy has made a villain of me."

He turns his back on the burning ship and all the men, staggers to the companionway, withdraws to his cabin, throws himself in his berth.

It's now he thinks of her, remembers that last time of love making in the glow of her coal stove on that bitter St. Valentine's night. The scents of fire, lavender, the faint mustiness of her hair rises in his nostrils. With trembling fingers, he covers his brow with his right hand, bites his lip, wonders if she still loves him.

13

USS Powhatan
JULY 3, 1861

Porter pushes back his chair, stands up, clears his throat. The first dog watch.

All the officers of the ship, except the third mate who has the deck, are assembled for the evening mess in the wardroom. Ten sets of eyes follow him. Each man seated at the long linen-covered table swallows a last bite of pot roast or boiled potatoes and puts down his utensils. Custom requires that dinner end when the captain leaves the table. The Negro steward snaps to attention at his sideboard.

He puts both hands in front of him with palms down as if he's literally holding the officers in their seats, thinks the whole bunch of Mercer's men look like Sunday school teachers in the starched white jackets of summer dress. Bearded deacons.

"Gentlemen, we are going to get up a full head of steam and sail southeast to double Cuba's Cape Antonio. Thence we're straight for Cienfuegos. Either there—or before—we shall find and destroy the Rebel cruiser calling herself the *Sumter*."

The officers sit still as statues in their seats. Their eyes leave their captain's in brief spurts and flash to the other men at the table.

He takes a step back, spreads his legs as if bracing against the roll of his ship.

"This Rebel captain Raphael Semmes is a menace, men. He is smart; he is desperate for glory. He knows the Caribbean like your mother knows her pantry. He is profoundly vain and arrogant. And he has always been a lone wolf, a seahawk."

The *Powhatan*'s officers shift uneasily in their seats, say nothing, ask no questions. They just stare at him.

So they want a sermon from me, want the Hijacker to sing and dance for their ruddy favor. Well, so be it.

"I know Semmes; he's a survivor."

When he lost the *Somers* in the Mexican War, rather than fade away into history after a humiliating court-martial, he volunteered for the army, joined the campaign against *Mexico Ciudad* just to keep himself in the fight. There's nothing he won't do, won't risk, for personal victory and—so it now seems—the Rebel states. Unchecked, there's no limit to the damage he may cause the Union's merchant fleet. No greater imperative right now than for the navy to stop Semmes. Porter says *Powahatan* is the right ship, at the right place, at the right time. He knows Semmes' tricks. Knows where the pirate's headed.

"I have the power of this ship to stop him dead in his tracks. Here ends the mess. There will be time for us to linger around this table in celebration after we sink the *Sumter*. Let's get underway. Look to your individual departments. Mess excused."

Nobody moves.

He feels his fingers start tightening into the palms of his hands.

"On the double, please."

The luff pushes back his chair but does not stand up.

"Begging your pardon, sir. Permission to speak?"

He nods his consent, a slight dip of the head.

"We want to know if the ship has received new orders, sir?"

The captain rolls his shoulders, cocks his head back, turns sideways as if to take a punch or throw his own.

"Yes, sir, you have just heard them. We get underway for Cape Antonio immediately. Is there something that is not clear, Lieutenant? Or ... are you flirting with disobedience?"

He thinks he hears someone curse under his breath, knows already that he should not have said that bit about disobedience.

Come on, boys. Cut me some slack. There is nothing less at stake here than saving the United States of ...

"I mean, Captain, the other officers and I want to know if our orders from the squadron have changed. If we are at liberty to abandon the blockade? We understand the dangers that the *Sumter* presents. But we do not feel that it is within our realm to take actions that run counter to the standing orders as we know them."

You little shits! Your realm? Good grief! You know I am freelancing here, and you want me on the record as saying so. You want to cover your own asses, want to protect your own pathetic careers, want to point the finger at me, call me the maverick if everything turns to night soil.

"The squadron's orders to me are for me alone, mister! Since when do junior officers have the right to question the nature of an order from a direct superior? If you want to play at being a sea lawyer, get off my ship and go start your legal inquiries into the nature of orders in some musty office. Otherwise, shape up and act like an officer and a mariner. Discussion closed. Get to your posts. We start the hunt!"

The *Powhatan's* officers stare at their hands folded on the mess table or in their laps, do not move.

He feels his cheeks catching fire.

"Have it your own way."

A knife slips off the table, hits the floor, clatters like breaking glass.

He spins on his heels, marches out of the wardroom. His officers can just stew in their own juices until they come to their senses. He will get his ship headed south with the help of the engineer and deck officer on watch. When Mercer's Sunday school deacons in the wardroom have listened to the hard and steady thumping of the pistons and side wheels for a while, then they'll take David Dixon Porter seriously. Then they'll know with what certainty he will stalk and sink Semmes. And they'll come around. Or he'll lock the lot of them in the brig.

The evening watch has started. The third engineer, who Porter has dragooned on some pretense into staying on in the engine room when his watch ended, still has not been able to get more than moderate pressure in the boiler. The ship jogs south.

When he calls the engineer on deck and presses him for more speed, he gets an earful, a rant like only an engineer can sling at a captain. The fucking tubing is already scaling and pitted so badly that pinhole leaks are more plentiful than shit specks in an outhouse, excuse the expression. Christ Almighty, up here on deck you can smell more steam than coal smoke in her exhaust, can't you? Six or seven knots is the best she'll do without a total tear down of the boiler to patch all the leaks. Even then, how long until new ones develop? Damned if the tubes aren't shot! Just corroded all to hell. And there are only a few spares. Hadn't *Powhatan* been sent up to Brooklyn for a refit, new tubes, valves, pipes? The whole shebang. But she was snatched away for this mission to Pensacola before her refit was finished. Just patched and jury-rigged for sea. Because some politicians had jerked her chain. Typical. And now all the pigeons are coming home to roost. What could you do?

He pats the engineer on the back, mutters something about doing his best, releases the exhausted man to return to his inferno. He leans against the mizzen shrouds, stands the deck watch himself. He searches the heavens for Betelgeuse. He wonders when Venus will rise up out of the black murk on the horizon, does some calculations. Cape Antonio lies over two hundred miles off. Well over a day away at this speed. Meanwhile, Semmes is getting further ahead, sprinting no doubt between bouts of raping and pillaging. Sailing for this steam frigate is out of the question. What wind there is comes at them on the nose now, and *Powhatan* sails like a garbage scow. When her paddle wheels aren't turning at near full speed, the ship staggers as if she's dragging a kedge on the bottom behind her.

You're doomed. Semmes will hit Cienfuegos, get his coal, and light out before you even get past the Isle of Pines. Then he will lose himself in the Lesser Antilles like a needle in the haystack. You've missed your chance, and you've all but provoked a flaming mutiny.

Staring into the swirl of faint stars overhead, he sees his brother Thomas' gray and lifeless face in an oak coffin, his cousin's bloody legs kicking at the air. Thinks about the Curse of the Porters. *Christ!*

Then he hears the rattle of musket fire and smells the sulfur fumes of cannon discharges sweeping over him. He sees the breastworks of a Mexican fort in Tabasco. It's 1847 again. He's leading a party of seventy seaman over the ramparts, driving out the Mexicans, raising the Stars and Stripes over the fort. The assault goes off without a hitch because he has spent days studying the maps, planning different scenarios, learning to think like his opponent. Like a boxing match. Just like. During the first rounds he keeps his guard up, tests his adversaries' weaknesses. Brains not balls. That's the secret. And for his victory the navy rewards him with his first command, the steamer *Spitfire*.

All ahead slow! Take her easy. This is just round one. Brains not balls. He talks silently to himself. *You are on the brink. But there is nothing done here tonight that has been written in stone. Semmes will not go away. Not while the hunting is good. You have time to plan your own hunt, the kill.*

He strides with sharp, clipped steps across the poop to the men standing the helm.

"Quartermaster, bring her around to three, five, zero. We've had enough adventuring for one night."

When he goes below to the wardroom, he finds his officers still sitting at the mess table like a pack of broken dolls. Some facedown with their arms folded on the table. Others sleep upright with heads in their hands or dropping on their shoulders or chins.

He steps into the wardroom. The luff looks up.

"Are you going to court-martial us, sir?"

Heads pop up around the table in the glare of the gimbaled whale oil lamps.

"Gentlemen, we've had a misunderstanding. Nothing more."

He feels, more than hears, their sighs.

"I have changed course for the *Minnesota*. She goes off station and back to squadron command at Pensacola shortly. When she goes, she will carry a petition from me to Secretary Welles to be released from blockade duty for a little *Sumter* hunting. Will you be game?"

The officers shoot odd looks at each other.

14

CSS Sumter
JULY 4-5, 1861

Captain Stout of the Maine brigantine *Cuba*, stands in the great cabin of the *Sumter*, feels the fire rising in his throat.

"Ye callest this an act of war?! I call it piracy. Has Stout made war on ye? No sir!"

Semmes sits at his desk, settles back in his chair. Looks away from the ranting Yankee. Twirls the left wing of his mustache and scowls out through the stern window at the blazing of noontime sun turning the sea a pale, milky gray.

"I don't care who ye thinks ye are, sir, or what renegade government pays ye keep. Stop my ship on the high seas, drag me at gun point and threat of my life aboard this infernal black hell ship, and ye shall find out of what metal Stout is made."

The young Maine captain puffs out his chest. He has the torso of an acrobat, long brown hair pulled back in a ponytail. His cheeks are clean shaven. Jaw muscles flex as he grits his teeth. Except for the long hair, the youth reminds Semmes of his own son, Oliver, who has left the Point to come south and enlist in an artillery brigade. Oliver, who might already be spitting fire like this at a Yankee. Oliver, who will fight to the death if cornered.

"Ye shall not get away with this!"

"I already have, Captain ... and this meeting is over."

"Pshaw."

He stiffens in his seat, points a stiff finger at Stout.

"You ... You are under arrest. Now, you will return to your ship with my senior midshipman Mr. Hudgins and a marine guard. And stay there, quiet as an obedient mouse, until we can deliver you, your ship and its cargo of sugar to a prize court. I've endured right much contumely from you, young sir. Not another word will you utter in my presence or I'll spank you like a young whelp, hear? Get out of my sight. This is a war ... not a schoolyard circus. Go!"

A guard nudges the Yank in the side with a musket. Stout slaps it away as if shooing a horsefly.

It's 0300 when Stout sees his chance. The *Cuba's* sailing close-hauled to the northeast under headsails, courses, topsails. She has been on her own for several hours after her towline from the *Sumter* parted. Captain Semmes told Hudgins to go it alone and meet the cruiser off Cienfuegos the next morning. Stout's bosun has the helm, under guard by two of the four marines Hudgins' has with him. The other two Confederates are sleeping. And so seems Stout and his crew of twelve who have been forced to lie side-by-side in the lee scuppers on the main deck.

The night is dark. Huggins long ago lost sight of the *Sumter*, which showed no running lights to betray her to an enemy. He tells his marines that he smells the scent of cane fields, knows they're closing with the coast, is going aloft to look out for the lights of Cienfuegos.

Stout almost laughs at the midshipman's stupidity of going up into the rigging while leaving just two guards in charge of a hostile crew. He nudges his first and second mates who are curled up on either side of him.

"We move as soon as the Reb's at the crosstrees. On my signal."

There's no plan in place. He trusts to common sense. The crew has been together for months, have an affection for the ship and each other. They're tough men like their captain, men known to clean house in the bars of sugar ports throughout the West Indies. Men not apt to give up their mates, their ship, their pay for five Southern boys playing soldier.

Stout feels a wave of energy spread among his crew as each man nudges the next to vigilance.

Aloft, Hudgins pulls himself over the futtock shrouds onto the platform of the maintop. He's out of sight from the men on deck and vice versa.

"Oh Lord, Lord! Help. Merciful Lord, Help!" Stout cries, his voice loud and full of misery. He sits up, presses his hands to his ears. "My head, my head! Help me. Help me!"

One of the marines guarding the quartermaster at the wheel comes running up the deck, waving his musket.

"Please. Help!" Stout howls with an unearthly shriek, staggers to his knees.

The rest of the crew lies motionless.

Stout rises to his feet, holding his head, squealing like a snared pig. He holds his head, sways madly.

"Stop that man!" shouts Hudgins from the top.

The two resting marines rise from their sleep and begin to follow their mate toward the madman luring them right into the middle of his crew.

"Stop. Stop that y'all, hear?"

The first guard is on Stout, hollering, threatening to club him with the musket butt.

Stout reels back.

"Boys!"

Before the marine can blink, the Yank grabs the guard's ears and head butts him. Someone tackles the marine from behind. The musket falls. The quartermaster at the wheel drops his marine guard with an open-handed chop to the throat as the *Cuba's* crew swarms over the remaining Rebs.

In twenty seconds it's all over. Stout's men have the Confederates lying on their bellies with muskets to their heads. Seamen tie their former-captors' hands behind their backs with sail gaskets.

"Give me thy gun." Stout begs a musket from his bosun.

"Down with ye, mate. She's my ship now."

He walks back to the poop for a better angle of the man at the maintop, fires at Hudgins.

There's a muzzle flash, a thwack aloft.

"Shit. Fucker!"

"Get ye down here! I've lost my patience with ye and ye lot."

"Never." Hudgins fires his sidearm. Stout hears the ball slap into the scuttlebutt beside him. He hands the musket back to the quartermaster.

"Don't kill him. Just get him down. I want to deliver this pirate to the hangman. Would that it were his better, Captain Semmes ... We go to New York."

Men cheer. The ship had planned to carry her cargo of sugar to England, a long slow passage; New York is much closer.

"Prepare to wear ship, boys. When we're squared away and the prisoners are locked below, those of ye who wish may splice the main brace and taste a little Cienfuegos *ron*!"

The men on the *Cuba* cheer again. In the east the first bars of morning light are breaking on the horizon. The quartermaster takes aim at the Reb in the rigging, fires.

15

District of Columbia
JULY 6, 1861

Fiona's chest heaves beneath a flimsy pink blouse. She towers over Maude, tries to catch her breath. Has a tightly rolled newspaper in her right hand, waves it in the air as if preparing to strike.

"Have you seen this?" Fiona slaps the paper down on the café table where Maude sits sipping her tea at Carley's Delicatessen. Since their school had ended for its summer break, the two friends meet at this lively breakfast spot on Tenth St. every morning at nine thirty for a cup of tea, a stroll.

"The late, great Raphael Semmes is all over this town!"

She feels something pound against her breast bone. She cannot comprehend what she's hearing. *All over this town?* It has been weeks since his last letter. He had been about to take his ship down the river from New Orleans. Raffy had sounded so proud and, though he would never admit it, anxious. She read the stress between the lines of endless chit-chat that was not like him at all, except when he was trying to cover for nervousness.

"*Read!*" Fiona sits down at the table, unfolds last night's *Evening Star*, pushes it over to her. "He's right there on the front page, love. Your knight in shining armor. I take back every mean thing I have ever said about him. My god, lassie, who would have ever thought? What a prince! The paper's demanding that Lincoln hang him."

She hears a loud buzzing in her ears, plows her left hand through the copper curls above them. She seizes the paper with the other hand. It seems to take minutes for her eyes to focus and scan the field of black words. Then, suddenly, a headline hits her like a dray-load of peat.

Rebel Raider Loose, Wreaking Havoc

July 5, Washington, D.C.—War Department officials confirmed this morning rumors that a Confederate commerce raider, the so-called Sumter, *has escaped through the Federal blockade of New Orleans and has begun seizing and burning American merchant ships.*

The raider slipped through the blockade almost a week ago under cover of a rain squall. Two days ago a Spanish merchant ship put into Tampico, Mexico, and reported having been stopped by the raider south of Cuba. After inspecting the Spaniard's papers, the Rebels let her sail.

Shortly after being released by the Confederate pirates, the Spanish crew witnessed the raider stopping another ship, which the Spaniards had met earlier in the day. According to the Spanish captain, the ship was an American merchant bark named the Golden Rocket, *from the state of Maine. The Spaniards stood off at a distance in case they could be of assistance.*

Sometime before midnight following the stopping of the Golden Rocket, *the Spaniards witnessed an enormous fireball burning to their east. Even from more than ten miles away they could see it was a ship. The next morning the Spaniards returned to the place where they had seen the fire. They found floating and charred debris, some clearly marked as property of the* Golden Rocket. *There were no small boats, survivors or bodies.*

The Spanish captain said there were a "multitude of sharks" swimming among the wreckage. He surmised that the American crew must have been forced into the water when their ship was burned by the raider and had fallen prey to the sharks.

Having fitted out in the port of New Orleans, the Sumter *is a converted packet steamer armed with all manner of weap-*

onry. Her captain is Commander Raphael Semmes, formerly of the Lighthouse Bureau, a man who quit a long, but undistinguished, career in the U.S. Navy to join the Southern cause in February. Her officers are also deserters from the navy. The crew is allegedly composed of mercenaries recruited in New Orleans for a mission of piracy and destruction.

"From what we hear, the whole lot of them are the worst kind of scalawags," said shipping scion Eliuh Bourne. "The navy must catch Semmes and his band of brigands, and hang them as the pirates they most certainly are. Let me make this perfectly clear: This raiding is not an act of war. This is a criminal act against private citizens and no such act ..."

Maude falls back in her chair, rubs her forehead with the back of her hand. In her pale green, linen dress and high-topped patent-leather shoes, she looks more like a woman dressed for a garden party than tea amid the steam of coffee pots, the clatter of plates, the scent of fried ham here in Carley's.

"He would never take an innocent life."

"What if he did? They're Yankee shippers and there's nothing innocent about that in my book, lass. They feed Lincoln's war monster."

During the last month Fiona has grown more and more outspoken against the North. On their walks she keeps track of the comings and goings of the Federal units camped around the unfinished monument to George Washington. Maude knows that Fiona's reporting what she sees to Rose Greenhow. But she still does not understand Fiona's passion, anger or spying against the Federal government. She thinks politics are irrelevant in the larger scheme of things, beyond the ken of a proper Irish lass.

"They are turning him into a devil."

Fiona takes a seat across the table, leans toward Maude. Her voice has a raspy hiss as she speaks. One corner of her upper lip twitches.

"The Yanks need to put a cruel face on the South," Fiona says. "They need to give ordinary people someone to fear and hate. No one will support their ridiculous blockade or volunteer for their army unless they are made to feel scared, vulnerable. Most people don't want to fight and die so Mr. Lincoln can say he held his precious Union together. Most people in the North could care less if the South goes its own way. Most don't care enough about the Negro to risk their lives for his freedom. They just want to be left alone to make babies, plant their gardens, go fishing, find their peace with God."

Maude suddenly sits up tall in her chair, tilts her head back, closes her eyes.

"I don't understand. I swear I don't ... "

Fiona reaches across the table and takes her hands. *These fingers, so long and dry, but so very strong.*

"You mark me: your Raffy is just the bloke these Yankee bully boys need to get a truly serious war started. And the newspapers are going to give the world a pirate to fear and hate. Tell them stories about death and destruction visited on their friends, relatives and neighbors ... until their blood rises. Let them picture a strutting little bloke who twirls his mustache like a matinee villain and ... you just wait and see. They'll cheer while their sons and husbands and fathers take up arms, while they fill up all the cemeteries with blood."

She hears Greenhow's voice echoing in her head. *You have ... a Southern officer grafted to your very soul.* She pictures Raffy yet again amid a cloud of cannon smoke, smells burning wood, hears the crash of falling spars slapping decks and ocean.

You may be in a position to do nothing less than save his life.

"Stop it. Just Stop!"

She hits the table hard with her fist. Her teacup jumps from its saucer with a bang. Heads turn toward the women.

"I'm trying, love." Fiona takes a napkin, dabs up the puddle of spilled tea. "I swear I'm trying, can't you see? But it's a bunch of bastards that's got this country by the throat now. Tyrants like King Billy and the rest of 'em that stole the old country from your own dear old mum. They say that they want to end slavery, but what they want to do is turn Americans into serfs, just like the English done to the Irish. I've run from the dandy lairds once. Now, I aim to fight them. These bloated self-serving aristocratic blokes, mill owners, government henchmen and their crews. Lincoln is just a pawn for their bleedin' machinations. And so is Raffy!"

Her body twists. Something inside her skin is fighting to get out.

"It's not fair. Raffy is a good and honorable man. They've got him all mixed up with someone else. They can't do this!"

Tears well up. Her face is flushed, blotchy. But she isn't melting. She throws back her shoulders, glares at a bloated dandy who has been watching the drama between the two women from a nearby table. He turns back to his eggs and toast under her withering glare.

"That's my lassie. Found your fire, haven't you?"

She blinks, seems to come out of a trance, knows with all her being that the time has come for a private visit with Rose Greenhow. Something deep in her belly trembles. She remembers how Greenhow held her in a spell, drew her so close that their petticoats crushed together at the waists.

"It breaks my heart, but you must not come here alone again, dear. It will raise too much suspicion. I am being watched."

Greenhow pulls her into an embrace, gives that little squeeze under the arm alongside the breast. A single shaft of dusty afternoon light cuts between the drawn curtains in the parlor, seems to burn a hole in the wine-dark carpet. She feels the heat of the older woman's breath on her neck, tries not to flinch. Tells herself to think of Raffy, only Raffy. Nothing else matters. She herself does not matter.

"I am moved beyond words that you have come back to me at last. I feared I ... the last time ... "

She feels the shadow of a disturbing memory and a sob rising in her chest. Hugs Greenhow harder, hoping to find her balance.

"I'm changed," she says. But she does not even know exactly what she means.

16

CSS Sumter
JULY 6, 1861

He hears the hiss of musket balls close overhead almost at the same instant he sees the smoke from a fusillade. It rises, a pale, blue cloud above the white ramparts of the Spanish fort guarding the river entrance to the harbor at Cienfuegos.

"They are rolling out a cannon, sir."

Kell points to a gun port in the fortress wall where a small gang of soldiers are working an antique twenty-four-pounder into place with pikes and rope. Atop the ramparts, officers in bright red and blue uniforms wave wildly at the Confederate cruiser.

"I think they aim for us to anchor, Mr. Kell. What say you? Shall we bow to the demands of our new hosts ... or blow their puny little fort into the next life?" He smells the sulfur as the cloud of musket powder drifts toward the *Sumter,* feels the blood rising in him. Finds himself remembering assaults against Mexican outposts on the way to victory in *Mexico Ciudad* back in '47.

"Be a pity to lose those seven prizes, sir!"

He stares aft from the *Sumter*'s poop, tallies his achievement, a parade of ships trailing in his wake, all now sailed by the prize crews he has placed on the captured vessels. The *Machias* and the *Ben Dunning* of Maine, the *Albert Adams* of Massachusetts, all captured two days ago. The *West Wind* of Rhode Island, the *Louise Kilham* of Massachusetts and the *Naiad* of New York seized just this morning as they left Cienfuegos. The *Cuba*, with midshipman Hudgins in command, trails behind ... out there in the haze somewhere most probably. And the *Golden Rocket*, gone but not forgotten, her crew still aboard the *Sumter*.

For a second his mind seizes on an uncomfortable memory. He had been within three nautical miles of the coast, within a league of the shore, in the actual territorial waters of Cuba when he spied the last three prizes being towed to sea by a tug from Cienfuegos. And he deceived them, flew the Spanish flag to keep them off their guard. The lawyer in him complains that he should not have misrepresented his ship's nationality, should not have given chase, not within the territorial waters of a Spanish colony. International law requires that he wait twenty-four hours before leaving the waters of a neutral nation to give chase to an enemy departing the same waters. He waited about an hour and a half. *Well, the deed is done. My crew was ripe for victories ... and prize money. Haven't I given the Yanks a chance to run five miles to sea, to sail beyond the territorial limits of Spain, before giving chase?*

"God strike me down if I lose those prizes, Mr. Kell."

Kell smiles his big teddy bear grin. Says the crew is bursting with pride. The *Sumter* has taken eight prizes in four days. No warship nor privateer has ever done such a thing.

"And we shall not end it here by picking a fight with our hosts ... Prepare to set your best bower. Send Mr. Evans ashore to invite the *commandante* aboard for champagne. Let us practice a little diplomacy. Now follow me."

He steps to the rail, faces the Spanish fort, snaps to attention, salutes. Kell does the same.

"Dip the colors, bosun!"

Aye, sir.

The Stars and Bars, which had been sent up upon seizing the last three Yanks, runs down from the spanker peak and back up again.

A brace of uniformed men ashore salute back from the fort.

As he lets his gaze roam the shore, he sees the hills dappled in a dozen shades of green, smells hibiscus, acacia, bougainvillea, oranges. *Most Merciful Father, dare I disturb this paradise?* Then for the first time since putting to sea, he takes stock of his appearance, how crusty he has become. His hair feels like straw, his cheeks burn from salt and sun, a boil blooms on the side of his nose, his mustache itches from wild hairs.

"This will not do, sir," he mumbles. "I am not a pirate!"

Suddenly, he craves a careful shave, a change of uniform, a bath, a fine party.

"Pass the word, Mr. Kell. We'll be receiving company. Dress whites for the officers, fresh togs for the jacks. I want the band playing 'Dixie.' And several bottles of champagne on ice. Let's see how the Spanish don takes to us now."

The *commandante* of *Fuerte Cienfuegos* takes a sip of the extremely cold and fragrant champagne, raises his glass.

"*Salud, señor.* I feared you were a *pirata*. But I find you a noble Quixote of the sea!"

He gives a slight bow of head to accept the compliment, raises his crystal flute in toast to the sweating, fat Spaniard come to roost in *Sumter*'s great cabin. He wants to counter that he's no tilter at windmills—*just count the prizes, man*—but speaks otherwise.

"I salute Your Excellency for his alert and vigorous defense of such an important port as Cienfuegos. It is an honor for my ship and my nation that you take time from your busy day to grace my cabin with your presence."

The Spaniard surveys the *Sumter*'s great cabin, adjusts the enormous scabbard swinging from his thick black hangar. He eases back in one of the empire chairs that the steward has brought out for the occasion. Amid the bars of light and shadow filtering into the cabin through the skylight, he smiles as he looks upon the gleaming brass of the clock and barometer, the polished cherry chart case, the captain's mahogany desk, the thick Persian carpet. He seems especially taken with the portrait of a young flaxen-haired woman in a gauzy, blue dress wandering barefoot in a field of violets.

"Your Dulcinea, *tu mujer?*"

"Just a picture, Your Excellency, a fantasy to keep a lonely sailor company!"

"She is a nymph, I think."

He says nothing, tries to smile, takes a sip of champagne. His cheeks flush a little with the memory of a dream he was having when the steward had woken him for the morning watch. He had been head to toe with Maude in a bed of cherry blossoms, bare as a pair of seals. Before setting out on the *Sumter,* he had thought only about the mission, its ten thousand attendant details, the crew and the inexpressible lightness that came over him at sea. He had not remembered this part of going to sea, the strange dreams, the longing for women and the fruits of the land. Wonders how it could be starting so soon.

"Cienfuegos has many refined and beautiful *señoritas,* who, no doubt, will be most eager to meet a dashing *capitán* who brings so many prizes into our harbor. Never have they seen such a victorious *caballero del mar.* And they are not fantasies, I assure you sir. But nymphs? Perhaps."

The *commandante* smiles a lecherous, lip-licking grin, winks. He drains off half a glass of champagne, raises it for a refill. Semmes beckons his Malayan steward with a quick nod to top off the Spaniard.

"Here in the colonies the women are infinitely freer with their favors than they are back in *España.* Some say it is the effect of the blood of Africans that courses through the veins of these *creollas,* though even the brown ones will swear to you they have five hundred years of *sangre pura* straight out of the courts of *Reina Isabella.* What does a gallant *capitán,* a Quixote of the world, think?"

He's baiting me, feeling for my weakness.

"I'm married."

"*Bueno.* Most excellent!" laughs the *commandante,* slapping his knee with his free hand. "I like you. You are *bueno*! But can you forgive my mistake? Already my second of the day with you. And I thought you were a pirate, too. What do you think? Perhaps it was the Spanish flag you were flying when first we saw you in our territorial waters.

But then you rushed off after the *yanquis* and returned here flying this new flag, which was unknown to me, on your ship AND on the *yanquis*."

He does not answer, knows he's about to feel the iron hammer of Spain on his head unless he can muster a silver tongue, a story with credence. He turns to his steward, gestures for a second bottle of champagne.

When the steward has withdrawn to the pantry, the Spaniard speaks again. "Señor, can you forgive me my mistake for thinking that since your ship sailed from Spanish waters flying a Spanish flag, that perhaps these prizes must now belong to the Spanish crown?"

The steward reappears. Semmes takes the new bottle of cold champagne wrapped in a linen napkin, dismisses the steward, serves his guest, flashes his poker smile. Lies.

"It was not a mistake at all, sir. I would forgive you a thousand times, Your Excellency. But there is nothing to forgive. You saw what you saw. You could not have known that we are the first ship in the navy of the new sovereign Confederate States of America."

He says the *commandante* could not have guessed that since the *Sumter* has but one flag halyard. That the ship had lowered her own national flag and raised the Spanish *bandera* as a courtesy flag when approaching Spain's territorial waters. Preparing to enter the port on a mission of peace, as ambassadors of President Jefferson Davis and the Confederates States of America, when the *Sumter* found herself face-to-face with three ships of the enemy.

The *commandante* takes another deep draught of champagne, wipes beads of sweat from his brow, lounges back in his chair with both hands holding the glass poised on the red sash girding his enormous waist. He has the look of a man hoping to be entertained ... even by desperate fictions.

"A leader such as Your Excellency could not have achieved so much respect and responsibility as to have the care of such an important fort without allegiance to the code of honor that rules the lives of warriors such as ourselves."

"It is the most important thing. What is a man without his honor?"

"Exactly, good sir. And my honor was put to the test when I found myself face-to-face with three of my enemies, perhaps armed, certainly carrying cargo that could aid my enemies in their perverse obsession with ridding the world of me, my ship, my crew and my country. What could I do but defend myself and all that is dear to me?"

The Spaniard takes another sip, swirls the vintage in his mouth, tastes it as if he's tasting the captain's story for its artistry.

He hopes the *commandante* is enjoying the champagne enough to overlook the little fact that the *Sumter* appeared on his doorstep with three prizes already in tow.

"I was on my way to Cienfuegos as a peaceful ambassador, but with the appearance of my enemy, honor bound me to face him or forever appear the coward in his eyes, your eyes and my own. Sir, I made the hard choice. War instead of sweet peace. I gave the enemy a fair chance to run. Then I hoisted my own colors for all to see. And I gave chase. Now, with the grace of God, I have prevailed over my enemy."

He sets his drink on a humidor, moves up to the edge of his seat, folds his hands. Stares without blinking into the Spaniard's face like a confident but humble brother-in-arms.

"Now, I ask for your understanding … and to let me make any and all amends on behalf of President Jefferson Davis, for any inconvenience or uneasiness I have caused you and the good people of Cienfuegos."

The *commandante* holds out his glass for more champagne. When it's topped off, he takes a swig, lets it play in his jowled cheeks. Then he cocks his head and gives Semmes a sidelong glance.

"You are *bueno*. I mean, you are truly *buenisimo*." He wags an index finger at Semmes. "What is it you wish, Quixote of the Confederate States?"

"To buy coal, water and provisions from your merchants, sir … and to leave my prizes in your good care." There. He'd said it. *Feed my ship that she might hunt again. Protect my prizes; they are my honor, my fortune, my future.*

The Spaniard smiles, drains his glass, holds it forth for refilling again.

He paces the quarterdeck, worried. It's already 0830 on a sweltering morning in the harbor at Cienfuegos. Midshipman Huggins has not shown up with his prize yet. And Lieutenant Chapman has still not returned from the mission he undertook the previous afternoon of delivering Semmes' letter of petition to the civil governor.

"Sir, I think I see the launch." Kell is at his captain's side, a long glass trained on the tangle of small boats bobbing near the quay at the center of town. "Yes, it's Chapman and his boat crew. He's standing in the stern. His shirt is unbuttoned; his coat is off and he is waving it. Ah ... he looks a little worse for the wear, sir."

Semmes reaches for Kell's glass, puts it up to his eye. He looks for several seconds at the stocky, black-eyed Don Juan waving his coat in the air as if he were in the midst of a *Mardi Gras* parade. His usually neat and trim jet hair and beard are in disarray. The *Sumter's* captain stifles a laugh.

"It seems, Kell, that our young *preux chavalier* has had a night of it, but returns with rich news. Let us hope that it favors our cause."

Chapman is begging his captain's forgiveness for his tardiness and his dishevelment when he climbs aboard the ship. He is still pleading his case as Semmes marches him directly below to the great cabin. The lieutenant lays out a tale of a party of which he has never seen the likes—a twelve-piece orchestra, a bevy of soft-eyed beauties calling him to dance, fruity rum potions to embolden the most restrained heart. All in his behalf. All to welcome the *Sumter* and celebrate her victories. Noble gentlemen and ladies called him *Señor Ambasador*. Sweet-faced *señoritas* and the governor himself begged him to stay the night.

"How could I refuse, sir? When the governor had not yet given me an answer to your petition? It was hard duty. I confess I was in dire danger of forgetting that I am a married man. And the governor wants to throw a ball in your honor tonight. He says we will be lavished with—"

"Leave off, Chapman." He slams the door of the great cabin, motions to one of the chairs left over from the *commandante*'s visit the day before. "Sit. What of our prizes? What of the coal? What of the Yankee consul?"

This last question has worked on him most of the night. What if the Yankee consul has wired his brother consul in Havana about the *Sumter*'s presence in Cienfuegos with six or seven American prizes? How soon until ships from the Federals' Key West squadron, ships that routinely visit Havana, are dispatched to hunt him down?

"We may buy coal, water and provisions. I have met the merchant, and all was sealed with sherry, good God, earlier this morning."

Semmes, now seated across the Persian rug from his dashing-but-disheveled emissary, begins to nod his head with approval.

"But his prices seem double what I remember paying in these Cuban ports."

The captain's mustache droops a notch.

"We are in no position to bargain." He speaks with tight lips. "The prizes?"

"The governor telegraphed his superior, Spain's grand dragon of the island, in Havana. Sent your petition word for word. Said you are a most persuasive writer. The governor in Havana is sending it on to Spain for final resolution. He says he knows that the British have already denied both the Federals and us the right to bring prizes into their ports."

His mustache begins to droop again as he stiffens for bad news.

"But ... but the grand dragon says that we may leave our prizes here, in custody of a Spanish prize agent. That, too, is arranged, sir."

The captain bows his head, claps his hands three times.

"Blessed art God Almighty, ruler of Heaven and Earth!"

Chapman smiles at his captain's pleasure. But it looks to Semmes like a sad smile.

"We may leave the prizes under the condition that a Spanish court will decide their fate, sir. Not a Confederate prize court as you had wished. We are enjoined to draw no funds from lenders here against the value of the prizes. That is absolutely forbidden us."

He sits back in his chair, folds his hands together under his chin as if in prayer, stares up at the blue sky above the skylight. The right tip of his mustache flicks.

"This is, I suppose, the best we could have hoped for." His mind turns to other worries. He thinks about the high cost of coal and the mere ten thousand in gold he has locked under a settee in the great cabin. *Unless I can get something of value from my prizes, I will soon be a pauper and reduced to the worst kinds of piracy.*

"We must be frugal, Chapman. Come, the American consul?"

"He's a knave certain, sir. I have made inquiries, bribed a telegraph operator. It seems the Yank wired his compatriots in Havana around noon yesterday to send a fleet after us."

"That whoreson. You're certain?"

"Saw the telegram itself. Written in plain Eng—"

Semmes jumps to his feet.

"They will be on us by tomorrow sunrise." He cannot wait here for Huggins and the *Cuba*.

17

Executive Mansion
JULY 12, 1961

E xiting the stables, Lincoln sees the Secretary of State marching toward him across the South Lawn and groans.

"What is it, Papa-day?"

The president smiles at seven-year-old Tad's nickname for his father. He knows that a speech impediment had been the genesis of the name, but it carries just the right mix of affection and whimsy to lift the president out of the thick stew of mid-summer heat, politics, war.

"Aren't we going to ride the pony?" Ten-year-old Willie eyes the bay Shetland the president is leading by the reins.

"Of course, boy. This will just take a minute. It seems Mr. Seward wants a word with your father."

He's coatless. His white shirt is open at the neck showing a tuft of black fur, the sleeves rolled above the elbows. Every afternoon that he can, he escapes to the barn with the boys and the family menagerie of dogs, goats, ponies and horses.

"Weasel-weasel. Pop goes the weasel!" Tad's yelling.

"That will be enough." He's well aware of Tad's compromising nick-names for some of the cabinet members like Seward, draws his face into a mock frown. He waves an immense finger in Tad's face, then hands the reins to the older boy. Still looking at Tad, he says, "Take the pony and go with Willie for a walk, Son."

Seward charges up, sweating in cravat and coat.

"Mr. President."

"Mr. Secretary ... What brings you in such an all-fired fit to disturb my boys' pony ride?"

"Have you not read the *Evening Star*? Can't you see what that pirate Semmes is doing?"

Lincoln watches his boys leading the pony through a glade of dogwoods, sucks on his cheeks.

"You mean the Reb sailor with his little raider down there in the Gulf of Mexico? I thought you told me to put him out of my mind at last week's cabinet meeting. And, no, I have not read the papers, sir. You know I can't stand their palaver."

"I never told you to put him out of mind, sir. This Semmes is big trouble for us. That must have been Gideon, sir. I would never have said such a thing. But Gideon seems slow to catch—"

He clears his throat with a deep rasping sound.

"Leave off Welles. I told you I've had enough of the cockfights between the two of you. Come. What news, sir?"

Seward does not wither under the president's challenge, thrusts out his lower lip.

"My ... our consul in Havana has sent word that Semmes sailed into Cienfuegos last week with six American prizes in tow. New York's insurance companies are in a panic. They've raised their rates two hundred percent this morning. I've gotten wires from ten of our biggest shippers demanding that we stop Semmes now and threatening to tie up their ships until we reach a settlement with the South. Without a merchant fleet we cannot sustain a war. Don't you see, Semmes is a vicious seahawk!"

Lincoln kicks a divot in the grass, stares across the South Lawn to where Elmer Ellsworth is training his Zouave regiment to the sound of fifes and drums.

"Why have I not been briefed on this?"

"I am trying to brief you, sir."

He rubs his hands through his hair.

"Why does it seem like everybody in the world knows about these things before I do? Why does every little Confederate initiative seem to burst into a bonfire in the press before this administration can put out the flames? Tell me that, Bill."

"The press intercepts our telegrams."

"Horse feathers! Somebody's leaking this stuff to make us look incompetent, and you know it! They want to turn public sentiment against this administration and force us to reach a compromise with the South. Is that not true, Mr. Secretary?"

Seward opens his hands before him, shrugs his shoulders.

"Well ... answer me, sir."

"I don't know what to say."

He feels his fists start to close and his shoulders rise.

"Say, yes, man! Say that from this time forth every sensitive telegram coming into your office will be delivered by you to me *post haste*. Say that we will then contrive a meeting with members of the Washington press to inform them of events and our response. Do you understand, sir?"

"Perfectly." Seward steps back from the figure hulking over him.

The president takes a deep breath, uncoils his fingers.

"Now, how do we put out this fire Semmes has started?"

"I don't know, sir. I'm just the messenger. You've told me that I shall not delve into naval affairs. I guess you better take this up with Gideon. Now ... if you'll excuse me, I have a staff meeting in a half hour."

He glares. "As you wish. Do me the goodness of asking my secretary to send for Mr. Welles."

Seward looks up into his boss' face, sets his teeth. Does not blink. There's the shadow of amusement on the secretary's face.

"I'd watch those boys nigh that water. It's a sea of pestilence and typhoid. Death to a child."

The president spins on his heels and begins lumbering toward his young sons who are splashing each other and their pony at the edge of the B St. Canal. It was designed for the delivery of fruits and vegetables from the country to the capital, but it has turned into the city's largest sewage drain.

⚓   ⚓   ⚓

Lincoln sits in an armchair, staring out the window toward the Washington Monument project, the army encampment, the Potomac. A white barber's cape covers his shoulders. His head tilts back. The barber's snipping the last ragged gray hairs from his beard when Gideon Welles appears at the office door. He feels like he is intruding, knocks softly on the open door.

"You sent for me, Mr. President."

Lincoln stiffens, pulls off the barber's cape in a flurry. A cloud of hair scatters. The barber jumps back.

"Sir?"

"Thank you, we're finished here, barber." His voice sounds abrupt, dismissive. "My tonsorial will have to wait for another day. Excuse us."

The barber, a thin black man, bows, backs out of the room with his cape and black tool bag.

Lincoln stands, gathers a pile of maps and books from his mahogany writing desk, carries them across the room. Drops them with a loud thud on a large walnut table in the middle of the room used for cabinet meetings on Tuesdays and Fridays.

"Sit, Gideon." The president motions to one of the two horsehair sofas.

He feels his scalp start to sweat. He has never seen his boss so petulant, so clearly perturbed. He settles into the couch in short order, folds his hands on his lap. Thinks two things simultaneously: *Has my wig slipped?* and *Am I going to be fired?*

Lincoln paces the length of the room to the west wall, pauses at the fireplace, reaches out with one of those enormous hands as if to touch the face of Andrew Jackson in the engraved portrait over the mantle. Welles hears the hiss of the gas lights, thinks he smells a leak—but maybe it's just the stench from the canal on this oppressive afternoon.

"I'm in no mood to beat around the mulberries, Mr. Secretary. How in the name of St. Francis have you let this raider calling herself the *Sumter* slip through your blockade? And why, with all these ships of war at your disposal, have you not brought this pirate Semmes to justice?"

He feels the sudden urge to sound in command of his fleet. But, in fact, his knowledge of how the *Sumter* ran the blockade, and her subsequent raids on shipping is shadowy, comes mostly from the papers.

"We're making every effort to—"

"I'm not finished, Gideon. Now you listen. Bill Seward burst in here earlier today, ranting about six more of our ships this Semmes has taken. Says the insurance companies and the shippers are fit to be tied and screaming for the government to take action against the rebel pirate."

Gideon takes a deep breath, shifts his derriere to the edge of the sofa, opens his mouth to speak ...

Lincoln doesn't let him get a word out. He stands in the middle of the room, spreads his arms in the style of a camp preacher. Seems tall enough to touch the ceiling. A giant who has descended to earth from a beanstalk.

"What in God's good name is going on in your navy? First they muck up the resupply of Ft. Sumter. Then they give away the navy yard at Norfolk. Everybody knows the blockade is leaking like a sieve. And now this cocky little Semmes is on the verge of shutting down our shippers. With one little five-gun raider. Didn't you tell me just last week to put this *Sumter* out of mind?"

He feels a knife in his back again.

"No, Mr. President. I said no such thing. That was Bill Seward. I said I was looking into the whole fiasco and the officers in command of the blockaders who let him escape."

Lincoln stands at the head of the cabinet table, rubs his right cheek and eye with a hairy paw.

"Lord. How am I to keep things straight? You and Seward, again. Finger pointing. I'm sick and tired of this tiff between you too. It is a damned distraction. And you know what? I don't give a bucket of oats who said what last week. The point is that nothing has been done."

The president is wrong. Ever since the names Semmes and *Sumter* appeared on the horizon, Welles has been after his commanders for intelligence. And at every turn he has pressed them to take care that the *Sumter* not escape through the blockade. But his boss is on a tear, and to protest would be suicide. Not that he loves this job so much, but he knows he could be good at it if given half a chance. He knows he could help the president hold the Union together.

Lincoln drops himself on the sofa, facing Welles. But even though the president sits, he feels no less threatening.

"Our navy is becoming a joke. And if it is a joke, then what's to deter the South from simply going its own way. We can't stop this rebellion with the army alone. And the South has already sent a legion of capable diplomats to curry favor in Europe."

Turn the other cheek. This storm may yet blow over.

"Yes, sir, I know."

The commander in chief makes a noise deep in his throat, a snarl.

"Let me be plain. I don't think your commanders are taking this blockade seriously. It is our most effective means of ending this conflict without bloodshed. But from what I hear, there are many of your captains who would prefer to steam into all the ports of the South, guns blazing. And not stop shooting 'til everybody's dead or surrendered. A damned bunch of glory boys. Well, I won't have it! Hear me, loud and clear. The people of the South are our kin. I will not preside over a blood bath. Tell your senior officers their duty is to maintain the blockade, not attack Southern shores. They have no excuse for leaving their stations ... nor letting ships slip in or out of the South. Make an example of those who have unleashed this maverick Semmes. Who was on watch when this *Sumter* ...?"

"The *Brooklyn*, sir. Captain Poor. The *Sumter* out-sailed him in a squall."

"Relieve him. Court-martial him if you can. Let your glory boys see how they will be humiliated if they cast a light eye on our blockade or fail in vigilance. This Semmes is for us to deal with ... not for some gold-braided sea boy to pursue on his own There were other ships, no?"

"Yes, sir. At least two more ships, as I understand it, were in the vicinity, guarding other passes at the Delta. The *Niagara*. Perhaps the *Minnesota*. And *Powhatan*. But I don't think they were directly ... "

Lincoln jumps to his feet, his face flushing.

"*Powhatan,* that's Lieutenant Porter again. He's got a nose for trouble. Pinch it!"

"It's *Commander* Porter now, sir. You promoted him less than two months ago."

Lincoln suddenly picks up a glass paper weight, looks ready to heave it somewhere. Hard.

18

District of Columbia
JULY 13, 1961

A roving violinist moves among the gaslit chambers of the Greenhow manse, playing melodies from Verde for the guests. Near the punch bowl in the parlor, two men press so close to Maude that she feels dizzy from their cologne.

Jean Claude de Saunier wears a tricolor chevron of red, white and blue across his chest and the most finely cut evening coat of creamy silk that she has ever seen. He's the *chargé d'affairs* for the French legation, a viceroy through his father, a Rothchild by way of his mother. For ten minutes he has been spinning the most entrancing tale of his posting in the court of a Sultan of Arabia and his harem. Almost Raffy's age, de Saunier has the manners of a fairy prince, the firm, lighted-footed body of a man who Maude thinks could waltz her all night. It's a shame that he bears the face of a hatchet.

The other man's younger, an assistant trade *attaché*. Hugh Riddley-Oak has a mischievous smile, a sparkle in his look, the unabashed forwardness of a blue-eyed schoolboy with cheeks of pink. He's ninth generation Harrow and Oxford, tells ribald stories—mostly loosely reworked sketches from *The Canterbury Tales*. And he has a fetching laugh. It echoes through almost all that he says, giving the impression that he still half-believes that the world has been made for his personal amusement. She can hardly take her gaze off him, thinks, *a lass could take a tumble for such a bloke ... even if he's a bloody Brit.*

But she fears he might read her mind. Turns her attention back to the worldly Frenchman, offers him her hand as Rose Greenhow sweeps into the midst of the trio.

"You can kiss it again, Mr. Ambassador."

The Frenchman beams at her flattery, takes her tender fingers in his own. There's a restrained hunger in his smile. She sees a gold ring with an immense sapphire on his middle finger, knows this man has the means to help her, help Raffy ... if she only knew how.

"Is she not a child of the gods, Madame Rose?" De Saunier holds her hand just shy of his lips, sights along her arm to the curve of a breast.

"An absolute angel, Johnnyboy." Greenhow kisses her on the cheek. "But I'm afraid you must excuse this charming creature for the moment. She's in high demand tonight. I have promised to introduce her to the good senator from Massachusetts."

"It has been my pleasure." The viceroy kisses her hand a third time.

She feels a queasy little flutter in her stomach, but flashes her most ingenuous smile.

"Perhaps, you could tell me more about Arabia, later, Your Excellency." She looks from Riddley-Oak to Greenhow and back to Riddley-Oak, watches a jolt of jealously twitch across both their faces, can't believe she's acting such the tart.

"Most certainly," says De Saunier.

"And what may I tell you, pretty lady?" Mischief dances in Riddley-Oaks' grin.

"Pray, not another country joke. But do you ride?"

"Like Gawain himself."

"Then perhaps you might give me a lesson upon some cool morning. I am but an eager novice."

She feels an involuntary blush rising in her cheeks. Then she suddenly remembers Raffy, why she's here. Turns away without really hearing her admirer's response.

Holy Mary, forgive me this harlotry.

When Greenhow has led her into the dining room, she pulls Maude into a corner. "You come to this game like a natural, sweet Maudie. But be careful, take two steps back from the edge, love. Ten steps back from your feelings."

"Aye. I did not know I would find it so easy or so much fun."

"It is the greatest gift and the greatest curse of the beautiful woman. But save yourself for the big scene. Your leading man's yonder in the navy suit hobnobbing with Senator Wilson over canapes. He's been watching you all evening."

She means to survey this new admirer, but spots Fiona across the room. Gives a little wave. Fiona lifts her chin a notch. Shoots back an ambiguous squint.

She has not yet been alone with Harry Burlow for thirty seconds or exchanged more than two dozen words with him, when the dashing, blond naval lieutenant stings her with a question and a caddy grin.

"You're Raphael Semmes' friend, are you not?" The man's not Adonis, but he has something that draws women to him like flies. Perhaps it's his fine Yankee features, generations of scrupulous breeding in the highest echelons of Connecticut society. Possibly it's the bravado and danger latent in the pointy tuft of dark whiskers on his chin ... and those eyes, pale as agates, burning with a dark fire. They settle on the Pillsing of her green satin dress where it marks the border between her neck and everything below, seem to look right through her.

She feels her heart seize but brushes a curl from her eye, gives him back a careless smile.

"I have lots of friends, Lieutenant."

The words are out before she can bite them off.

My god, I sound such the saucy drab.

"Like the elegant Miss Fiona, Queen of the Amazons?"

He cocks an eyebrow and a suggestive little smirk. She knows exactly what he's getting at, decides to let him think what he likes about her amorous preferences.

"Yes, Fiona ... among others." She winks at him.

He bursts into a belly laugh that jolts him with such a spasm that he spills a touch of his champagne.

"Precisely. Among others. Then, all the worse for me that I am not included in the circle of the chosen."

Yes. She has her fish on the line. Now suddenly remembers the fan in her left hand. She draws it across her face in a flutter to screen her amusement.

"I don't think it's too late, Lieutenant."

He tosses his head back on his neck, blinks at the ceiling, laughs again.

"Then may I tempt you with champagne?"

"You may try."

She gives him her arm, lets him guide her into the parlor to the punch bowl.

Twenty minutes and two glasses of bitter *brut* later, she's still hanging on his arm. They have paraded from room to room of Greenhow's cotillion, chatting. She has learned that it's through his job that Burlow knows Raffy. As assistant detailing officer at the Navy Department, Burlow has the everyday responsibility of writing the orders for most of the service's senior officers.

"That must be very exciting," she says as he pauses with her on the threshold of the grand staircase to the living quarters upstairs. "You know everybody's fate."

"Sometimes I am fate himself. I can stick a man off in a dark corner of the Lighthouse Service for the rest of his career. Like your Raphael Semmes."

"How wicked."

He shrugs. So it goes.

"After a while it gets dreadfully boring. They don't seem like real people. You never see them bathe in glory, crumble in defeat, wither away in oblivion. They're just names. A bag full of toy sailors."

"From what I read in the papers, Raphael Semmes is no toy sailor these days." She cocks her head, arches an eyebrow.

"Sometimes they break the rules. They surprise you. It's the only thing that keeps me from going stark raving mad. Your Semmes, he's breaking all the rules. He's a dirty word around my office of late. Old

Folkwattle Welles doesn't seem to know how to stop him. Don't you wish you could be there to see how it ends for the good commander? Do you think he'll go down in a symphony of barking cannons or drift off with the tide like a drowned rat? A mercurial fellow to be sure!"

She remembers a man of snow crumpling at her feet in a dark hallway, feels him shiver in her arms. Then bit by bit warm to plow her like the wet, green earth of Shannon. Feels a pinch in her loins.

"Who can guess what the hungry wolf will do, Lieutenant?" Her voice sounds far away to her. She feels the champagne rising in her, a warm bath. A dreamy smile crosses her face.

"My thoughts exactly, madame. But wouldn't you like to know?"

Her mind pictures a gale driving gray waves over a black ship, sails in ribbons.

"Aye."

He smiles. "Here before you stands a hungry wolf. Shall we see what he will do?"

She feels his arms circle her waist from behind. His hips press against her buttocks. She has missed such holding frightfully, likes the sense of forbidden pleasures waiting to catch her from some dark place.

"Do you have a carriage, Lieutenant?"

19

CSS Sumter
JULY 13, 1861

Waves the size of tobacco barns bury the deck in the dark. For three days and nights she has been beating toward Barbados into the teeth of a gale. The ship's steaming hard on the wind with the fore topmast staysail, fore topsail, main topsail, and reefed spanker set to dampen the roll. Now the wind has clocked from northnortheast to east-southeast, increased from force eight to force ten. The rain comes in sheets. The larboard running light casts a dull red glow against the night. The midwatch has nearly run its course. Lieutenant Evans has the deck. But Semmes cannot sleep, will not leave the deck. He's in the season of the great Caribbean cyclones. There's now, with this ever-increasing wind, every sign that his ship has come afoul of more than an ordinary gale.

The *Sumter* has already burned through most of her coal and has not yet cleared the north coast of Jamaica. By engineer Freeman's calculations, there's less than a full day's supply of coal left. At the noon sight, Semmes discovered that his ship has actually been set backward on her course over the previous twenty-four hours. Barbados and a fresh supply of fuel seem impossibly far to windward now. Soon the *Sumter* will have to go it with sails alone.

Still the storm continues to gather strength. The cruiser rumbles, creaks as the waves press her. Sea chests, furniture, pots and pans clatter around below. Men yell to make themselves heard. Over the sound of everything comes the howling of the wind in the rigging. For two days he has listened to the high-pitched scream of the wind and not worried. But in the last few hours the wind has dropped its note to a deep whir, begun dismantling the *Sumter* piece by piece. During the second dog watch the inner jib carried away with the sound of a thunderclap. On the evening watch two of the new t'gallant sails split their seams, shredded. The jacks fought for more than an hour aloft to clew up and furl the remnants.

With some of the steadying sails now gone, the ship rolls in thirty-degree arcs, pitches like a hobby horse. Even the most seasoned seamen in the crew, including the luff, have put themselves on a course of bread and water for fear of numbing bouts of seasickness. Semmes has taken nothing since noon, feels his stomach tightening into a stone.

Little by little the caulking in the decks is working loose. Everything below in the ship's wet. Six inches of water sloshes through the fo'castle and the galley. Even the wardroom and the great cabin, usually the driest places on the ship, are not immune. Every time a wave rolls over the deck, officers' country down-floods through deck leaks, the scuttles, the skylights, the companionways. The steward has been fighting a losing battle to keep the cabin soles and ladders dry. The officers have to walk from hand-hold to hand-hold to keep from falling. Still men lose their footing. Evans goes head-over-tea-kettle in the wardroom on leaving his cabin to start the midwatch, finds himself stuffed, in the wink of an eye, under the mess table with a bloody lip and aching elbow.

On deck a boarding sea rips a bosun and the carpenter right out of their harnesses on the windward jackline, would have washed them overboard through a gun port if a cannon had not broken its lashings and plugged the port first. Instead of running from the careening cannon, the half-drowned men grab its loose lashing, resecure it even as another sea almost washes them over the lee rail.

All this the captain sees. He has barely left the deck in thirty-six hours. An hour into the midwatch now, he finds his mind losing a grip on the struggles of this ship and these men, returning again and again to December 8, 1846, the last minutes of life on the stricken *Somers*. It seems some cruel agent of fate has taken him back to the hour when he lost the brig. He knows that injury or death is coming to his crew just as surely as the crashing of another wave. The old names and faces begin to clutter his mind. More than thirty lost. He sees the fat cook

Seymour coming out of the only lifeboat to make room for two other men, watches sailing master Clemson strike off on his own so that weaker swimmers in the crew might hold on to a studding boom and be saved, feels Midshipman Clark pluck him off the upper half-port on which he has been floating and drag him into a lifeboat.

I couldn't stop shivering, couldn't stop, God help me.

Now he clings to the windward mizzen shrouds, staring into the raging darkness, shivering again.

There's a flash of lightning. The deck shudders. First a knee wobbling tremor, followed by distinct heavy thuds and a grinding as if the ship has struck a reef full on, is driving herself high onto a jagged ridge of coral.

He looks around him, isn't sure where he is.

The grinding stops. A faceless, hooded figure is shouting at him. Evans.

"Fore topmast has sprung, sir. Torn clean away."

He stares aloft, sees a tangle of yards and rigging, flicks the rain from his brow with the back of the hand. Begs the Most Merciful Father to give her a little more life.

"Assemble the watch. Alert Mr. Freeman. Tell him we are going to need all of his engine's might directly. She can't take this much longer. We've got to run her off to the southard while we still can. Prepare to wear ship, Evans. Three men on the helm. These are wicked seas. Can you handle it? You aren't just going to be a mate all your life, are you?"

Evans stiffens. Throws back his shoulders, bulls out his thin chest, sets his teeth.

"Aye, sir. Wear ship it is. Count on me, Captain."

"That a boy! Have at it ... I must get below to the charts for a spell. Ever been to Curaçao? There is peace and plenty at Curaçao, Evans. Bank on it."

"And coal, sir."

"The Devil's own coal."

He salutes his deck officer, wobbles across the poop toward the wardroom scuttle. His long watch coat trailes a stream of water, must weigh twenty pounds. He's still murmuring a prayer of contrition when he gets below and realizes that he has not told Evans to take in the spanker before wearing ship. Once again he starts up the ladder for the deck. Near the top he feels light-headed, leans against the scuttle wall, buries his face in the crook of his right arm. Then everything goes black, and he falls ten feet back down to the cabin sole.

The next thing he knows he's splayed out on the wardroom floor. Kell, Chapman, the doctor, Pills Galt, all standing over him. He tries to gather himself and rise. But he can't move.

20

District of Columbia
JULY 17, 1861

"What do you think of this, Burlow?"

Welles sits at his desk in the Navy Deparment, passes the letter with its painfully small, neat script across the blotter to the assistant detailing officer.

He knows the service taboo of sharing confidential information with a junior officer, but he needs a sounding board on this delicate issue and almost none of his senior men are trustworthy. Either their loyalties to the North are tenuous, or they seem to be angling for career advancement, glory, power, a change of leadership. Maybe all of the above.

Burlow, on the other hand, is an ardent champion of the Union, fervently anti-slave. And from the first, he seems to have taken to Welles like a young man in search of a mentor. True enough, young Harry is a bit of a rake-hell, loves a party and his tarts, but isn't that just youth? Connecticut roots and good family have to count for something in the end. Most importantly, no one else in the entire navy knows its personnel—their strengths, weaknesses, histories—like the assistant detailing officer. Besides, the boy has a refreshing candidness that seems altogether free from guile. So Harry is his man of the hour.

Burlow brushes a blond lock out of his eye, gives his boss a look of studied earnestness, surveys the letter. It's from David Porter on the *Powhatan,* and it lays out what the recently frocked commander claims to be a fool-proof plan for bagging Raphael Semmes. Since the near mutiny on the *Powhatan,* Porter has taken time to refine his plan. He prophesies Semmes' first stop as Cienfuegos. Says that Semmes, with years of experience in the Caribbean and the Gulf, will hunt the shipping lanes south of Cuba. He will patrol near the major passes into the Caribbean, like the Mona Passage west of Puerto Rico and the Sir Francis Drake Channel south of Tortola. The *Sumter* will lurk around islands like Barbados which have fuel and lay to windward of the shipping lanes, giving him the crucial weather gage on Yankee shipping bound to and from the Spanish Main. And he will never be more than a week away from a coaling station.

Porter claims that he knows these waters as well as the Reb. Put him in command of five or six warships, and his flotilla will stand guard at the major entrances to the Caribbean, forcing Semmes into the Caribbean basin. Once they have Semmes penned in the Caribbean, they can practice a little naval diplomacy. Sailing into foreign coaling stations like Danish Charlotte Amalie on St. Thomas, they will make a show of force, back up the local consuls' pleas to refuse the Confederate pirate refuge, provisions, water, coal. In such fashion they will tighten the net around Semmes until he has to come out and fight. Then they will blow his little, black, raiding barge to kingdom come.

When he has finished reading, Burlow sits back in his seat, arches both his eyebrows, blows out a breath.

"Come, Harry, what do you think?" He fingers the curls of his toupee that just now seem to prick at his ears.

"Quite a plan."

"It could work, could it not?"

"Naval strategy is not my area, sir."

"But it makes sense. And, good God, I must do something about this bugger Semmes. The president, not to say half the country, seems mad to catch him."

"So I've heard." Burlow frowns ... ever so slightly.

"What's that look? Come, young man, be straight with me. Let me hear you."

"Off the record, sir?"

"Of course, speak up."

Burlow takes a deep breath, seems to be counting to ten in his mind. "Well, it's Porter, sir."

"Bit of a problem, isn't he?"

"He's as much a maverick as Raphael Semmes. Not one for follow-ing orders if they don't suit him, I'm afraid."

"That stunt with Secretary Seward to hijack the *Powhatan*. Seems like he's out to look after his own hide."

"Exactly, sir. That wasn't the first time. Porter pressed the navy for a leave some time back to go captain on steamers making gold rush runs to California. But when that business went flat, he came back pestering us for command and promotion. Just last winter the scuttlebutt was that he planned to quit the service and sign on as a master with the Pacific Mail Steamship Company. But then he slithered to the helm of *Powhatan*. His father destroyed his own naval career by disobeying orders and raising all hell between the U.S. and the Spanish crown at Puerto Rico."

"Cheeky bugger."

"Exactly that, to my way of thinking, if you want to know the truth, Mr. Secretary."

Still holding Porter's dispatch in both hands, Burlow nods with his whole body.

Welles suddenly rises up from his slouch. He stretches across the table, seizes the letter.

"But the man gets things done! Maybe we need a maverick to catch a maverick. Not one of these slow and plodding graybeards who pass as our squadron commanders, eh?"

"Can you trust him not to go off half-cocked, firing his guns in some foreign harbor and starting a war between us and France or England?"

Welles drops the dispatch on his blotter, kicks out of his seat, struggles to his feet, an aging giant. Turns his back on Burlow and walks to a window, massages the chin wattle under his massive beard with both hands. He looks like he's milking his neck.

"And who does he really work for?" Burlow asks.

Welles spins on his heels, glares at Burlow as if stung by his *protégé*. In his mind he revisits that mad night when he learned that the Secretary of State and Porter had diverted *Powhatan* from the mission to resupply Ft. Sumter.

Jesus Christ, Bill Seward. Does that bastard have a hand in this somehow?

"Not me. Porter never worked for me. That's the sad truth."

Burlow shrugs, pretends he doesn't know. Pretends he did not intend to hit his boss below the belt. "If you gave Porter his dream, would the president support you?"

He feels his stomach turn. Hears Lincoln. Powhatan*, that's Lieutenant Porter again. He's got a nose for trouble. Pinch it ... Or I'll find someone else who can do the job!*

"I'm jammed."

"Beg your pardon, sir?"

"Never mind. You're excused, Harry." He fondles his wattle again, stares out the dirty window in the direction of ships masts rising above the Washington Navy Yard.

"Will there be new orders for Commander Porter?"

21

Curaçao
JULY 17-21, 1861

Semmes smells the hibiscus and oleander of Curaçao, lying a quarter mile off to larboard, breathes deep to inhale the scents of the land as he sits on his berth and struggles into his service coat. Pain shoots up his back, tightening in his chest.

After his fall four days ago, Pills Galt found two ribs totally dislocated from their moorings. Galt popped them into place, but shooting pains still come back at him with each breath. He chokes, wonders if this is how life will be forever hence. Is this how it feels to get old?

Sumter arrived here off the port of Willemstad on St. Anna's Bay at dusk last night, and signaled for a pilot. He had arrived in due course, but said it was too dark to take the ship into the harbor. So the *Sumter* lay to outside the harbor for the night. Now, it's just past sunrise. Kell knocks on the door to the great cabin to say that the pilot has returned with a message for Semmes from Governor Crol.

The captain buttons his coat, brushes back his bushy brows with his finger tips, gives a twist of beeswax to each corner of his mustache. Lurches to the door, swings it open. He squints at the luff and the Dutch pilot, trim and proper in his dark suit and close-cropped blond beard.

"Are you alright, sir?" Kell winces in sympathy.

He grits his teeth, steadies himself on the door jam. Then he turns away and waits for the pain and nausea to pass.

"God willing, man. We've been waiting out here all night under light steam. Our coal is most used up. Can we take her in now?"

"I'm afraid not," says the pilot. "His Excellency the Governor says he cannot permit the *Sumter* to enter, having received orders from Holland to that effect."

He feels his chest hardening. Struggles to inhale.

"This is a pretty kettle of fish!" There's no wind. The sea's slick calm. Would they have him row his ship thirty-five miles to Venezuela to beg coal?

The master of the *Sumter* turns to the pilot. "Will you excuse us, good sir. Have a seat. Please let my steward get you some fresh coffee."

He rings the bell for his steward, orders coffee and johnnycakes for the pilot. Then he leads Kell forward to the shadowy wardroom. Each step jars him with pain.

"What do you think, Kell?" His voice sounds hollow, forced. Not an intentional whisper, but a whisper still. With an edge.

"I smell a rat, sir."

"The American consul, no doubt. This tinpot governor has no orders from Holland. Some picayune Yank has bullied him right much, threatened that Lincoln will send a flotilla in here to blow his precious little trading port all to hell if we are granted our just due."

"Aye."

He clasps his hands, squeezes them together beneath his diaphragm as if the action could force precious air into his lungs. Slowly he feels his chest rise, open. His back straightens, his shoulders cock back.

"Lincoln's foreign service is a nest of whores and panderers! God help us, Kell. The Yanks pray to the god of commerce. There is no hole, or corner of the earth, into which a ship can enter, and where there is a dollar to be made, that has not its American consul. And he is the smallest of men, eager for self-aggrandizement and his puny profits, shrouded in a cloak of jingoistic patriotism. Holy Jesus, but it makes me mad!"

He spits these last words with such vigor that the luff takes a step off to the side.

"I can picture it. Some simpering, caviling little ferret has got word of our presence, most likely from this pilot, and beat a path to the good governor's door." His voice gains timbre. "There he has puffed the Dutchman full of William H. Seward's hogwash. To wit: we are pirate outriders of a rebellion that will be soon put to rest. That we are not deserving the belligerent rights of safe harbor, provisions and fuel accorded a commissioned warship of a legitimate government. Yet we come in peace. Foul, Kell. Most foul!"

Kell nods, wonders what is coming next.

"Get me my secretary, sir. I shall dictate a letter to send ashore to the governor with Chapman. It shall spell out our case for belligerent rights with such clarity that this Dutch *burgermeister* will fear he has marched all of Holland into a war with the Confederacy should he refuse us. Hold the pilot here under some pretense. And beat to general quarters. Clear for action. Don't you think it's time our jacks have a little practice with the guns?"

Kell smiles. Old Beeswax has found his high note again.

The *Sumter* shakes with thunder as the first gun in the larboard battery discharges, slams back eight feet against its breaching tackle, launches a cloud of light blue smoke outward, boiling up and over the deck. Wadding falls like snow. Four cables to the west a geyser erupts from the placid water as the twenty-four-pounder sends up a plume of spray thirty yards short of its target. It's an empty pork keg, flying a red flag, that the ship's cutter has anchored down-range. Just to the north of the line of fire stands the government house. Most of Willemstad's men rushed here to assemble in council shortly after Chapman delivered Semmes' letter to Governor Crol.

"Gunner. Ready on number two. Raise her a touch. Silence on deck." He stands, watching the target with his glass. "Prime. On the up-roll, fire."

On the gun deck, the sponger and powder boy stand opposite the fireman and the gun captain on either side of the cannon. Everyone claps hands to their ears, turns away. The gun captain pulls his lanyard, touching off the percussion cap at the prime hole on the number two gun, then leaps backward away from the recoiling carriage. The white kerchief tied over his head already glistens with sweat like his dark back. A jet of water explodes beyond the target.

"Too high. Gunner walk it back a bit. Ready on the pivot gun."

"Captain, look to the shore." Kell has his eye on the government house and fortifications. "We have an audience."

He swings his glass toward the island, sees the windows of the council building, the parapets of the fortress, filled with faces peering around corners as if fearing that at any second the *Sumter* might turn her guns ashore.

"Splendid. Amazing what a little gunpowder diplomacy can do, isn't it, Mr. Kell? Let's show them what happens to those who come afoul of the Confederate States of America, men. Silence on deck. Careful aim, gunner. This time on the down roll. Skip it home. Fire away."

He holds his long glass on his audience, spreads his legs to keep his balance, feels the ship lurch to starboard and shiver as the eight-inch pivot gun spits fire. Thunder echoes. Through the smoke he sees men ashore erupting with spastic grasps for their heads as if to make sure their hats had not been blown away. Down range the ball hits the water like a goose skidding in for a landing, skips twice with the same effect, smacks the target into a cloud of kindling.

"Fucking, yes!" shouts the gunner.

Semmes pretends not to hear, tries not to smile, spins his glass down range just in time to see the last of the debris settling.

"Chapman's boat's coming back out from town, sir. And there's a squadron of bum boats in his wake. I'd say His Excellency Governor Crol and his minions have seen the wisdom of your argument."

The captain swings his long glass toward the harbor. A swarm of small rowboats are pulling toward his ship. And in each boat are women. Chocolate skinned women in red, green, blue and yellow head scarfs. Wearing muslin dresses you can almost see through. They have the faces of fallen angels. Breasts like the mounds of melons, mangos, guavas filling their boats. Pretty soon he knows that he will hear them calling to him in their lilting creole—"*Dushi, mi dushi*, sailamon"— and he will be carried beyond all pain and worry to those days he spent in their arms as a buck midshipman on the Old Lex so many years ago.

Fucking yes! "Secure your guns, gunner. Mr. Kell, have Mr. Freeman get his steam up. Pilot, to your post, if you will." He heaves a sigh, feels something breaking up a bit in his chest. He's a man who has been waiting half his life to come home to a scene like this. He suddenly thinks of Odysseus among the Lotus Eaters, bewitched by Circe.

"And Mr. Evans, you can let the ladies aboard."

He cannot take his eyes off her. She's tall, willowy with skin the color of cinnamon. And she has a tangle of black coils that frame a face made slender by high cheekbones, a thin nose, fine jaw. It's her fifth day visiting the ship. She carries baskets of guavas and shell jewelry to sell, and she plays a concertina while dancing for the jacks who throw coins in her tin cup. He thinks this is the snake dance of Eve in the garden. When she dances, she returns his stare with a gleaming smile.

He feels a stirring in his loins; a thing wild, haunting. He thinks of Maude, his sweet selkie, and curses. Tells himself that he will love her forever, but wonders if there's even a remote chance of seeing her again. Then he thinks of Anne who will never let him go ... but whose breasts have become indifferent to his touch. Now, he wonders if loneliness, like this infernal pain when he heaves a breath, will be his lot until a bullet finds him, he drowns, loses himself at the end of a Yank's rope. Or sails home to Dixie as a king of the deep.

"Mr. Evans, I think I'd like some guavas. Could you send that whirling dervish to my cabin, please?"

The officer of the deck gives a little salute, turns away so that the captain cannot see his look of surprise and amusement.

The tart calling herself Villie sets her basket of fruit on the table in the great cabin, puts her hands on her hips, smiles at the *Sumter*'s master who contemplates her from his empire chair. His elbow rests on the arm of the chair, the forearm stretching up to support his jaw, fingers toying unconsciously with the tip of his mustache.

"Can you eat wit dat ting?" She holds her hands over her mouth and wiggles her thumbs out to the side like a cat's whiskers.

"It depends what you've got for me to eat, my dear."

Lord Jesus, I am become a ruddy bucko.

"Dis gal got da sweetest guava in all dis island, *mi dushi capitan*."

She puts both hands into her basket, comes up with two plump, yellow orbs. Cups them right in front of her breasts and walks toward him. Her head droops a little and tilts to the left, giving her smile a seductive look. He watches how her hips sway, how the flame-colored fabric of her skirt catches on her thighs, swings in counterpoint to the motion of her body.

He reaches out for a guava. But as he reaches he hears something in the center of his back crack.

"Damn!"

"You hurt."

"It's nothing."

He feels a guava fall into his lap. Her hand slides along the side of his neck. He opens his eyes.

She's bent down on one knee, face-to-face with him. He can smell the scent of tamarind in her hair as her hand continues its strong, slow exploration of his neck, testing the knots in his muscles with her thumb and fingers.

"You jus a snarl of flesh, *dushi*."

He puts his head back. The other guava falls into his lap. He feels the smooth tip of each of her fingers on the cords of muscle rising to his ears, spreading out across his shoulders.

"It's my back. I fell."

"Please, take off da coat, *mi capitan*. Lie on da bed. Facedown. Villie can help."

S O U T H E R N   S E A H A W K

He feels her breath on his cheek. Sees her untying his cravat, closes his eyes. Falls into a little half dream.

It's a Saturday morning in the spring not long after he met Maude. She loves to take long walks so he invited her on one of his favorite tramps north out of Georgetown along the towpath of the C&0 Canal. They carry a picnic basket of pastries, strawberries, cheese, two bottles of chilled apple wine. At the Great Falls they find a clearing near the Potomac, spread a checkered tablecloth, feast. And when they have taken their fill of food, they take each other. Not in the sense of the carnal beasts they will become in later days, but in the sense of explorers in a dark and sumptuous garden. It's the touching of the miracle of flesh that he craves. The unlacing of the dress, the unburdening of hair. His fingers combing through the roots of her copper mane, her smooth, moist hands plowing the furrows along his spine, across his shoulders. The promise of new life, youth, immortality.

Now he feels that promise all over again, buries his face in his pillow. The cinnamon-skinned woman works the pressure points in his lower back with one hand, teases the inside of his upper thighs with the fingertips of the other.

Semen is already starting to weep into his small clothes when a rough knock comes from the cabin door.

"Captain. Kell here. Most urgent that I talk with you!"

"Kindly come back in half an hour, when I have roused."

"Sir, look to the wench. She has a knife!"

Jesus Christ on the cross.

He rolls. Scrambles upright in the bed, feels a rib pop loose from its moorings in his back again. Tries to ride through the pain, harness its power. Grab for the woman's wrists.

Her eyes are wide with terror as she spins free of his grasp. She stretches for her basket of guavas, sitting on the cabin sole near the captain's berth. Her right hand comes up with a paring knife. She slashes with it at his chest. The knife catches on a button hole of his shirt, slits it to the tail.

But if he's cut, he doesn't feel it, only the pain searing in his back, shooting into his chest, burning now into his arms and his legs. He summons it, calls it twelve times an ape, until he feels his nostrils flare and the gorilla explode. He pounces on the girl, drives her to the floor, a rag doll. Straddles her chest. His knees pin her arms.

"Who sent you? Who sent you, gal?!" He's shouting as his left hand tears the knife from her fingers, flings it across the cabin with a clang.

She bites her lip in defiance, the blood and tears already starting to flow.

Kell kicks open the door.

"The Yank consul sent her. Freeman just heard about it from his moll."

He slams one hand on her throat. His other reached beneath his mattress. He comes up with the Naval .44 service pistol Sam Colt gave him back in March, puts the barrel right between her eyes, draws back the hammer.

"Did he? Did the Yank send you? Speak or die, gal!"

He feels her starting to convulse beneath him.

Something warm and wet spreads over the inside of his thighs.

"Aw, Mother Mary!" Kell sees a pool of golden fluid spreading over the cabin sole. "She's pissed herself."

"Speak, gal!"

Her eyes squeeze closed.

"He say he give me a hundred guilders." The voice small, far away. A child or an old woman.

The pain and the excitement jolt through him. He smells the sharp scent of urine.

"I'll eat him for breakfast, hear? I'll have satisfaction at twenty paces with the monkey!"

Kell bends, put one hand on Semmes' shoulder. He extends the other, asking for the gun.

"Sir, let it go."

He looks into the luff's broad, bewiskered face. Smiles.

"Good Kell, loyal Kell."

Give me that man that is not passion's slave, and I will wear him in my heart's core.

"The ship's ready."

22

New York
JULY 21, 1861

A swarm of reporters and Federal naval officers in their summer whites are surrounding Captain Stout of the brigantine *Cuba* on a pier at the Brooklyn Navy Yard. He has just finished telling the story of how he and his crew overwhelmed a Confederate prize crew and reclaimed their ship.

"Ye must not paint an heroic picture of the little *Cuba* and her crew; by bringing this brigand Albert Hudgins and his consorts to justice here, we do naught but our duty to the republic. Hang 'em if you will, but their blood is not on my hands. They are mere boys, deluded into playing at piracy by a man calling himself Commander Raphael Semmes."

"Tell us about Semmes," shouts a whiskered young reporter from Horace Greeley's *New York Tribune.*

"Is he a villain?"

Stout surveys his audience, looking slowing over the crowd from left to right. He wears his white shirt unbuttoned at the neck and dark trousers ending in sea boots that come almost to the knee. His long hair is pulled back into a tight queue.

"A villain? Yea, boys, he's a villain of the blackest sort. And a cunning corsair. The man doth make love to the image of piracy. Why, ye see, he has a mustache beneath his nose the size of a raven's wings. And a goatee like Satan himself. Semmes stands as big as a bull and carries a cutlass on his belt. Of which, I must say, he is fond of brandishing in the faces of both crew and captive to make a point or gain his way."

In the collected group, the sound of scratching pencils, copying every word.

"How did he treat you, sir?"

Stout squints for a second as if remembering a terrible pain.

"Worse than any among ye might treat a stray dog."

He says that the pirate tied him in a chair in the great cabin, seized him by the hair, held a cutlass to his neck, demanded gold. When he said he had naught but some two hundred dollars in paper money, letters of credit and the cargo of sugar, the pirate whipped him with the hilt of his cutlass, knocked him onto the cabin sole, kicked him in the ribs, uttering the most outrageous blasphemies. Then he sent Stout back aboard his ship in chains with his prize crew ... such as they were. After picking his pockets. The scoundrel stole his watch and a gold locket given him by his wife.

"So would you call him a common thief?"

"Aye, sir. That he is. One gone stark mad with greed, too. Ye tell me he was once a ranking officer in our navy. Why that is almost impossible to believe."

"The pirate Semmes showed none of the sense of the decorum and respect common among two ship masters. He did not conduct himself or his crew according to the codes of discipline and honor for which the naval service is famous. Indeed, the flag of the so-called Confederacy seems but a flag of convenience for the blackard. He's a man you don't want to meet alone in a dark alley. All threats, cursing, weaponry. And boasts. The man bragged about his conquests. Said he'd burned four ships just to light his way on a dark patch of ocean the night before. God knows what he did with the crews."

"Where was he headed, Captain?" The question booms over the heads of the assembled crowd. An odd silence settles over the multitude as their faces turn to the speaker. He's a naval officer of considerable age, a full head taller than anyone else, with an arresting baritone voice, a thin, chiseled face, bags beneath the eyes like an inveterate drinker. A lock of gray hair falls over his forehead, giving him the look of an aged Romeo.

"Beg pardon?"

"I say, did Semmes say where he was bound?"

Stout rubs his chin, nods, seems to know that the footlights of this scene now cast their glow fully on another. Stout is Semmes' past; the speaker Semmes' future.

"He was towing us east along the south coast of Cuba when the towline parted, and I heard him tell young Hudgins to rendezvous off Cienfuegos, sir. No doubt he aimed to go hunting in the sea lanes around Cuba's south coast for awhile."

The tall naval officer speaks again. This was no longer a gathering of the press and naval brass to meet the hero of "The *Cuba* Incident." This has become a public conversation between two plucky roosters.

"There are many merchant ships there and along the north shore of Haiti," says the naval officer. "The Old Bahamas Channel—pirates have grown fat in those waters for two hundred and fifty years. Why would Semmes go far from those cruising grounds until the pickings get slim?"

"I don't know. Why don't ye tell me?" Stout's feeling feisty.

"I doubt he will, sir! He's a rogue wolf in the lamb yard."

The reporters make sure that they get that quote down.

"But when he's plucked the Old Bahamas Channel clean, I can well guess where he'll go next." The tall naval officer has a smug grin on his face. "This would-be Blackbeard can be stopped. With a fast ship and some big guns, and the help of God, a man might drop him in his tracks."

"Hey, Admiral, who are you?" one of the reporters asks.

The naval officer smiles smugly and looks down on the assembled multitude.

"Captain Charles Wilkes, captain of the United States sloop of war *San Jacinto*. Write it down. I'm the man who discovered Antarctica. And I am the man who has received authority from Secretary of the Navy Welles to hunt down the pirate Semmes. The Rebel reign of terror shall be short lived. You can quote me on that. Charlie Wilkes gives no quarter to pirates and Johnny Reb."

"What will you do when you find Semmes and his gang?"

Wilkes smiles.

"Exterminate the vermin!"

23

USS Powhatan
LATE JULY

Preposterous!" Porter stands the quarterdeck four bells into the noon watch, snarls at the dispatch in his hand.

The luff casts his captain an uneasy glance, knows another blow-up's coming, shuffles forward to be out of the line of fire. It's a good time to have a talk with the bosun about splicing the chafed spots in the foretop buntlines. When the skipper's in one of these moods, his officers avoid him like the yellow jack.

The massive canvas awning that spreads over the *Powhatan* from foredeck to transom offers shade but not relief from the humidity of the Gulf in high summer. Both the officers and men are dripping sweat in the light afternoon breeze. Everyone's feeling wretched from the heat, not to say pissed about the new water rationing plan the captain has instituted. The horizon in all directions is a pale blue haze. Not a squall in sight to bring cooling winds and rain to fill the water casks. There's nothing on the horizon at all except the ghostly outline of the Mississippi Delta to the north. The schooner that has just tied alongside *Powhatan* with her dispatches from squadron command at Pensacola, thumps against the sloop of war as the two vessels roll against each other in the lazy swells.

Porter crunches the dispatch from the Secretary of the Navy into a ball, throws it overboard with a wicked back-handed toss. He closes his eyes to clear his mind, but sees the words again.

As per your request to leave your station to pursue the raider Sumter. *... Your request is hereby denied. The* Powhatan *shall maintain the blockade of the Delta with all due vigilance. G. Welles.*

"Fuck all!" Porter kicks the bulwark.

"Bad news?" The master of the dispatch schooner.

"It's nothing." He scowls, looks right through his guest as if he were a ghost.

The trim, bantam cock of a man was once a middie with Porter back on the Connie during the Med Cruise in '31. He's a superb mariner, but he lacks political influence and has not got on well in the navy. Still a lieutenant. He came aboard to deliver the dispatches in person, see his old shipmate, catch some shade under the awning. No doubt, he hoped Porter would treat him to the courtesies usually due the master of a dispatch boat. A cigar and conversation between masters below decks in the great cabin. The life of a captain is a lonely one as protocol keeps him aloof from both his own officers and men. So sharing scuttlebutt with a fellow commander comes as a welcome antidote to a cloistered existence, the pressures of command. So ... a cool libation, trays of smoked oysters or deviled eggs often appear from the pantry. But in this regard, things are not looking promising on the *Powhatan* today.

Porter rolls his massive shoulders, gazes off to the south.

The smaller man watches this, keeps silent until he's almost sure no invitation is coming.

"I'll have your dispatches for squadron, Commander. And be off then. This light air has put me days behind my schedule."

The schooner captain extends his hands for the leather dispatch pouch stamped *Powhatan* that Porter clutches in his hand. It bears little of import. He has seized no blockade runners. Only seen what might have been the shadows of smugglers slipping along the coast by night, bound in and out of shallow Barataria Bay, the one-time outpost of the pirate Lafitte.

All he has to report to squadron command are the particulars of men treated in sickbay and those punished. Just this week, six more men felt the cat for fighting. The crew's in a surly mood, and things do not promise to get any better unless he can provide them with something more meaningful to do than bobbing around off the Delta, enforcing this ridiculous blockade.

He looks at the schooner captain's extended hands, starts to pass him the dispatch pouch, then suddenly takes it back.

"Sir?"

He slams a fist against the pouch.

The schooner skipper twitches. "Is there a problem?"

The captain of the sloop of war suddenly shoves the dispatch pouch at the schoonerman, lets loose a horrendous sound. Perhaps just a clearing of the throat, but quite possibly a growl.

"Forgive me, Salty. I am much distracted and perturbed." He claps a thick arm around the shoulder of the smaller, thinner man. "I have nearly lost my sense of hospitality. Surely, you have time to step below with an old Connie boy. Shall we get clear of this heat for a bit of a gam and refreshment? The steward's got a pitcher of sangria. What say we utilize it?"

A smile spreads over the schoonerman's sunburned face.

"Most assuredly, Commander. There's much news adrift in the squadron these days."

He inhales deeply on his Key West cigar, holds the smoke, then lets it escape in a perfect ring until it makes a cloud against the white ceiling of the great cabin. He takes his time with a sip of sangria, tries to make his question sound offhand.

"I suppose there must be some news of the *Sumter*."

His guest raises both eyebrows, nods with an air of significance.

"Semmes has stirred up a hornets' nest of public outcry. His name is all over the front pages of the papers we get from New York and Washington.

"The *Sumter*'s already taken two score prizes. Maybe more. And now it seems Old Man Welles is sending some boats after her. Charlie Wilkes on the *San Jacinto* has gotten the nod. The press has made much of Welles sending the great hero of the Antarctic after the pirate.

The captain of the dispatch schooner snorts into his porcelain mug of sangria. It's clear he's skeptical, thinks Welles' choice to send Wilkes *Sumter* hunting is just a ploy to get the newspapers and shippers off his back. It may not even be his own idea.

Porter's blood begins to boil.

"Christ, Whipping Charlie Wilkes? What a self-important prick. And a goddamned antique. Hell, he must be sixty-two or sixty-three years old. One of the old boys' club. A stinking curmudgeon. Grist for this new retirement board they're making up under David Farragut!"

"I remember his court-martial for the illegal punishment of crew following the Antarctic expedition back in the forties."

His officers didn't even stand up for him. But he was a hero. Like Perry. And he had suck with the admirals and bloody pols. So he got off with a reprimand. Pure poppycock. Standard operating procedure in this man's navy.

Porter feels his fingers beginning to cinch tight around the handle of the sangria jar as he pours off another cup for himself and his guest.

"He'll muck it all up. Hell, if he's even been to sea in about fifteen years. Fucking flogger. Christ, they'd be better off sending Mrs. Lincoln."

The dispatch captain pulls the cigar from his mouth between two fingers, stares at the smoldering tip.

"Friend of mine sailed with him in the Pacific, said his own private opinion of Wilkes was that the man was little removed from an absolute buffoon. I hear he claims he'll find Semmes along the West Africa route or the Old Bahamas Channel."

He feels like something just smacked him in the back of the head. He bites off the end of his cigar, spits it in the brass ash stand.

"Bilge! My god, is Wilkes fucking daft? Why in the name of Hell would Semmes take that tea kettle of his off soundings into the middle of goddamn nowhere when he can't have more than about a ten-day supply of coal aboard? And why would he haunt the Old Bahamas

Channel when he knows his only coal is in Havana or Nassau ... and the Key West Squadron will be watching those ports like hawks? If you were Semmes, Salty, where would you go hunting?"

The bantam cock smiles to think of such an opportunity. He has clearly seen far too much service as an errand boy for commodores and admirals.

"Mona Passage. East of Culebra. Sir Francis Drake Channel around Tortola. Anegada Passage. Work on down the Leeward Islands."

"Exactly. Then run for South America when things get too hot for you in the Caribbean. It would be a feast of Yankee ships, and all the coal and water you wanted ... We should be chasing Semmes!"

"Fat chance. Since when has the navy ever put the right men at the right place at the right time except by pure accident?"

Porter grunts. "Welles is a political hack."

"What's new?"

The master of the *Powhatan* knows his cynical friend speaks the truth, but can't focus on the boss. It's Semmes who seizes his imagination.

"But what in Hell's name is Wilkes thinking?"

"He's not; he's just grandstanding," says Porter. "He imagines he'll get a good cruise out of the Old Man before they force retirement on him."

This is Wilkes' ticket to get the hell out of that observatory where he's been rotting in Bethesda. He doesn't give two shits about Semmes. He's going to just use it as an excuse to do a little freelancing. He'll stir up a heap of shite before this is all over. Welles has plenty of enemies in Washington. They may well be sponsoring good ole Charlie.

Porter thinks of Bill Seward and his own caper with hijacking the *Powhatan*. Wonders if he has been made a gull by the Secretary of State. A disposable pawn in some dark Washington parlor game.

"We're fucked, Salty. Lincoln's fucked. Semmes is going to raise holy hell!"

The dispatch captain swills his sangria, takes a deep breath.

"He's far from the president's only problem. A week or so ago the Union army squared off with the Rebs at some place called Bull Run in Virginia. Got their asses handed to them by a fellow they're calling Stonewall Jackson."

"So the unraveling begins."

24

CSS Sumter
JULY 27, 1861

He paces the quarterdeck, the luff at his heel. Feels his back tighten, start to burn as he watches the paymaster riding back to the ship from shore in the gig. The man wears a stony scowl on his face that makes him look dead in the late afternoon shadows falling over the Moorish looking port of Puerto Cabello, Venezuela.

"Merciful Christ, not again! Would they have me rot at sea? Burn my prizes? Damned, but I have belligerent rights!"

Kell says nothing in response, gives a sympathetic look with his warm, open face.

Semmes has already been driven out of Puerto Cabello once with no coal or provisions. Told in no uncertain terms by the local potentate, a flabby consort of the U.S. consul, to take the prize he then towed, the New York schooner *Abby Bradford*, and leave. *¡Inmediatamente!*

But now he's back. Maybe it wasn't the smartest move to return to a place that already showed him the door, bared its teeth. But he desperately needs coal, and he has seized another prize, the Philadelphia bark *Joseph Maxwell*. He has been in an impulsive mood since leaving Curaçao, playing everything from moment to moment, as if he has lost sight of any plan. And before steaming in here a second time, he argued against his officers' misgivings. He claimed that the locals would take the *Maxwell* back for safe keeping rather than see her burned since she carried some cargo for a Venezuelan merchant. And surely their humanity would prevail to take the bark's unruly crew off his hands.

But from the look on the paymaster's face, and the hustle of gunners pulling tompions from a brace of rusty cannons in the fortress ashore, he must have been wrong in his assessments. It seems the local *commandante* has grown even more resolute in denying the *Sumter* everything but the taste of gun smoke.

"Those pea shooters are a joke, Kell. I ought to beat to quarters, clear for action, blast this town to hell and claim a colony for Jeff Davis. Get the whole lot of us ashore for awhile." His mustache jumps up and down as he barks.

A new thought seems to cross his mind; he cracks a giddy smile. "What say you to setting ourselves up like emperors? These Spanish *payasos* seem to do it with impunity along this coast. Music, wine, dancing girls ... "

"Wouldn't that be a pretty prospect?" There's a winsome note in the luff's low voice.

"Oh, Lord. The world has gone mad! If we weren't in such dire straits, I could just laugh. Just flat out laugh, Kell!" He coughs into his hand—or perhaps it's a snicker.

The luff looks at his skipper sideways, wonders if Pills Galt has given him a bit too much laudanum for his back pain and sent the master halfway round the bend.

"You OK, skip? How's the back?"

"Progressing." A lie.

The laudanum helps, pushes the pain to the back of his consciousness. But he hates the opium powder. Hates its bitter taste when mixed with alcohol for ingestion. Hates the curtain of golden fog it draws between his mind and everything else. And now, after days of hot rainy weather he has a wicked cold. Every time he coughs, his back feels ready to split in twain. So between the busted back, the laudanum dreams and the cold, he has barely gotten more than two hours of sleep at a stretch for days.

Kell looks skeptical.

"You want me to deal with the *Maxwell*? Send her crew ashore in the boats and burn her?"

Semmes feels sick, tired, angry. Everything seems a half-forgotten dream. The warrior in him wants to say, "Yes. Burn the fucker, Kell. Light up the night with her. Let the flabby Venezuelan and his American bum buddy see what happens when you cross the Confederate States of America and Raphael Semmes."

But something else in him tugs on the reins, calls for caution. This is complicated. There's neutral cargo involved. And perhaps he needs the *Maxwell's* crew as hostages. On his last venture into Puerto Cabello he learned from a New York paper that the Yankees captured the Confederate privateer *Savannah*, were calling the crew pirates, aimed to hang the lot. Well, what would Lincoln do if the captain of the *Sumter* threatened the same fate for the *Maxwell's* crew? Did he have the right to execute? *What would Jeff Davis say? And what about the woman; the captain of the* Maxwell *had his wife aboard. God, imagine if Anne or Maudie ...*

Kell sees his commander slipping off into a cloud.

"Sir, skipper? You want me to fire her?"

He suddenly snaps a heel on the deck, draws himself up to attention. But his gaze avoids Kell and settles on the horizon.

"I must think on it," he says. Almost adds, *I fear I've made mistakes of late. Possibly fatal ones.*

The *Sumter* stops her retreat from Puerto Cabello in international waters beyond a marine league of the coast where he has anchored his prize the *Maxwell*, left her crew aboard under a guard of Confederate marines. Now he paces his quarterdeck, glaring at the setting sun. He claws the unshaven stubble under his chin then beckons to his boarding officer.

"Get the people off the *Maxwell*, Mr. Chapman."

"Aye, sir!"

"You can tell them that it has been our custom to treat crews from our prizes as worthy guests who we will land and repatriate at the earliest possible convenience. But their government has now set an unfortunate precedent, ignoring the rules of warfare and condemning the crew of our duly commissioned ship of war the *Savannah* as pirates.

According to Mr. Lincoln's view of the world, the *Maxwell's* people must be pirates as well since they actively aid and abet, with their commerce, a government who robs the South of its freedom and who intimidates, starves and impoverishes our citizens with their infernal blockade of our ports."

He hunches over in a coughing spasm.

"Sir?" Chapman's concerned.

He draws himself upright, gives his officer a hollow look.

"Tell them, hear?"

"Yes sir. Consider it said, Captain." Chapman searches his captain's face for something, perhaps the light of reason. "Permission to get my boats underway to the prize?"

He runs his hands through his hair, leaves it a thicket of gray spikes.

"Wait, son. Just a minute ... Make a space in one of the boats for me." He walks across to the larboard mizzen chains where Kell is in conference with Pills Galt. "Kell, I'm going over to the prize. I may be there some time. You have the deck."

He hacks again, puts his face into his hands, buckles over.

Kell and Galt shoot each other questioning looks. It is not customary for the master of a warship to leave his vessel and board a prize. Who knows what dangers await on a captured ship? Sometimes there are booby-traps. Then there's the issue of Semmes' wretched health.

"Are you sure this is wise?" The doctor breaks military protocol, challenges his senior officer. The man's his patient, and he's clearly in distress. "Can I at least give you something for that cough?"

His head suddenly snaps out of his hands. He fires the doctor a red-faced glare.

"More of that goddamn laudanum? You think I don't know what that opiate is doing to me? You don't think I know that the two of you are wondering whether I'm fit for duty? Mother Mary, I pray. Just give me some peace. Not more of your poisons. Peace. Peace to gather myself. Peace to decide!"

Now he's alone. He stands back aft near the bark's magnificent steering wheel, inlaid with birch details. He reaches for the brass compass cover on the binnacle, opening and closing it as if it is a child's toy. Chapman has harangued the crew of the *Maxwell* as ordered, hauled them off to the *Sumter*. The sun has set. There's no moon. The lights of Puerto Cabello light the southern sky. To the north, he can just make out Ursa Major on the horizon with Polaris on the lip of its cup. The *Maxwell* creaks as she rolls at anchor in the easterly swell.

"Talk to me, Maudie," he says aloud. "What do I do, now?"

He doesn't know why he has invoked the spirit of his lover. Maybe it's the laudanum. Or, more like, the lack thereof, as he swore off the drug this very noon. It's crazy thinking of Maude. She knows nothing of ships nor war. And with no letters from her Raffy for months, she probably has given up on him, moved on to a man who's more available and younger. She's just a memory. A pretty picture like the girl on his cabin wall. Still ...

He feels his way along the starboard rail to the bows of the bark, coughing up phlegm and spitting over the side as he goes. He started trembling hours ago. First just the fingers. But now he feels like his whole body's a swarming hive of fire ants. These aren't the tremors he felt months ago back in Montgomery begging for a ship, nor the trembling of fear, although there may be some of that. Nor is it like shivering in a storm such as the norther that had claimed the *Somers*. It's more like he's in the grips of fever, hot flashes followed by icy chills. But not quite that either.

When he comes to the bowsprit, he takes off his coat, folds it, lays it over the capstan. Then he mounts the sprit, clambers out past the triced-up staysail to the cap, where he squats, straddling the jib boom with his legs and feet dangling. He used to come to this spot many a time as a middie on the Old Lex, even as a sailing master on the Connie, just to get off by himself and think. So here he is again, perched on the nose of a windship with nothing but stars above, inky sea below. He wonders if he remembers how to talk to God or

Maude or even himself. Can't remember how the litany went? Hail who? Our father what?

A convulsion of coughs seize him. He hugs his chest, feels the pains tearing his lungs and his back to pieces. The shakes really have him now, too. And when the pain and the tremors come together like the jabbing of a thousand hot needles, he forgets where he is. He feels his whole body shuddering as words begin to bubble from his mouth.

Now he confesses. Confesses to the memory of a woman he still thinks of as a West Irish selkie, confesses to himself, confesses to the Holy Redeemer and the Mother of God.

"Our Maudie full of grace, blessed art thou among lovers ... Mea culpa, mea culpa ... The avenging angel of the Confederacy has made a royal mess of things. I am almost out of coal and water and food. And I have lost my way.

"I have exposed myself ... and my ship. I should have burned the *Abby Bradford*. Good God, I sent her off to Louisiana under quartermaster Ruhl carrying a dispatch to the Secretary of the Navy. A dispatch I wrote in plain English because I was too sick and tired to compose it in cipher. Damn me! What if Ruhl runs afoul of the blockade and the dispatch is found? What then? The *Sumter's* cruise will be an open book to the Yanks."

Just as bad, he let on that he was heading off to the northeast for Cuba or Barbados to deceive the Yankee consul and the Venezuelans the first time he left Puerto Cabello. Only to return from the southeast with a new prize. Even the dimmest wits could follow his trail, see through his lies about Cuba and Barbados, see that he has been heading south and east, following the trade routes through the West Indies to the Spanish Main.

Where he has stalled? Where he sails in circles taking prizes he cannot manage. Making a spectacle of himself. How long will it be until Lincoln and Gideon Welles sick their biggest sharks on his trail? Then, by Christ, he'll get an old-time war of belching cannons, splintering oak, decks of blood. And there's little to be done except to keep his powder dry.

"What do I do with you, darlin'?" Now he's talking to the ship, and he spins around on the bowsprit so that he can look into the spider web of the bark's well-kept rig. "Take your flag, label it, put it in the trophy bag? Confiscate your chronometer for my collection, and burn you? Turn your lovely shape and all the money I could get from you to ashes?"

Don't even think of it.

The mariner feels a hot flash of fever or whatever it is searing through his shoulders again. Now the voice in his head is Maude's or God's or the Holy Mother or Raphael Semmes, Esq. formerly of Mobile, Alabama, former Attorney at Law. He can't tell. Things are all tangled up in his mind. The voice of the woman who rescued him from a slough of despair. The voice of the Sky Father. The voice of his lawyer self who made a naval tribunal see Kell's innocence back in '49. The same. The same voice.

Trust to the rightness of the law. Honor it and it shall honor you. You cannot be judge and executioner with impunity. Yank though she may be, she has a neutral cargo. You cannot condemn her to the flames.

"I am short on men. I cannot give up one of my officers to manage a prize crew."

What about a midshipman? Hicks is a good navigator. Ready for command.

He grits his teeth, fights off a wave of the shakes.

"He's just a boy."

Delegate. Trust your crew.

"Goddamn. Goddamn the laudanum."

He floats into a dream, pictures himself not much older than Hicks as sailing master on the Connie. Sees Stout, captain of the *Cuba,* who all but bit off his nose. He was Hicks' age. Maude was like that, too. And his son, Ollie. Fiery.

A cough starts deep in his chest. Rides a wave of tremors up his raw, hot throat, flooding his mind with a blinding light. Then as he hacks, and hacks some more, his mind rises from his tortured flesh, begins to soar on silver wings. And he sees.

"Alright. It's Hicks. It's Hicks … Jesus, Maude!"

He gasps for air, fills his lungs. They hurt like hell. He takes another deep breath just so he can feel the very roots of his pain. Then he wipes his hot, wet mouth on the sleeve of his shirt and stares aft into the hawse pipes of the ship. They look like a pair of eyes.

"Hicks is taking you to Cienfuegos. I'll put your master and the lady ashore tonight. I am not going to hang anyone. I don't have the Yanks' stomach for such cowardly feasts of vengeance. I've got to run. But where?"

25

Santiago De Cuba
EARLY AUGUST, 1861

Fifty-three ships at anchor in the harbor at Santiago de Cuba, but none of them is the *Sumter*. Or has seen her. James Palmer knows because he has asked. Each confounded vessel.

He's the captain of the USS *Iroquois*, one of the navy's newest and fastest steam frigates. She's a fifteen-hundred-ton rocket capable of steaming in excess of twelve knots. She carries eleven-inch smooth bores, side batteries of thirty-two-pounders. With this sled, three times the size of the *Sumter* and twenty percent faster, Palmer has been methodically trying to track down the Rebel cruiser through a process of elimination.

He has received the same vague orders as Charles Wilkes on the *San Jacinto*. Go out and sail around for a while, at least make a show of trying to catch Semmes. Superiors at the Key West station counseled him to circumnavigate Cuba in a clockwise fashion in search of Semmes. They said it was a surefire plan. So, always one who has heeded the advice of his seniors, Palmer spent the last two weeks patrolling Cuba's north coast and east end, stopping at each major port in search of news about the Rebel. But after almost four hundred miles of fitful cruising, he has come up empty-handed in his search for Raphael Semmes. It's as if the *Sumter* vanished after sailing out of Cienfuegos.

Mounting from the gig to the stone quay in his summer whites, Palmer looks like a poster drawing of the modern naval officer. He's trim, middle-height, with a full head of sandy hair, although he's some years beyond forty. His thin, clean-shaven face often wears a smile, especially when he needs to buck himself up to face a new challenge.

His thin lips smile now as he strides across the tracks of the cane railway and heads into the dense, steaming city. It's a little past five in the afternoon. The flower ladies, fruit vendors, shops, stalls, cafés and restaurants are just beginning to reopen after siesta. His official reason for coming ashore is to take dinner with the U.S. consul and to learn if any word of Semmes or change of orders for the *Iroquois* have arrived at the consulate via another ship or by telegraph from the chief consul in Havana.

But what he really wants is a long walk. He wants to lose himself in the strange earthiness of Santiago. He wants to disappear among the shadows of colonial balconies on narrow streets, vanish among the scents of *tostones* grilling, *puerco asado* roasting over open fires, burning sugar crusting on flan. The tart smell of limes. He wants to submerge in the melodies of street musicians strumming *quatros* and breathing notes into their clay jar *botijas*. Mostly, he wants to live life for a while without a gaggle of junior officers looking over his shoulder, judging him for his failure to fulfill these new orders from Welles to find Semmes. It seems Welles is starting to feel the heat from press coverage of Semmes' depredations and has decided he needs to send more ships after the rebel raider.

"I need a cathedral," he mumbles as he scans the skyline for the tower and cross that he remembers from another visit.

He has succeeded at everything he has ever done, until now. It isn't that he gloats or brags on his accomplishments. They simply give him a quiet confidence with which to face a new day. But now Semmes, or the lack thereof, upsets all that. He feels like a barefoot wanderer in a sea of glass, and he needs to get down on his knees in the house of the Lord to beg God's wisdom.

As always, he has a plan. Making prayer is the first thing he has to do to reclaim his balance and prepare himself for a horrendous butchering at the consulate. Second, he will seek out a bookshop to buy volumes to feed his hunger for words. Third, with his new books, he will find a secluded café. There he will take a table in the evening sun. Order some smooth *añejo* from the vats of the local Bacardi family to stir into a *cafecito*—black as night, hot as hell, sweet as sin. Then he will make a little career out of sipping his brew and watching the *palomas* picking the cobblestones clean of bread crumbs.

Until the setting sun and duty call him across town. After that he must face three hours of bullying—over dry ham and starchy pastries—about this *Sumter* business, by a poor imitation of Ben Franklin. Only after a thorough flaying will the consul offer any new information about Semmes or new orders for the *Iroquois*. If there is any.

This last thought makes him stop dead in his tracks in front of an old lady seated on sacks of coffee beans, offering to tell his fortune with a handful of cowry shells. He gives her a sad little grin.

He blinks as he steps out of the Catedral de la Nuestra Señora de la Asunción into the light and noise of the city. He thinks the visit has gone well except for some awkward and embarrassing fumbling for pesos when he decided to buy a candle to light for his late Uncle Joe. He always likes the insides of cathedrals. The press of the knee boards reminds him of the absolute need for humility in this life. He loves the scent of incense and cool musty air, the hush of prayers rising from the lips of the penitent, the women with their lace *mantillas* covering their heads.

His own praying goes about as well as can be expected under the circumstances, but praying for guidance never makes him feel instantly whole again. It isn't like confessing your sins and saying prayers for forgiveness. God might show him a way out of this wild goose chase after Semmes, but it will not be now. It might not be soon.

So on to phase two.

"Bookstore," he announces to himself as he stands on the top step of the threshold to the cathedral. His left hand shields his brow from the glare of the evening sun as he looks east across the adjacent park, tries to read the name boards over the doorways of shops.

At last his eyes bring the words *Libréria Mozo* into focus. Beneath the wooden banner he sees book carts brimming with volumes set like open gates into a vast *tienda* that promises a cavern of books. He imagines the soft dry feel of the leather covers and the sharp scent of ink in wondrous novels—perhaps one he has not read by Dumas or possibly something from a *Cubano* if the Spanish is tame enough. So he's almost in a trance, thinking of how he might spend his pesos on handfuls of dreams, as he descends the steps of the cathedral and starts toward the Promised Land.

An instant later he's almost trampled to death by a team of four prancing *paso finos* dragging an enormous black *calesa* around the corner. In the wake of this open carriage, stuffed with soldiers and men in black blindfolds, come hundreds of uniformed *guardia*, wearing patent leather Napoleonic hats, brandishing muskets, knocking people out of the way. One almost breaks his ribs with a rifle butt. He stops his swinging weapon short only when he recognizes Palmer's uniform, then growls, "*Gringo maricón.*"

The next thing the American knows, he's being rushed down the street in a screaming mob. He feels their spittle and the heat of their words on his cheeks.

"*¡Asasinos!*"

"*¡Hijos de putas!*"

"*¡Fuera España. Fuera España!*"

"*¡Pendejos!*"

"*¡Autónomia!*"

"*¡Libertad!*"

At first, he thinks they are ranting at him, but then he sees that the mob has its eyes on the *calesa*, the blind-folded men and the *guardia*.

Shots crack over the din. Lots of them.

The scent of musket smoke fills the air as he feels the crowd freeze then begin stampeding back in the direction from whence it came. People fall. Scream. Claw at their neighbors.

It's when he sees a gang of men scrambling toward him, clambering over the heads and shoulders of a thousand frightened faces, that he finally lowers his head like a bull and breaks out of the seething crowd in front of the bookshop.

"Good God, what is happening?" he asks out loud.

"Possibly the revolution," says a voice in English at his back. "The Spaniards take another group of intellectuals to face a firing squad in the Plaza de Marte ... But they cannot kill us all. As you see, the *gente* are rising."

Palmer spins on his heels, comes face-to-face with a black-eyed sprite. The man has a neat, pencil strip of a mustache, an immense forehead, bald dome. He wears a white *guayabera* shirt over dark trousers.

"Fernando Mozo at your service, Captain." The small man with the puckish grin speaks with a thick Cuban accent as he gives a little bow before extending his hand.

Palmer takes it. Feels the firm, warm grip.

"Things are falling apart!" he says before he can govern himself.

The Cuban lets go his grip and shrugs, a gesture both wistful and sad.

He suddenly feels like a discourteous clod, offers his hand again. He tries to muster some Spanish, not to signal that he's a man of the world, but to show respect.

"*Mucho gusto, señor.* Forgive me. I am James Palmer."

The Cuban takes his hand again and nods.

"*Yo se.* I know."

He toys with his empty glass, eyes the dark bottle of *añejo* that stands in the middle of the small marble table between him and his host. But he's not in a café. He all but forgot his plan the instant Mozo showed him this little courtyard within the extreme reaches of the bookshop and offered him a *copita* of Bacardi's finest.

"I wish I did not have to go so soon."

"We all must answer to a higher power, Captain."

Mozo corks the rum.

He leans back, stares up at the evening sky that has begun to fade fast from violet to indigo. The cicadas have started their buzzing high in the ceiba trees. There's barely enough time for the officer to reach the consulate for his appointed drubbing ... but something holds him here. He feels like the fates have not yet finished with him. That he has been brought to this place for more than good conversation about the revolutionary fire burning in the hearts of *los Santiagos*. More than the talk of favorite tales with this humble bookseller, more than a bag-full of seductive volumes by Victor Hugo, Nathaniel Hawthorne, the Cuban Cirilo Villaverde.

"I am about to fail, Fernando."

The Cuban rubs his hands together on the table as if intending to pray and releases a soft sigh. This is not really such a big island. Everybody has heard of Palmer's hunt for the *Sumter*.

"Failure is the common theme of our days. I think it is only the Americans, and maybe the English, who dream that life is otherwise."

"Then I am still a dreamer. I admit it. But I cannot accept failure as a matter of course. I must find the *Sumter*."

"You will never catch this Semmes, my friend."

He feels like someone has just smacked his cheek. He stands to go. He's regretting he ever entered the *Libréria Mozo*. It's time to take his new books, say thank you, move on. At least he knows what to expect from the consul. This Cuban's an utter mystery. First all the hospitality, then this slap in the face. Suddenly, he wants to just grab the little fellow and shake him.

"I have to leave," he says in flat tones. Then something fills his mouth and he blurts. "Why? Why won't I catch Semmes, Fernando? What do you know?"

The Cuban swallows and purses his lips.

"I'm afraid I have made a bad end for our evening ... But I think you must hear the truth, James. If you want to catch the rebel, you must change the way you fish. Think of history. Think of all that you have read."

"I don't understand. I've stopped at every port, spoke to every ship ... "

"Exactly. You are a good military man."

"So?"

"So you hunt your enemy like he is another warrior. But don't you see? He is not. He has quit your navy. He is not acting like a warrior. He has gone to the other extreme entirely."

Mozo says Semmes has become Stead Bonnet, Calico Jack Rackham, Thomas Kidd all rolled into one. He's a pirate. To catch him, a man must stop thinking like a warrior. Think like a buccaneer. What would those old *piratas* do if there were here? Where would they hunt? Where would they hide? Certainly not around a major port like Santiago where they might easily be overwhelmed, caught, hung.

For about the fifth time since meeting Mozo, Palmer feels a loss of words ... and just plain dumb. He looks into the Cuban's eyes, feels their sympathy and truth. Brutal truth. It's as if the little man has read the whole story of Raphael Semmes' life ... Palmer's too.

He wants to ask, *Who sent you into my life?* But what he says is, "You are an amazing man. I owe you more than I ... "

Mozo shrugs, dismisses the compliment with the wave of a hand. He puts his arm through Palmer's as he escorts his guest through the *tienda*, back toward the street pulsing with lovers making their evening *paseo*.

"Think like a buccaneer," Palmer muses.

"Yes, my friend."

Mozo suddenly stops at a cart of English books. He fumbles through a pile of volumes until he finds one he's looking for, hands it to Palmer.

"A little *regalito*, from me to you. It may hold the keys to your quest, James Palmer."

The American looks at the volume. Its red pigskin is hard-worn. He has to strain to read the gold leaf of the title: *A General History of*

Pirates, by Charles Johnson. He's heard of it. It's supposed to be the best book ever penned about the so-called Brethren of the Coast.

Riding back to the *Iroquois* in the gig at midnight, he's smiling again. Tonight, the consul's condescension and bullying bounced right off him as if he were made of burnished steel. The man did not so much as dent him when he spoke of the lack of promotion and wretched posting that would come to those who failed to stop the *Sumter.*

His mind has already begun to catalogue the haunts of the old-time pirates of the Caribbean, and he knows that hence forth his sailing's leading him not into the Meccas of contemporary commerce but to the backwaters, places where Calico Jack, Bonnet, Blackbeard tarried. Places like Tortuga Island north of Haiti, Bahía Samana on the east end of Hispañola, Isla Mona in the Mona Passage, Culebra. There are more hideaways in the same neighborhood. A man could find them in Johnson. He cannot wait to dive into the book when he gets back to his berth.

And there are other places further south to consider searching. St. Barts, Guadelupe. Maybe Martinique.

26

USS Powhatan
AUGUST 13, 1861

The shout comes down from the foretop lookout.

"Sails."

Porter raises his megaphone. "Where away?"

"Hull down, three points off the larboard bow, close inshore. Three-masted schooner. Downeaster."

He feels his blood beginning to burn. It's not yet eight in the morning, the air is light. He has all day to run down this sorry bastard. Here's a chance at last. In his mind he calculates an intercept course.

"Engine all ahead full. Helm right to north, northeast. Luff has the deck. I'm going aloft."

Porter compresses his long glass, stows it in an inside breast pocket of his jacket. Starts up the larboard ratlines on the mainmast. The air's nearly calm and the sloop of war doesn't have so much as a riding sail set. She steams on her lines, making the climbing easy. The wind begins to tease the curls of his beard, the hair around the side of his head.

The scent of smoke rising from the funnel reminds him what a coal hog his ship is. She's already critically low on coal, and he wonders if he will have enough for this chase if the stokers pour it on. But they must. The alternative's too painful to consider. How could he leave his station off the Southwest Pass and head back to Fort Pickens to fill his bunkers ... with not so much as a single prize to show for months of blockade duty?

As soon as he mounts the maintop and extends his glass, he sees the schooner, perhaps ten miles off to the northwest, ghosting along in a light shore breeze blowing off the bayous and low coast. She's the biggest thing he has seen approaching the western side of the Delta since he got here back in mid-June.

"You tried to run in last night in the dark," he says aloud, "but the air fell out on you, didn't it? And now here you sit, fat, dumb and screwed in the full light of morn, eh? Who are you, sweetheart? Why's a Yankee girl like you sailing down here in the Cajun Cradle? What have you got hidden inside those pretty, white topsides?"

No doubt she's heading toward the entrance to Barataria Bay. She's too far inshore to make a run for the Southwest Pass, and there's virtually no other port on this corner of the Delta except the old pirates' bay. But Barataria's entrance by Grand Isle is more than eight miles to her northeast. She'll have to catch a fresh breeze and do some fancy sailing to make the safety of the bay's shallows, where *Powhatan* can't go, if she wants to escape Porter now.

He remembers his days as a middie on the Mexican *Guerrero*. There was something the Mexican boys liked to say when the chase was on, when they could almost feel the prize gold within their grasp. *De puta madre.*

Exactly. Now all the heat and the waiting pays off. You are not Raphael Semmes, but de puta madre, *you will make my day, mother whore. If the goddamn engine doesn't fail me.*

He has been gaining steadily on the schooner for more than an hour. But now a sea breeze is coming up. Suddenly, the schooner has a bone in her teeth, racing northeast toward Barataria Bay. In a mile she will be home free. Still, the *Powhatan's* wheels are churning with a fury, and he's almost close enough to read the name on the schooner's trail boards through his glass.

"Beat to quarters, luff. Clear for action. Double shot the larboard battery. Train your bow chasers on her jibs."

He smiles. Since he was a boy playing at navy with his brothers, he has loved the commands that call a ship to action.

"Ready on the chasers. What's your range gunner?"

"Mile and a half, sir."

"Alright then. Quiet on the deck. Across her bows now. Standard distance. Fire as you will. Both chasers if you please, gunner. In succession. Reload on the double. Larboard battery to the ready."

The luff cocks an eyebrow at the second officer as the powder monkeys scamper below into the magazine for more powder and shells. Two shots? This is more than a signal to stop; it's a challenge.

The men on the bow chasers swivel their weapons, aim. Fire.

The antique chasers cough. Smoke and wadding drift back over the main deck where the gun crews are sighting along gun barrels, sliding the elevating quoins under the barrels of their cannons and adjusting the angles of the gun carriages with pikes.

Two plumes raise a cable in front of the schooner's bowsprit. But the schooner shows no sign of slacking sheets or rounding up. Men on the deck are heaving sacks of something overboard to lighten her.

"I believe she aims to run for it," says one of the midshipmen to a mate.

Porter wheels, shoots the boy a withering look for disturbing the peace of the quarterdeck. Then he listens to the beat of the side wheels and frowns. They've begun to sound sluggish. The schooner is still a mile off the larboard beam holding her own in this race. And a mile closer to the bay entrance than the *Powhatan*.

"Signal officer, run up your heave-to-and-stop flag. Gunner, reload your chasers. Boat speed, quartermaster?"

"Seven knots, sir."

"Damn it to hell. Did I or did I not call for full speed? What in God's name is going on in the engine room?"

A midshipman brings the news.

"The engineer reports his boys can't stay ahead of the leaks, and the stokers are down to mostly dust. Can't keep up the pressure, sir."

He looks aloft at his ship's bare masts, curses himself for not already setting sails. If the engine was doing its job, they would be superfluous, even a nuisance in close quarters, but now …

"Men aloft, let go topsails. Prepare to square away. On the double."

The luff shouts orders. A horde of men scurry up the ratlines. Waisters gather in columns at the braces and sheets.

Canvas cracks aloft. He feels the ship lurch forward a bit and heel as the waisters sheet home.

"Ready on the chasers, gunner ... "

"Flag going up on the schooner, sir. Good God, it's the Stars and Stripes."

"Hell it is! Lying sacks of horse dung. Who do they think we are? Chasers, fire at will. Both shots. Let her know we'll sink her if she doesn't stop this charade. Right under her bows this time! Luff, larboard battery at the ready. Quiet on deck!"

The officers on the quarter cast side-glances at each other. Suddenly a routine stop has become an all-out attack ... on a U.S. flag vessel.

He can almost hear their unasked question hanging in the air. What if she really is an American, come from afar and has not heard about the hostilities or the blockade? Such a thing is possible. Foreign flag ships already stopped by the *Powhatan* have made such claims. Some seemed valid. A ship at sea becomes a world unto herself, cut off from dramas of the shore.

"Americans would not run!"

But he knows what Mercer's men would say, "Unless they think that it is we who fly the false flag. That another spat with Mexico has broken out, and we are a Mex raider in disguise."

Damned these milquetoast mariners, damned their endless second guessing. Who are you, girl? Who are you, you little slut?

The bow chasers cough again. One ball skips right under the schooner's bow. The other takes out her flying jib.

A cheer goes up from the gun crews.

Still, she presses on. Her crew jettisons cargo.

Now with the sails drawing, *Powhatan* closes the distance. She's just a bit more than a cable off the schooner's starboard quarter. But the wind has freshened yet again, and the schooner is holding her own against the frigate.

On the schooner the crew has begun to dip and raise the Stars and Stripes furiously. Men on the schooner's rail are waving the *Powhatan* off with their arms and hats.

He tries to read the schooner's name and hail off her transom, but shadows and his own rigging block the view.

"Chasers again?"

Porter hears a cautious conservatism in the luff's question. It makes him snort. The time for caution has run out, isn't that clear? Hadn't he been patient long enough? For months? Damn it to hell. In another three minutes the schooner would be across the bar into Barataria Bay ... and home free.

"No, sir. Forget the chasers. Something's foul here, luff. I'll wager my stripes on it."

He tells the luff to record the time and place in the log. Note that the unknown schooner failed to heave to and stop after four shots across her bow and a flag signal. Note that she has been tossing her cargo for more than ten minutes and that she is running for shoal water where she can elude the *Powhatan*.

"Prepare the grapnels, luff. Marines armed, loaded and forward, sir."

"We're boarding?"

He pulls himself erect, sucks in a tremendous breath.

"After we slam her with a broadside. It's the moment of truth, is it not man?"

He grabs the megaphone from the luff's hand.

"Quiet on deck. Larboard battery at the ready, gunner. Rake her rig. On the up roll, fire in sequence!"

On the schooner two men are grabbing for the flag halyard ... with a white sheet readied as a flag of truce.

But they're too late. *Powhatan's* five nine-inch smooth bores explode with rolling thunder and a hail of hot iron.

It's only as the smoke begins to clear and the first of the grapnels clatter aboard the schooner to pull her alongside, that he takes his gaze off the Downeaster's shattered spars and shredded, smoldering sails. Now he reads her name. *Abby Bradford. New York.*

"We found him in the galley trying to stuff the cook's stove with this, sir!"

The marine lieutenant hands a smoking leather pouch to Porter as he stands on the quarterdeck eyeing an unshaven, bare-chested ruffian with his hands cuffed behind him. Blood drips from the corner of his mouth. His forehead red and swelling. There has been some resistance to capture. Now, a marine clasps each of his arms.

Porter opens the pouch, takes out a thick letter addressed to the Honorable James Mallory, Secretary of the Navy, Confederate States of America. He breaks open the sealing wax, reads. The dispatch, dated 23 July, 1861, comes from Puerto Cabello, Venezuela. The words of the letter swim before his eyes, the last sentence echoes through his mind. *We are all well, and doing a pretty fair business, in the mercantile parlance, having made nine captures in twenty-six days.* The signature at the bottom, Commander Raphael Semmes, master CSS *Sumter.*

He says nothing, passes the dispatch to the luff now at his side. There's no longer any mystery concerning the nature of this schooner. The captain of the *Powhatan* has struck gold.

"What is your name, man?" Porter's voice, which has been loud, shrill for hours, is now low, quiet and soft.

"Eugene Ruhl, sir."

"Well, Eugene Ruhl. Are you the master of the Bradford?"

Ruhl stares at his feet until one of his marine guards shakes him. "So to speak, sir."

"It seems you have quite a tale to tell, Captain Ruhl."

The master of the *Powhatan* pauses and shoots a smug grin at his luff. He pictures Raphael Semmes and his wicked moustache. His upper lip begins to tremble slightly.

"Will you tell your tale to us?" His voice begins to swell. "Or shall we hang you from the yard arm here and now as an example to the world of what the United States of America does to pirates like you ... and Raphael Semmes?!"

Ruhl talked for hours. And so did the rest of the prize crew captured off the Bradford. Their tales of life aboard the *Sumter* were remarkably similar. Everything they said supported what Semmes had written to Mallory in the dispatch. So now the history of the *Sumter*'s cruise is a matter of public record. And while capturing eight ships in the first five days of cruising is impressive, to Porter's way of thinking, Semmes has squandered away the last few weeks, with only the Bradford to show for a thousand miles of hunting.

"Now he's in trouble," says the luff as he and Porter sit at the wardroom table in the late afternoon, reflecting. "He's running out of time ... and everything else. He's not found the prizes he needs to survive, and he has all but run out of places to secure them. I foresee a puny end to a poor and misguided adventure."

Porter folds his hands, presses them to his forehead, wants to believe in the rightness of the luff's words. But something nags at him. He thinks of the colorful tale his old shipmate Salty painted of the *Sumter*'s reign of terror—dozens of prizes to fuel the raider's belly and spirit. It's so different than the picture he gets from this captured message ... or from Ruhl and his crew.

"Don't write his obituary yet. Semmes knows many tricks. Why would an officer of his experience send a dispatch to his superior in plain English and not in code? What if the dispatch and the Bradford are meant for our eyes? Decoys? This Ruhl claims that the *Sumter* aims to head for Barbados. The rest of the prize crew seems in disagreement about such a plan. But if you were Semmes, would you give out any accurate information about your future plans to your crew? It goes against all the protocols of command."

The luff shrugs. He sees the point.

"So now what, sir?"

"We get a cable on the Bradford. We nurse the remains of our coal and tow her to Pensacola. There I will present my report to the flag-officer, send another dispatch to Secretary Welles and petition them both to let me refuel and go in search of the *Sumter*."

The first officer nods, no emotion in his face. He's a man who has crossed swords with his skipper too many times, and now he has no energy for it. After all, look what he has achieved today ... when other men would have held their guns.

"Mark me, luff. Semmes has not sailed for Barbados as is given out. Sending this dispatch in English shows that he's either shaken ... or practicing a ruse. Perhaps both. But it also shows that he may now have information that the *San Jacinto* and others are after him. At some point, he will circle back north, try to get home. This I firmly believe. But not now. Not when he knows the hounds are on his trail. He aims to lead us on a merry chase."

27

District of Columbia
AUGUST 5, 1861

Burlow eyes her over his glass of Riesling, gives a wicked grin, promising he has more in mind for this evening than the dinner he will buy her in a riverside crab house. It's a dark, hot night in Washington, and the only relief comes in a carriage ride south along the Potomac where a breeze stirs off the water.

The couple lounges back in separate corners of the rear-facing bench in their cab. He has not changed out of the whites he wore to work, but he has the buttons of his collar undone. She unfastens the neck of her baby-blue blouse, shakes her shoulders until the high plane of her chest bathes in the damp air. Her glances avoid her companion, settle on the lights of the District twinkling to the northeast.

Stretching an arm out over the top lip of the carriage, Burlow seizes the tip of the cabby's buggy whip dangling there. His fingers stroke the strands of braided leather.

"Do you use a crop when you ride, Maudie?"

She knows he's talking about more than horses. It's almost always his way to speak in code. She likes the challenge. It sends jolts of excitement and—sometimes—fear through her. So now she plays along, pretending not to hear, to see where this unusual man's mind might take her next ... and how she might snare him.

"Well ... ? A crop, love?"

"If he's sluggish."

She winks, drains off her glass of wine, then takes a sip from his glass.

He bursts into laughter.

"Naughty girl."

"I suit myself to the company."

He laughs again, reaches across the seat, takes her hand, raises it to his lips for a long kiss. She feels his blue eyes reeling her in and shifts her body toward him, knowing the time has come for fishing again.

"You better be careful."

"I think you're all talk."

"You have no idea." He wraps her in his right arm, kisses her.

Kissing has been common between them during their carriage rides together since meeting at Rose Greenhow's party. But now he comes on with the force of a starving animal. Dropping the half-full wine glass on the floor, his left hand slides between her legs.

"I have someplace I want to show you."

She pulls her face away ... but strokes the hand between her legs.

"This better be bleeding good, Harry."

"You've brought me to church?"

The carriage stops on his instructions in front of a redbrick chapel deep in the back streets southeast of the Capitol. A white wooden plaque to the right of the double doors announces the place as the Church of the Crucifixion.

"I call it the Tender Trap."

She catches his bawdy insinuation, thinks it sounds disgusting, sacrilegious. But says nothing.

"Come on."

He drops out of the carriage, passes a rolled greenback up to the cabby then takes her hand as she steps down.

She tilts her head to the side, raises a skeptical eyebrow at him. She has never been to this part of town before. All she knows about it is that great clans of Negroes live here, but she sees no one on the dimly lit lane. The only thing she hears is the twang of a banjo in the distance, the muffled sound of a pipe organ filtering out of the church. The music might be Bach, she thinks, but she isn't sure. She still counts on Fiona's passion for classical music when it comes to naming composers. Still thinks of herself as more of a jig-and-ballad girl.

He knocks five times with his fist on one of the heavy oak doors.

Eventually, she hears the clatter of footsteps on flagstones inside. Then a small window opens at eye level in one of the doors.

"Yes, sir?"

The flash of white teeth and a black face at the window.

He pulls a card from his pocket, hands it through the window along with a twenty-dollar gold piece.

The door swings open.

"Blessed is the Lord," says an immensely tall black man dressed in a sexton's dark robe.

"And blessed art the sinners who come unto him," says Burlow.

This exchange seems more code to her. But the instant her eyes begin to focus, she loses that thought, gasps. The sanctuary of the church blazes with hundreds of candles, casting flickering shadows on the walls. The shadows dance across both mammoth and miniscule sculptures of Christ on the cross that are hung from every available inch. Each sculpture streams with the crimson blood of the Lord Jesus in his hour of need.

The organ swells from pipes somewhere in a balcony overhead.

"Satan, Prince of Darkness." Her breath explodes through her lips. "Follow me, love."

He leads her by the hand to an alter at the front of the church beneath an absolutely life-size crucifix on which the face of Jesus seems to howl in pain. The blood—but surely it's just red paint—has dripped from the wounds in his hands and side, leaving splatters on the marble alter itself.

Two ribbed and fleshy candlesticks light either end of the alter. In the middle stands a silver chalice.

Burlow drops to his knees before the alter. She hitches up her skirt and kneels beside him.

He lifts the chalice. A brass key has been hidden beneath the chalice base. He pockets the key then holds the chalice in both hands and takes a long, slow drink from it before passing it to her.

She watches him. His eyes closed, cheeks giving an involuntary shudder when he swallows. *I must be bloody daft.* Then she remembers Raffy, pictures him on a Yankee gallows. Knows that she might never see him again if she loses her nerve now. Still, part of her wants to run away as fast as she can.

But she has to know where all this is heading, whether Harry Burlow is going to back himself into a corner where he can never escape her. So she opens her mouth and lets the liquid from the chalice flow in.

She has prepared herself for the tepid, salty taste of blood. But what rolls around her tongue is sweet, fiery blackberry brandy. She smiles at her silly fears as she lets the brandy slide down her throat.

For what seems minutes, he leads her by the hand through dark passageways beneath the church. The air smells of incense and a strange, sharp smoke. It's so cool that she wants his jacket over her shoulders. Candle lanterns, hung at intervals, cast pools of light along the way. Every so often they pass a door trimmed in red or green or purple cloth. Organ music echoes through the corridors. Once she thinks she hears the sound of a woman groan with pleasure or pain. But maybe the brandy has just loosened the screws a bit on her imagination. Finally, they reach an alcove and a door covered with black velvet.

"Welcome to my secret world." He unlocks the door, swings it open with a rakish twitch of his eyebrows.

She follows him into a chamber. Candles set in tall sconces near the doorway light the space. It has a low, beamed ceiling, fieldstone walls decorated with the hides of large animals, antique pikes, spears. Suits of chain mail armor, black leather battle masks hung as decorative pieces. There's a huge, rugged-looking four-poster bed in the far corner. Three bearskin rugs cover much of the slate floor. An assortment of trunks, couches and large feather pillows fill in around the edges. Like the covering on the door, all the fabric is black velvet. Even the thick cords twined around the bed posts. Even the bull whip and cat-o'-nine-tails coiled atop a trunk.

"Bloody Jesus." For a second she feels the chill of absolute terror racing up her spine, but she recovers. "Where's the wolfhound, Harry? Are we in the hall of the mountain king?"

He closes, locks the door.

"Not quite yet, love. But soon." He picks up a clay pipe from a table and lights a match. "Very soon. Let me introduce you to a mild stimulant that the darkies call Mary Jane."

28

CSS Sumter
SEPTEMBER 6 & 7, 1861

They've been heading east. Passed the Amazon delta two days ago. Now the hazy, green coast of the province of Maranhão, Brazil, lies off to starboard across four miles of muddy water flowing out of the Rio Anil.

"Another river!"

He does not have to elaborate to Kell as they stand the quarter-deck during the forenoon watch. The luff has heard his captain's rant against rivers at almost every one of the *Sumter*'s landfalls. And he understands Semmes' irritation. For a seafarer, a river's a poor third choice as a port of entry. It offers none of the ease of approach you have at an open roadstead such as at St. Croix, nor a natural harbor with the predictable depths and a protected, current-free basin like St. Thomas. A river's a bottleneck above and below the water, fraught with twisting and shifting channels, currents, bars. Snags. Logs and wrecks swept into your path to snare or hole your vessel. When you take your ship into a river, you always have to play the tides and currents ... and you have to pay beyond all reason for a local pilot, often arrogant and imperial, to take command of your own vessel and guide the way.

Now the ship wallows in the ocean swell where a frothy current rip divides the green sea water of the Atlantic from the muddy outflow of the river, leading to the sugar and cotton port of São Luís.

Semmes feels the pain in his lower back, stabbing him right through the hips. He's a little dizzy. Since leaving Puerto Cabello a month ago, the cruiser has met with one frustration after another as he searched for coal and a place to leave his prizes. In Trinidad the British relieved him of his prisoners from the *Maxwell* and sold him coal and provisions at exorbitant prices, all the while hemming and hawing about the legalities of such transactions and side-stepping diplomatic courtesies.

It was worse when he tried to buy coal in Cayenne, Guyana. The American consul had the coal monopoly there, and turned him away with threats. Then a wind in the face and foul currents had stopped the *Sumter* cold on her route to Maranhão, and he had to backtrack to Surinam to buy coal and regroup. He had lost weeks there, and his black steward Ned was charmed into desertion by the American consul. Perhaps worst of all, he has not taken a prize since the *Maxwell*.

But at least he got his coal and a bit of news from arriving ships in Surinam. Beauregard had whipped the Yankees at Mannassas Junction and driven them back to Washington. And a Federal cruiser, the *Keystone State*, had lately stopped at Barbados proclaiming her part in a dragnet of ships hunting the *Sumter* that now included the *San Jacinto,* the *Niagara,* the *Crusader*, the *Iroquois* and the *Powhatan*. The *Keystone State,* and perhaps others, were so close. he could almost smell their Pennsylvania coal.

He blinks, purses his lips for a second, then speaks.

"We are almost out of coal again, Kell. We must make port, but I see no pilot vessel. Truth be told, I have precious little money for a pilot. Get me my charts from below. I'll take her in. By God, I hate being such the slave to black diamonds."

Kell salutes, goes off to fetch the charts while he calls for more steam, gives the quartermaster a course change toward the only landmark on the horizon, the green peak of Mt. Itacolomi. The orders given, the captain makes his way to the starboard mizzen chains, raises his arms, faces the fresh trade winds and steadies himself between a set of lanyards, as if hanging from a cross.

The tide has just started to ebb out of the river. He orders the ship to full speed so as to ride as much of the high water as he can while entering the port. He pushes off another wave of dizziness. Is starting to congratulate himself on skirting the outer shoals of the river and the middle ground, when he feels the bump ... then a sickening grinding along the keel. The force of the strike knocks him to one knee. He breaks his fall with out-stretched arms. Men stagger to stay upright on deck. The ship bucks to starboard, stops. Hard aground on an uncharted sandbar. The tide racing out from under her. The engineer stops the screw even before Semmes can order it. Excess steam blows off from the funnel with a loud hiss, a plume of thick, white vapor.

Good Christ, I've lost her.

He imagines the faces of the officers at his court-martial as he offers no excuse, except zeal, for wrecking the only warship in the Confederate navy. They're the same faces that had judged him when he lost the *Somers*. Yankees. They laugh in his face.

As he gets to his feet, he feels every man of the crew looking at him. So silent on the deck, he can hear the current rippling around the ship. Knows what he does next will make or break him as a commander. Forever. But suddenly, he senses a giddy lightening in his soul. The back pain remains, but he no longer feels dizzy. It's as if the worst has already happened.

He puts his hands on his hips, lets a little grin spread beneath his mustache. He looks forward, slowly surveying his men with a new clarity of vision. Then he makes a show of twirling his mustache, gives them a little bit of the Old Beeswax they have learned to love. Or at least respect.

"Welcome to Brazil, boys!"

The men laugh in spite of themselves. Even Kell.

Now he plays a hunch. He guesses that deep water must be off to starboard where the current runs swiftest.

"Engine astern, Mr. Chapman. Full steam, please. Quartermaster, hard left rudder. All crew to the starboard rail to heel her over."

The screw begins to churn up a cloud of gray marl astern. The *Sumter* lurches backward a foot or two. Stops. Begins to list to starboard. Lurches again. Then she backs off the bar as the current catches her bows, swings them to the right.

"Eight fathoms." The leadsman.

He smiles again.

"Let her go ahead, Mr. Chapman."

When the ship's free and clear, the skipper sees fishermen waving frantically from their small sailing *jangadas* near shore.

"Now set your hook, sir. And send a boat to those fisherman with someone who knows Portuguese. I think we're about to get a little lesson in local pilotage."

Five minutes after one of the *jangada* fishermen has guided the *Sumter* through a maze of shoals to her final anchorage off the quay at São Luís, Dr. Galt approaches him on the quarterdeck. Galt is a small, thin man with black hair who reminds the captain of a picture he'd seen of the writer fellow Poe.

"I think you are going to learn to love this town, Captain."

His eyes settle on the red tile roofs of the classical colonial buildings with their iron balconies and pastel walls of red, green, yellow, blue. His mind loses itself in the warren of streets that snake up the hill to the cathedral. He can already smell the anthuria and imagine the confetti of butterfly wings on his cheeks.

"Beg pardon, sir?"

"The town. You will learn to love it."

"Hmmmmm. Why is that, Doctor?"

"Because as your physician, I am sending you ashore."

Semmes cocks his head, doesn't understand.

"I want you to look for a hotel where you can escape the demands of the ship and heal yourself."

"That's not possible."

"It is not only possible, Captain, it is essential. You are hurt and sick. You refuse my medicaments. And you are on the very edge of exhaustion. You cannot drive yourself, as you have done these last two months, much longer. You are a man, not a weapon, sir. Do you understand?"

He wants to dismiss this gadfly. There's much to do. He fears the ship may have started a plank weeping with the grounding, perhaps even sheared off the false keel. Repairs will take ...

"Do you understand me, sir? If you do not rest yourself, we will lose you before the year is out. Perhaps you care not for your life. But I assure you most fervently, the officers and crew do. The South does. Your family and loved ones do. We cannot abide the space you would leave in us. Now will you arrange for a shore leave voluntarily, or shall I call Mr. Kell and pronounce you unfit for duty?"

Semmes looks at the doctor, then at the cathedral bell tower ashore. Hears Maudie say, "Come on ... before you catch your death of cold." She reaches out and brushes his brows, his mustache, with her long, dry fingers.

"You are a right persuasive fellow, Pills. Perhaps you should have studied law ... "

He lurches forward as the two-horse gig reins suddenly to a stop in front of the Taberna Branca on the outskirts of São Luís. The late afternoon sun casts a golden glow in the pollen-rich air. Sounds of drums, odd stick-like percussion instruments, guitars, singing spill from the low, white, stucco building trimmed with blue *ajulejo* tiles.

It's September 7, Brazilian Independence Day. The gig's driver, the dark, compact Hernand Porto, is in more than his usual holiday mood. He reaches down from the gig, smacks the neck off a champagne bottle with a quick rap on a stone hitching post, pours the bubbling contents into two pewter goblets that Semmes holds forth. It's their third bottle since Porto offered to show the town to the new and prestigious *americano* guest at his hotel.

"*Como vai agora?*" Porto calls to a brace of young women hanging out the open French windows. "How are you, my beauties?"

"*Ta. Ta bom. Tudo bem*, Hernand!" The women giggle.

"*Beijame, amor.*"

A beauty with sun-streaked, long, dark hair darts to the gig, flings herself across Semmes' knees, throws an arm around the neck of the cavalier Porto. Begins a long passionate kiss. Her hands move over his body as if searching for hidden sweets ... until one accidentally slips beneath Semmes' belt.

He stiffens.

"*Opa!*"

The woman slides her hand off the *americano*. Eyes his uniform.

"*Desculpe, Capitán.*" She pecks him hastily on both cheeks as if to kiss away a wound.

He shakes his head in amusement, lets out a gale of laughter from someplace he has not opened since leaving Maude.

"Commander Raphael Semmes, meet Gabriela," smiles Porto. "Eighth wonder of Brazil."

The woman straddles the two men's laps with her firm buttocks, gives a little smile, shrugs with outstretched hands. There's an openness, an innocence in her every movement that lifts him further out of his pain and worries than all of the champagne has.

"What do you think, *amigo*?" Porto cocks an eyebrow rakishly at his guest.

"I love this country." The miracle of womanhood just inches from his face. Tiny bubbles of vintage flicking from his mustache.

"If you want her, you can have her," whispers Porto not so quietly, as the men sit at a rough wooden table in the *taberna*. "She works for me. They all do. Don't you just love her?"

He listens to the beat of the drums, watches the barefoot Gabriela as she dances a slave's *samba* with another first-rate beauty on the dirt floor. Their low-slung peasant blouses hide little of breasts like pomegranates. Loose cotton dresses flicker from pulsing hips in the candlelight.

"She's lovely." He has been looking at Gabriela, watching her every move as she brings more than fifty patrons to life with her songs, dances, guileless touching.

Evening turns to night. He and Porto sup on the *taberna*'s fresh *siri,* crab shells stuffed with seasoned meat bound in manioc paste, drink several bottles of *vinho verde*. And still he watches her as if looking long enough would bring on some feeling he lost long ago, far away.

But now his brain is buzzing with thoughts of obligations. He frowns.

"What is the matter my friend? You don't want Gabriela?"

He waves a hand in front of his face.

"Nothing. It's nothing, Hernand."

Porto wags a finger.

"Don't tell me nothing. A man does not turn down Gabriela for nothing. I am your host. It is my pleasure and my duty to help you mend from months of war. Surely, you will not deny me the chance to be of service. Raphael ... speak to me from your *alma.*"

The *americano* puts his face in his hands, releases a shallow breath. Then he tells Porto half of what's on his mind.

"I am right much in the thrall of your most gracious hospitality and friendship ... But I have grave fears for the future of my ship and crew, to put it frankly, Hernand."

He says he must repair his ship after a serious grounding, provision her, coal her. But he is almost out of money. How can he find a bank to lend two thousand dollars on a bill against a country that almost no one has heard of or will recognize?

Porto reaches across the table, pours off another glass of green wine for Semmes.

"Toma! Drink up, my good friend. I thought you had a bigger problem. Love, perhaps. But money? Money can always be gotten."

They must go see Tom Wetson. He's Texan. A patriot who will do anything for the Southern cause.

Semmes' head rises out of his hands, and he gives the Brazilian a bleary-eyed look of humble gratitude.

"Gods and angels, man!"

"I'll drink to that. To gods and angels, Raphael ... Now shall we call upon the lovely Gabriela?"

He shakes his head no. In his mind he sees a cinnamon-skinned woman slashing at his chest with a paring knife. Then he hears the voices of two good women calling him, speaking his name in desperate prayers.

"I must go back to the hotel ... There are letters I have long needed to write."

"Ah, love," nods Porto. As if this explains everything.

29

District of Columbia

MID-SEPTEMBER, 1861

Welles opens the door to enter, spots the envelope, frowns. It's lying on the floor, just beyond the threshold to the place that has been his home since coming to Washington. The glow of a gaslight in the corridor of the Willard casts a yellow cloud of light into the evening gloom of Room 8.

"Oh Lord, now what do they want?"

It has been a maddening day at the Navy Department. First, the tedious planning for a secret offensive on the Rebel outposts at Port Royal Sound in South Carolina. On top of that, hammering out the details of a contract with a crazy Swede named John Ericsson. The man claims he can build a bizarre little ironclad pillbox of a boat that will split the Rebel fleet at Norfolk into match sticks in half an hour.

He stoops, picks up the envelope, perhaps a petition from an office seeker. Or, as had been the case recently, the letter might well be yet another solicitation from Senator Hale of the Committee on Naval Affairs urging the Secretary of the Navy to buy useless or rotten ships from Hales' cronies.

He throws his suit jacket on the coat tree by the door, shuffles across the room to light the oil lamp on the bed stand, tumbles on top of the lilac bedspread.

For several minutes he lies there with letter in hand. His thick, white beard heaving on his chest with each breath. The locks of his wig look like a gray nest of feathers around his pale, wrinkled face. Barely a breath of air comes through the open window. He's dripping sweat in the heat and humidity that is suffocating Washington.

Finally, he blinks twice, sits up on the bed. Opens the envelope in fitful jerks with his fingers. Flakes of wax splatter on his trousers from the odd seal of a dove in flight.

"Spare us. You cannot sell me garbage, Senator," he mumbles as he unfolds the single sheet of vellum. There's a point when he will cease even reading Hale's endless petitions, and it's coming soon. But this letter has invaded his home, such as it is, and he knows he can neither eat nor sleep until he brushes it out of his mind.

He finds his spectacles in his vest pocket, puts them on, reads the words.

Pay close attention!

Did you know that mrs. Rose Greenhow has been placed under house arrest for spying against the government of the United States of America?

Do you recall a certain tintype taken of yourself being kissed by this same lady at a party in her salon?

Unless you withdraw ships from the naval blockade around mobile, New Orleans and cape fear, your dear wife and your president shall see this picture.

Do not try to mislead us.

Do not share this letter with anyone.

We are watching your every move!!!

We must see quick and meaningful action on your part to do as we ask, or you will be exposed as a consort of a traitor and a woman of ill-repute.

Raise the shade and lower it three times in your window if you understand.

The last gulp of coffee from the afternoon rises in his gorge. Something's loosening in his bowels. He finds the porcelain bedpan, drops his trousers just in time.

"Oh Christ, oh Christ!"

He bites his forearm to keep from retching until the spasms subside. Stays this way, elbows on knees, head in hands. Perched on the bedpan in the middle of the room while his body purges itself.

To his surprise, the terror of being exposed as a traitor and whore monger begins, little by little, to give way to clearer thinking. So ... he has fallen into the hands of bullies. He has felt their sting before, as an awkward boy back in Connecticut and as a player on the political scene for decades. He does not know who has him by the throat now. The Curmudgeons, Seward, Hale: all are possibilities.

They all have reasons for weakening the blockade. The Curmudgeons want ships released from the blockade for more offensive campaigns.

Seward? Seward wants the blockade to just plain fail ... and to bring down Lincoln, and Welles with him. That's certain. Seward has hopes of being the next president or, perhaps, the king maker.

And Hale. Hale stands to make a lot of money taking a cut from all the naval contracts that will multiply like rats if the blockade fails and the war drags on.

Who has the balls for blackmail? He doesn't know. People do strange things for power and money. One thing he does know is that he can't fight his own private war against all of these foes. There are too many. He has to find out who sent the letter, who's watching him. But he will learn nothing through defiance.

Bullies just hit you from behind and vanish into the dark when you come out swinging. To catch a bully you have to pretend to be weak, take their abuse. Then they will swell with confidence, come at you again. And again. Until you know everything about them ... and you use your knowledge of them to spring your trap.

He gathers himself, turns up the flame on the oil lamp by the bed. Then he goes to the window and grabs the draw string to the shade.

30

USS Powhatan
SEPTEMBER 21-22, 1861

"Have you seen the *Sumter*?" Porter extends his hand to help a wiry, brown-skinned man over the rail.

The pilot has come out by sailing *jangada* to meet the Yankee off São Luís. And now, even before he has finished climbing the Jacob's ladder to board the frigate, Porter is on him.

The Brazilian pauses at the top of the ladder and rears back, startled by both the brashness of Porter's welcome and the lack of protocol. Ship's masters rarely meet pilots anywhere but on the quarterdeck.

"Your hand, man. Do you speak English?"

"*Sim,* yes, I speak English, Captain." He stares at Porter's hand for several seconds more, as if weighing the consequences of touching such a disgusting thing. At last, he seizes the Yankee's wrist and swings aboard. A smile begins to brighten his face.

"Captain Raphael Semmes said that a distinguished Yankee captain and a powerful ship of war would soon come asking for him. In this regard, he has requested that I extend his compliments to you for a hunt well-done. He is a true officer and gentleman ... And, I might add, a very generous man when it comes to compensating his river pilot."

"Semmes? My god, man. Semmes? Here?"

The pilot nods. "You did not see him? He left port just five days ago. He was sailing back and forth off the mouth of the river for several days more. He let us believe that he was waiting for you. Perhaps to make a battle. But I have not seen or heard of the *Sumter* now for two days."

"All stop!" The slow rush of the side wheels ceases. Steam lines clatter, thump beneath the deck. "Which way did he go?"

The Brazilian shrugs. "That I could not tell you, sir."

Porter sucks his cheeks between his molars and bites down until the blood comes. After almost five weeks of searching along the entire chain of the Antilles—after tracking Semmes from Cienfuegos to Curaçao to Puerto Bello, to Surinam to here—*Powhatan* is only two days behind the *Sumter*. And now after racing all this way, one of her two boilers has failed. *Powhatan* is too weak to head back to sea for the final chase. She needs time at anchor for repairs. It's beyond maddening to Porter, but if pausing here is something that has to be, he thinks that he might use a few days in São Luís to his advantage.

Everywhere Semmes has stopped he has made a spectacle of himself as the gallant knight errant of the Confederacy. He leaves friends, enemies, false clues for his pursuers. And an open book as to the condition of his ship, his crew, his finances, his health. All pieces in a puzzle that might reveal the Reb's next move. Clues that have gotten Porter this close to squashing his enemy. There was a fat *commandante* in Cienfuegos, a bum boat siren in Curaçao, an angry governor in Puerto Cabello, who each talked freely about the pirate Semmes for hours. Now when he plots his quarry's next move, Porter feels Semmes' lingering back pains, knows his frustration over finding no home for his prizes, hears the hollow echo in the *Sumter*'s money chest. And misses the tenderness of a woman's touch. Soon he thinks he will taste Old Beeswax's blood.

"Take her in, pilot, as you will. And tell me, sir, who did keep company with the gallant Captain Semmes in your fair port?"

He has a crisp ten-dollar Federal note on prominent display in his hand.

The rhythm of the guitars, the beating drums. He watches a wench with sun-streaked, long dark hair dancing a samba with another beauty in the Taberna Branca. Hips pulse. Cotton dresses flicker in the shadows.

"If you want her, you can have her," Hernand Porto smiles at Porter across a table in a hot, dark corner of the *taberna*.

"She is a saucy moll."

"Eighth wonder of Brazil."

The American licks his lips, tastes the coarse hair of his beard.

Porto pours his guest and himself another tumbler of cool, crisp *vinho verde*, looks at the wad of paper money that Porter has just pulled from a pocket inside his white service jacket.

"How much, *senhor*?"

"Gabriela will be yours for as long as you want for twenty dollars. She will open the Brazilian book of love to you. And she is fresh from the country."

He shoots Porto a hard look. He has heard rumors. "Semmes had her. I know Semmes had her."

Porto suddenly realizes the girl would be more valuable if he lies. "Just once."

The American drives a fist into his open hand. He wonders what secrets Semmes let slip with this tart, feels his manhood stirring below his belt with the prospect of tumbling the drab, wringing every ounce of Raphael Semmes from her memory.

"Bring her on." He slides a twenty-dollar note across the table.

"A room will be another five, amigo."

Porter glares, knows he's paying five or six times the going rate for a *puta* and a bed. He hates always being taken advantage of by the locals.

"You're robbing me, *senhor*."

"Brazil is a poor country, and a fresh girl like Gabriela ... a man could sell his soul for such a piece of paradise. But if money is a problem, I have other ... "

Porter hesitates, looks at Gabriela again. She has stopped dancing, sits on a stool at the bar across the room, beaming a black-eyed grin at him. He feels his arms and legs starting to tingle the way they always do before a boxing match.

Fuck it. Gideon Welles is going to buy me a tart. Abe Lincoln is going to purchase us a few secrets.

"Let's not quibble, man." He passes another five across the table. The Brazilian smiles.

"Jesus Christ, she only speaks Portuguese!" Porter stands in the middle of the public room of the *taberna,* glares at the Brazilian pimp. He has just spent his hot milk in a darkened cubicle with a tongue-tied goddess. When he asked her about Semmes, she only giggled and touched him in places, ways, unknown to his wife.

Porto puts down a deck of cards he has been shuffling as he sits at a table.

"Of course, Captain. What did you expect of a girl from the country? Or is it that you desire more than a private tour of her garden? Come, *senhor.* Hernand Porto is at your service."

The Brazilian nods to a seat at his table, pours a fresh glass of *vinho* for the American.

He feels the old urge to cripple or break something pulsing through his arms, curling his fingers. But he counts to ten, then sits.

"I want to talk about the Confederate pirate Semmes." Porter has his wad of green American bills in his hand again. He peels off a ten-dollar note, lays it on the table.

The pimp gives a little smile.

"Of course, the pirate. Interesting fellow. But he has his troubles, I think. The ship, *Sumter,* she had a hard grounding here. On a bar coming in. I cannot remember, but I think she might have damaged something?"

"What, man?"

"It isn't clear in my mind."

The American puts another ten on the table.

The Brazilian makes a show of racking his brain.

Porter wants to reach across the table and grab him by his skinny, sun-burned throat.

"I think it was something about, what do you call it? The false keel, the worm shoe? It got ripped off."

The *Sumter* was leaking. Semmes had local *estaleiros* working with his carpenter for several days. But the repair was of the most temporary nature. The ship will start to leak again as soon as she meets any kind of rough weather.

"But Captain Semmes had other worries. Let me think."

"Come on, man!"

"I can't quite seem to remember. I wish I could, but my life has been so full, you see, what with the hotel business, and the *Taberna Branca*. The girls. I'm sorry. I just … Let's have another bottle of wine?"

"I don't want any more of your sorry-ass wine, Porto. I want answers. What does it take to get people in this backward flea pit to talk to me?!"

The Brazilian pushes the money on the table back at Porter. Stands up.

"A little more courtesy and human decency than it seems is in your nature, *senhor*! I think we are finished here. Have the best day that you can!" He turns to walk away.

The American does not hesitate for an instant. He reaches for the service pistol he wears under his jacket, draws it, cocks the hammer.

With the click of the hammer, Porto stops in his tracks, turns slowly with his hands up.

The whores, watching from the bar, begin to shuffle away through a curtained doorway.

"Sit down, *Senhor* Porto. Let's get something straight between us."

The Brazilian sees Porter's hand gripping the pistol as it lies on the table, pointing at him. He sits down slowly, his hands still raised.

"I will have answers. Either you will tell me all you know about Semmes … or you will have an accident with a firearm. Now talk!"

Beads of sweat suddenly speckle Porto's brow. He wipes them away with the flick of his hand.

"Semmes is nearly out of money. He borrowed two thousand dollars from a Texan living here to pay for his coal, provisions, the work of the *estaleiros*."

"What else?"

"Nothing."

"Damn it to hell, fellow. What else?" His right hand tightens on the pistol grip.

"He has pains in his back that never quite seem to stop."

"Tell me something I don't already know for Christ's sake. Where is he going?"

Porto shrugs.

The American jumps across the table. He seizes Porto by a tuft of his long black hair and drives the barrel of the pistol right into a nostril.

"Where, you slimy bastard?"

The Brazilian casts his eyes up to God.

"I do not know. I swear I do not know. Please! Sometimes Semmes talked about going north to the Windward Islands. Sometimes he spoke of sailing east to Cabo São Roque. I swear!"

He lets go of the pimp's hair, holsters his gun. Stuffs the two ten-dollar notes in the breast pocket of Porto's shirt, walks out into the dusty street without another word.

He knows Semmes has been lying to Porto. But now the Rebel has made his trail obvious to anyone willing to read between the lines. By giving out two different stories, Semmes has made clear exactly where he is NOT heading.

"The bastard is on the Equator, hunting. *De puta madre*!" Porter mumbles to himself as he hails a cab. Then a new thought crosses his mind, and he frowns.

What if Semmes is leaving these breadcrumbs for me to follow? What if the pilot's right? Could Semmes actually want me to find him? Is he bored with raiding, spoiling for a fight?

31

CSS Sumter
SEPTEMBER 27, 1861

He sits at his desk in the great cabin, scooping up a mound of gold coins in front of him. Listening to their clink as he drops them one by one back onto the mahogany. The time's just past six bells into the forenoon watch.

As she has been doing for days, the ship is gliding along at a stately three knots under working canvas and stunsails, boiler fires out, her funnel lowered, stowed on deck. From a distance she looks like an innocent merchantman as she stalks the sea lanes in the doldrums just to the north of the equator. In this guise she hopes to snare more prizes along the direct route between New York and Cabo São Roque, the Horn of Brazil.

There have been problems. The long windward beat out to sea from Maranhão opened the ship where she was damaged during the grounding. Now she leaks. The watch is pumping fifteen minutes in every hour. And there's no telling how badly the leak has poisoned the powder magazine with dampness. Surely, some of the explosives have been rendered useless.

Just as bad, the crew has been in an ugly mood. There have been fights, and he has assembled the men almost daily to witness Mr. Evans apply the cat to some poor lubber.

Two days ago, with the *Sumter* disguised as a Federal warship, he hailed the Boston brigantine *Joseph Park*, then seized her, the cruiser's first prize in about a month. But there had been no thrilling chase and little swag aboard to distract the *Sumter*'s jacks from restlessness. The *Park* was six days out of Pernambuco in ballast, almost an empty shell except for a small bag of gold. Now the jacks are back at each other. Just this morning the bosun broke up a knife duel between a Brit topsman and a Scot waister. The men were both drunk. Kell believes that the crew has brought aboard no small amount of a Brazilian aguardiente called *cachaça*.

All of these troubles, and something more that he cannot name, nag at him as he tries to face off with his daily chores as ship's administrator. This particular chore, counting the gold confiscated from the Yankee captain of the *Park*, is hardly more satisfying than tallying the various daily inventories of ship and crew health. Even without counting, he knows that there's not enough gold here to pay his fuel and provisions bill in his next port of call even with the loan that Porto arranged for him.

He must seize another valuable prize ... soon. To this end he has placed Lieutenant Evans in charge of the *Park* and set him sailing seven to ten miles to the westward as a decoy and lookout for the *Sumter*, but after two days neither ship has sighted anything. Now he toys with his mustache and listens to the cries of drowning men in his mind as the *Somers* slips beneath the sea. He has been at his desk for the better part of an hour, scooping and dropping the gold. Still he has not stacked it into neat piles to count. Each time a coin falls out of his hands and strikes the table, he feels the back pains starting their assault on him anew. He pictures sand sifting through an hour glass.

"Captain, you should see this." Kell is at the doorway to the great cabin. "Most amazing."

He glares, does not wish to be disturbed.

"Really, sir. A bird has come aboard. All the way our here. Imagine, five hundred miles from the nearest land. Some of the crew are calling it a sign."

He has always taken an uncommon delight in the mysteries of the sea and nature, and for days he has been praying for guidance from God. Now this. A thing of the air has found his ship. In the middle of nowhere. What is this winged creature?

It's a petrel, a tiny black and white Wilson's storm-petrel, the kind of bird he has watched feeding among the great whales in their calving grounds near the Mona Passage. And now it flits from the finger of one seaman to another as the jacks stand in a circle on the main deck, offering up crumbs of hard tack. A little welcome party has already started. One of the men has begun to pipe the melody of "Aura Lee," and a sailor off the *Park* has joined in with his fiddle.

"'Ere, sir. Give it a go!" The *Sumter*'s Irish cook hands the captain a bit of stiff bread and a tin cup of water.

A sailor casts the bird into the air from his hands. It flutters twenty feet overhead, then settles on the main yard. The music stops.

The captain takes the bread in one hand, the cup in the other. His mustache cocks in amusement as he gives a two-note whistle.

The petrel twitches its head left and right at the sound of the whistle, places its origins. Flies right to Semmes, perches on the lip of the tin cup as if it's a trained canary come home to its master.

Semmes can't help himself. He beams.

"Drink up, little voyager."

The bird pecks at the water, flutters into the cup, splashes itself in a flurry of tiny beating wings. Regains the lip, drinks more. Then the bird jumps to the crotch between the thumb and index finger of his other hand, nibbles at the bread he holds.

"Now back to your natural element."

He launches the petrel into the air with a heave of his hand. The bird soars aloft, circles the mainmast then comes back to the captain's hand again.

"It is the food he wants," he says.

He lets the bird eat and drink for a minute longer as the gathered crew watches. Then he tosses the bird aloft again. Only to watch him circle the *Sumter*, return to a perch in the crotch of his left hand.

"Astonishing."

"I think it is more than the food, sir." Kell says.

Gently, he raises his hand until the bird is less than a foot away, eye to eye with the mariner.

"Look, Kell. He is like ourselves. A hunter. Far from home and alone on a vast sea." He suddenly remembers his much-loved poet Tennyson, quotes, "'Made weak by time and fate, but strong in will.'"

"Aye, sir. What will you call him?"

He doesn't hesitate, doesn't need to reflect. "Ulysses."

"What say you, sir? Is it a sign from the heavens?" One of his crew wants to know.

The captain looks out at the gathering of men. He's surrounded by his own crew and that of the *Park*.

"Aye boys, this little Ulysses is indeed a gift from the Creator. And like his namesake in the poem by Alfred, Lord Tennyson, I do believe he calls to us in the poet's immortal words: 'My mariners, souls that have toiled, and wrought, and thought with me—that ever with a frolic welcome took the thunder and the sunshine ... some work of noble note, may yet be done, not unbecoming men that strove with Gods.' What say we 'sail beyond the sunset, and the baths of all the western stars'?" He puffs his chest. "What say you, men?"

A cheer not unlike a battle cry rises up from the assembled multitude. The piper, then the Yank fiddler, too, break into "Dixie." Men dance.

Only he knows that he has left out some somber words when quoting his poet: "You and I are old, old age hath yet his honor and his toil. Death closes all." He feels those absent words rattling in his chest. Knows why.

"This creature has truly picked the strangest of all days to arrive, Kell."

He eyes the bird now perched calmly on his index finger.

"How so, sir?"

"Today is the anniversary of my fifty-second year."

"The Lord works in mysterious ways," says Kell. "May the little Ulysses be the bearer of God's blessing on you today and all those days to come."

He sits alone again at his desk in the great cabin, the bird perched on his shoulder. The gold finally counted, bagged. All $1020 of it. Now a letter lies open in front of him. It has come out of the *Park*'s letter bag, a missive from the captain of a Yankee merchant brig, the *Asteroid,* to the ship's owner. In it the captain speaks of his fears of being seized by the *Sumter* and vows to steer wide of the usual rhumbline course on his way back home.

"We have done our job too well, Ulysses. We have scared off the prey. The name *Sumter* has struck fear into ships from Boston to Brazil until they take desperate measures to hide from us. We must change our hunting strategy or perish for lack of sustenance."

The bird nips at the shaggy hair over the captain's ear as he twirls his mustache, stares out through the stern windows at the slate gray sea of late evening. The ship wallows in the light air. The joiner work creaks. Pans clatter in the pantry. The oil lamp squeaks against the brass chain that holds it as it swings over the desk, casting fitful shadows on the ceiling.

He blinks as if coming out of a dream. He shouts for his steward to summon the first officer.

When Kell appears at the doorway, he beckons him with the wave of a hand to enter. There's no offer of a seat, and the first officer stands before his captain's desk at attention.

"Mr. Kell, we're finished with this desolate and infernal Equator. Call back Evans and the *Park* to us. She has not served her purpose as a decoy or a watchdog, and now I fear we must obliterate her. By my reckoning we have exhausted almost all the current possibilities of finding an ally to accept our prizes. Nor can we spare men for a prize crew just on a chance that the venture will come to something. From this time forth, the *Sumter* will destroy every enemy in her path ... unless we know in advance that some nation, some port close at hand, will accept our prizes."

Kell nods.

"We will proceed under sail to conserve fuel. It will be right slow going through the doldrums, and we will continue to hunt along the way. But my aim is to veer back north to the French West Indies where the hunting will be better ... And perhaps, just perchance, the French will come to our aid in our hour of need."

The luff nods again. Tries not to show the excitement he's feeling for a change of plans.

Semmes strokes the crown of the petrel that has shifted its perch to the index finger of the captain's left hand, clears his throat.

"Every man among us must understand the Yankees are even now close at hand. Thanks to our friends the journalists who send their reportage around the world with the fleets, we know at least some of those who would destroy us. Old shipmates and brothers in arms, eh?"

"And rivals, sir."

Semmes smiles as if remembering butting heads as a middie and young officer with the men who now pursue him.

"Just so, Kell. David Porter in the *Powhatan* is right clever, and an angry man, as you well know. He will eventually see through our deceptions. Charlie Wilkes in the *San Jacinto*? The fellow will stop at nothing when it comes to his personal quest for glory. James Palmer in the *Iroquois*. As solid, steady, and thorough a naval officer as ever commanded a ship of war. He has the perseverance of a man who will make up with initiative for any lacking creativity of mind. And there are others the papers tell us of, too."

"The *Shepherd Knapp*, the *Keystone State*, the *Niagara*," says Kell, who has learned his captain's habit of keeping track of his enemies.

"We must be ready to fight for the honor and success of our sovereign nation. The men are hot and tired and dissatisfied with our cruise of late. They must be brought into line, Kell. They must see that the cruise of the *Sumter* is no longer a fishing expedition. Soon we all will be fighting for our lives. God help us if we are not ready. Y'all hear?"

"Trust me, sir. We will be ready." Kell salutes.

The captain's right hand returns the salute from his own forehead. Then from the bird's.

Kell can't help himself, gives a startled look.

32

District of Columbia
SEPTEMBER 28, 1861

She has been smoking the Mary Jane with him, sitting on the bed, passing the pipe back and forth. Only afterwards, when their room in the church Burlow calls the Tender Trap has become a red-rimmed blur, does she ask him if this herb she has now smoked with him on three separate nights is as addictive as opium.

He dissolves for a few seconds into laughter, tells her not to worry. It's just a kind of hemp. Just a little something extra the good sexton threw in for the price of the room. Just something to set you free.

Bloody transform you, more like. Into a beast. Or, who was that fella that Fiona talked about, the Marquis de something?

She cannot remember, for the life of her, how what began as a bit of giddiness, and a little craving in her loins, has come to this. But now her mind's spinning in smooth, fast arcs. She feels her almost unlimited power, sees her chance to maybe steal from the navy, something for the South, for Rose, for Fiona, for Raffy.

"Hit me! Hit me, you slut!"

He lies splayed out facedown and naked on the bed, wrists and ankles bound to the bedposts, squirming and bucking.

She towers over him, riding his rump in a leather bodice, black mask. The velvet cat-o'-nine-tails hangs from her hand. She's already used it a lot. The red welts rise like the tracks of a little animal on his back. Each whack brings him closer to the carnal release he howls for. She's not quite sure she understands this pain for pleasure insanity. But she knows the terror of being poised for a free fall down a mountain of ecstasy, wanting it more than life itself. And she knows the madness that comes when a lover holds back ... when one's right at the threshold. Harry might do anything, say anything to get over his edge ... if she holds off on the whip now. Taunts him about his work.

So she does. Instead of ripping into him again with the cat, she bends down over him, her leather bodice to his back. She grabs him around the throat with her left hand, squeezing off some of his air, biting his ear.

"Do you want to die, Harry. Want to die?"

"Kill me. Kill me." His breath frantic.

She hates Harry's sick code talk, but she gives it to him. She presses him on the subject of the navy, presses him on the boss he likes to ridicule. He's hiding something.

"You want to kill the navy? Kill it dead, Harry? Kill Old Folkwattle. Hack the bleeding boss?"

His eyes, huge and wild, look back over his shoulder at her. Pleading. Afraid. Hungry.

She squeezes his throat harder. Bites into his ear, keeping up her low challenge.

"Why don't we gut Gideon Welles, Harry? Slay the bugger?"

His fingers claw at the bed sheets. His body pushes, pulls against its bindings. He whips his head at her, snaps at her with his teeth.

"Kill me. Jesus, hit me slut. Cat me!" He's almost screaming.

"You want the cat, Harry. Want the bloody cat, love?"

"Hit me. Hit me. Whore!"

"Are you afraid to butcher the boss? Slaughter Welles, Harry?"

His right arm breaks free of its velvet rope. He swats, scratches at her.

Now she lays on the cat. She hits him so hard across the shoulders that he wails.

"Are you afraid, Harry? Afraid to kill Welles?"

His free hand sinks its fingernails into the flesh on the back of her right thigh.

"Kill Welles? What? To hell with Welles. Kill you. Fuck you, fuck you, you slimy Irish twat!"

"What?"

"Welles is skinned already."

Her ears perk. She knows he's right on the razor's edge.

"You want to die, Harry?"

"Jesus Christ Almighty, end it."

"What?"

"Fucking end it!"

She raises the cat over her head. Whacks him.

"Why is Welles skinned, love?"

He digs his fingers further into her hamstring.

She hits him again. His back is beginning to bleed.

"Why, Harry? Why?"

"We've got him by the balls. Jesus. Kill me."

She holds off the whip, yanks at his hair.

"Who's *we*, you worm?"

"Hit me!"

"Who's *we*?"

He gives a tremendous kick, breaks a leg loose from its binding, almost throwing Maude to the floor. But she holds onto his flanks with her knees. Goes to the whip again.

"*We*, Harry? Who's *we*?"

She can't help herself now. She just lays on the whip. Again and again and again, trying to beat the secrets out of him. But he's too far gone. His whole body begins to jerk, a man struck by lightning.

He screams. Long and shrill.

When her heart stops pounding, and the sweat, the blood, the semen have grown cool and sticky on the sheets, she hears him say, "My god, love, you are the queen of the night."

I wish we were both dead.

Her mind skips to a picture of the only other man who has shared a bed with her. A gentle man, a brave man, an honorable man.

"Do you ever want to see me again, Harry?" She puts her lips on his cheek as he lies beside her.

"I'd slay a hundred dragons."

"Then tell me who has Welles by the balls. And how."

He shrugs, sees no harm in boasting a little of his wickedness to such a jaded hussy. He doesn't know why she's so stuck on Welles. Doesn't care. She can tell no one of consequence. She's not Semmes' whore anymore. She's his ... And he's hers.

"Me. Me and a few good friends of the navy. We have the bugger by his grapes, love. We've got a tintype of Rose Greenhow kissing him, and we're going to blackmail the whore monger to hell and back with it. Then get the navy in fighting trim."

So this is it. A shadowy tale of blackmail is what she sold herself for. She wonders if this scrap of information is worth her current state of humiliation. She wonders how she might turn her scrap to the advantage of a knight long-gone over the blue horizon, a new nation surging to life across the Potomac.

"You're a clever Judas."

"And I'll tell you something else." He gives her a vulture's grin. "Your glorious Raphael Semmes will soon be shark bait. Right now there are a half-dozen warships closing on the old boy, Maudie."

She feels the insides of her chest freeze. Feels a sudden urge to run all the way to Fiona's room across town and beg for help.

"You really crave the scent of spilled blood, don't you?"

"That's why you love me." He kisses her neck, slides his hand along her bare thigh.

"You might be surprised." She closes her eyes, prays to the Holy Virgin for forgiveness for what she has already done. For strength in what she and Fiona now must do.

33

The Horse Latitudes
SEPTEMBER 28-29, 1861

The Yankee brigantine *Joseph Park* wallows in the swells a hundred yards to the west of the *Sumter*. All of her best sails have been stripped, transferred to the Reb's locker. Her yards dangle at odd angles.

"This is the last of her valuables, sir." Lieutenant Evans reaches into a sailor's cotton sea bag, pulls out the *Joseph Park*'s chronometer.

Semmes stands beneath the sun awning over his quarterdeck. The petrel Ulysses paces back and forth on his right shoulder. He takes the instrument in hand, opens its rosewood case—lined with form-fitting green velvet—and listens to the delicate ticking of this marvel of precision. Chronometers always remind him of an enormous replica of his uncle's gold pocket watch. He loves the idea that tiny emeralds, rubies and diamonds are at the heart of the time-keeping movement.

"What a beauty, eh, Mr. Evans?"

"Yes sir. We have salvaged everything. Shall I fire the *Park*?"

He gazes at the hands on the chronometer's twenty-four-hour face, sees that it's not yet 0800 and the start of the forenoon watch.

"Leave me to think on it, Lieutenant. Haste could be our undoing."

When Evans has saluted, marched off, Semmes strokes the wings of his mustache. Powhatan, San Jacinto, Iroquois *and others are out here combing the horizon for the smallest sign of us. Watch your step, man.*

He reaches up to his shoulder with his left hand, rubs the crown of the petrel. The bird ruffles his wings, puffs out his chest.

"What shall we do, bird? Scuttle her? That would be the least conspicuous, eh? The safest course. Send the carpenter over to make a mess of holes in her bottom and just let her fill and sink? Leave her behind, while we sneak off to the north, disguised as a flyblown merchantman with our funnel stowed out of sight on deck?"

The petrel jumps onto the captain's left index finger, cocking its head in swift jerks.

He looks into the little black eyes, sees the image of himself reduced to the size of a flea. He feels a pain rising in his back, wonders why it has chosen this moment to haunt him again. This pain that squeezed the breath from his lungs after his fall down the companionway ladder in the gale north of Jamaica. The pain for which he nearly blinded himself with laudanum, the pain that was tearing at him when he ran the *Sumter* aground at Maranhão.

Now the pain carries another memory.

He feels the rock hit the small of his back with such force that it knocks the wind from his lungs, sends him sprawling into the dirt. The scents of mule turds and stale hay on the towpath clot his nostrils. It's the summer of his eleventh year, his first year as an orphan living with his uncle in Georgetown, across Rock Creek from the capital. He's been fishing for bass just below the rapids on the Potomac. Now he's walking home along the C&O Canal with four keepers on a string when three boys start taunting him from a glade of trees. "Hey, sissybaby. Hey, shitty knickers, give us your fish!"

He has always been told to ignore the catcalls of other children so he continues west along the towpath, hoping to slip away among the drays and shopping parties clogging Wisconsin Avenue where it meets the canal. But the scallywags have begun raining stones in his direction. At first they are just pebbles that clatter like hail as they hit the ground around him. He walks faster, dares not run because instinct tells him that these boys will stalk him all summer if he shows fear. He throws back his shoulders, raises his head and marches forward, telling himself that he has just a mere one hundred-or-so yards further to go. Now the rocks come. First, hitting the towpath at his back, sometimes skipping up against the back of his knickers to sting his legs. One sails by his head so close that he hears it whir like beating wings. Then something sharp socks his back with a dull thwack. He goes down.

As he gets up on his knees, he hears laughter. The rock throwers are on the towpath running toward him shouting, "Get his fish."

When they're almost on him, he rises to his feet. He was intending to leave the fish and run, but his left arm has other ideas. It hauls the string of bass out of the dust and swings them like a whip at his assailants. It catches the nearest of the boys around the neck, draping him in muddy fish. Even before the fish quiver to rest, he lets go the string, takes his fishing pole in both hands, swings it sideways like a bat, catching all three boys hard across their bellies. One boy loses his footing and nearly falls into the canal.

He cocks his pole to strike again.

"Get out of here," he screams. "And leave the fish!"

It's only when they've skeedaddled, and he has rinsed the dust from his fish in the canal, that he feels the pain in his back shooting into his chest.

"My back hurts, and I'm in a scrappy mood, bird. Know the feeling? Not a thing we can do about it except scratch this itch, Ulysses."

He beckons to the luff who's in earnest conference with Evans and Chapman about the wisdom of setting stunsails.

"Mr. Kell, tell the men that we will beat to quarters and clear for action after the noon mess. Thereupon we shall test the accuracy of our guns and the strength of our powder on the prize. I aim to blow her to pieces in short order, and make a funeral pyre of what is left! The *Park* shall serve as our *Powhatan,* our *San Jacinto,* and our *Iroquois* today. They cannot be far afield."

Just after two bells into the morning watch, Porter hears a knock on his cabin door.

"Goddamn it, yes. What?"

"The maintop lookout has seen something to the eastard, sir. Possible flames."

He sits up in his sheets, feels *Powhatan* rolling as his gimbaled berth sways to the swell. A dull pressure in his crotch, has to pee.

"Just a minute. Tell the deck I'm coming. Have them keep a sharp eye on the flames."

He looks out the stern windows. The sky is still the charcoal gray of false morning. The cabin itself all but dark save the glow from a low flame of a wall lamp near the door.

Probably nothing at all. The sky can play a lot of tricks on a man's vision.

He gathers his long nightshirt up in a fist so it will not trip him, shuffles to an open stern window and tries to make water. At first nothing comes. Then the urine begins to flow. He feels a pain like a white hot poker branding the inside of his member.

"*De puta madre!*"

He grinds his teeth. The pain at urination started about a week ago, just a few days after leaving Brazil. He knew the trouble immediately, had contracted his first dose of the French pox as a middie sowing his wild oats in a Mexican cat house. It was a right of passage back then, and he was on a long shore leave with local root doctors to sooth his burning flesh. But now he's at sea, in the midst of a great hunt, and the quinine sulphate mixed with whiskey that the ship's surgeon prescribed has done nothing but make him feel tired. The pain seems to be growing thorns in his balls.

"*De puta madre!* Fucking Semmes' ruddy slut!" *I need to find a root doctor who knows his ass from a teacup. Quinine sulphate! Christ, it's what the ship's quack prescribes for everything, even the grip.*

"Is everything alright, sir?" The steward at the door.

"Hell's blazes, yes, man. Now leave off. Can't a man take a piss in peace?"

When he reaches the deck he finds the second officer and a midshipman training their long glasses toward the eastern horizon. It's growing a whiter shade of gray with each passing second.

"Where away?"

"The lookout marked it at the horizon, five points off the starboard bow."

He puts his own long glass up to his right eye, scans the horizon.

"I see nothing."

"I believe we have gained on it, sir. It should be nearly abeam now, sir," says the midshipman.

"Flames, you say?"

"That's what the lookout reports. Thought I saw them once, but only for a moment." The second officer's voice sounds ragged. "Also thought I saw some smoke. A light trail streaming just above the horizon, like a little plume drifting off to the north."

He keeps scanning the horizon, still sees nothing.

"Do you think it is the *Sumter*, sir? Has she taken another prize and burned it?"

The questions grate at the back of his brain.

"I have no idea, boy. Just tell me, do you see it? Where? Come, show me what you dragged me out of bed for!"

"There, right off the beam. I see the flames again." The middie holds his glass with one hand, points with the other.

The captain brings his long glass to bear, twists the last cylinder for focus. Finally, he sees something. A tiny orange flare. And the black dot of a sail or hull near to it. Just for a second or two. Then they're gone so quickly that he can't be sure he has truly seen anything. He waits, thinks the strange images will reappear with the next roll of the ship. Pictures Semmes standing smugly at the quarter rail, watching his enemy crumbling to ashes. He changes his footing to better level his glass against the force of the dipping deck. But as he shifts his weight, he feels something give in his bladder. Just the slightest discharge of urine, but it sets off the sting of the pox, starting in his groin, shooting to the back of his eyeballs. Everything in the telescope turns red.

"Jesus Christ!"

"Sir ... " The middie. "I see something again. Flames. Do you?"

"I've got the smoke too, right above," says the second officer.

He grinds his teeth together, Drives the sting back into his gut. *Damn it all to hell, this fucking whore's gift. I need a root doctor. I could find one for a farthing in St. Thomas. But here? Christ. And what if this is goddamned Semmes? It could be he. We have just crossed the Equator to the west'ard of the rhumbline between Brazil and New York. A turnpike of ships. Any hunter would come here to catch his limit.*

"Where are those flames, the smoke?"

"There, just midships."

The captain feels the pain clawing at his belly, tries to focus. The image in the long glass remains a blue-brown blur.

"See it, sir?"

He grabs the sailing master's megaphone.

"What see you, there aloft?"

"A fair morn and a vacant sea now, sir."

He continues to squint into his glass. At last, his eye catches something as he scans from northeast to southeast. The sun, bursting over the edge of the planet, burning like a golden galleon. It nearly blinds him.

"Afraid the sun swallowed him, sir. Must have gone over the horizon by now." The second officer begins collapsing his long glass into itself. "Should I alter course to the eastard and run down this mystery?"

Porter drops the glass from his face, rubs his closed eyelids with his middle and index fingers until he can see the web of veins glowing like fine shadows in front of him. He wants to go aloft for a look himself. But when he draws his spread legs together, he feels the sting of pox searing right to the ends of the hair on his head. His brain is a hive of hornets.

When the buzzing in his head finally lets off, he sees a shiny blue morning, smells the coal smoke from his stack, the coffee brewing. Johnny cakes frying in the galley. It seems he's was waking from a dream. Suddenly, he's all but certain that what they have seen through their long glasses is nothing more than flares from the rising sun. That, and its reflections in clouds that form like mares' tails on the horizon with the coming of a new day on the Equator. Suddenly, he doesn't care if it is Semmes out there burning his way to glory or baiting him to a fight. Porter's gut ripped. Trapped on a ship with leaky boilers.

The poxy bastard has left his calling card in my gut. I had not imagined such a thing might even be possible.

How can a man fight like this?

34

The Executive Mansion
MID-OCTOBER, 1861

Walk with me, Gideon." Lincoln stands up at his desk. He has a letter, something else small, in hand.

For the first time since he was called on the carpet for letting the *Sumter* escape, Welles sees Lincoln's right cheek twitch, his upper lip curl. He flashes his Secretary of the Navy a sharp look, then turns away. Starts outdoors toward the South Lawn. The president looked just so that night back in April after the *Powhatan* confusion, when he threatened to break off Bill Seward's finger.

Lord Almighty, what have I done now?

Thirty yards out onto the lawn, Lincoln pauses, waits for him to catch up. Takes him by the elbow with one immense paw.

"I ... I ... I am so infernally agitated, I can hardly speak of this, Gideon. I certainly cannot speak of this in the executive mansion. I cannot have these *things* in the executive mansion." The president shoves the letter that he has been carrying in his left hand against Welles' chest. "Look at this and weep for us all, sir!"

He opens the one-page letter. Finds a small tintype, two by three inches, the image dark, blurry. He takes his spectacles out of his vest pocket to bring it into focus. A gust of wind drives a swirl of yellow and red leaves around his feet.

At first he thinks he's looking at the image of a lynched body suspended from a tree. Then he sees a second figure in the picture. He still cannot make out what he's seeing until he turns himself so that the light comes over his shoulder, illuminating the tintype.

Now it's clear. There's a young, white male bound by his hands to a willow branch over his head. He's naked. And there's a woman in what

RANDALL PEFFER

looks like a leather mask and bodice flailing at his back with a whip.
The whip seems both frozen in her cocked arm and in blurry motion
at the same time. The camera catches the action from the figures' left
sides. The man has his face turned over his shoulder toward the camera.
His eyes are cast upwards and his mouth seems to be shrieking to the
heavens. A tousle of light blond hair falls over the forehead, girlishly
handsome even in its agony. The man's aroused penis stands up in
full-blown ecstasy.

"Is that your Lieutenant Burlow?"

He feels his chest withering as the true nature of what he's seeing
becomes clear. He has heard of such depravity, but never seen anything
like this. Now his heart turns to dried petals and stops dead.

"Good God, man! Do you understand what he's doing with that
trollop? In all my life I never ... " Lincoln's voice booms. "Such wanton-
ness is almost beyond my ... Damn it, Gideon, what kind of people
do you have ... ?"

"This is a hideous embarrassment."

"You have no damned idea, Gideon. No idea. Read the letter."

His hands shake as he raises the letter to read. Lincoln looks
over his shoulder, his hot breath fuming. It stinks of coffee, bitter
marmalade.

In delicate blue ink and fine script the letter details the dates and
places Harry Burlow has been seen in the company of women of ques-
tionable morals. It also names him a member of an exclusive club for
flagellators secreted beneath a Negro chapel in Southeast called the
Church of the Crucifixion.

"Behold. The North and her unholy legions shall soon repent their
wicked ways!" are the last words of the letter.

"What do you know about this boy, Gideon?"

He feels his heart crumbling. Then he tells a lie of omission. "Nothing. I swear. He is one of the few in the department who puts in a full
day's work. A Connecticut boy. I know his family."

He does not say how Burlow once ushered him to the home of
the Reb spy Rose Greenhow. Does not mention how Burlow encour-

aged him to take a tart, how Burlow sometimes brags of his drabbing around the office.

Lincoln gives him a withering stare.

He feels the need to offer more words in defense of his own ignorance. "He has been extremely useful to me in trying to bring order—"

"Horse shit, Gideon. Horse shit!"

The president kicks the grass with his shoe, sends a clod of earth flying ten feet across the lawn.

"Do you think this all ends with a dirty picture and a declaration of moral outrage? Have nearly four decades in politics taught you nothing? This stinks to high heaven. Our enemies have just begun to toy with us. The blackmail will come. The demands. The extortion."

"I'm going to fire him. Cut him off from us."

"Oh most certain, sir! You *will* do that! But don't you think it is closing the barn after the horse is out? For all we know, someone may already be blackmailing your boy Burlow. My word, there is a war on, man! How much has he already given the Rebs? Do you think he has sold out the plans for the assault on Port Royal? How many good boys will die because one naughty little lieutenant in the Navy Department is making a filthy hobby of getting himself spanked? Tell me that, Gideon!"

"I am responsible for this mess. Would you like my resignation, Mr. President?"

"You're damned right you are responsible. And no. *No*, confound it, Gideon, I don't want your resignation."

The president's hands fly up to the sky as if driven by an explosion.

"You are the only one around here I can remotely trust. The rest of the cabinet ... and McClellan ... Lord Almighty, General McClellan! They are most ambitious men who would give their right arms to see me hoisted on my own petard. Don't leave me, Gideon. You have no idea how much I need you at your post. But, tarnation, man! Get your house in order. Cast out the scum. Protect yourself against even the slightest rumor of impropriety. Control the damage caused by Burlow. Redraft your plans for the capture of Port Royal ... and anything else of a delicate nature that Burlow might know of and betray."

He heaves his frame erect before his president, then bows.

"I am your most humble and indebted servant."

Lincoln shoots him a little smile. "They underestimate us, Gideon. That is our secret strength. We are more resolute and more cunning than we look."

He still feels his chest swelling with a humble pride when he gets back to his room at the Willard. But then he unlocks the door, finds a gleaming white envelope addressed to him in graceful, light-blue script. The note inside turns everything left in his chest to dust.

Your picture is next, Mr. Secretary, unless you recall the ships chasing the Sumter. *Forget about Raphael Semmes!!!*

35

CSS Sumter
OCTOBER 27, 1861

They have been a month more at sea without sighting land. Try as she does to make her way north toward a new hunting ground off the Windward Islands, the ship has been making slow progress.

She's ghosting under canvas in the fluky breezes north of the Equator, her fires out to conserve fuel for chasing prizes. Along their course they have spied, run-down, and boarded more than a half-dozen vessels. In each case the cruiser, with no name boards or transom lettering, flew the Stars and Stripes and masqueraded as a Yankee warship in search of an infamous Confederate commerce raider called the *Sumter*. But none of the overhauled vessels belonged to the enemy. And none, save the English brig *Spartan,* bound from Rio to St. Thomas, carried any useful news about the course of the war. When boarded by a Reb officer wearing his old Yankee uniform, the *Spartan*'s captain complained bitterly about Yankee audacity in stopping and boarding his neutral vessel. Then he scoffed at the phony Yankee boarding officer, told him that his Northern comrades in arms were about to get whipped like hell. The Confederate army was advancing on Washington.

This distaste for Yankees has been the common sentiment expressed against the boarding parties. It is the source of wardroom mirth aboard the *Sumter* that even when she's not destroying enemy shipping, she's sullying his reputation among mariners. But there's no more laughter when the ship moves above seven degrees north latitude and runs smack into a series of storms bringing wind, rain, sheet lightning. For twelve days the *Sumter* faces nothing but northerly gales and half-gales right on the nose. The ship leaks. The crew pumps—a half hour on, a half hour off. Men wretch their guts out. To conserve dwindling stores, rations for officers and men are reduced to moldy, worm-eaten bread and a tough form of dried beef that the jacks call *old horse*.

North of fourteen degrees, the weather breaks. The first clear, steady breaths of the northeast trade winds begin to fill in. On Sunday, October 27, the ship is sailing north toward her new hunting grounds between Barbados and the Windward Islands. Officers and men are trying to dry out. Breeze light, seas calm. It's just about three bells into the forenoon watch, the sun coming on warm, but not yet scorching. On deck the jacks are shaving and bathing in cups of wash water. Some have already begun shaking out their best mustering shirts and beating their best hats into shape for the weekly inspection.

Semmes stands in the "sick bay," a stuffy, little cabin next to the powder magazine, conferring with Pills Galt about the alarming number of cases of inflamed gums, loose teeth, and swollen joints the doctor has seen in the last week.

"Scurvy is about to run rampant, and the men are in a foul—"

"Sail ho." The shout from the lookout echoes from aloft, cuts off Galt mid-sentence.

The captain feels his soul dance.

At last! Most merciful God, let this one be a fat Yank. We have been long in the wilderness, as thou knowest.

"Beat to quarters, Kell. Clear for action." He spits orders as he rushes on deck.

Even before the fife and drum begin their battle cry, the jacks stuff away their pretty gear, toss their kits into the fo'castle, run to stations. They are stripped to their waist. Do not want their wounds sullied by dirty shirts.

"Chapman has the deck. Come, Kell! Come!"

The captain wiggles free of his dress jacket, tosses it to his steward, mounts the starboard main shrouds. His joints ache, but he climbs like an ape with his long glass tucked beneath the waistband of his trousers. Kell, now in shirtsleeves, too, races upward at his side.

"What a thing to get aloft again," Semmes says as they reach the hounds. His mustache curls into a smile.

"Grand, sir. Most marvelous."

He pulls himself up the futtock ropes onto the platform of the maintop.

"My god, but I feel a boy again."

Kell's already on his feet, long glass up to his eye.

"Where away?" He calls to the lookout who's twenty-five feet further up at the topmast crosstrees.

"Two points to leeward, sir. Schooner."

"Can't quite ... "

"Come, Kell. We can make her out better from above."

He begins scaling the ratlines to the topmast hounds. When he mounts the crosstrees, the Irish lookout gives a big gap-toothed smile.

"She's a bleedin' Yank, sir, or I ain't been at sea these twenty-nine years man and boy."

The captain takes up his glass, eyes the distant shape. Peering through the lens, he can make her clearly. A two-masted schooner. The whitest kind of cotton canvas in her fore-and-aft rig. Gaff topsails tight as drums. Sharp clipper bow. Low-slung, white topsides, with an easy finish at the stern. New England-built.

"Unmistakable."

He squints into the freshening breeze, nods in agreement. Braces himself with an arm looped around a shroud as the *Sumter* trips a little in a gathering swell, makes a sudden lurch to leeward.

"Bone in her teeth and a white quarter wake. She's riding stiff with a cargo and fast as a witch. We've got a race on our hands to catch her by nightfall in this breeze, Kell."

"Bring it on then, sir!"

"Aye. Let's have at it. The Lord helps those who help themselves. Ahoy below! Men aloft to take in the stunsails. Funnel up and braced on the double. Tell the engineer to light his fires and get up a full head of steam. Alter course to leeward. Make it northwest by the compass. We are going hunting."

⚓   ⚓   ⚓

"Sir, the engineer begs a word with you."

He jumps, coming out of a dream. It's already past two in the afternoon. He has not taken coffee, sipped water, eaten, spoken, moved from the pilot's perch of the starboard horseblock for hours. He has just stood there like a statue with his long glass on the Yankee schooner, measuring the miles he's gaining on the prize by the dryness in his mouth. Loving every minute of it. When the midshipman spoke, a picture of Maude was just crossing his mind. He saw her beckoning him to bed, thick copper hair covering her milk-white shoulders. What a charmed life he once led, he thinks, prays that it might be so again. On a day like this, with his ship about to snare a fat prize, a life with Maude almost seems possible.

He feels his ship charging into short, cresting seas, looks around at the men gathered on deck to watch the *Sumter* pulling to within three miles of their prize. He smells the sharp scent of sulfur in the coal smoke, hears the steady rush of vapor pouring off the funnel.

"Where is he?"

"Sir?" The midshipman standing before him looks confused.

"The engineer, man. Mr. Freeman. Did you not say ... ?"

"Right, sir. Sorry sir. He cannot leave the engine room. Humbly asks that you come there if you will, sir."

He scowls, stomps toward the engine room hatch. Even from yards away he can hear the grinding of machinery. As he starts down the ladder the withering heat hits him. The *Sumter*'s engine space always seems hot as an oven, but here in the tropics the place is an absolute Hades. The draft of the fire boxes sucks a half-gale of wind down the hatchway.

"What would you have of me, Mr. Freeman?"

A ragged silhouette is cranking a pipe wrench on a fuming joint in a steam-return line. In the background, flames roar from a half-dozen open fire boxes. Blackened figures, wearing nothing but head rags and their small shorts heave shovel-loads of coal into the monster's mouth.

Piston rods beat up and down. An oiler with his long-spout squirts down shaft bearings.

As usual Freeman hears nothing through the beeswax in his ears. He doesn't look up, keeps at the pipe joint, spits out a mouthful of black phlegm onto the pipe where it sputters up and down until it vaporizes.

Semmes wipes the sweat from his brow, steps off the bottom rung of the ladder onto the catwalk. He aims to grab the engineer by the elbow to get his attention, when suddenly he feels his feet go cold. Soot-speckled, oily water sloshes over the iron catwalk, splashing his best muster shoes. His last pair of clean socks.

"Goddamn! Goddamn it to hell!"

"My thoughts exactly." Freeman has somehow heard his captain's beef. The engineer now stands within a foot of him, his hands cupped around his mouth like a sailing master's megaphone. With his slicked-back black hair and dripping pointed beard, the man looks like the fallen angel.

"Bloody leaking to beat the band, sir. And she's down a bit by the head, sir. Look there, would you?"

Freeman points forward toward the feet of his black gang. Semmes sees that the stokers are up to their ankles in water.

"How long, man?"

Freeman throws his hands in the air. He has lost all track of time.

"Something's let go."

"That it has, sir. Noticed it when it come up on our feet, we did. That's when I sent for you. If I had to guess, I'd say one of the engine mounts has started to come adrift. Probably got a little loose when we slammed that sandbank in Brazil. Now it's worked looser with all the storms and this hard running. Maybe busted some frames and started a butt leaking."

He remembers that the deck watch has been sounding the bilges every half hour. There was a gang on the pumps when he came below.

"Pumps aren't holding it."

"No sir, I fear not. The leak's getting ahead of us. How close are we to the prize?"

He squints into the blazing fire boxes, calculates. Knows what Freeman's thinking. If they catch up to the prize and seize her soon, the *Sumter*'s crew could move aboard, abandon their little black cruiser. A warrior who goes to sea always knows his ship is expendable. The trick is not to feel sentimental about her and do what you have to do to stay afloat and fight another day. But, still, to lose the *Sumter* in the glory of this chase seems a cruel slap of fate.

"We could be on her within the hour."

Freeman screws up his cheeks and shakes his head.

"We'll have water in the fire boxes before ... and then ... "

Then the cool seawater hits the hot boilers and she blows us all to Fiddler's Green. With the Yanks standing by to cheer us on our way.

"If we knew where she was leaking, we could sling a sail under her as a patch. Get ahead of it with the pumps and a bucket brigade. Chink her up from inside and lay in another patch and some shoring on the inside. But it's too late for that."

"Aye, 'fraid it is, sir."

"Goddamn it! I'll get the deck ready to abandon ship, launch the boats, fire a signal shot, haul up the distress flag for the Yanks."

He can save the men. But the Yanks will not take him. He will not let them hang him from a yard arm. Will never allow it. In his mind he sees himself freeing little Ulysses from the great cabin, then settling into his bed to dream of Maude while he waits to go down with his ship. He wonders what it feels like to be blown to bits—probably right much better than drowning.

The Welsh engine man claws his forehead with a black hand.

"Can I try something, sir? It would contaminate her system, but it's a chance."

"Sir?"

"Let her feed-water line drop into the bilge."

"Run her on salt water? Brine? God, man! She'd foam all to hell. Clog her valves with salt. Scale up everything to a fair-thee-well ... or let the crown sheet go dry and blow sky high."

"Aye, sir, that she will. But not right away maybe. She's a thirsty bitch, and she'd suck up twenty-five gallons a minute ... or a little more. Maybe I can manage the foaming if I back her off half to about thirty revolutions. That might be enough to give the deck boys a chance to get another pump started. What say, sir? Can we catch the Yank with thirty revolutions? I don't think the old girl wants to dance with Davey Jones yet."

Semmes' head bobs forward as if something has cracked him from behind. He blinks, pictures the fat Yank heaving to and striking her colors ... unaware that she's surrendering to little more than a ghost of a warship. The preposterousness of it all! He slaps his forehead with both hands, lets a single laugh burst from his lips.

"You are a genius, Mr. Freeman. Do it! Do it by all that is holy in the sight of God and the Devil. Run her on brine. Suck it out of her."

Freeman throws his arms in the air in a little cheer.

Then Semmes bends close to his ear. "Don't tell a living soul. The crew would think us mad, run right into the arms of the Yanks if they knew we even thought of such a thing. We'd be the laughingstock of every wardroom from here to Calcutta."

"Count on me, sir. Bit of our secret. You go fetch us a plump prize, Captain. I got to feed me engine a little of Neptune's love juice."

Nightfall. There's fiddle music, jigs on the fo'castle deck, a fine pig turning on a spit over a makeshift fire pit near the funnel. Jacks are fetching roast potatoes and ears of sweet corn from the coals, gnawing on fresh apples or mild New York cheese. The quartermaster has set up kegs of rum and apple cider on trestles near the main fife rail, pours it off to the ship's company without regard to any sense of rationing. To leeward, the Yank schooner *Daniel Trowbridge* from New Haven, a prize crew aboard and their captives locked below, lies hove to under riding sails, swinging a single lamp at the masthead. The wind has gone light. A half-moon hangs in the sky.

Kell stands with his captain at the taffrail and raises his pewter mug of rum-spiked cider for a long swallow. "I counted over a dozen live lambs and pigs, not to mention all the geese. Hogsheads of beef and pork, canvassed hams. Sacks of flour, cases of crackers and wheels of cheese. A cache of tart Macintoshes. Mess of corn. Enough to feed us five or six months in style!"

"The Lord saw the goodness of our cause today, Mr. Kell. He looked on us with right much generosity, that is certain."

He smiles to himself, thinks of soot-stained Freeman and the salt-water diet for the engine that turned certain catastrophe into this carnival at sea. He knows that even as the crew feasts, Freeman is secretly flushing the brine as best he can from his beloved Merrick engine. And Freeman was right. After they seized the prize and got the *Sumter* pumped out, the carpenters found two broken frames. There was a loose butt block under the port engine mount, where the hull leaked like a basket. Now if the carpenter's gang can just shore her up enough to stay afloat ... and let him taste his enemy's blood again.

36

District of Columbia
NOVEMBER 1-2, 1861

"What about the *Sumter*, Mr. Secretary? The public wants to know when you are going to catch the Reb pirate, sir!"

Welles rocks back on his heels, does not speak. He smiles at the reporters whom he has been inviting to his office every Wednesday afternoon for the last six weeks to brief them on current naval operations. The idea came to him too late to gloat over the details of how one of his squadrons attacked and overran the Confederate positions, took seven hundred prisoners at Cape Hatteras back at the end of August. Nor could he yet respond to questions about the huge fleet—seventy-seven ships, if truth be known—whose sailing was announced in the October 26 edition of *Harper's Weekly*. He hopes that as he speaks, Sam DuPont's boys are already pounding the Rebs at Port Royal, South Carolina. But "mum" is the word until he gets reports from the field. A few of the supply ships foundered in a gale off Hatteras on their way south. Discussion of that must be avoided too.

But, still, the gathering works. The topic of the *Sumter* can always be exploited ... even though he has quietly sent out recall dispatches for all the ships who are currently hunting the Reb. He needs those ships at home for a major assault as early as January, perhaps, against the Confederates on North Carolina's Outer Banks. Still, at the moment David Porter, Charlie Wilkes, James Porter, others are still at sea. Some, no doubt, still in search of the *Sumter*. There's a chance that they might get lucky.

Playing up the hunt for the Confederate cruiser has always been his hidden agenda in hosting these press gatherings. The story of a swashbuckling Southern renegade torching innocent American merchant ships seizes the public imagination. It distracts reporters from bigger issues at hand. Best of all, he has discovered that any mention of the *Sumter* to the press seems to salt a wound in his blackmailers. Each time that he releases information about the *Sumter*'s predations, known ports of call or the navy's attempt to catch and destroy her, he has received another threat the next day from his blackmailers.

The last one had read in part: *Don't be a fool, Mr. Secretary. Do not attempt to play games with us. We have lost all patience watching your pathetic attempt to make political profit with your pronouncements to the press about the* Sumter. *Unless you give up IMMEDIATELY your ridiculous obsession with Raphael Semmes, we shall, as we have said before, expose you to the press as a consort of a traitor and a woman of ill-repute. How* Harper's *will love this story. It should be fascinating to your wife and Mr. Lincoln as well!*

He pictures Burlow dangling buck naked from a tree, taking the cords of a cat on his back. The image makes him wince.

They are bluffing. I am worth too much to them as a puppet for them to toss me away ... at least, at the moment. But they are boiling with frustration. They will not be able to stop themselves from wanting to attack me with a quiver of threats if I stick it to Semmes one more time. And this time I'll bite back.

He clears his throat and shoots another one of his best simpleton, Father Christmas smiles at the reporters. Having been a reporter and part-owner of *The Hartford Times* and founder of *The Hartford Evening Press*, he understands this game.

"Yes. What about the *Sumter*, my good sirs? I have some news there! This very morning dispatches place the Confederate pirate in a noose surrounded by the *Powhatan*, the *San Jacinto*, the *Shepherd Knapp*, the *Keystone State* and the *Niagara*. I have it on good authority that a most-careful captain, James Palmer on the *Iroquois*, has narrowed the search to the Eastern Caribbean. Semmes cannot now escape. His callous but pathetic little reign of terror is most certainly about to come to and end ... somewhere in the vicinity of the French islands, Guadeloupe or Martinique perhaps. This is my prediction."

He sits hunched over in a stiff ladder-back chair with a .32 caliber Smith & Wesson pocket pistol in his lap. Someone gave him the gun back in '56 as a good luck gift during his unsuccessful run as a Republican for the governorship of Connecticut. He has never used the weapon, and he never got the hoped-for support of the Connecticut River Valley gun makers. He fears, hates firearms. But today the weapon's loaded. It might buy him some credence.

His face leans so close to the inside of the door for Room 8 at the Willard, that the side of his immense beard brushes the knob. His head tilts his ears to better hear any footsteps approaching on the carpet in the hall. He fixes his vision on the crack at the bottom of the door, as he has done for the better part this entire day, and squeezes his teeth together to stifle a yawn. It's already half-past two in the afternoon.

Come on you bastard, show yourself.

He has been two months setting this trap. Now it's time to spring it, time to catch the wretched blackmailer dipping his fingers in the pudding.

A rush of footsteps over carpet approaches from the far end of the hall. Faint at first, then louder. A floorboard creaks. The footsteps stop as if the walker is unsure of his progress, having second thoughts or attempting stealth.

Welles squeezes the handle of his gun, wonders what he will do when he confronts his blackmailer. He knows that as soon as he sees the first white flash of the envelope sliding toward him under the door, he will rise to his feet, fling open the door, point the pistol at the blackmailer and say, "Don't move, please." This much is clear. But after this, what? He can't exactly plan his next move. It will depend on the blackmailer. What if he has a gun? What if he runs? What if he's a colleague like Bill Seward or a powerbroker like Senator Hale? Or one of the Curmudgeons? What then?

Will he shoot? Will he threaten violence? Maybe. Will he pledge his own dirty tricks in retaliation? Certainly. But what if he holds his gun on a mere messenger? How will he get the messenger to divulge the name of those he works for? How? He isn't sure. But he hopes he knows what to do when the moment of truth comes. He's counting on his intuition for backroom political dealing to pull him through.

The steps begin again, come closer. They pause for about ten seconds. There's a slight clattering sound. A rustling. Then the steps approach the door to Room 8.

He holds his breath. Hears the rustle of clothing as if someone's stooping. The muscles in his shoulders tighten.

Then he hears the soft tinkle of silverware against porcelain. And the footsteps pad away down the hall. When he can hardly hear them, he cracks open the door softly, looks out. At the end of the corridor is a bellman with an arm-full of room-service breakfast trays he has finally gotten around to collecting from outside guests' doors.

A half hour passes without a noise, save the rattle of the pipes sending a burst of steam to the radiators to take the evening chill out of the hotel. Then, suddenly, the door across the hall creaks open then slams shut abruptly. He hears heavy breathing as someone approaches his door. He barely has time to pull his weary head out of his hands when he hears a key enter his lock ... and turns.

He jumps to his feet just as the door swings open.

An immense Negro chambermaid stands before him with an armload of towels. As she stares at the gun in his hand with wide eyes, ashen skin, he suddenly realizes that he has not put the "Do Not Disturb" placard on the outside doorknob.

"Forgive me," he stutters, lifting the towels out of her arms with both his pistol hand and free hand. "Cleaning my gun, you see. Thank you, ma'am, but I have no need of your service today."

He cradles the towels in his gun arm, fumbles in his pants pocket with his free hand until he finds a clutch of coins. Without taking time to see what he has, he presses the change into the maid's hand, bows slightly, withdraws. He closes the door with his back.

"Good God!"

37

District of Columbia
NOVEMBER 2, 1861

She approaches Room 8 from the service staircase in the Willard, dressed as always in the maid's uniform that Fiona bought for her. Her walk is swift, deliberate. In her hands she carries a feather duster and dustbin. The letter is tucked in her waistband, beneath her white apron where no one can see it.

As she always does when she sneaks with her threats toward the quarters of Secretary Welles, Maude flicks her feather duster along the top of the wainscoting as she hurries along the hallway. A charade in case someone might see her. It's four thirty in the afternoon, and she knows that the regular floor maid has finished her rounds, departed.

Once, the very thought of her deceit and treason had set her hands to sweating and her heart galloping. Just as they did before her craven interludes with Harry in the Tender Trap. Just as they did the day she had lured him to the Women Warriors' picnic grove along Rock Creek, seduced him with apple brandy, tied him to a tree, whipped him ... while Fiona took photographs with her box camera from the bushes. Now, while she dusts, she hums "Danny Boy" softly in tones that remind her of her dear mom's singing on cleaning day. In her mind she's picturing Raffy with the tropic sun on his face, the trade winds ruffling his hair.

Reaching Room 8, she grabs the note that she has penned in pale blue ink on Fiona's best vellum. Bends to slip it under the door. But even before her fingers have eased their grip on the envelope that holds the note, the door swings open. She has not even heard the crackle of the bolt.

"Please do not move!"

A huge ghostly man with a fluffy white beard is pointing a gun at her. His toupee of long, gray curls sags off his ears. He wears a morning coat, wrinkled and lint covered. As he holds her there at gunpoint, his gaping mouth closes. The look of total surprise vanishes from his face. In its place, the single arched eyebrow of recognition.

"Get in here this instant, girl! Good God, I know you. Burlow pointed you out, said you were Semmes' Irish truffle, claimed you and he had been making the beast with two backs all over the parks and … And … Lord. You're the girl in the hood … with the whip! Get into this room this very instant!" His cheeks have begun to flush.

"Bugger off, mate!"

The words are out before she can think. She throws the feather duster and the dustbin at his chest. Runs. Runs to round the nearest corner as fast as her legs will carry her.

She wonders when he will shoot.

But he screams instead.

"I know you, you scullery tart. You can't hide from me. You have no idea how fast I am going to have your frisky little fanny locked away in jail like that Greenhow woman … or stuffed in steerage on a cattle boat back to Ireland. Who in Heaven's name do you think you are … ?!"

A lassie and a selkie, a bloody tigress of the first magnitude … and a fool for love. She answers in her mind.

Then she flies down the front stairs to the lobby, disappears into the crowd of carriages and cabs on Pennsylvania Avenue.

"What do I do now?" she asks Fiona.

The dark, slender woman runs her fingers through Maude's curls, hugging her to her breast as they sit on the bed in Fiona's flat.

"Maybe it's time that you think of yourself. Maybe we should head out West, maybe even get on a ship to California."

She loves it when Fiona holds her like this. She feels like nothing can hurt her with this strong, hard woman to protect her. But she knows that even after all that she has been through, after all the ways that she has compromised herself, she cannot give herself up to Fiona in the way that her friend desires. She could kiss Fiona, kiss her like a lover. She did it that first night when she had come back to Fiona after Raffy left her. So she knows it's not the physical touching that bothers her. It's just that she absolutely knows that she cannot feel complete living solely in the company of women. Surrounded by the Women Warriors she finds her mind sometimes slipping away to Raffy. Just as it is now.

She nuzzles the ruffles on Fiona's blouse.

"I have to save him."

"I know, love ... But I wish it were not so."

"You saw the paper today. Welles says that his navy will take Raffy somewhere in the southeastern Caribbean. Around the French islands, around Martinique."

"Aye."

"What can I do?"

"You cannot go back to your flat. And you cannot stay here. Welles may already be sending bully-boys for us. You need a safe place to hide until we can get out of this town."

"No. How can I help Raffy? He needs to know what the Yanks are doing to him. He must steer clear of Martinique and the rest of those places.

"Do you really think I care, lass? Do you know what a cloud of gloom that man brings into my life? Sometimes I think he's the blackest ... "

She throws her arms around Fiona's neck, presses her face to her friend's cheek, kisses her softly beneath the ear.

"I'm so so sorry. I wish I could get him out of my mind ... but he's always there. I know it is crazy. But help me to save him. He's in grave danger. Help me for the South."

Fiona sniffs back tears, strokes her friend's curls again.

After a long time she says, "Alright, love, for the South, then. You need to write a whole pack of letters."

38

Old Bahama Channel
NOVEMBER 8, 1861

Lieutenant Donald Fairfax sees smoke on the horizon, licks his lips. He's the luff on the screw frigate USS *San Jacinto*. She swings to her light anchor in the open sea five miles off the north coast of Cuba near the Paredon Grande lighthouse.

"Today we snatch glory from the jaws of defeat." The ship's captain Charles Wilkes smiles. To get a better view of the smoke, he leads the luff to the bows of the frigate, lying head to the moderate northeast wind.

Wilkes consults his pocket watch. "Is it not as I predicted, Lieutenant Fairfax? I said we would see her at noon, and it is but twenty minutes shy that she steams right into our arms."

Wilkes' craggy frame has a stiff attentiveness as he watches the smoke through his long glass. But when he drops it from his eye, his face has the washed-out, gaunt, blurry look of a man coming off an all-night drunk, still giddy with fantasies.

Fairfax stares away toward the dark coast of Cuba, trying not to picture the life of extreme seclusion that his captain leads day-after-day behind the closed door to the great cabin. There have been rumors for years about Charlie Wilkes tippling. They say that during his sea commands, and at his naval observatory in Bethesda, Wilkes sometimes locks himself away for days with a bottle of Russian vodka and writes wild and wondrous things. Certainly the second part of the rumor's true. Wilkes' five volumes on his exploration, his discovery, of Antarctica are works of legend. His *Theory of the Winds* a must-read for deepwater men.

"Why look so glum, Fairfax? We shall write our names in the history books this day, man!"

"Yes, sir. We may well do just that."

"Then why the sour puss? Look, she races toward us like a lover. Like destiny."

"Aye."

"Well, then what can it be that drags you down? Is it all of this legal business? Do you fear that we exceed our authority here?"

Fairfax pauses, clears his throat before answering.

"Come, speak man, I do most depend on your counsel!"

"Well then, yes, sir. I have not changed my opinion since we first talked of this operation. I know you have consulted your legal texts for days, and that you think we have our rights here according to maritime law, but I feel we are on the shakiest of ground. Our standing orders were to hunt the *Sumter*. And now we are recalled to squadron, not this!"

Wilkes spits on the deck.

"Semmes be damned, man. He's a ne'er-do-well sham of a pirate who has not been worth the time and effort of this magnificent ship. Thank God, Welles has finally seen fit to recall us. We have been to West Africa and back, mucking around the Old Bahamas Channel, in search of Semmes' sorry little ship. In hurricane season, man. Hurricane season! Beat all to hell. And seen nothing of him, heard nothing of him being here in the northern Antilles since July. The man's already lost one ship. Most like he's done it again."

"I wish I could believe that."

"What do you mean?"

"When we met the *Powhatan* near the beginning of October in St. Thomas ... Commander Porter said he had been within a few days of seizing Semmes until his engines began to fail."

"Balderdash. Porter had no sight or word of Semmes for some weeks. As you well know from our own pasting, this is the season of great storms in the tropics. To stay at sea in this region for so long at this time of the year is suicide in a little Gulf packet such as Semmes' boat."

Fairfax thinks of how his own massive frigate struggled for her life just weeks ago against seas like mountains, how Wilkes is an expert on the global patterns of storms like hurricanes.

"Yes, sir."

"No one has seen the *Sumter* for about six weeks. If she has not made port in all this time to recoal, then she has buried herself at sea. She cannot still be out here. All the odds are against it. Porter knows that. That's why he has given up his search and headed home for Key West and New York. He cares nothing for the recall dispatch; he would keep hunting if he thought the fox was still loose."

Fairfax shrugs. He wishes he were convinced.

"Listen. It stands to reason that if Porter thinks there's a chance the *Sumter* is still out here, he would have refit in St. Thomas and taken up the hunt again. Jesus, never has a man been so obsessed with such a little mission. The story of Semmes' half-assed raiding will be little more than a footnote to history. Forget about Semmes. Here comes the grand prize."

Wilkes waves his glass at the ship now just hull-up to the northwest.

"We could end the war here. Mothers will name babies after us!"

Fairfax seizes his bearded chin with the palm of his hand. Rubs it feverishly.

Christ, he's off. He's gone down the river this time.

Shortly after 1300 hours, the *San Jacinto* weighs anchor and throws two shots across the bows of the British mail packet *Trent* as she steams within range. The first shot a blank, the second a live shell that splashes just a half-cable in front of the Englishman's headsails.

The *Trent* turns to windward, heaves to, awaiting the Yank boarding party. Now the stratagem that Wilkes has been hatching for more than a week begins to unfold. Stopping at Cienfuegos for coal on his way back north from St. Thomas, and still searching fruitlessly for Semmes, Wilkes learned from the U.S. consul in that port of a major new development on the diplomatic battle front. At the moment the State Department was in a furor to catch two Confederate commissioners running to Europe with dispatches proposing all kinds of cooperation between the South, Her Majesty Queen Victoria and France.

These men—former U.S. senators, their secretaries, and families— had escaped through the Federal blockade of Charleston Harbor to Nassau, then to Havana where they were awaiting passage to England aboard a mail packet of the British Royal Steamship Company. Wilkes saw that if he waited in ambush at the narrowest point of the Old Bahamas Channel, he could stop the English packet and snatch the commissioners. Under the international laws of belligerent rights, he could seize any of his enemy's "contraband of war" off a neutral vessel. Dispatches were such contraband, and so were those who carried them, Wilkes reasoned.

Fairfax argued otherwise. He said that to seize the commissioners off the *Trent* is in contradiction to U.S. interpretation of international law. It is, in fact, doing simply what the English did by impressing sailors off American merchant ships—the events that precipitated the War of 1812.

But Wilkes is sticking to his interpretation.

Now the *San Jacinto* and the *Trent* are face-to-face, the Yank with her guns run-out, loaded, manned. And in his current mood, Wilkes might do anything.

Fairfax volunteers to lead the boarding party himself. He hopes that his calm, steady presence will bring some measure of respect and rightness to the kidnapping. But no sooner has Fairfax arrived at the *Trent* by cutter, been ushered to the quarterdeck to meet Captain Moir, than he knows he's in for a fight.

"This is a neutral ship. You have no right to stop me nor to demand my passenger list. I am unarmed!" Moir is aloof and poker-faced.

"I have orders to arrest the Confederate commissioners Mason and Slidell and their secretaries."

"What will you do if I refuse to give them up?"

"I have orders to take the ship if necessary." He nods toward the cutter and the detail of armed marines waiting there.

A crowd of officers and passengers begin to press around him, shouting.

"This is an act of piracy!"

"Go back to that bastard Lincoln!"

"You fucking cove!"

"Enough of that!" Moir to the crowd. "Take this man below." He points to the man who had cursed Fairfax.

The crowd protests. Calls of "Yankees, go home" ring out across the main deck.

Suddenly, American marines scramble out of their launch and rush with fixed bayonets toward the crowd surrounding Fairfax.

Women and children scatter. Moir rises up on his heels.

"This is outrageous, sir."

"I must have those men."

"Never," says a waxy old gentleman. His white hair falls over his ears in the style of an actor playing King Lear at Ford's in the District. "We are under the protection of the British flag, and we will not leave this ship except by force of arms!"

Fairfax recognizes the man as Slidell, looks around and sees Mason and the secretaries too.

"Then I'll take you by force. Make your farewells with your families, sirs."

Slidell's jaw drops.

"You should be ashamed of yourself," says his teenage daughter.

The ship rolls, throws her against Fairfax. Both of them almost fall.

"Hit him again, child!" Someone from the crowd has misinterpreted what had just happened.

Good Lord, deliver me from this.

He moves the girl, and puts a hand on Mason's shoulder, "Come with me, sir!"

"I yield by force." The long-haired Mason is making sure his witnesses get it right.

Slidell spouts something similar as two other American officers take him by the arms.

"You damned Yankees!" A woman passenger makes like she's going to hit Fairfax with her knitting bag.

A man of the cloth shakes a Bible. "May you rot in Hell!"

"Arm us, Moir! Give us guns!" Someone in the crowd.

"Throw the pirates overboard!"

The English captain glares at Fairfax. "Do you see what you've done?"

He opens his mouth to beg patience, but the English captain turns, walks aft out of the fray.

Fairfax feels someone grab his elbow even as he stands amid the crowd holding Mason by the shoulder. It's the *San Jacinto*'s marine sergeant.

"Come on, sir. Let's get out of here."

"Do you have the dispatches?"

"What dispatches?"

"The Rebs'. They're what we came for."

The crowd presses closer. Someone spits at him. Women are still shrieking. A baby bawls.

"Let's take 'em!" A voice roars from the crowd.

He looks at the red-eyed anger surrounding him, knows he will have to break through that horde to search the staterooms. Probably never find what he's looking for, blasted things are likely tucked under some woman's petite coat. And he isn't looking there. Good God, in how many ways could taking these hostages from the *Trent* offend the English Queen? She might well just take up arms with the Rebs.

39

St. Thomas, Danish Virgin Islands
EARLY NOVEMBER, 1861

After almost two hours of plodding upward over tracks of dirt and crushed coral, the surrey creaks to a stop.

"This is it?"

James Palmer arches his back to stretch the kinks out of his shoulders, eases himself out of the surrey. The mid-morning sun almost blinds him. He shades his brow with a hand to the forehead even though he wears his black-billed service cap. Here on the high spine of St. Thomas, he guesses he's a thousand feet above the fuming port of Charlotte Amalie lying to the south and the pale blue paradise of Magen's Bay stretching out to the north. The trade winds whir over these heights, cooling him instantly, nearly carrying away his cap until he tucks it under his arm. His sandy hair flutters. He carries a worn red book in one hand.

"Dis dat Drake's Seat sure, Captain!"

A smile breaks over his thin, clean-shaven face. He knows that no matter how long he sails the West Indies, he will never cease to delight in the melodies, rhythms and variations in the island Creole of these one-time slaves.

"I've heard that the great Drake came here almost three hundred years ago to watch for Spanish treasure ships and plot the passage of his own fleet among the islands to the east."

"So dey say. A mon he might do a whole world of lookin' and tinkin' up here."

Palmer cocks his head, listens to the wind, looks east at the purple humps of St. John, Jost Van Dyke, Tortola arched above the sea like a pod of immense whales, dividing the waters—Caribbean to the south,

Atlantic to the north. Then he hands the surrey driver three of the island's Danish coins.

"Would you be so kind to come back for me in an hour?"

The black man is on the verge of speaking, seems about to say he has nothing better to do than wait up here among the clouds and look down on God's own world like the Creator himself. But he must sense that the American captain wants to be alone. He nods, taps his horse with the buggy whip, starts away to the west along the ridge track.

For several minutes Palmer paces back and forth, watches a pair of humming birds flicking among the bougainvillea. Then he follows a short path to a nest of large rocks and takes a seat on one. He closes his eyes, takes a deep breath, opens his volume of Captain Johnson to the chapters on Calico Jack Rackham, Mary Read, Anne Bonney. He loves reading about this unholy trio. Feeling this book in his hands reminds him of the spritely Cuban who tendered it as a *regalito* back in Santiago. He pictures Fernando Mozo, wishes he were here to enjoy the magnificent prospect of the view ... and give counsel.

"I'm alone, Fernando."

A mongoose flushes from a bush at the sound of his voice.

Wilkes and Porter have abandoned the chase. Welles wants me to come home. Now what do I do?

Arriving at St. Thomas yesterday in the *Iroquois* to recoal, he harbored hopes that he might rendezvous here with his comrades-in-arms, that together they might form a dragnet and test Welles' hunch that Semmes would eventually head for the islands of the French West Indies.

But he was met by yet another officious consul with a secret dispatch from Welles calling him—along with the *Powhatan, San Jacinto, Niagara, Minnesota* and *Shepherd Knapp*—back home to their squadrons.

"Something big is brewing at home, you can be certain. Welles needs every ship," the consul said. "He needs a victory."

The Rebs are gaining momentum on the water. There's news that they recently used a ram called the *Manassas*, clad in iron and shaped like a floating cigar, in foiling a Yankee plan to build a fort to control the Head of the Passes on the Mississippi. Porter and Wilkes were both in St. Thomas during the second week in October to get their change of orders. They had recoaled, given their crews a little liberty, then started north.

"I wouldn't say they were exactly disappointed to be heading home," the consul said to Palmer. "Wilkes, in particular, seemed completely sick of chasing this pirate Semmes. Porter ... Porter seemed distracted. Came to dinner at the consulate and hardly talked. He was keeping something very close to his chest, let that damn Wilkes ramble on about all his achievements. Insufferable man."

The news of being recalled felt like something crushing in on his lungs yesterday, and now, sitting up here at Drake's Seat, he feels his chest tighten again.

So I am to go home as Porter and Wilkes have done, call off the chase, forget that just two months ago Welles had said we must catch and destroy the Sumter *at all cost. What has changed? I am so close. I can almost smell the* Sumter's *smoke. If I quit now, the last two months have been for nothing, my life has meant nothing. The pirate has won.*

Palmer rises from his seat amid the nest of boulders, kicks at the dirt until he dislodges a rock. Then he bends, picks it up and flings it way out over the steep, green slopes falling away below the ridge to the north.

"Damn it. Damn it!"

He's not a man who ever minded spending massive amounts of time to accomplish his goals. He knows he's not gifted with flashes of brilliance like Wilkes or the ambition and hunter's intuition of Porter. But he learned early that persistence and attention to detail can carry a man a long way. He believes that victory almost always falls to the tortoise, not the hare. So now, being recalled, being cut short in the race when he thinks the finish line might well be right over the horizon, tears at his guts.

He pictures the charts of the Caribbean he has spread all over his desk in the *Iroquois'* great cabin. He thinks about all the reading he has done in his pirate book. He remembers the list of pirates' haunts he has made stretching from the Isle of Pines and Tortuga Island to the north all the way to Bahía Mochimo in Venezuela to the south.

One by one he has been checking off these places. He has met the great grandchildren of the old-time pirates at Tortuga, Bahía de la Semana, Culebra, Vieques, Anagada. Seen in their lives the common stamp of buccaneering. More than the approval of their fellow humans, the love of family or even the judgment of God, what has shaped the lives of these freebooters is an abiding impulse to be free. In particular, they enjoy freedom from the tyranny of governments in all its shapes and forms. It's not his own essential conviction. But he can understand it, especially at moments like this when a man's government seems to jerk him around like a rag doll, snatch him out of the race just when he has made it his own. Win or lose, hunting the *Sumter* is what defines him now, maybe forever.

At each backwater placed he has asked after the *Sumter*. And if he didn't actually visit one of these haunts, he has spoken to ships that have come recently from those places. Now he knows that no port in all of the Caribbean—large or small—north of Dominica has seen or heard of the *Sumter* in months. Tracking Semmes this way is tedious, slow, but little by little he is reducing his field of search. He sees himself and Semmes both running out of options.

In his mind, it's a near certainty that if he keeps hunting the Reb in this fashion, he and Semmes will eventually find themselves face-to-face. Then it will be simply a contest of wit, will and guns. He has the advantage in guns. He and the pirate may well be evenly matched in will. And wit? That remains to be seen.

So why should I go home? He tosses another rock. *How much time might I steal from Gideon Welles to continue my search? Surely, it will take the navy some weeks, if not a month to learn that I have received the recall dispatch. I am so close ... I could just pretend that I misunderstood the dispatch and ...*

He has never ignored an order before. Not in his whole career. This is a monumental choice.

"Forget about Semmes," the consul said yesterday. "He has no doubt gone so far up some wretched river in Brazil to hide, or made a party with the natives, that he is not even in our war anymore."

That would be just like a pirate, wouldn't it? Why not let be? Why not just go home to hearth and kin? At least go back to the squadron for a new assignment, one that fits his training better, like convoy protection for some grand assault on the Rebel coast.

A tempting prospect. The *Iroquois* will be fully coaled, watered, provisioned in two days or so. She could report back at the squadron in Key West within a week. Would be at the dock in Brooklyn or Boston a fortnight after that for a thorough refit. And he would be at liberty, free.

That word again. Nothing can match its seductiveness. It is what keeps Semmes going past all resources, past all reason. He is free, and he sees himself as a sacred knight of freedom for his beloved Southern States. He knows that as long as he keeps himself at sea, no government, no enemy, not even family or love can hold him back.

The consul is wrong. If there is one thing that Johnson teaches in his volume about pirates, it is that the land never serves them for long. They are creatures of the waves. Freedom is their drug, and the only place the pirate can really find it is at sea. Semmes will not hide long in some river. He will stay at sea, raiding as he can. Raiding with the full knowledge that his enemy always labors at a great disadvantage. He labors in the shackles of the Navy Department, Gideon Welles, Abraham Lincoln, the tax payers. He does not have the lure of freedom to keep his men going when resources, personal comfort and the recognition of other men is in short supply.

"I am beaten."

He feels his skin boiling, tears at his jacket buttons, grabs a sleeve, rips the coat off his body as if intending to fling his stripes and campaign ribbons to oblivion. He raises his arms until the whirring trade winds lift them, almost like wings. The cool wind tickles his ears, the skin on the back of his neck.

He kicks the soft, dry ground. A deep furrowing gouge that buries his black service shoe for a second. When the shoe resurfaces, it's scarred with cuts and scratches that no amount of polish will ever make pass muster.

"I must be crazy as a loon."

His eyes wander to the small mound of earth that he has kicked free of this mountain top. Amid the dark soil, sun-dried grass and roots, he sees something shiny, like a diamond, catching the sun. It seems to be moving in tiny little bursts. He bends, scoops it up. Takes the small, shiny thing in his hand. Can't believe what he's seeing. A sea shell, a spiral snail's shell. Something tickles the skin in the palm of his hand.

He jumps. Then he realizes what he holds. A hermit crab. There's a hermit crab living in a seashell on top of a mountain.

My God, how did the crab and the shell get to the top of this mountain?
He shakes his head in bewilderment, laughs.

The hermit crab scuttles toward the edge of his hand, pauses for just a second at the prospect of the free fall that lies just a step away, then launches itself into thin air.

He knows not what will come, and yet he leaps. Just because there is a rightness in it, because it is his nature.

He pauses, looks around him as if in a strange place he's seeing for the first time. "And so it is my nature, too. Though I have not known it until now." *What if I too am free, Raphael Semmes? What if I too am a pirate of liberty? What then, my enemy?*

40

Martinique
NOVEMBER 9, 1861

This French governor seems a bit snarky, sir. Some sort of admiral in their navy. Old boy would give me neither smile when I presented our credentials and request for safe harbor, coal and provisions. Said he was holding a dispatch for you, personal-like. 'Quite an original,' he called it. Requested you visit him in person to retrieve it."

The captain of the *Sumter* takes a deep breath, gives a sideways glance out the stern windows of his great cabin. A clutch of fishing smacks bob alongside the market quay at Fort-de-France.

"Here we go again, eh, Mr. Evans? Fifty-odd days at sea almost makes a man forget the petty pomp and ceremony by which the shoreman measures his life."

"It is a different world, sir. Especially this here French colonial one on Martinique. All croissants, baguettes, concertina music and that little Napoleon parading around in his chevron, on one hand. All hordes of free blacks milling about everywhere with nothing to do, on the other. Lovely green mountains and a lot of pretty flowers, though."

Semmes twists the ends of his mustache with both hands.

"I guess it's time for the Captain Cornpone show."

Evans squints, shakes his head in confusion.

"Sorry, sir?"

"Never mind." He waves Evans off, talks to himself in low tones. "A dispatch? For me? Personal-like ... ?"

The lieutenant turns to take his leave, is just two steps from the door when Semmes breaks out of his fog. Calls.

"Send me the steward, sir. Ask him if he can come up with a pressed set of my dress blues ... and a polished hanger. I am ashore to see ... "

He reads the name on the card of introduction that the governor has sent back with Evans. "His Excellency M. Maussion de Condé." *And to find out what the Sam Hill is going on.*

A thick manila envelope in a leather pouch—like the ones the old navy sent out as dispatches to its captains—this is not. It's a letter, a light blue envelope, like eighteen others that Maude has sent him. She has charmed her admirers, Riddley-Oak and de Saunier, into whisking the letters off in diplomatic pouches to the port captains on all their islands in the Caribbean.

Each addressed in smooth, looping script to:
Commander Raphael Semmes, Captain
Confederate States of America
Steamship Sumter
URGENT!!!

The envelope reeks of perfume. Lavender. Her lavender. As soon as he catches his first scent of her, his heart begins to breathe. He sees her curls, the light freckles on her pale shoulders. Can almost taste her sweet breath.

"You blush, Captain." The governor stands at the sideboard in his office at Fort Saint-Louis. He has a broad grin on his face.

Semmes knows the bastard's enjoying this moment.

"I don't know what to ... "

"It is not necessary, my good sir. You are a Frenchman. Semmes is a French name, from Normandie, *n'est-çe pas?* One Frenchman understands another. And we are both men of the sea, *oui?*"

The governor, still smiling, raises a glass of pale Sauvignon in toast.

"You must forgive—"

"No apologies from the world's most famous corsair. I am delighted to have been the custodian of your correspondence. A toast, sir. To wives and lovers."

Semmes raises his glass of wine. Sees the smile on the governor's face, knows what's coming next, the old sailor's refrain.

"May they never meet," say both men in unison. Then they clink their glasses, drain them dry.

Adjacent to Fort Saint-Louis stands a large park called La Savane. All green lawns, benches, tall shade trees, stands of bamboo. A place for evening concerts, idlers, lovers. The citizens of Martinique have erected a statue of their most-famous daughter, Josephine Tascher de la Pagerie—mistress, wife, and scorned lover of the Emperor Napoleon.

Semmes retreats into La Savane to read his letter. Gives a little laugh, thinks it most ironic that of all places in the world to read his first letter from home—his first letter from his mistress—it is here. He stands almost in the shadow of the stone empress who's holding a locket with the image of her long-lost love.

2nd of November, 1861

> *My Dearest, Sweetest, Heroic Captain,*
> *MY RAFFY! My heart and my soul. I pray that this letter finds you quickly ... and in good health and spirits. And I pray that you trust me in what I am about to tell you even though it may sound fantastic. Please!!! You must not question how I know these things. But they are as true as the pledge I made to you on that St. Valentines' Day that now seems so long ago. As true as my love for you, the love that informs everything I do these days, my sweet. Trust me without question.*
> *If you are in possession of this letter, you are in grave danger!!!*

*Washington has become an insane place since you left. It is
full of spies, dark threats, betrayals, drunkards, perversions of
every sort. Legions of Northern soldiers. The men presiding over
this cesspool govern by assuring the people that they are protecting us from monsters. And with the help of the journalists, the
potentates have made you a most celebrated villain. They have
called you a pirate who will stop at nothing to feed his appetite
for wanton destruction of innocents.*

*Now the Secretary of the Navy Welles is boasting that a half-
dozen of his ships are closing in on you. In particular, he has said
that a captain, James Palmer on the Iroquois, has narrowed the
search to the Eastern Caribbean. That the navy now believes
they will find you in the vicinity of the French islands.*

He feels a lightning bolt shoot from the tips of his mustache to the
tips of his toes.

*At all costs, my love, you must keep clear of those French
places. This Palmer is sure to be looking for you there. Hide.
Cross the ocean. Flee for your life, your future. For me.*

Then she tells him, in words he will never confess even to his God,
how she loves him. She writes of Heaven and Hell, all their raptures
and tortures. The letter is so full of wild longing and devotion that he
leans his back against a ceiba tree and squeezes his eyes shut.

Suddenly he can no longer stop the tears. He weeps silently out
of great guilt. Knows that he has abandoned the very best thing in
his life for a scrap of glory. Knows without her telling him that her
information about the Yankees who pursue him comes at the cost of
pandering her body and her mortal soul to the enemy. Knows that she,
too, is now in great danger.

The hand holding the letter falls to his side. As he leans against the tree, he looks and feels every bit as much a stone statue as the Empress Josephine.

At last his eyes open, shift to see his ship swinging to her anchor off Fort Saint-Louis. The harsh light of midday makes him blink. In all his dreams he never imagined that news of his executioners would come to him like this. In a letter from his impossible love.

"My Irish angel," he says aloud. *What have I done to deserve you?*

He turns his gaze away from the bright sea, stares into the darkness of the shade trees overhead. Then he lifts the letter to his nose, smells the lavender, tries to picture her. Once again he sees the copper curls, the light freckles on the shoulders. He sees her green eyes, full pink lips, even the tiny dark cave in her belly. But as hard as he tries, he cannot see her whole, cannot conjure a full-blown image of his Maude among the trees. He cannot remember the notes of her laughter, whether they rise or fall. Once, for a second, he thinks he can hear the music of her soft, slow breathing. But then it's gone.

I'm losing her. Bit by bit. Just as I lost Anne during the Mexican War, never found her again even when I finally came home. Only a bastard daughter, another man's child. Only Anna ... Most gracious and merciful God, show me what must be done for my love, my family, my country and my ship.

No divine sign comes to him out of the trees. No disembodied face of his lover floats among the leaves, no storm-petrel circles down from the skies. He's alone. His heart and soul feel dead.

A little grunt escapes his throat. He suddenly understands something that should have been clear to him the day he sailed free of the Mississippi Delta.

All I have left are my ship, my men, my wits ... and my balls. Sweet Jesus.

41

District of Columbia
NOVEMBER 10, 1861

If you're looking to give me a little personal work, it is my sad duty to tell you that I no longer have private clients, Mr. Secretary. The government, it seems, has appropriated all of my time ... and that of my associates."

Welles tries not to scowl at this news. He surveys the short, slit-eyed man in the tight, brown suit who stands before him on the stairs, shrugging. Heavy Scottish brows obscure cold, blue irises. The short-cropped, black hair and beard put Welles in mind of a muskrat trapper he knew on the Connecticut River.

"No such thing, sir."

"Then I am mistaken. Forgive me. But my antennae naturally go up when a fella requests a meeting such as this at an evening lecture. Especially when the lecture is on the somewhat obscure topic of building a national network of observers to forecast changes in the weather. Especially when the point of rendezvous is a particular darkened stairwell off a cloister in the Smithsonian Castle, eh?"

The little man's words bear the lilt of his Glasgow roots.

"Then what will you be needing, sir? I am most afraid I have certain promises to keep. And I am never late."

He feels as if his tongue is swelling in his mouth. This mangy, little Allan Pinkerton has set him off balance.

"It is just ... just one small thing that ... "

The detective raises his right hand, waves it as a signal to stop, turns away to head back down the stairs toward the lecture hall.

"Wait! Please, sir. This is a matter of national security."

The detective spins on his heels, mounts several steps until he's eye to eye with the taller Welles.

"Why didn't you say so? I don't get on well with those who talk around the issue, Mr. Secretary. Just don't. Makes me all itchy inside. It's the Scotland in me, see. Plain speaking. That's the best way. No misunderstandings." The detective looks at his watch. "Speak, man. My promises will not wait."

Welles has a mind to throttle this impudent bulldog, but George McClellan says Pinkerton's the best. Already a legendary figure in Washington. The man who saved Lincoln from an assassination plot when his victory train passed through Baltimore on the way to the presidential inauguration back in April. He disguised the president as the invalid brother of one of his female operatives and slipped Lincoln through the menacing mobs unrecognized. Now Welles needs a man with such pluck. He will humble himself ... speak plain as he can.

"Well then, to come to the point, I am being blackmailed, Mr. Pinkerton."

"I'm Allen, these days, sir, Major E.J. Allen."

"Of course, Major. You are in the employment of the War Department now, I gather. And you have nailed down the case against those Southern spies, Captain Elwood and Rose Greenhow. Imagine! They intended to pass off diagrams of the District's fortifications, with lists of armaments, to the Rebs. What audacity!"

"Sesech trash of the worst kind! Got Elwood wishing he were never born at this very moment in the Old Capitol Prison. I think the lovely Mrs. Greenhow shan't be far behind him, eh?"

Pinkerton—Allen—growls a little. He speaks as if the very thought of the Reb spies stirs something foul in his belly.

"But come. How is this blackmail an issue for national security?"

"If I told you, I would have to have you killed." Welles cannot believe he had just said this. So dramatic. Such a cliché. But this Pinkerton, or Allen, or whoever he's decided to be today just gets under his skin.

"Go to hell, Mr. Secretary. Life's too short for your palaver. Good night, sir!"

Welles picture Semmes' and Burlow's tart, suddenly imagines her surrounded by shadowy figures.

"Stop, man. Shall I tell the President that you knew there were rats in the pantry and did nothing about it? Is that what you want?"

The detective pulls up with a jerk, just two steps from the bottom of the staircase and escape. "Never ... never challenge my loyalty!"

"Then you must catch me a rat, Mr. Allen."

"Just one?"

He thinks of his enemies like Seward, Hale, the Curmudgeons. Tries to banish the thought that he's up against a cabal of evil ... but can't.

"She'll do for starters, sir."

The detective's eyelids lift a bit. "Why did I know that it was a woman?"

"Yours is not to reason why, sir. Will you find her ... or ..."

"Give me the name."

He suddenly realizes he does not know it, feels stupid. But then has an idea.

"Get it from the Greenhow woman. Seek out the blackmailing moll of Raphael Semmes, find out who she's working for. Bring her to me!"

When he's alone again, he permits a little smile to escape his lips. It's been a bit of a satisfactory day. The first news from the Port Royal Expedition arrived this morning. On November 7 Samuel Francis Du Pont led the largest fleet of U.S. warships ever assembled against the Confederate forts guarding the entrance to Port Royal Sound north of Hilton Head island, South Carolina. Seventeen warships, sixty support ships and over twelve thousand troops have executed a brilliant coordinated attack, seized Fort Walker on Hilton Head and driven off four Confederate warships, losing only eight Union sailors and marines. Now the Yanks are on their way to capture the port of Beaufort. Du Pont has driven a bloody stake right into the heart of the South. What a desperately needed victory.

And this Scott terrier Pinkerton, who calls himself Allen now, is off to put the bite on a cunning Irish tart. With a little luck Welles might have all this blackmail business cleared up before Mary Jane and the children move to Washington later in the month.

God has finally heard his prayers. Now he can return to the lecture hall and actually listen carefully to this idea about building a national network of observers to forecast changes in the weather. Such a weather service might have huge implications for the navy ... if it could be organized soon enough to help quash the current national emergency. If the Washington cabal of evil does not try to sabotage it, the way they're trying to quash the hunt for Raphael Semmes.

42

St. Pierre, Martinique
NOVEMBER 14-15, 1861

Semmes paces slowly back and forth across his quarterdeck, watching an interminable parade of black women shuffling aboard—with their fruits, their trinkets, their pussy—when he hears the shout from aloft.

"Steamer ho! Round the north point of the island, sir."

The women freeze momentarily. The baskets of coal they carry on their heads wobble. A fat Frenchman curses at them. They continue filing across the deck toward the coal chutes to dump their loads into the nearly empty bunkers.

The silhouette of a barkentine-rigged ship, cruising under steam alone, is still five miles away, slinking south. It looks black and hazy through the hot mist of the showers that have been blowing over Martinique from the northeast all day. She flies a Danish flag. Her yards have been disarranged to make her look like a short-handed merchantman. Her gun ports closed and painted white to blend in with the cove stripe. But he sees immediately that she has the sweet lines of a new Federal screw sloop of war. The *Iroquois*, he's certain. He saw her at the Brooklyn Navy Yard during the rigging out shortly after her launch in '59.

"She comes for me. God Almighty, she comes for me!" he says under his breath ... and wonders how it is that death sometimes stalks the living in such beguiling shapes.

He's not surprised to see *Iroquois*. He's had Maude's warning. And just this morning a pilot came aboard with a rumor of a strange warship having been sighted at the south end of the island off Diamond Rock. But what good are such warnings? There's nothing he can do to escape, even if he wishes it. The *Sumter* needs a rest to recover from almost two months at sea. Freeman has both pistons and half the valves on the ship torn apart, trying to truly cleanse his Merrick's innards of corrosion and scaling from their salt water feast while pursuing the *Daniel Trowbridge*. The carpenters still struggling with the leaks in the hull.

And even if the hull and engine were ready, it would be foolhardy to put to sea without replenishing his nearly empty coal bunkers. He has spent the last four days badgering the French governor to let him buy fuel. Only yesterday he was refused coal—again—from the government stocks at Fort-de-France, told that if he desires coal, he must purchase it commercially at the north end of the island from a merchant at Saint Pierre.

So he has come to Saint Pierre, the capital and main settlement on Martinique, to take on over sixty tons of English anthracite. In fifty pound baskets. One at a time. Now it's five bells into the noon watch. The *Sumter* is moored just off the quay, not yet full of coal ... her machinery in pieces. A sitting duck for her enemy.

"Look how she meanders. I don't think she sees us." Kell's at his skipper's side near the taffrail with his long glass trained on the *Iroquois*. "She cannot see our black hull against the shadows of the mountains here."

"Would that it could remain forever so ... " Semmes feels his back tighten and a pain shoot down into his thigh. "Pass the word, quietly, Mr. Kell. No fife and drum. The enemy has shown himself at last. Clear for action. Crew to quarters, except those involved with the coaling. Keep on coaling ... by all means."

He sees it all through his long glass. It's as if a demon has suddenly taken possession of the *Iroquois*. One second she's steaming lazily along the coast some two miles distant, the next her quarterdeck's crowded with officers in white, pointing at the *Sumter* and shouting. The decks and rigging begin to swarm with men. The funnel belches a fat black cloud. The warship takes a bone in her teeth, veers southeast toward the quay at Saint Pierre. Gun ports flop open.

"Arm the men, Kell. The shark has caught our scent!"

He goes below to find and load his favorite Colt revolver. When he opens the cabin door, something grazes his head as it flies by him. Turning back toward the companionway, he sees the shape of the little Ulysses winging toward the sun.

"Fair winds, friend!" He watches the storm-petrel flittering away high in the air. Becoming a mere dot, nothing. Wonders if there will be more desertions before James Palmer calls him to battle.

When he comes back on deck with his loaded pistol tucked under his belt, he sees that the *Iroquois* has closed to within a mile, slowed. The Danish flag comes down. Up goes the Stars and Stripes. Her crew runs out the guns. Meanwhile a crowd of citizens, both white and black, have begun to gather along the shore of Saint Pierre to see what will happen next. Some islanders have begun swimming out alongside the *Sumter*, alternately shouting encouragement to the crew to whip *les barbares du nord* ... or flee for their lives.

He tries to focus on his enemy, tries to gather himself and think what he must do now—whether to rally the warrior ... or consult the lawyer in his soul. The air fills with the clamor of shouts from the shore, the water, the deck. He feels surrounded, can't even get a clear view of the *Iroquois* through the pack of officers around him.

A red-faced middie starts up the ratlines with a musket.

"I'm going to bag me a pack of Yanks."

Pains shoot up Semmes' back, blood buzzes in his ears. He can see nothing but the black shape of the boy in the rigging, smell nothing but the sour scent of panic in the men around him. One shot from the *Sumter*, just one, that's what Palmer wants. That's all it will take to give the Yank the right to defend himself. The right to bring a full broadside of thirty-two pounders and eleven-inch smooth bores to bear on the little Southern cruiser. It will be a slaughter. It will be within Palmer's legal right. And it will mean that the French emperor will never again welcome a ship of the Confederacy to one of his ports.

The *Iroquois* comes on, the beating of her pistons and the deep-throated snorting of her funnel growing louder with every second. Two hundred yards and closing. Nearly within musket range. A clutch of marine sharp shooters stand, bracing rifles across their chests on the foretop.

He sees the boy in the rigging stop his climb short of the hounds and start to raise his gun to his shoulder.

Suddenly, everything's still. He's back aboard a Hudson River side-wheeler watching a lumpy-looking purser in a powder-blue uniform lighting a firecracker to murder another bird. Then his hand's on his gun, drawing it swiftly, cocking it as he raises it over his head, takes a bead on the boy.

"Drop that gun! And get the Sam Hill out of that rigging, boy! Or I'll have your life before the Yanks can take it from you. I will not provoke a brawl, hear? Drop it! Now!"

An ashen, stricken look comes over the boy's face, as if waking out of a nightmare in the middle of church. Then he drops the musket, and jumps.

A gunner's mate catches the weapon. The boy seizes a backstay, slides to the deck. He has tears spilling over his cheeks when he crashes to a stop. His legs buckle under him, and he falls to his knees.

"Forgive me, Captain!"

Semmes pictures his son Ollie, the rosy cheeks, thick chest, fresh face eager for approval. He uncocks his pistol, tucks it back in his belt. Strides to the boy. Takes a deep breath.

"No harm done, son. See yourself to my cabin. We'll talk."

The captain's back stiffens. His chest swells as he takes command with the voice of a stump preacher.

"All hands as you were. Continue coaling. If the Yank wants a fight, he must start it. We shall give him no cause. Not here. Not now. Or I'll put a bullet in the first man who tries. By God Almighty, I will!"

"Look to the Yank." A voice from the foredeck.

All heads turn seaward ... in time to watch her sheer off to the south. She's just one hundred yards away. Palmer stands his quarterdeck in dress whites, snaps a salute at his former comrade-in-arms as the *Iroquois* veers seaward.

Semmes turns his back, stares at the green mountains of Martinique.

Three bells into the midwatch, a bright moonlit night. He's lying in his berth in sweat-soaked sheets and long-johns, twirling the tips of his mustache, missing the bird Ulysses. Wondering if he has done the right thing by not publicly punishing the gun-happy midshipman, when Evans beats on the door.

"*Iroquois* is coming again, sir."

He throws off his top sheet with a tremendous backhand flourish, swings his feet to the floor.

"Crew to quarters, man. Clear for action. Quiet as you can. Personal weapons ready. Both batteries run out. Swivel gun aimed and loaded. Don't give us away. I'm coming."

He rubs his eyes with his fingers. Finds his trousers, shirt, shoes, service coat in the moonlight shining through the stern windows. *To hell with a cravat.* Dresses in seconds, grabs his Colt .44, heads on deck. Climbing the companionway ladder, he feels something scratching his feet, realizes he has forgotten his socks. *Well, fuck it.*

The broad Bay of Saint Pierre is a pool of silver with the bright moon lighting it from high up in the western sky. As the *Iroquois* approaches, he thinks she looks like a great sea-monster crawling toward him under cover of night, eyeing his ship, licking its chops in anticipation of a feast.

"I've never seen the men so primed," says Kell.

Semmes sees his gunners in the dark head scarves. Waisters poised at the rail with muskets and sharp, little Roman swords. Most men bare-chested. Some have already found a few minutes during the late afternoon and evening to shave their heads for battle.

"It's the breathing time of day for me. Let the foils be brought ... " Semmes quotes Shakespeare.

"Aye, sir."

The men give a nervous chuckle at their exchange. If ever there were a time to buck themselves up with words from *Hamlet*, it's now.

Every face on the *Sumter* watches the monster puffing straight toward them. It's now just two cables off the starboard waist. Closing. Slowly, steadily, silently ... aiming straight at the cruiser's engine spaces as if she intends to ram and board her. Lights are going on in the French forts ashore. No doubt they have men at their guns, too. But who will they serve?

"He violates the sovereignty of France and the laws of neutrality even now, sir, with such a show of belligerence. Perhaps the French will fire on him."

"Would that it were so. This governor is too timid by half to join the fray unless the brawl is altogether begun. Palmer spits in his face, as he spits in ours. Because he knows he can." His whisper has a cold metallic ring to it.

"Bastard."

"The Yanks always feel like they get to make the rules. I know this game. God will judge him for this insolence. Palmer aims to make us panic and defend ourselves. But he does not have the balls to actually attack."

Kell stares wide-eyed at the *Iroquois*, now just a cable off, still on a collision course for the *Sumter*'s waist. She looks big enough to steam through the cruiser and keep right on going.

"Come on, man. Sheer off!"

Semmes feels his mouth go dry. *My God, Palmer's running out of space to turn away even if he wants to.*

The flats of each hand fly to the sides of his mouth, brush back the wings of his mustache. He wonders how he and his crew will show themselves in a fight. He has stood up to the whiz of bullets, the slash of sabers, the blinding explosions of shells, the utter chaos of battle well enough when he went soldiering in the Mexican War after the loss of the *Somers*. But that was some fifteen years ago. How will he face the near-certain destruction of his ship under the pounding of a ship twice her size? The splintering wood, the screams, the spattering of blood? And if the enemy comes aboard, how will his boys repel a crew of Yanks who outnumber them two to one? They aren't from the South. They're mercenaries. Why should they fight? What would light their fires?

Semmes leaps to the starboard horseblock.

"Look to your pikes, men. Repel boarders. And show them what a man might do to protect his home and brothers!"

"Give 'em hell, Old Beeswax!" somebody shouts.

The *Iroquois* looms so close she's all but blocking out the moon. Gunners bend toward their cannons, lanyards in hand, ready to fire when ordered. Men grab for any handy piece of rigging to brace themselves for the shock of collision.

For a second or two it seems everyone and everything in the Bay of Saint Pierre holds its breath—even the fuming engine in the belly of the Federal battle ship.

Then, the ringing of an engine-room telegraph bell shatters the silence. There's the muffled clanking of machinery. The thunder of the *Iroquois*' thrashing screw as it beats full astern. The ship begins to skid sideways ... until she slips off the *Sumter*'s starboard quarter. And stops. By Semmes' estimates, the rails of the two enemy ships are only twenty feet apart.

For several minutes the officers and men of both ships face off in the dark across the narrow void, totally silent. Weapons in hand. Nobody blinks.

Finally, the Iroquois' engine-room telegraph clangs again. The enemy moves off from whence she came, cutting a graceful curve with her wake on the silver water.

Lieutenant Chapman arches his eyebrow at Pills Galt. "Wasn't that fun?"

The *Iroquois* makes two more false charges before sunrise then retreats further out into the harbor. In short order, Semmes gives his men permission to stand down and get some rest.

Some hours later a French steamer of war arrives at Saint Pierre from Fort-de-France. That afternoon the French captain joins Semmes aboard the *Sumter*, and Semmes learns that the Frenchman has delivered orders to Palmer to immediately cease and desist from his menacing behavior in French territorial waters, under threat of being fired upon by French batteries ashore and afloat. Palmer has also been warned that if he chooses to anchor in French waters, he will be required, by the statutes of international law, to delay any departure from the port for twenty-four hours after his enemy has departed. If he chooses not to anchor, he needs to take his ship into international waters beyond three miles, a marine league, of the shore. Within minutes, the *Iroquois* steams out to sea.

"I do not think this is over," says the French captain.

"Why?" Semmes hands Captain Duchatel a glass of champagne in the cruiser's great cabin.

"Your enemy has petitioned the governor through his consul here for permission to, as he says, 'liberate Martinique from the scourge of a villainous pirate.'"

43

District of Columbia
NOVEMBER 15, 1861

It seems a good place to hide. Mary Ann Hall's bawdy house on the southwest side of Capitol Hill. According to the army's provost marshal there are now over four hundred houses of prostitution in this city of sixty-one thousand, more appearing every week. By some estimates the District has almost as many whores as soldiers. A whole neighborhood of bordellos, called Murder Bay, infests the city blocks east of the executive mansion, just to the north of the encampments on the Mall.

But Hall's establishment is no wham-bam-thankee-mam kind of place. It's three stories tall, features an ornate parlor for socializing, a piano player, maid service, chilled champagne. And a chef serving up ribs, caviar, blue crabs, Maryland terrapin. Hall's place looks more like a small hotel or hospital than a house of love. It has stood in an area known as Reservation C at 349 Maryland Avenue since 1840 when Mary Ann came to town as a twenty-year-old to seek her fortune. Her clientele are senators, congressmen, lobbyists. And with eighteen young lovelies living and entertaining on the premises, hiding Maude amid the daily fandango is no problem all. Especially when it's helping Hall's old friends Rose Greenhow, Betty Duval and Augusta Morris. Especially when it helps the Southern cause.

Twelve days ago, Fiona told the head teacher in their school that Maude could not come to work, was deathly sick with a grip. Then Fiona brought her here to hide among Hall's backroom staff. She's never returning to her teaching position. She's going to Richmond with Fiona as soon as someone can be found to ferry them across the Potomac at Port Tobacco. As soon as friends of the Women Warriors further South can be enlisted to aid the fugitives.

But it has taken Allan Pinkerton only five days to catch the scent of Raphael Semmes' Irish tart.

Smack in the middle of the afternoon, Lulu, Hall's black housekeeper, bursts into the kitchen, throws herself into the old ladder-back chair next to the pantry with a great huff and sigh. The chair creaks under her ample weight as she looks around for Maude, finally spots her bent over the wash stand. Her hair is now dyed a glistening black, pulled back in a bun under a white kerchief. She wears a full-length brown leather butcher's apron. In her hand she holds a gleaming paring knife as she helps the cook, Jonah, pick out the meat from a bushel of Chesapeake Bay blue crabs to make deviled appetizers for the evening rush after Congress closes shop for the day.

"They's a gentleman in the parlor asking after you, Miss Maudie. He say he your cousin. But I don't likes the looks of him. Reminds me of what's they calls a warthog. Talks like he got a mouthful of taters. Sounds a bit like your own speech, sure."

Maude drops the jimmy crab she is holding onto the counter of the wash stand with a loud thunk. She knows no men with accents like her own, nor a cousin who looks like a warthog.

"Mistress Mary Ann, she be chatting him up, introducing him to Flossie, Belle, some of the other girls. She give me a sharp, secret look and say, 'Have the kitchen gal make us up a fresh bowl of turkle soup. And send out some Irish whiskey.' Fella say he no drinking man, but he do enjoy Patuxant River turkle."

Maude slips across the room to the swinging door that separates the kitchen and the parlor. Hall's use of the word "Irish" is a signal to her, an alarm to hide. But she has to see this warthog, has to know the face of her enemy. The description does not fit Gideon Welles.

She cracks the door just a hair, presses her face to the slit. She sees brilliant shafts of golden sunlight washing over the ruby walls, vermilion brocade fabrics of the divans and sofas, a jungle of potted ferns and palms. A crystal chandelier sparkles. The piano player has just launched into an up-beat version of "Camptown Races." The scents of cherry pipe tobacco, candied oranges, dipped chocolates, sherry and rose water fill the air. Flossie relaxes on a couch. She's a sandy blond with sleepy green eyes, hardly twenty years old. Leans on her right elbow, her right hand toying with a curl hanging over an ear. Her legs cross under an elaborate black silk dress, flashing the hem of her pink petticoat. It clashes with the green carpet.

Maude hears voices rising, but cannot make out the words over the doodahs of the piano. Cannot see Mistress Mary Ann ... nor the warthog. Then she hears a rush of footsteps coming her way. Eases the door closed, presses herself against the wall next to the hinges.

"Stop! I told you I do not know anything about someone named Maude Galway."

"Please, don't take me for a fool, good lady. Haven't you heard that Mr. Lincoln doesn't look as favorably as the previous administration on houses of entertainment such as you are keeping? Have you heard what happened to Rose Greenhow when she came afoul of the government?"

"Are you threatening me, sir?" Hall's voice sounds more surprised than angry.

"I just want to see where you keep your Irish whiskey. That is all, then I'll trouble you no more. You might be making the mistake of storing it improperly."

"You said you do not drink."

"I have the interest of others in mind."

The door swings half-open. Through the crack by the hinges, she sees Hall block the entrance to the kitchen with her body. She's a petite woman, in her early forties like Rose Greenhow. Her frilly, russet French gown cannot disguise the hard, tight body of a woman who welcomes a tumble in the sheets or fisticuffs with equal enthusiasm.

"My kitchen is not on the tour, Mr. Allen. Now, will you kindly rejoin me in the parlor? Or shall I ask Jonah to help you leave?"

The black cook picks up a meat cleaver. Suddenly, Maude realizes that she still holds a paring knife in her hand.

The sole of a man's brown brogan wedges itself under the door as Hall tries to pull it shut. A hairy little hand with neatly manicured fingernails grabs the edge of the door behind which Maude hides.

"Where's the tart, you whore monger? Where's Raphael Semmes' dirty little moll? I know you've got her here."

Hall swings a left hook at Pinkerton's face. He ducks, slams his shoulder against the kitchen door, flinging it wide open. Pinning Maude against the wall behind it.

The cook charges across the kitchen with his cleaver raised. But before he can take three steps, she raises her paring knife and pounds it between the knuckles of the detective's hand that still grips the edge of the door.

He roars, falls back. Blood flying.

She casts off her butcher's apron, starts to run for the back door on the far side of the kitchen.

A gun fires.

The bullet buzzes by her ear, smacks the plaster wall by the back door. She dodges to her right. Keeps running.

Something slams into a wooden cabinet behind her with a terrible thud. Jonah has thrown his cleaver at the detective, missed.

Now she's at the door, starting to fling it open, feeling the cool wind of late autumn in her face ... when the gun fires three times. The first shot smacks the ceiling over her head. The second splits the wooden trim of the back door casing. The third strikes a crock of pickles stored on a shelf next to the door, sending an explosion of pottery and vinegar into her eyes. She falls.

When she brushes the debris off her face, she sees a man standing directly over her with a pistol in his right hand pointed at her. His left hand is wrapped in a bloody kitchen rag and grasps Jonah's meat cleaver. He does indeed look like a warthog. But she has no idea who this warthog is.

"Back off!" He cocks the cleaver as if ready to throw it. The cook and Mary Ann Hall freeze where they stand in the middle of the kitchen. "Back off, hear?"

44

Palmer wanders aimlessly in his cabin. Stern windows to desk. Bookshelves to wash stand. Barometer to chronometer.

At the looking glass on the bulkhead, he stops, stares. Sees the dark circles under his eyes, the gaunt cheeks, the sun-cracked, bloody lips. Turns away. He hates this time of day. Especially on an overcast evening when you cannot even see the sunset.

His head pounds from the heat, humidity. And, especially, this waiting on Raphael Semmes to make his move. He drops on his berth, yawns. He hasn't really slept since finding the *Sumter* here at Saint Pierre five days ago, just cat-napped off-and-on a few hours each afternoon. At night he's always awake and on deck. Night is when Semmes will run for it.

Don't lie down, he tells himself. *Don't drop your guard. This is Semmes' game. He aims to tire you out to distraction, then bolt for open water. It's the only way he can beat you.*

The cook's dinner rumbles in his belly. He tastes the peppery grease of the mutton stew again. Feels a vague pain beneath the waistline of his trousers. Falls back on his berth to ease the gas, covers his face with his hands. His service coat's still on. One shoe rests sole-down on the sheets, his knee cocked in the air. The other foot remains on the floor, feeling the bucking and the rolling of the *Iroquois*. The foot on the floor is his hedge against falling asleep. But tonight it does not work.

RANDALL PEFFER

He wakes to the pounding of rain on deck. Winds and seas have been building all afternoon out of the south-southeast, sending white combers ashore. The weather's bad enough that the *Sumter* might be at risk if she remains in her anchorage. What will Semmes do?

Three miles at sea, Palmer feels the *Iroquois* rolling heavily even though she has the spanker sheeted in tight and some head sails backed to steady her, keep her hove to the weather. The oil lamp, with a leather jacket fixed to keep the captain's night vision sharp, casts a pool of light that skates around the ceiling.

He listens to the beating of the rain. Pictures the black night outside. A pirate's night.

"Christ, Jesus Christ, he's going to run! What time is it?"

It's all coming true, the nightmare he has predicted in the dispatch he sent Gideon Welles via the consul. *"I feel more and more convinced that the Sumter will yet escape me, in spite of all our vigilance and zeal, even admitting that I can outsteam her ... "* His eyes dart around the dark cabin for the hourglass, but can't find it even though it stands a mere ten feet away beside the logbook on his desk. He fishes in his coat pocket for his watch, holds it over his head to catch the lamplight, squints. It's not quite nine o'clock. Not quite two bells into the evening watch.

"Can you see signal lamps ashore?" he calls to the officer of the deck as he stumbles on deck, pulling on his long, black slicker.

"No, sir. Can't even see the lights of the town. Not even a glow. This squall has—"

"He's going to try his luck! Mark my word, man. We have to get in there. He'll run in these showers when he knows we're blind. Any pirate would." *God knows I would. I'd run off the wind. Sail north. Run like a bunny for the first time in my life.*

"Yes, sir."

"Beat to quarters. Clear for action. Double the lookouts. Signal the engine room, all ahead full. Helm, steer east-by-northeast. Take in the sails. Prepare to run out the guns, but don't open the gunports or pull off your tompions. Let's try to keep the guns as dry as possible."

"Aye, aye."

He hears the clang of the engine-room telegraph, wipes the rain from his brows with the back of his hand. Stares forward into the downpour. He can just make out the gun crews assembling around the thirty-two pounders with their pikes and swabs. Powder monkeys slipping, sliding, skidding on bellies across the rain-slick deck as they try to get below to the magazine with their canvas slings to carry the shells and charges.

Except that it's a dark night with the moon not yet up, this is not how he pictured his duel with Semmes. He has commandeered a Yankee lumber schooner at the quay into doing his bidding, placed his own man on the schooner with orders to keep a close watch on the *Sumter*. When she heaves her anchors and starts to move, the lookout is to show one red light at the mainmast of the schooner if the Reb is heading north, two if heading south. With such a warning, he's sure to intercept Semmes as soon as he crosses into international waters. He pictures the stars in Orion's belt and the sparks from the *Sumter*'s funnel lighting the black sky ... just before he pounces on her, raking her decks with a massive barrage of canister and battering her hull with detonating shells.

But now he's a blind man chasing a phantom, steaming at eleven and a half knots toward a bold, unforgiving coast he cannot see, an enemy whose course he can only imagine.

"Lights three points off the larboard bow!"

The rain's rapping so loudly on the hood of his slicker, the shout of the lookout seems like a call from another world. He curls an arm around a mizzen shroud to steady himself, puts a hand up to his forehead as a visor. Peers into the gloom.

His first thought is that if the *Sumter* is off his larboard and heading north, then she's already ahead of him. He has a stern chase.

"Guns loaded and out. Standby both batteries. Crack on more speed." He gives the orders before he sees anything other than the raindrops clotting on his lashes.

"Steaming light ho. Starboard running light ho. Half mile."

He keeps staring into the black squall. Still nothing, and he wonders if his lookouts are seeing things. This does not make sense. He has not changed course. Semmes should be moving away from him, should be four points off to larboard, not two points. And showing lights? What pirate ever showed a light at night?

"Lookouts confirm! What see you, boys?"

Shouts from the bows, the foretop, the maintop.

"Green light. Brighter now. Still two points off to larboard."

"Two steaming lights—high and low, same position, and closing with us."

"Spark shower. She's coming fast."

The squall eases a little, starts to move off to the northwest. He sees the lights of Saint Pierre twinkle through the murk off to starboard. They look very close. Damned if he isn't at least a mile within French waters. Well screw all. He will fight where he has to.

Now he sees the lights, the sparks swarming above a black shape, charging toward him. Has Semmes gone mad, turned back, when his escape was all but assured, to fight? *Is there no end to this renegade's bravado?*

"Sharpshooters aloft. Bordering parties to the ready."

Sergeants shout. Platoons of marines in full battle gear gather at the larboard rail and load their muskets.

"Two cables off. Coming hard."

A chill shoots through his arms and shoulders. The two ships less than a quarter of a mile apart, in easy range of each other's guns already, closing at a combined speed of over eighteen knots. If each holds to its course, they will ram each other's bows within a minute.

Why doesn't he shoot? Or is he taunting us to fire within the French jurisdiction, as we taunted him some days ago? Does he mean to sacrifice his ship, his crew and himself for some vain hope of dragging the French into the war to aid his cause?

"Does he aim to attack, sir?" The mate has joined Palmer at the mizzen shrouds. "Or does he just not *see* us?"

Such a thing's possible. The *Iroquois*, of course, is on the hunt, showing no lights. And she has a fine new spark arrester in her funnel. Maybe she's invisible from the deck of the *Sumter*. The element of surprise is something to be treasured. But Parker would rather not risk a collision. And an unannounced ambush in French waters would not play well with the higher ups. That's certain.

"Show your lights. Hoist the colors. Let 'em be clear who will destroy them!"

The ships are barely a cable apart.

"She's flying the Union Jack, sir."

Palmer squints. Such a trick was standard pirate procedure. Hadn't he used it himself, coming into Martinique disguised as a Dane? *But what if she actually was … ?*

He stares harder at the black shape emerging from the night. Sees the Union Jack rippling at her peak. She's a schooner-rigged steamer with all sorts of top hamper and cabins.

"Hard to starboard. Engine full astern!"

My god, he knows her, had seen her back in St. Thomas! She's a British mail packet.

The rain has stopped. He sees the other ship clearly, the tense cheeks of the men on watch in her bows. Both ships careen away to avoid a collision. As they veer away from each other at less than thirty yards, he sees the packet's captain on his horse block with a megaphone to his face.

"Where the hell are your running lights, ye damn fool?"

"Piss off," he says under his breath. Feels immediately ashamed, glad no one has heard his terror speak.

When the sun finally rises over the lush mountains around Saint Pierre, he sees that the *Sumter* still swings to her anchor off the quay. The British mail boat lies nearby … with the Rebel's cutter just now pulling alongside the packet. Semmes, it seems has found an ally. How soon will Palmer's own arrive? He sent off a dispatch almost a week ago to the consul at St. Thomas, saying that he has the *Sumter* trapped at Saint Pierre, he needs more ships to secure the blockade, to assure the kill. And he needs them soon.

45

She feels the wet chafing between her legs, smells the rank odor of the menstrual cloth her captors gave her three days ago. Wishes someone would just smother her in her sleep. Her job's done. Somehow Raffy will get one of her letters. Then he will know what to do next to save himself. He cannot save her.

Her hair's knotted in clumps around a gaunt face, specter pale. The white kitchen dress she put on five days ago at Mary Ann Hall's is now gray, straw covered. She has been sleeping on the floor of this little stable in Murder Bay for the better part of a week. Pinkerton, and the thugs he hired to keep watch over her, have fed her nothing but cold rice, navy beans, stale coffee. One of the men gave her an old horse blanket a couple of days ago to keep out the chill of November.

She huddles in a corner of the small tack room, bridles and traces dangling from nails on the wall. She does not move, refuses to talk even when taunted by her keepers. She cannot count the times she has been promised a real meal, a glass of applejack or a bath if she put out, sucked a cock, revealed the names of her conspirators. But they can all bugger off. After her interludes with crazy Harry Burlow, her body isn't going to cooperate with any man, unless his last name is Semmes.

As for conspirators ... ? She thinks the little warthog expects to hear about some dark web of evil among the rich and powerful in Washington. Why bother telling him the truth? He would not believe her if she told him that she acted alone in blackmailing Gideon Welles ... with a little help from Fiona and her camera. She isn't giving them Fiona. And she sees no reason to speak of a shadowy group Harry called "Friends of the Navy." She knows nothing of them. Harry's bragging about their plans to blackmail Welles merely gave her an idea, inspired her very own plan to help the man she loved. So now the only time she speaks is to ask permission to relieve her body, to squat next to an old mare amid the piss-soaked straw and dung of her stall.

"Get up, missy. Supper time. Boss wants to have a bit of a chat with you."

Her guard, a fat country boy about her own age with an Ohio twang to his voice, pokes her gently in the side with his musket.

She opens her eyes, sees through the bars of a small window that night has fallen on the city again.

The door creaks open. In walks the warthog, carrying a tin of beans in one hand and two bone cups of coffee in the other. The mare whinnies.

"Let me make this perfectly clear, Miss Galway. This is your last chance to tell me everything you know. Or you are going to the Old Capitol jail for acts of treason ... and never coming out."

He stops in the middle of the room, gives her a hard, dark look.

"Who put you up to this misguided blackmail? Why did you do it? Was it Harry Burlow? Or was he just a pawn in your game? Were there others? Your friend Rose Greenhow, perhaps? Southerners? Foreigners? Members of our own government or military? Did they speak of others? How was it all planned? Who took the tintypes?"

The detective sets the beans and a cup of coffee on the floor boards in the middle of the room. He nods for the guard to leave, takes the man's seat on a blacksmith's bench. If she wants her first food of the day, she will have to rouse herself and come for it. Come close enough to the warthog to smell his sour breath and hair oil.

She glares at him. Makes no move to leave her blanket or her corner. Her stomach aches for food, but she will be damned before she shambles across the floor in her rags and bends down at his feet to pick up a platter of food that looks and smells like cur's swill. She will not be his dog. If he wants her, he can come for her. Can see what she will give him with the horseshoe she has found among the rotten straw in the mare's stall. Now she holds it in her right hand, hides it beneath the blanket, the folds of her dress.

Pinkerton takes a sip of his own coffee, looks at the bandage on the knife wound she gave him at Hall's place, sighs.

"Why must you make this so hard on yourself? Give me the answers I seek and you shall sleep in the bed of a first-class hotel tonight. My organization can help you start over among your own people in Philadelphia, New York or Boston. Would it not be good to get back among the Irish? I like your pluck, Miss Galway. Under the right conditions I might even have a job for you in my organization. So what say we try to put the past behind us now? Tell me your story, and let's move on. You will find me a gentleman if you give me a chance."

She closes her eyes, doesn't have to listen to these lies and palaver. *Gentleman? Now there's a laugh.* She knows gentlemen. Some of the best. Men like white knights. Gentlemen like Hugh Riddley-Oak, Jean Claude de Saunier. Gentlemen like Raffy. This warthog can't even buy a jacket that fits him. He always looks pinched in by his clothes, an orphan child in itchy brown hand-me-downs.

He spits a mouthful of coffee on the floor.

"Alright, have it your way, you pathetic tart." He draws his pistol from the shoulder holster and starts across the tack room for her. "You'll talk one way or the other. You think I don't already know about your black-eyed girlfriend?"

She opens her eyes again, tightens her grip on the horseshoe. *Come on you bloody bastard. Now I have nothing to lose.*

"Stop! Stop there this instant, Mr. Allen!" A husky male voice.

The detective freezes in the act of reaching for her hair, thrusting the pistol at her nose.

Standing in the doorway on the far side of the room is Gideon Welles. With his huge fluffy beard, red cheeks, and green overcoat, he looks more like Father Christmas than ever.

"Get a grip, Allen. Leave her alone this instant. I asked you to bring her to me ... not beat her."

The detective growls to himself.

"She doesn't listen to reason. The use of force is all she understands. She's already put a knife in me!" He waves his bandaged hand at Welles.

"You don't have to tell me." Welles is remembering how she nailed him with a feather duster and dustbin at the Willard. "Put that gun away, this instant. I have news that changes everything."

Maude feels wide awake. Everything about the tack room and the men facing her looks magnified, crystal clear. Even in the yellow glow of the stable lamp. Welles holds a glistening bottle of cognac in one hand, three glasses in the other.

"Let's have a little toast."

He sets the cognac and the glasses on the blacksmith's bench. Bends to the floor, picks up the plate of beans. Walks to Maude.

"I have just received a dispatch from the captain of the USS *Iroquois*. He has the *Sumter* trapped at Martinique."

She feels her heart seize.

The detective looks confused. But he holsters his gun as directed.

"Pour us a drink, will you, Allen? This is indeed a special occasion."

Welles seems almost jolly as he swaggers up to her, bends down until he's eye to eye with her ravaged face. He places the plate of beans on her lap. He has clearly been drinking already.

"The end is near, my dear, for you and your jackstraw lover. The only difference is that he's going to wind up on the end of a rope, and you are going back to Ireland as an undesirable ... "

She hits him with the beans full in the face. The tin plate makes a soft crunch as it smashes his nose. Then she tosses off the blanket, jumps to her feet.

An instant later she clocks the detective across the left side of the head with the horseshoe as he stands mid-room, bottle of cognac in one hand, cork in the other. He has a look of total surprise on his face as he spins off balance.

46

Martinique
NOVEMBER 23, 1861

Almost everyone on the *Sumter* and ashore is watching the sky with intense silence. As if it might show them a sign.

Sunset comes just before the ship's officers assemble for the evening mess. Comes like the drawing closed of a pale curtain without a cloud to make a bank of violets in the west. Venus is three hours high, shining almost as bright as a waning moon on the glassy bay of Saint Pierre.

"Be seated, gentlemen."

Kell, Evans, Chapman, Galt and the rest take their places at the wardroom table, with Semmes at the head. Every man's eyes stare at the mess set with its china, silver, linen. Each officer wrapped in his own thoughts, perhaps of the dinner parties ashore that they have been abruptly asked to miss.

"I had hoped for some clouds, some rain. A dark night, sirs. But it is not to be. The best we can do is make haste before the moon comes up at seven minutes past eleven. There is no question in my mind. We cannot delay further. We must go tonight, gentlemen."

The officers stare at their captain. No one moves except Semmes, who gives the right tip of his mustache a little twist.

He says that the *Iroquois* has sent out dispatches requesting reinforcements. It, indeed, is only a matter of a day, perhaps only hours, before they arrive to compound the *Sumter*'s problems immeasurably. Freeman finally has his engine in shape. The leaks have been tended. The ship has been coaled, watered. Provisioned for two months at sea.

"We have played our waiting game to a fair-thee-well. The captain of the British mail packet claims our enemy, Captain Palmer, looked as one of the walking dead when he mistook the packet for us last night and came at the Brits like a drunken Mars."

A couple of the officers snicker as they picture a wild-eyed, deluded James Palmer with his gunners posed to fire on the innocent packet. Most of them know him from the old service as an "officer's officer." But Raphael Semmes has rendered him dazed and anxious.

"Is every department of the ship ready?"

"Aye," says Kell. He has checked everything with the officers and men several times since this afternoon when his captain gave orders to recall the crew, cancel all shore leave, prepare the ship for a sudden departure.

"Then eat hardy, gentlemen. We have a long night ahead. At eight tonight when the French garrison fires its usual evening cannon, we slip the anchor, an axman cuts our stern cable from shore. We run like a hound from Hell!"

"Aye, aye, sir."

Semmes smiles as his officers speak in unison. After supper he will assemble the ship's company and tell them that he has never been so proud to sail with such a tight crew of ready mariners. They are the stuff of legends. Tonight they will prove it.

All of Saint Pierre, and the Yankee's spies, are watching. Each of the past three nights, the islanders have gathered on the shore to stare out at the *Sumter* and the *Iroquois* and argue. They know that the time's coming for the *corsair du sud* to try to outrun or fight his enemy. Some hope for the *Sumter*'s improbable escape. Others yearn to see the *Iroquois* maul her. Who they favor depends on whether they feel more strongly about slavery or the rights of a group of people to self-determination. Either way, they're excited by the prospect of witnessing a contest between titans.

The rapport of the eight o'clock cannon is still echoing among the mountains surrounding Saint Pierre when the *Sumter*'s sternman swings an ax and severs the last cable tying the ship to the shore.

The funnel gives a deep cough. Black smoke billows aloft. The deck shudders with the grinding of machinery below. Then the ship begins a slow turn to larboard. She has not moved twenty yards before a deafening cheer rises from the citizens gathered on shore. It sounds as if the whole town has turned out. Thousands of voices howling into the night, a haunting, warbled battle cry as the signalmen hoist the *Sumter*'s massive Stars and Bars to the peak. No doubt the shoremen see that all hands aboard the corsair wear dark clothing. Perhaps they notice that the guns are manned, loaded, run out. The swivel gun already trained toward the west, the *Iroquois*.

Semmes stands on the starboard horseblock in his full dress blues, gold braid and buttons glistening from a fresh polish, cutlass at his side, service cap cocked over his right eye, mustache waxed into rapier points. Maude's letter lies next to his heart, tucked in the inside pocket of his coat. He does not think about how likely it is that his flight tonight will end in death and ruin. He just thinks of that day some five months ago when God showed him how to outrun the *Brooklyn* coming clear of the Mississippi Delta. For the last hour he has prayed mightily on his knees before the crucifix on the wall of the great cabin. He has said one hundred Hail Marys and beseeched his Lord for guidance. Now it's up to God to show him the way to freedom, or give him courage if he must meet the enemy gun-for-gun on a dark sea.

"Steady as she goes, quartermaster." His voice is quiet, without emotion.

"Aye, sir. Due south she is."

The *Sumter* presses straight ahead through the anchorage at five knots. The only sound's the wash of the screw.

Kell, long glass up to his eye, stands near his captain, looks to sea.

"The *Iroquois* still lies off about three miles. She is almost in the center of the bay, sir. But tending to the north, pointed that way, sir."

"Very well. Watch her. Palmer may be shaken, but he is not asleep."

"Aye, sir."

Semmes searches the dark off the port bow. He's looking for something among the black shadows of the mountains that come right down to the sea along the south rim of the Bay of Saint Pierre.

There it is. The twinkle of an anchor light. A ship looms out of the darkness ahead. The French steamer of war lies to her anchor nearly in the *Sumter*'s path, closer than he expected.

Damn it!

"Hard to starboard, quartermaster. Quickly now!"

The quartermaster hears the urgency in his master's voice, jumps to aid of his helmsman. They spin the helm like a lottery wheel. The *Sumter* saws to her right.

He holds his breath, hopes Chapman has shifted and resecured the provisions correctly so that his ship will not trip over her bows and stall when she makes a hard turn.

The bows swing slowly, too slowly. A pain stabs him in the back.

But then the rudder catches, and the *Sumter* slips clear of the Frenchman.

He closes his eyes for just a second and exhales.

The Lord is my shepherd ...

At the French ship's rail her officers and men are waving their hats and arms.

"Vive le Sumter!"

"Signalman, dip your colors. Officers, salute."

The *corsair du sud* snaps to attention on the horseblock, holds his salute until his ship has passed along the whole length of the other.

When the ship has glided deep into the shadows of the mountains close to the south coast of the bay, Lieutenant Evans, who has been posted as a special lookout, runs aft.

"I see them, sir. I see them. Look, sir, there are two red lights, one above the other at the Yankee schooner's masthead."

Evans points aft toward the lights of Saint Pierre. There, just as he has suspected, Palmer's spy aboard the slab-sided, Yankee lumber schooner has raised a signal to the *Iroquois*. Two red lights: "*Sumter* underway, standing south!"

"Good job, man!"

Still peering into his long glass, Kell speaks. "*Iroquois* is putting about, sir. Turning to the southard."

"They have taken the bait, gentleman!"

Now to set the hook.

"Quartermaster, take the jacket off your binnacle light. Helmsman show your white shirt now. Tell Mr. Freeman to give us a little cloud of sparks. Let Palmer see us for a bit."

Standing nearby on the quarterdeck, Chapman shoots a smug little smile and winks at Pills Galt, as if to say "I told you so." The old seahawk has a bag of tricks.

"She comes hard now, sir. Bow wave visible. I think she sees us. Damn it, she just doused her lights."

"Aye, jacket the binnacle. Helmsman as you were in that dark sweater of yours. Quiet on the deck."

Through the gloom he can see the outline of the craggy coast drawing near. A mile ahead lies the southern-most point of the Bay of Saint Pierre where it meets the open sea. If the *Iroquois* catches him here, he knows she will attack ... even if he tries to run along the coast of Martinique within the three-mile limit of French territorial waters. Palmer will not be able to resist the temptation. The trick's not to get caught here.

He counts slowly to two hundred. He's so close to the rocky coast he can hear the wash of surf among the rocks.

"At the helm, hard to starboard. Steer due north. Have the engineer bring us up to full speed. No sparks, please."

With these commands the seahawk reverses his course. He aims to sneak toward the northern pass out of the bay ... while the Yankee sprints south according to the signals from his spies and the little trail of lighted bread crumbs that Semmes has left. This is a simple ruse, but how often the fox has lost the hounds with just such a trick. Now, it remains to be seen how long it will take Palmer to realize he has been gulled.

"Engineer says we have to stop or lose everything, sir." The midshipman who bears the news has his hat in his hand. His cheek twitches involuntarily. His tone is low, a whisper so that his voice won't carry over the water to the enemy.

"Come again, boy?"

He still stands the starboard horseblock, grinds his teeth so he does not utter the blasphemies raging through his head.

Kell, who had been searching the horizon for signs of the enemy's smoke, drops his long glass from his eye, braces his legs as if expecting the boilers to explode. The ship's now almost at the point when she is abeam her southbound enemy. Perhaps as close as a mile and a half. Where's the enemy? If she sees the *Sumter* now ...

Chapman comes running up.

"Been to the engine room, sir." His voice is too loud, excited.

Kell and Semmes shoot him evil looks. The midshipman looks relieved. Someone else to take the heat.

"Whisper, man. What ... ?"

Chapman wipes a slick of sweat from his forehead.

"Main bearings can't take this speed, sir. Overheating. The oiler was pouring on his grease ... when it caught fire. Still burning. Mr. Freeman can't put out the fire unless—"

Semmes' face is ashen, the anger in his voice barely muted. "Stop the engine, Chapman. Blanket the fire. Kell, you have the deck."

Chapman gives the order. The screw stops. The only sound on the ship now is the hiss of excess steam blowing off through the funnel.

Sail combinations run through the captain's mind. How fast could he set his sails? He could sail out of here. He has done it before. He has out-sailed the *Brooklyn*. He turns his head and feels for the wind with his mustache. But there's not a breath of air.

Damn it all!

He follows Chapman to the engine room hatch. Freeman clambers up out of the smoke. The crusty old Welshman has tears on his cheeks.

"I'm sorry, sir. I swear to Heaven I ground and polished those bearings meself. But they are just tired. Too scored from hard running all these months, from our chases, Captain."

Semmes shakes his head, doesn't want to hear apologies.

"The fire?"

"Snuffed her, sir. The boys are greasing everything down again proper now and ... "

He's hardly listening. Staring off to starboard. The lights of Saint Pierre abeam not even two miles away. He sees the pale glow of Venus on the slick sea, knows that it will be moon up in an hour. Sooner or later, Palmer's lookouts will spot him lying out here silhouetted by the lights of the shore and the heavens.

"Just give her fifteen minutes to cool down. We'll get you out of ... "

He wants to shout that he does not have fifteen damned minutes, doesn't have five to spare. Jesus, this is not an exercise. It's life or death. Like the time the *Sumter* started tearing herself apart, sinking out from under them all, while chasing the *Trowbridge*. Freeman saved the day. And Freeman knows the stakes. He does not need scolding from his captain. He needs a show of confidence. The whole crew does.

Yea though I walk through the valley of the shadow of death ...

He twists both ends of his mustache as if preparing himself for a night with the ladies ... or battle.

"Work your magic, Mr. Freeman ... This too shall pass."

"Aye, sir. On the double, sir." The engineer smiles.

Semmes is watching Freeman slip back below into the smoke and steam when he feels a drop of water on the back of his neck. Then another, and another. Until the deck's being pelted.

"It's raining." says Chapman as if he's announcing the birth of his first son.

He turns to the south, sees the blackness of a squall coming on. It's moving from the south to the north ... shielding him from his enemy.

"God bless. God has blessed us, Mr. Chapman." The words explode from his mouth.

He feels hot tears of joy and humility. And for the second time in a week, he does not even try to squeeze them back.

When he reaches the quarterdeck, he finds Kell with his face up-turned to the heavens, smiling as his cheeks stream with rain.

"I prayed for a miracle," says the luff.

His fingers are still laced together when Freeman sends word on deck that the bearings are ready ...

The *Sumter* starts speeding north again, a phantom amid the thick, black rain.

It's almost an hour before the ship breaks out of the squall. He looks around. Moon glow is beginning to outline the summit of Mont Pelée to the east. The lights of Saint Pierre twinkle astern. The *Sumter* is now at sea, five miles beyond the Bay of Saint Pierre. Far ahead, Semmes can see lights at the town of Rousseau on the island of Dominica off to the north. The *Iroquois* is nowhere in sight.

Suddenly he pictures his enemy. Passing strange. For a few moments it's as if he's on Palmer's quarterdeck, can see the Yanks that clearly.

The Iroquois *lies drifting at the intercept point off the south pass out of the bay. Her gunners ready at their cannons. The marines in the tops, muskets loaded, poised. Almost every man on the ship listening for the* Sumter. *Middies down in the hold with drinking glasses pressed to the side of the hull, hoping to catch the first faint churning of the* Sumter's *screw, the beat of her pistons.*

"She should be here by now," says Palmer.

"If she is making better than seven knots, yes sir ... But maybe she has slowed on account of the squall."

"I know him. He would not slow for a sea of devils. He should be here. Damn you, Raphael Semmes. You should be here."

A brief gust swirls over the quarterdeck of the Iroquois, *clears away the last of the rain. The squall moves off to the north. The moon's just now edging over the mountains, illuminating the whole bay.*

He scans the breadth of the bay with his long glass, sees nothing.

"God help us!"

Kell moves shoulder to shoulder with his captain.

"Permission to speak freely, sir?"

"Granted."

"Are you thinking what I'm thinking, sir?"

He clears his throat. Just a few minutes past he was feeling the ache in James Palmer's heart. Now his mind's veering in other directions. He's wondering how Anne and the girls are making out, whether they are still in Cumberland with her brother, how his sons are getting on in the army. He remembers the scratchiness of Ollie's beard when they hugged at West Point. Now he's feeling Maudie's letter against his chest, smelling her lavender. He craves her. It's that simple. He has written her a long letter telling her so. This very morning he left the letter ashore for the governor of Martinique to post to her, as she directed, care of a French diplomat in Washington. Maybe she will get it. A sailor never knows.

"You first, Kell."

"Pardon, sir?"

"What are you thinking?"

"I'm thinking it's going to be a long time before we get home to our loved ones. I'm thinking now that it seems we have shaken the *Iroquois*, you don't want to risk another go with the Yankees here abouts. You aim to take us across the pond ... "

Semmes smiles. It's a warm smile, a sad smile. He remembers words from Maude's letter. *Hide. Cross the ocean. Flee for your life, your future.*

"Good Kell. How you do read me sometimes. What say you to the Azores and the Med? Might we not find some good hunting yonder?"

EPILOGUE

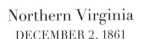

Northern Virginia
DECEMBER 2, 1861

The lurching of the carriage shakes her. It clatters over the rickety wooden planks of a bridge. Even though it's noon and sunny, a wintry chill hangs in the air.

But she's warm. She has an iron foot warmer beneath her toes, two downy carriage blankets over her and Jean Claude de Saunier to hold her in the cove of his torso and right arm. The dram of cognac she took an hour back has helped too, but it has made her feel confused.

"Where are we?"

"I believe we are crossing the Rappahannock River, my dear, a place called Fredericksburg. We make good time. The driver has promised us Richmond before *la tombée de la nuit*. By this evening you shall have a warm bath, a little *pâté foie gras* and a glass of Graves in the new capital of the Confederate States of America. Tomorrow we shall meet President Davis."

She nuzzles his shoulder.

"How can I ever thank you for your kindnesses, Jean Claude?"

"Your presence and your radiant smile is all the reward I seek."

She looks up at his sharp face, crooked nose, tells herself there's a certain austere handsomeness here. And there's a generous and noble heart beating in this chest. Raffy, of all people, would understand if she finds some comfort with this man. He would understand why she has agreed to keep house for de Saunier while he sets up the unofficial French legation to the Confederacy in their new capital.

Still, her hand trembles as she squeezes three sheets of folded vellum to her breast beneath the carriage blankets. The sheets are a letter from her sailor, written just before his flight from Martinique. And the words tear at her heart.

... Tonight I must run the gantlet, my love. If I fail, they will surely kill me outright ... hang me from the yard. If I succeed, I must vanish for some time. Either way, please know how deeply I care for you. By your letter, reaching me here in Martinique, you have humbled me with your love and devotion. What you have done for me and the cause for which I labor, is quite simply the most wonderful gift I could ever imagine. You have surely risked your life in giving it. Now, if you still love me, do all and everything that you can to keep yourself safe from harm. Try to get South where you will find friends. When this horrible conflict ends, if I survive, my first act will be to search for you. You are my sun, my moon, the star I steer by. The angel on my shoulder. Fair winds.

The Frenchman passes his fingers softly through her curls.

"Why such a deep sigh, my dear?"

She's picturing a girl hidden beneath a seal's skin.

"I was thinking of selkies."

"*Comment?*" He doesn't understand.

"It's a West Irish fairytale." Her lips break into a smile. "Of the sea."

HISTORICAL NOTES

This novel is set against the backdrop of real events in the American Civil War during 1861. The naval action, the infighting in the Lincoln Cabinet, political intrigue in the Office of the Secretary of the Navy, and the clandestine operations of secret agents like the Confederate Rose Greenhow and Federal Allan Pinkerton described herein are based on well-documented facts. Even specific locales used in this novel (especially in Washington) such as the Ebbitt Grill and the Willard Hotel—which are still in operation—and Mary Ann Hall's bordello near Capital Hill have been the subject of intense analysis by scholars.

All of the historical figures is this novel—Raphael Semmes, Gideon Welles, William Seward, Abraham Lincoln, David Dixon Porter, Charles Wilkes, James Palmer, Allan Pinkerton, Rose Greenhow—were real people. The dates, places and action of all major war-related events are drawn from actual occurrences as revealed through the journals, published memoirs and correspondence of the major characters. Semmes' *Memoirs of Service Afloat* and *The Cruise of the Alabama and the Sumter*, as well as the three-volume diary of Gideon Welles, have been invaluable research tools.

Biographers have often revisited the lives of Semmes, Welles, Lincoln, Porter, Wilkes, Seward, Greenhow and Pinkerton. Among Semmes biographies, Stephen Fox's *Wolf of the Deep* stands out for its deep and meticulous research ... as well as its courage to air guarded secrets about the man the Semmes family often refers to simply as "The Admiral." Specifically, Fox documents that Raphael Semmes' wife Anne bore a daughter Anna in 1847 who could not have been fathered by Semmes. He was away fighting the Mexican War during the time of conception. Fox also details the existence of a "romantic connection" between Semmes and a young English woman named Louisa Tremlett, a relationship that persisted through years of correspondence.

These illustrations of marital infidelity resonate with a picture of the Raphael/Anne Semmes marriage that biographers and contemporaries have observed as layered, complex and not totally monogamous. While Anne obviously strayed during the Mexican War, perhaps she may be forgiven since her husband was away from home for years at a time and, by many accounts, was a man who delighted in the company of attractive women wherever he traveled. In short, the Semmes union was like many marriages among the gentry during the Victorian era.

These discoveries led me to make an intuitive leap and imagine that Raphael Semmes may well have had a mistress at the outset of the Civil War. Maude Galway is that character in my novel and is entirely a fictional creation. My intent in adding her to the mix of historical figures is not to sully the reputation of Raphael Semmes or cause hurt to his descendants. After reading his books, memoirs and relevant biographies, I simply cannot picture him without the affections of a fresh, young love energizing his spirit.

Maude burst onto the page unbidden on the first day that I sat down to draft this book. I immediately liked her spunk, admired her loyalty to her man. So she stayed, blooming in the novel. Fictional flesh-and-blood, heart-and-soul. But also an emblem for the many women who kept company with Rose Greenhow and played crucial roles as spies against the Union in Washington during the early years of the Civil War.

—RANDALL PEFFER
February, 2008

Randall Peffer established himself with his first book, *Watermen*, a documentary of the lives of the Chesapeake's fishermen. It won the *Baltimore Sun*'s Critic's Choice award and was Maryland Book of the Year. In 2000 he published *Logs of the Dead Pirates Society*, a literary memoir that evokes the natural drama of life aboard a traditional research schooner sailing the coast of Cape Cod.

Randy is the author of over three hundred travel-lifestyle features for magazines like *National Geographic, National Geographic Traveler, Smithsonian, Reader's Digest, Travel Holiday, Islands* and *Sail*. His travel features appear in most of the US major metro dailies. He is also the author of a number of travel guides for *National Geographic* and *Lonely Planet*.

For fourteen years he was the captain of the research schooner *Sarah Abbot*. He teaches literature and writing at Phillips Academy/Andover and has spent his summers on Cape Cod and the south coast of Massachusetts since his youth.

Killing Neptune's Daughter, his first mystery novel, appeared in 2004 accompanied by strong reviews. *Provincetown Follies, Bangkok Blues*, his second literary mystery, was a finalist for the Lambda Award in 2006. *Old School Bones* is his third novel in what is now called the Cape Islands Mystery series.

Visit www.randallpeffer.com for more information.